Heart of the Viking

Band of Bastards, Book 2

Lois Templin

ARE YOU SIGNED UP FOR DRAGONBLADE'S BLOG?

You'll get the latest news and information on exclusive giveaways, exclusive excerpts, coming releases, sales, free books, cover reveals and more.

Check out our complete list of authors, too!

No spam, no junk. That's a promise!

Sign Up Here

www.dragonbladepublishing.com

Dearest Reader;

Thank you for your support of a small press. At Dragonblade Publishing, we strive to bring you the highest quality Historical Romance from some of the best authors in the business. Without your support, there is no 'us', so we sincerely hope you adore these stories and find some new favorite authors along the way.

Happy Reading!

CEO, Dragonblade Publishing

Additional Dragonblade books by Author Lois Templin

Band of Bastards Series
Heart of the Hawk (Book 1)
Heart of the Viking (Book 2)

Also from Lois Templin
The Knight, The Lady, and the Curse (Novella)

Chapter One

Oswestry, England – November 1284

G ALIENA MERCER HAD been in the depths of despair for long enough. It was time to start living again.

But the guilt of moving on was like a knife in her belly.

She would never forget what had happened or fill the hole that would forever mar her heart. But neither would her heart stop beating, nor her lungs stop breathing—which is what she had fervently hoped for each day of the last three years.

The numbness that had protected her in the years since she'd lost everything had dissipated months ago. In its wake had been an uncontrollable grief and the fervent wish she would just die. But, as in so many things, God had refused her that solace, too, leaving her no choice but to continue her dismal existence.

She wanted more than to just exist, though; she wanted to actually *live*. That was the longing keeping her awake at night of late, and that had forced her to venture beyond her widow's cottage on the edge of the churchyard and into the village.

To live she must be among the living.

If she were honest with herself, it wasn't just the realization that she may well continue to live and breathe for decades to come that forced her to leave her cottage. Anora, her only friend in this world, deserved her due credit.

It was because of Anora that she'd started venturing beyond the threshold of her tiny home, and eventually agreed to help the innkeeper with cleaning the tavern, the rooms above stairs, and other odd jobs in return for meals and a few extra coins each month. The innkeeper was a stern man who grunted orders and wasn't afraid to throw patrons out of his establishment if he didn't like the look of them. He hardly acknowledged Galiena, but he was a fair employer and left her alone as long as she kept up with her duties.

As much as she did not want to be alone any longer, experience had taught her to avoid most people, because most people didn't seem to approve of her unusual upbringing or her uncommon opinions. Their disapproving looks and cutting remarks had taught her it was best to keep to herself.

Besides, she hadn't needed a lot of people in her life up to this point; she had been quite contented if she had just one person with whom she could be completely herself. At one time, that had been her father. Then she had had her husband, Adam, and Nahara, her daughter, both accepting her and loving her just as she was.

And now, she had Anora.

But lately, she started to wonder if she had mistaken numbness for contentedness. She'd withdrawn into herself to avoid the pain, but now being withdrawn felt lonely instead of safe. Her routines which had been a comfort in the past had begun to feel mundane. In truth, she was bored and restless and longed for a change.

She sighed and wrapped her arms around herself to ward off the cold and looked up at the patch of blue sky breaking through the late afternoon clouds—an unusual occurrence for early winter when the rain could go on for weeks without ceasing. After adding an empty barrel from the tavern to the pile in the alley behind the inn, she stopped to appreciate the break in the cold drizzle and bask in the small piece of clear sky in the waning of the day. She was learning to stop and appreciate the small things that brought her joy—including a hopeful patch of blue struggling to break through the endless clouds.

This was why she was standing in the narrow alley that came to a dead-end behind the inn, leaning against the damp stones next to a stack of empty barrels, enjoying the brief reprieve from the rain, when she heard the men.

She knew they hadn't seen her standing behind the column of wooden crates in the dimness of the cramped alleyway, because if they had seen her, they wouldn't have been having the conversation they were having now. At the sound of the voices, she'd pressed herself completely flat against the wall, anticipating they would soon be gone. She considered taking the two steps required to cross to the back door of the inn, but that would have caused an awkward situation, and it was easier to just stay hidden. Not wishing to draw attention to herself, she quieted her breathing and waited.

She'd expected them to conclude their business—whatever that may be—quickly and be on their way. What she didn't expect was for them to start discussing the king and queen of England and some lord whose name she didn't recognize. Conversations about the ruling monarch and lords of the realm weren't unusual and typically were nothing to be concerned about.

Unless they were taking place in dark alleys with hushed voices....

"You're late."

"I had other matters to attend to."

The men spoke in low tones, but Galiena was hardly more than an arm's length from them and could hear every word clearly.

"Next time you arrive late will be the last time you do anything for me."

"Give me the missive," the other man grumbled. "And the gold you owe me for delivering it."

Galiena heard the distinctive sound of coins in a pouch changing hands and then the metallic jingle of them pouring out, presumably onto a man's palm. She wanted to peek but shrank back against the wall. This was getting even more dangerous.

"This isn't what we agreed upon."

"You get half now, and the other half once I have proof the missive has been delivered."

"I want it *all* right now."

"You get half now or you get nothing."

"And how will you get the missives to the lords you need for your plan? You refuse to speak to Lord Dacey yourself, or any of the other lords. Your anonymity depends on me and the few other men in your employ."

"Quiet."

"There's no one around to hear us," the man snapped, then continued his argument. "I've proven myself. I've even delivered messages right under the king's nose at times. I've kept my eyes and ears open, and I know things, things that are worth more gold than you're paying me."

"Is that so?"

"Aye. There are more lords who resent the king and queen as much as you and your little network of rebels. I can give you names for the right price and negotiate meetings for you."

"You think you know better than me who can be trusted and what needs to be done?"

The men's growing irritation was evident in their harsh whispers, and she feared it could erupt into bloodshed at any moment. Galiena wracked her brain for a way out of this situation but came up with nothing other than praying the men didn't find her.

"I know of your plan, and I can help you."

"What plan?" Even without seeing the man's face, Galiena could hear the ominous warning in the flat tone of the words.

"I know you are planning to have the queen's babe murdered."

At the mention of the queen and the royal heir, Galiena's gasp caught in her throat and her neck prickled with dread. It was silent for a long moment, but she knew the men were still there. She held her breath, not daring to move for fear they would discover her.

"And I know you are planning to make it appear as though the Welsh rebel Rhys was responsible," the man continued. "My mother was Welsh. I have blood relations who could be of use to you. Think about what I have said and do not waste my talents or my resources."

There was a scuffle, and then a noise like someone gasping for breath. Galiena could see the edge of a cloak against the outer wall of the inn. She shifted slightly to peer through a gap in the crates to see a man pressed up against the wall with another man's hand clutching his neck. His eyes bulged, trained on the man choking him. His hood had slipped back, and she could see his face turning purple, the veins popping on his forehead and temples. His hair, cropped close to his skull, revealed a scar that stretched over his ear, leaving a bald patch on his scalp.

"Do not question me or think to give me orders again," the other man said. His hood was pulled forward, draping over his forehead, and hiding his features. "Take this message to Lord Dacey. And if you are ever so fucking dim-witted as to speak of what you *think* you know about me to anyone, I will kill you. Do you understand?"

Galiena was very much regretting her decision not to go back into the inn when the men entered the alley. They would have seen her, but it would have been before they started speaking of things that were not meant to be overheard. If they discovered her now, she questioned if she would live to see the morrow.

And just when she had decided it was time to start living again!

"Aye," the man against the wall gasped.

"Do not fail me on this mission."

"I will not," came the choked reply.

Galiena heard a sharply indrawn gasp for breath as the man was released, then the scraping of footsteps as he stumbled out of the alley. What seemed like an eternity later, she heard the measured, steady footsteps of the other man. She stood complely still, hardly daring to breathe, until she was sure the men were gone.

After a long while, she carefully peered around the stack of crates to be certain the alley was empty. Seeing no sign of either man, she was about to step out from her hiding space when little Tommy Cutpurse came barreling into the alley at a full run. He shoved his ill-gotten gains into a crevice between two stones on the back wall of the inn, then squeezed through an impossibly small gap between the inn and the bakery. The buildings were so close to each other that no one other than an underfed child could ever fit between them.

She heard the pounding of more footsteps entering the narrow alley and quickly flattened herself against the wall behind the crates again.

"Wait, you rotten scoundrel," a voice called. Galiena recognized it from the clandestine encounter she'd overheard just moments before. It was the man who had been shoved against the wall.

After letting out an oath of frustration, he ran back out of the alley, presumably to look for the boy, unaware that what he really wanted was within his grasp, hidden in a hole in the wall.

Galiena stared at the opening between the two stones for a long moment. The light was too dim to see what was in there, but all of her nerves were buzzing with the certainty that it was the pouch that she'd heard the men exchange.

Carefully, quietly, still afraid for her life, she stepped cautiously forward to stick her hand into the opening in the wall. Reaching in, she felt smooth leather, and her pulse pounded as she extracted what she'd found to reveal a small, lightweight pouch. Squeezing it with her hands, she determined that it contained a few coins and something more pliable. Like the rolled parchment of a missive.

She took a deep breath, her heart beating rapidly in her chest as she weighed her options. She could put the pouch back and pretend she knew nothing about it, that she didn't overhear the men in the alley, and that she had no knowledge of a threat to the king's infant son, the only surviving heir to the throne.

Or she could take the pouch and do something about it.

She thought of her own child, how she'd felt snuggled in her arms warm against her chest, so helpless and beautiful with bowed lips and full cheeks. Losing her daughter had broken Galiena, and it sickened her to think of the queen losing her child. She knew that pain and knew that it didn't matter that the queen had lost other children before. Each loss had to be just as painful as the first for any mother.

As curious as she was about the contents of the missive, she dared not open the pouch in the alley. Instead, she tied it next to her own on the thin leather belt she wore beneath her kirtle, determined to make her way to her little cottage by the church as inconspicuously as possible. There she would pour out the contents of the pouch and determine what to do next.

As she opened the back door to the inn, a soft scuff of a boot against stone caught her attention. She turned her head to see a tall, hooded figure with a long cloak billowing out behind him round the corner into the narrow passageway.

She slipped through the back door to the inn, pulling it shut behind her, then ran through the tavern toward the front door. She said a quick prayer that the man in the alley hadn't seen her clearly in the dim light and that the lane in front of the tavern would be full of people enough for her to escape into the crowd before he could find her.

As she burst through the door and out into the lane, her heart sank.

There was only one person in the lane, and he looked like something terrifying, like a barbarian from the tales told to children to scare them into behaving.

Or worse, he looked like a *berserker*.

But when he turned to look at her, a smile transformed his face. There were crinkles at the corners of his eyes and mouth as if laughing and grinning was something he did often. As intimidating as he looked, she decided to trust her gut as an idea started to form in her head.

✦

Chapter Two

"**A**RE YOU IN your cups again, Husband?" A woman appeared from seemingly nowhere at his side and tugged at his arm.

For the first time in a long time, Viggo "Red" Algarssen was rendered speechless. He looked down into a pair of startling silver-gray eyes ringed in black, and wide with what he assumed was fear. She had that look he recognized. Unbidden, his heart clenched at the intense way the woman stared up at him, unblinking and earnest, as though pleading with him not to reject her. She'd placed her hand familiarly on his chest, and she seemed to be trying to turn him back in the direction from which he came.

He'd come to Oswestry looking for vengeance, not a wife, but he'd play along. It was laughable, really. She was tiny, puny even, and completely intriguing. "It is you who intoxicates me, *Wife*," he said with a loud lusty growl, as he wrapped an arm around her shoulder, draping the end of his fur cloak over her. He tucked her into his side and started down the lane. If she was seeking an escape, he'd give her one.

He'd seen the man come bursting out of the inn behind her and noticed the way her body had stiffened. Frustratingly, the man's face was obscured by his hood and Red wasn't able to get a

8

good look at him as he turned his head from side to side, obviously looking for someone.

The woman turned to look over his protective arm as they walked, presumably searching for the hooded man.

"Do not look his way," Red ordered in a low voice as he feigned stumbling down the lane a few more steps, keeping up the pretense of being drunk. When they got to the end of the lane, he leaned his back against an open wall and splayed his legs wide enough to pull the woman between them and into his chest. He wrapped his cloak tighter around her to hide her as he warily watched the man stalking down the street in their direction.

The woman tried to peek her head out to see what was happening just as the hooded stranger slowed his steps and turned his attention to them. Red didn't know what the man in the street was to the woman in his arms, but he could feel the tension in her body as she stood straight as a spear against him. He concluded they were not well-acquainted, or she would not be trying to hide from the man in plain sight.

He was doing his best to hide her face from the man's view with his bulk and cloak, but short of stuffing her head down into the fur he'd wrapped around them both, he could think of only one other way to shield her from vision without arousing suspicion.

"Kiss me, Wife," he said with a drunken laugh as he leaned his face down close to hers, covering her cheek with his hand and tucking her into his shoulder as he pressed his lips to hers. Kissing an unwilling woman did not hold any appeal for Red, but it was the most effective way to shield her identity from the man. He couldn't stop the twinge of guilt that stabbed at his stomach as his mouth touched hers, even as he told himself that it was the lady in his arms who started this preposterous situation by calling him "Husband".

The woman hesitated for a breath, then played along with more enthusiasm than Red anticipated, clutching his shirt in her fists as she pressed her lips against his. He tried to ignore the jolt to his body that made his heart beat faster as he kissed the woman while at the same time watching the man on the street through slitted eyelids.

"*Oi*," the man called out rudely.

Irritation shot through Red's veins at the man's audacity. The woman in his arms went rigid with fear and clenched tighter to his tunic. He could feel her trembling and the rapid beat of her heart against his stomach. He lifted his head to look at the man but kept the woman's cheek pressed to his chest. "What do you want?" he growled.

"Did you see a woman come out of the tavern?" The man's voice was gravelly and rough like he was purposely lowering it to make it unrecognizable. Red noticed he also deliberately hid his face under a heavy hood pulled low.

"I have eyes only for my wife," Red said with a drunken slur. "We're celebrating my return and I'd like to get back to it. Go away."

The man's hooded head stayed turned in their direction as Red dipped his head to nuzzle the top of the woman's head. He studied the cloaked figure to remember him for later; he would track him down and teach him a lesson in courtesy. The man was doomed, as far as he was concerned: first, for daring to hesitate after Red told him to move on; second, for causing the woman in his arms to be terrified. And third, for interrupting a passionate moment between a man and his wife, even though they were neither. In Red's opinion, this was the most egregious thing of all.

Finally, the man moved away, stomping back up the lane in frustration as he turned his head side to side, looking for anyone hiding in the doorways or behind corners.

Red was yet to know who the hooded man was to this woman, or why she was trying to escape him, but he would find out.

He held the woman close to him under his cloak, shielded from view, as he kept a watchful eye on the lane until he was sure the man was gone. He'd held other women in his arms before, but for some reason that he couldn't fathom, he was reluctant to let this one go. He kept rubbing his chin over the top of her head while he watched the man walk away. Her hair was particularly silky and soft to the touch, much like her lips. Perhaps it was the danger of the situation and his need to be a protector, but the woman in his arms was completely intoxicating, like a siren's call.

No, not a siren's call. More like the pull of a she-wolf on her mate. Red knew that when an alpha wolf found her, only death could part him from his she-wolf. He believed the same held true for men and women if they were willing to believe in Fate.

His mother told him often as a small boy the tale of how she'd known the moment she saw his father that no other man would ever have a place in her heart. It had been like a lightning bolt the first time they had locked gazes. He chuckled, remembering how she'd said it took his father a little longer to admit they were fated to be together, but they'd been inseparable once he'd quit fighting it. It had broken her heart when he'd been killed in battle before either of them even knew she carried his child, and she'd never loved again.

Small hands pushed against his chest and the woman slowly tipped her head back to look up at him. Those eyes! They were the most beautiful he'd ever seen, especially now that the fear had drained from them. Her lips parted as though she planned to say something, but then she paused, and an expression of bewilderment crossed her delicate features. Red smiled at her then, a slow, knowing grin. Did she feel it, too? Had she recognized him as the match to her soul?

"Let me go," she said evenly, as a sweet smile crossed her lips.

She had the slow, languidly sensual moves of a she-wolf. He stared at her, mesmerized.

"I said: *Let...me...go.*" Her tone was fiercely determined as she spoke through clenched teeth. Beautiful, white, perfect pearls of teeth.

Red couldn't stop looking at her, wanting to touch every curve of her face. He opened his mouth to ask her name, taking his time to release her, when her sudden movement and an explosion of blinding pain made him flinch and bend toward the ground as the breath whooshed out from between his lips.

His breathtaking she-wolf had kneed him in the balls!

GALIENA HASTILY STEPPED out of the protection of his fur cloak, feeling a twinge of guilt when the massive, red-headed oaf pursed his lips as his eyes bulged. One hand moved to his tender private parts—she supposed to protect them in case she decided to knee him again—while the other clutched at his chest as he gasped for air.

She hadn't meant to knee him in the groin as aggressively as she had, but it would make him think twice before ignoring her demands again. In truth, a portion of her defensive vigor came from the unexpected urge to lean into him as he kissed her. He was big, warm, and smelled like a fresh autumn morning, and she'd felt safe and not so alone for the first time in a very long time when he wrapped her in his arms.

It also felt wrong.

Wrong because she didn't know this man. Wrong because she'd not been wrapped in anyone's arms since her husband died. Wrong because she had thought her body beyond responding to the touch of a man who wasn't Adam.

The frigid air enveloped her now that she didn't have the luxury of his fur around her, and she hugged her arms around her middle to stay warm. She looked up the street where the man who had been looking for her had disappeared, then turned to go in the opposite direction. She wasn't safe in the streets. And even once she rid herself of her current nuisance in the form of a tall, red-haired, bearded Viking, she knew she was still in danger.

"Whoa!" the oaf called, putting his hand on her shoulder. She stopped and looked down at the place where he was touching her, then glared over her shoulder at him. He lifted his hand and held it aloft in a gesture of surrender.

"I am not your horse." Nothing irked her more than men putting their hands on her uninvited, but she'd learned well how to deal with unwanted attention from working at the inn. Though to be fair, she had been the one to approach the Viking first, even to put her hands on him in a familiar way. Her tone had been unnecessarily rude after he had helped her hide from the hooded man, but she felt peevish and unsettled. In the years since her world fell apart, she'd isolated herself from others, and she'd developed an instinct to inwardly cringe and outwardly steel herself when men tried to get impudent with her.

She'd kept her distance from men since her husband died lest they misinterpret her intentions. She rarely had to interact with the crowd at the tavern or the guests staying at the inn, and she usually kept to herself, cleaning or helping in the kitchen. As gruff as the innkeeper was, he did seem to have some mercy, rarely sending her into the tavern to serve food or assist with pouring tankards of ale. The few times she helped in the tavern, the moment the male patrons started making her uncomfortable with their propositions or putting their hands on her, he would send her to the kitchen and out of view of the offender. It was an unexpected kindness, but one she welcomed.

But when this giant of a man had wrapped her in his cloak and held her against him, he'd made her feel things she thought buried too deeply to ever experience again. His warmth and strength brought back memories and feelings from a time when her life made sense. A time she fought every day to keep buried lest the memories bring her to her knees.

She increased her speed when she heard him following her but to no avail. In a few long strides, he was in front of her, turning to walk backward so he could face her. She hid a satisfied smile to see the stiff gait that she suspected had more to do with his encounter with her knee than with the awkwardness of his backward shuffle.

"Accept my forgiveness, my lady," he said, attempting a grin that looked more like a crooked grimace. She wanted to be put off by the mischievous charm, but something about the way his lips quirked, and his light-blue eyes glittered gave her an unfamiliar feeling in the pit of her stomach. It wasn't fear, dread, or wariness—those she knew well. She didn't know what this was.

"I am not a lady," she said, averting her gaze as she tried to skirt around him.

She couldn't go back to the inn—the man would be looking for her there. Out of habit, her footsteps started in the direction of her cottage, but the thought quickly crossed her mind that if the man inquired about her at the tavern, he would know her name and where she lived before sunset.

The only other place she knew to go was the goldsmith's, but the thought of bringing danger to her only friend, Anora, and her kind father, Frode, made her stomach twist.

Galiena's fingers touched the pouches hanging beneath her tunic. One contained all the coins she dared to carry on her, and the other contained a bit of gold and a small roll of parchment that could mean her death.

Unless she managed to evade the man until he quit looking for her.

Perhaps he'd given up when he continued down the street. She wasn't sure if he even got a clear look at her in the fading light of day in the dim alley. If he had, then he wouldn't have been fooled by her wrapped in the arms of a stranger when he stopped to talk to them. He either didn't recognize her and wasn't exactly sure for whom he was looking, or he knew it was her and would be back.

"Can I at least know your name?" the charming nuisance asked, still facing her as he walked backward.

Galiena pressed her lips together and shook her head. "I do not expect to require your services again, so there is no need for you to know my name."

"'Sweeting' it is then," he said, turning to walk at her side. Though his attention was back to scouring the lane for danger, he did flash her a lopsided grin. "Isn't that what husbands call their wives?"

"I am *not* your wife." She should have been annoyed by his brashness, but she found him quite disarming with his awkward smile, one corner of his mouth curving higher than the other and forming a dimple in his left cheek.

Galiena stopped abruptly. She didn't want to notice anything about him. It would lead to no good. She suspected he knew well how handsome he was, with his charming grin and pale blue eyes that sparkled with mischief. He kept his beard trimmed close, but his hair was a wild mane of deep red.

She reminded herself that she should be more concerned about the stolen pouch hidden under her tunic and the ominous hooded man who wanted it back than the handsome stranger who made her stomach uncomfortably jittery.

She put her head down and continued walking, determined to get away from the charming Viking, but he continued to match her stride easily with his long legs. She pursed her lips in frustration and was about to tell him to leave her alone when he suddenly grabbed her hand and pulled her into a narrow lane between the apothecary and the baker's shop. A yelp of protest started to escape her lips but was cut off by his huge hand covering her mouth and most of her face. She wriggled to break free as he pressed her into the wall of the bakery, but he would not release her.

"Shhh," the Viking said in a hushed voice. He kept his fingers pressed to her lips, but he was peering around the edge of the stone wall into the main lane. He pulled back into the shadows of the narrow lane and looked down at her, one eyebrow arched disapprovingly. "Your pursuer is persistent."

She could feel the pulse pounding in her head as fear came over her again. She pressed her hand against the folds of her tunic, reassuring herself both pouches were still secreted there. She knew not what was written in the missive, but the sinister details she'd overheard, and the fact that the man seemed relentless in finding her indicated it was important. The gravity of the situation was making her heart drum in her chest, and she feared the hooded man wouldn't be satisfied until he found her and retrieved the letter and the gold.

But what would he do to her once he had the letter? If he caught her, could she feign ignorance, pretend she hadn't overhead anything? Would he believe her and just let her go? She would bet what little silver she possessed he would rather wring her neck and search her lifeless body for the missive than ask questions.

Her gaze darted to the side and she looked down the passageway, measuring the distance and speculating whether she could reach the other end before the hooded man found her. She could disappear quicker if alone. She looked at the giant of a man pinning her to the wall, his fingers lightly pressing against her lips, and pleaded with her eyes that he release her while at the same time, she tried to slide out from under his grip.

Instead, he grabbed her hand and pulled her along the narrow lane. He was surprisingly quiet for his size, his boots making hardly a sound as they hurried to the other end and rounded the corner. He looked over his shoulder ensuring they were not being followed as they emerged into the main lane of the village. Then he looked left and right, as though trying to determine which way to go, obviously not overly familiar with the lanes through which they moved.

Galiena felt a spike of hope as she noted that bit of information. Distracted, he didn't appear to be holding tightly to her hand. The foolish giant thought she was a complacent woman. She took advantage of his inattention and pulled her hand free, then took off running toward the lower part of the lane, away from the center of town. Darting into another small corridor that was barely visible just beyond the butcher shop, she felt a twinge of satisfaction, certain the wide-shouldered Viking wouldn't fit in the narrow passageway. After all, even with her petite frame, she had to run with her shoulders angled. A man of any size, like the

Viking or the hooded man, would have to struggle to get his body to fit through the cramped space.

She reached the far end of the corridor and turned onto another lane leading toward the edge of the village where the smithies were located. Looking over her shoulder as she went, she was shocked to see the huge redhead was only a few strides behind her.

Saints above! How had he stayed so close behind her without her hearing his footsteps? How did he fit through the alley? Had he gone around the building? And if so—how did he catch her so quickly?

It didn't matter. All that mattered was getting to a safe place, away from the hooded man and now—perhaps—the Viking, and the only way to do that was by being fleet and canny. She knew the village; he didn't. With that in mind, she continued to dart through the lanes until she rounded the back side of the goldsmith's shop. She stopped when she was out of sight of the lanes but was immediately dismayed to see the Viking round the corner and enter the alley right behind her.

"Would you, please, just go away!" she hissed at him. "You are far too conspicuous with your...your...." Her hands were whirling in circles in front of her indicating his size, his huge fur cloak, his flaming red hair, and all the rest of him.

"My what?" he asked, looking down at her. His insouciance, she decided. That was too conspicuous too.

There was nothing to be done for it, she decided, so she ignored him, as she rapped on a wooden door. A moment later she heard the snick of a panel being slid to the side and a small opening in the door appeared at eye level. A heartbeat later, she heard the scrape of a heavy bolt followed by the scrape of the door being thrown open against a stone floor. Glancing to the end of the alley to be sure it was still clear, Galiena stepped into the warmth of the goldsmith's backroom.

She groaned in frustration when the door did not budge as she tried to close it behind her, knowing full well the oaf had followed her into the shop. Her one and only friend, Anora, stood with her mouth agape, staring up at him wide-eyed.

Galiena spun to face him. "What are you doing?"

"Waiting for you to answer my question," he said with a smug grin over his shoulder as he pressed the door closed and slid the bolt back in place. The man was daft.

"What question?"

He turned back to her and crossed his arms over his chest. "I'm far too conspicuous with my *what*?"

"*That's* what you want to know right now?" Galiena asked, her voice rising. "With all that has happened, that is your concern?"

He shrugged, the left side of his mouth curving up in that distracting lopsided grin. "I would have been happy just knowing your name, but you wouldn't answer. So…"

"All of you," she huffed, tearing her focus from his handsome face with its sharp jawline framed by that neatly trimmed beard to look at something less unsettling, like his chest. Except now he had his arms folded across that broad expanse. It made her think of how it had been to be pressed against that chest, by those arms.

There was a fine dusting of red hair gracing the contours of his forearms, highlighting their muscles and tendons as if on purpose. Exasperated with herself for noticing, she folded her hands demurely in front of her in an attempt to regain her composure and said in the sweetest voice she could muster, "Thank you for your assistance, kind sir. As you can see, I am now safely deposited out of sight, and you may be on your way."

She wanted to look at the parchment secreted away in the pouch. She couldn't go back to the inn or her little cottage, which left only the goldsmith's shop belonging to her friend Anora and her dear father. But she was regretting her choice now, fearful that she would bring danger to the only people who were kind to her. At the same time, what choice did she have?

"Not yet, sweeting. Who is the man in the hood?" he asked, stepping closer to her so that she had to tip her head back to look at him.

"Someone only a little less annoying than you."

Chapter Three

R ED TOOK IN his surroundings. The other woman who worked in the shop didn't seem concerned. She'd settled a hip against a work bench and was watching them with interest as an amused grin curved her lips. He liked her already. And her delight with the situation suggested she probably wasn't going to pick up any of the sharp tools he saw to use on him. There were fine chisels and hammers, pitch pots, sheets of silver and gold, brushes, and a small forge—the tools of a goldsmith. Besides the back door, there was a stairwell on the side of the room, and another door leading into the front of the shop. He heard a rustling in the other room and braced himself for a new confrontation, even as he turned his attention back to the woman in front of him.

"Who was the man? Why was he following you?" he persisted.

"Spurned lover," she said flatly, arching one fine, dark eyebrow. An unexpected surge of irrational rage gripped him at the thought of any man having touched her. Jealousy? He supposed he couldn't blame himself for that. Even as she taunted him, he found her eyebrow arch and her cocky attitude quite alluring. The little vixen lied to him. He wasn't surprised. This situation just became more and more intriguing.

Knowing he'd get nowhere by forcing her to give him the information he sought, he decided to play along. "Your lover? I'll kill him," he growled.

She huffed a disgruntled sigh. Definitely not the response of a woman regarding a lover, spurned or otherwise. "Kill him? For what reason?"

"As your husband, I must kill any man who dares touch you." He meant it as a jest to irritate his she-wolf. He had no claim over her, but he nudged good sense aside and let himself pretend for the time being that she was his to protect.

His *wife*—he'd yet to find out her name—planted her hands on her hips, drawing his gaze to the curves of her body and making him swallow hard at the indecent visions that were filling his head.

"Do you plan to kill every man who came before you, *Husband*?"

He dragged his gaze up to her face when she called him "Husband" in a sarcastic drawl. His she-wolf had a bite to her that he found completely delightful. And—unexpectedly, again— arousing.

The other woman pushed herself away from the work bench to step to her friend's side, her mouth wide in astonishment. "*Husband?*"

His she-wolf glanced at her friend, making an *it's-of-no-consequence* motion with her hand.

"Aye. And *Wife*," Red growled, fully aware that he was being unreasonable, but unwilling to do anything about it. "As such, I will gladly kill every man who has ever touched you."

She glared at him for a long moment with those incredible silvery eyes snapping. Then she shook her head and appeared to shrink, bluster gone. "This is a preposterous argument, considering we are not married," she muttered.

"Where I'm from, it merely takes a declaration to be married. You already declared me your husband. And I now declare you as my wife." If he wished to be an utter brute about the matter, there were many who would support the claim—they had said the words to bind them, even if hers were said in desperation and his in jest.

He heard a door in the front of the shop open and the rhythm of heavy footsteps headed in the direction of the back room. Despite the oncoming threat, he kept his focus on the most enchanting face he'd ever had the privilege to look upon, though his hand shifted to the heavy axe hanging from the back of the belt at his waist.

A tall, dark man with a leather apron and formidable forearms stopped in the doorway between the front and the back of the shop, clutching a hammer in one hand. The head of a shorter man was barely visible over his shoulder.

"Wife? Husband?" His new wife's friend gasped, all amusement gone from her voice. He gazed down at two women staring up at him, one with eyes wide in astonishment and the other—his she-wolf—with the fire back in her level gaze. Since neither woman appeared concerned about the newcomers who were obviously known to them and likely here as protection, Red relaxed his stance, but only slightly.

"Anora," the man in the doorway growled to the other woman, "does this man need to be shown the door?"

The words were heavily accented and, from his time journeying through Spain and into northern Africa, Red guessed the man to be from somewhere in the region of Morocco.

"I honestly cannot say, Sumayl!" The woman's response was tinged with laughter. "Galiena? What say you?"

"*Galiena…*" Red exhaled and arched a triumphant eyebrow at the little vixen. "'Tis a beautiful name for my bride."

"Bride?" The woman and the two men in the shop all exclaimed simultaneously.

"I am not your bride!" Galiena snapped.

"What is your name, good sir?" Anora asked, a broad, eager grin lighting up her face.

"Viggo Algarssen, loyal servant of Sir Grogan of Hawkspur, at your service," he said with a formal bow of his head in the direction of Anora and the men standing in the doorway—his small effort to make up for his previous rude behavior of ignoring them in his quest to get a straight answer from Galiena. "But you may call me 'Red'."

"Viggo Algarssen," Galiena drawled. "Calling you 'Husband' was nothing more than a ruse, and you know that. You've served your purpose and may leave now."

"*Red*," he reminded her. He shouldn't provoke her, but he enjoyed the way her gray eyes frosted with anger almost as much as he'd enjoyed the glint of bewilderment that had lingered in them after he'd kissed her. "Ruse or not, you declared me your husband and I now declare you my wife. We are legally wed." He winked at her for good measure as he said the last.

"That is *not* how it works." She flicked her hands at him the same way she would if shooing a goat. "Be gone. Be on your way."

Besides his instinct to ensure her safety from the man pursuing her, Red was having far too much fun to be on his way. This woman was beguiling, intriguing, and completely intoxicating. It had been a long while since he'd felt this exhilarated for any reason other than going into battle. Never before had a woman made him feel this invigorated, especially while still clothed! It matched the rush he felt when he faced death, and it confirmed one thing: this tiny, enchanting creature with silver-gray eyes, silky black hair, the face of an angel, and a tongue as sharp as a dagger was most definitely his she-wolf.

THIS MAN WAS pure frustration! He had a certain charm that in a different place and time she may have found appealing, but in this situation and in this moment, he was a huge, red-headed nuisance.

"Why are you doing this?" she asked the man staring down at

her with ice-blue eyes. "Why will you not leave? If it is from some overly chivalrous sense of duty to see to my protection, you have done that. As you can see, I am safe now." She gestured toward the large blacksmith and Anora's father, barely visible behind him.

At that moment the front door of the shop opened. Galiena startled, and she felt the color drain from her face. She said a silent prayer it was not the hooded man come to find her as the blacksmith pivoted in the doorway, hammer still in hand.

"Good day, sir. How can we help you?" Anora's father, Frode, asked. Galiena still could not see the older man, nor the person who entered due to Sumayl blocking the doorway. Tamping down the fear rising in her throat, she scooted to a corner of the room away from the doorway and pressed herself to the wall where she was out of the line of vision of anyone peering around the blacksmith. The Viking—who suddenly seemed so much less annoying and far more welcomed than she would have imagined—was in front of her, shielding her with his body as soon as she squeezed herself into the corner.

"You should get out of sight, too," she hissed at him. "The man saw more of you than he did of me."

"I want him to find me," Red said, keeping his face turned toward the door. His tone was far less worried than she felt. As if he was confronting a fly and not a threat. "So, I can kill him for threatening you."

"Greetings, Sumayl," the newcomer said, then called in a louder voice, "Do you need my assistance, Red?"

Galiena did not recognize the voice, but she was positive it was neither of the men from the alley. Whoever it was obviously knew the blacksmith from next door since he'd addressed him by name. She let out a breath of relief and slumped her forehead against Red's protective back before she realized what she had done. Then she jerked her head up when she realized the man had also addressed Red by name.

"Is all good here, Anora?" she heard Sumayl ask from the

doorway.

"I don't know, Sumayl," Anora said, her voice entirely too gleeful. "I believe Galiena needs to answer that question."

Red slowly turned, as though trying to keep her from startling like a scared chickadee, then put his hands on either side of her shoulders. "Are we good here?" he said to her in a low voice, all traces of mischief gone from his expression.

She was staring back at Red, unsure of what to say. She didn't really know anything about the man, or his true intentions. She'd wanted him gone, but when it seemed the hooded man may have found them, she'd been happy to have his protection.

"I can vouch for him, Sumayl," the newcomer said.

"And you are?" Anora asked in her characteristically bold manner.

"He is called Hunter," the blacksmith answered.

Galiena stepped out from behind Red to see the other man. Sumayl had stepped fully into the work room and no longer blocked the view into the front of the shop where Frode stood with the other man. He was taller than average, but not as big as Red or the blacksmith, and he had wavy brown hair. He looked nothing like the men she'd seen in the alley. "You know him, Sumayl?"

"Aye. Hunter has purchased my wares and I've done work for him on several occasions."

"From what you know of *him*," Anora asked, pointing a finger to indicate Hunter, "would you trust the giant hovering over Galiena?"

Sumayl seemed to contemplate the question for a long time as he studied the big Viking standing at Galiena's side. She looked up to gauge Red's reaction, surprised to see he stared directly at Sumayl with a steady gaze as though unbothered by the blacksmith's scrutiny. Sumayl was a large and powerful man with undeniable strength from years of hard work with heavy tools. There were not many men who would dare challenge him—but apparently Red was one of them.

"Aye," Sumayl finally responded, "if Hunter says he is to be trusted, I will believe him."

Galiena's shoulders relaxed, and she let out a sigh as a measure of tension eased from her body. Red must have heard her reaction because he leaned a little closer to her. She turned to look up at him, only to find him smiling broadly at her in a manner that she decided was both arrogant and mildly charming.

"My deepest gratitude, Sumayl," Anora said. "I believe all is well here."

"If I'm wrong, you know the signal," the blacksmith said, his voice low and menacing. "Give it and I'll be back to crack open their heads."

"I know, and I thank you," Anora responded.

"Thank you, Sumayl," Galiena echoed, appreciative of his protective presence.

Frode and Hunter stepped out of the way to let Sumayl pass by, but then immediately returned to stand in the doorway as though watching a curious spectacle presented by one of the traveling troupes who provided entertainment at fairs.

"As you can see, Viggo," Galiena said in a calm voice, using the Viking's given name as a means of putting some distance between them, "we are well protected, and I do not wish to detain you any longer from your duties."

She tried to sound convincing, but the truth was that the thought of being found by the men from the alley was terrifying. The way she'd hid behind him even a moment ago showed that she was growing accustomed to the Viking serving as her personal guard, but in truth, she didn't know who he really was or if he could be trusted. And trusting the wrong person with what she'd overheard could be deadly.

She looked at him when he didn't immediately respond to her statement.

He tipped his head to the side and arched an eyebrow at her. "You ran into the arms of a stranger, me—asking me to pretend to be your husband. You have a mysterious man chasing you and your face is still pale with fear. I am not going anywhere until I know what makes you so afraid, why you are in danger, and who the man is. What did you get yourself into, Galiena?"

She pondered this for a long moment. What was the best way to answer? And if she involved him even more, would she put him in danger? Was that a risk she was willing to take? *No.*

"I'm not exactly sure. But it does not concern you." With that, she turned and stepped toward her friend, only to find Anora, Frode, and Hunter watching her and Red with intense interest.

She heard Red step close behind her. "It became my concern the moment you tucked yourself into my cloak and looked at me with those pleading eyes."

"That was my mistake," Galiena said, refusing to turn to look at him. Instead, she was looking at the man next to Anora. "Sumayl said your name is Hunter, but who are you?" she asked, suspicious of him despite Sumayl's assessment that he could be trusted.

"His friend," he responded with a nonchalant tip of his head toward Red. There was something in the way he was standing that reminded Galiena of a cat—quiet and unassuming but with the ability to turn lethal in the blink of an eye. Who were these men she'd unwittingly encountered and brought into her life?

"Why are you here?" Galiena asked the men, looking from one to the other. "Why are you in Oswestry?"

"We are looking for someone," Red responded.

"Who?" she asked, hoping to turn his attention away from her predicament. "Perhaps we know the person and can direct you where to go."

She wanted a moment of quiet, alone with her friend, to get her opinion about what had happened that day. She'd not had any time to process what she'd overheard in the lane, nor to look at the missive tucked in the pouch on her belt.

"At this moment, I'm more interested in the person after you," he said turning to face her again. "You've yet to answer my questions about why he chased you out of the tavern and into the lane."

"It really does not concern you," she said, lifting her chin. If he became any more involved, he could be placed in danger, and she was unwilling to allow that to happen to him. He'd done enough by getting her here. He didn't need to do any more. "I thank you for your assistance, but you can be on your way."

Red crossed his arms over his chest, stood with his feet apart, and slanted his brows until they formed a menacing *V* over the bridge of his nose as he peered down at her. She knew he was trying to intimidate her, but he was about to learn she wasn't so easily daunted.

Galiena matched his stance, crossed her arms in front of her, and drew her own brows together to meet his gaze. "What is *your* business in Oswestry? And why were you lurking conspicuously in front of the inn?"

Red's lips quirked as though he was holding back a laugh as he shook his head at her. "You tell me first who the man is that chased you from the inn. And—I am not conspicuous."

"Aye, as I said before, you are far too conspicuous. You were conspicuous when you were standing in the middle of the lane in front of the inn, and you were conspicuous when you followed me through the village to here."

"You still haven't told me who the man is," he persisted. She was learning he was a very stubborn man—but she could be just as stubborn.

She jutted her chin out at him and slammed her fists onto her hips in frustration. "I can't tell you who he is because I've never seen him before today."

He raised his eyebrows then. Obviously, he didn't believe her. "Why was he after you?"

She shrugged. "I answered your question, now you tell me why you are here and who you are looking for." She wasn't convinced yet that it was wise to reveal to Red what she'd overheard—for all she knew, he could be an enemy of the king as well.

He furrowed his brow and sucked his upper lip between his teeth. He appeared to be contemplating what to tell her, so she stayed quiet. Beside her, Anora and Hunter were standing completely still and in complete silence, only their heads moving as they swiveled between Red and Galiena. Anora's father still stood near the doorway and watched them just as intently.

After a long moment, Red finally broke the silence. "We're looking for someone who took something from me."

"And you think the hooded man is him?"

It was Red's turn to shrug. "You tell me."

She needed to come up with some kind of lie. Keep it simple, she told herself. "As I said, I've never seen him before today, so I cannot tell you."

"What happened before you came running out of the tavern and into my arms? I wager it was more than a rude proposition that had you running for your life," he said, arching an eyebrow at her.

She wished he would quit referring to her "running into his arms". It sounded far more intimate than it was. But as to his question, it was fortunate she'd seen enough during her time working at the tavern that it wasn't difficult to come up with a story. "He was a drunken idiot who dropped a pouch of coins in the alley behind the tavern while taking a piss. He didn't realize I was there, so I took them after he left. But he returned, likely when he tried to pay for another ale in the tavern."

Red didn't look like he believed her, but she raised her chin defiantly, daring him to call her a liar. He turned to look at his friend, then turned back to her with a sigh, his face taking on a bland expression. No suspicion or skepticism, just neutral indifference from whatever message passed unseen between the two men.

"So, you're telling me that you are nothing but a simple thief?"

Galiena nodded hesitantly. She hated the idea of being

thought of as someone who stole from others for no good reason, but it was the only story she could come up with that sounded believable.

And she shouldn't care what he thought of her—he would be gone from her life soon.

Red studied her for a long, uncomfortable breath, but she refused to squirm under his scrutiny even when a slow smile spread across his face. An uneasy feeling started to grow in the pit of her stomach. She didn't know this man well, but in the short while she'd been in his presence, she'd learned that when he grinned in that unsettling and charming way that set his eyes to twinkling, he was up to mischief.

"A wife skilled in the art of thieving can have its advantages." He had the audacity to wink at her after making that proclamation.

"I agree!" Anora interjected before Galiena could respond. "I *must* know what this is all about." Her voice was tinged with more amusement than Galiena thought appropriate for the situation. "When did you find yourself a husband, Galiena?"

"I did *not* find a husband!" In any other circumstance, her friend's ability to not let anything rile her was welcome. And her never-ending quest to find as much merriment in every situation as possible was one of the things that Galiena admired most about Anora. It was something she herself struggled to do and she needed more levity in her life. But at this moment, when *she* was the brunt of Anora's amusement, she was not enjoying the situation at all.

Anora turned to Red's friend, addressing him as though they were lifelong friends. "What do you know about this?" she asked, tipping her head toward Galiena and Red.

Hunter's lips parted as though to speak, but then he said nothing. He simply stared at Anora, seemingly mesmerized. It wasn't an uncommon reaction; Anora had a way of enchanting people. When he continued to stare at her, mouth slightly agape and not responding, Anora turned back to Galiena. "You and I have much to talk about."

"Aye, we do," Galiena agreed. "But first, someone needs to find Tommy."

"The cutpurse?"

She nodded at Anora, keeping her attention directed away from Red. "I fear he may be in danger."

Chapter Four

RED WANTED TO throttle Galiena. "Who is Tommy, and why is he in danger?"

He knew in his gut she lied to him when she said she stole coins from the man and that was his reason for chasing her. She might be flippant with him about her situation, but this was proof she was in more danger than she was telling him.

She looked up at him with those silver-gray eyes that shimmered like the snowscapes under a full moon he so loved from his childhood, and he lost his breath for a moment. He tried to believe the sudden ache in his heart was longing for his homeland, but he knew it had more to do with the woman standing before him with desperation and suspicion etched clearly in the set of her jaw and the crease between her brows.

"I can see it on your face," he said to her in a gentle voice, "you need me, but you don't know if you can trust me."

She hesitated a moment, her lips parted as if to respond, and he knew whatever she said next would be another lie.

"I do not need you," she said, her voice strained.

He lowered his face down until he could feel the warmth of her breath, locking his gaze with hers. "I think you do."

He couldn't stop the triumphant grin he felt curling his lips when she turned away from him and he saw her mouth press into a straight line as she swallowed hard. He also couldn't stop from letting his gaze skim down the seductive curve of her throat, cursing silently at the high neck of her tunic which hid the rest of her from his sight. The curves and swells beneath the material hadn't escaped his notice, but it was the smooth skin below her ear that was captivating him at this moment.

He watched her throat bob as she swallowed. Then she turned her head back to meet his gaze. "How do I know you can be trusted?"

"What does your gut tell you?" he asked her. He'd noticed the way she looked at him, how she seemed more at ease when he was near, and he was confident she would conclude that he was trustworthy. Before she could respond, they were interrupted by the old man standing in the doorway to the front of the shop.

"Do you want this man to leave, Galiena?" the old man said from the doorway. Red turned his attention toward him and noticed for the first time that even though Frode's gaze was directed at him, his eyes remained unfocused.

As much as it galled Red that the old man thought he could force him to leave, he stayed civil, remembering that he was standing in the man's shop. "I am at a disadvantage, sir. You know my name, but I do not know yours."

"I am Frode, and this is my goldsmith shop." Frode's voice was strong and his words resolute as he stepped closer to Red— close enough for him to see the man's milky pupils. Frode did not let his failing vision stop him from taking a stance on behalf of Galiena, and for that Red admired him. "You've met my daughter, Anora."

"Indeed, I have," Red said with a sidelong glance at Galiena's bold friend. "Pleased to meet you both," Red said, but before he could say anything more Frode continued speaking with an air of authority that could not be denied.

"Galiena is like family to us. I've known her since she was a child traveling with her merchant father. In the absence of her father and husband, it is I you will have to contend with if you do not behave with decorum toward her."

Red's attention shot to Galiena. "You are *married*?" he heard himself bark, his hackles raised in agitation.

Galiena didn't seem to hear Red's outburst. She was looking at Frode wide-eyed and with her mouth open in astonishment. "I did not think you remembered me as a child."

He was about to repeat his question, frantic to know if his she-wolf was already married to another man, but a gentle touch stopped him. He looked down at Anora's hand resting reassuringly on his arm. He tried to calm himself, realizing he probably looked like a snarling beast ready to pounce.

"Widowed," Anora whispered.

The anger receded and his shoulders slumped in relief. He knew it was absurd to feel this possessive about a woman he'd known for an hour at most, but he reminded himself of how his mother had told him as a boy that when he met the woman destined to be his, he would feel it in the marrow of his bones, just as she had.

And today, there was no doubt that he had felt something in the marrow of his bones. When she'd flung herself into his arms looking for protection, the instinct to kill anyone who would dare harm her overwhelmed him, and then he'd been jolted to the core when he'd kissed the little raven-haired vixen.

Widowed he could accept. Married? Absolutely not. Because then she couldn't be his—and she needed to be. It was destiny.

"When Anora brought me to your home not so many months ago," Galiena said, "I thought I recognized you, but it was too difficult to explain that when we first met, when I was a child, that my father had dressed me as a boy for my safety. But you knew, somehow, that I was the boy you once knew. Is that why you were so kind to me? Because you knew my father?"

"Aye. Your father and I did a lot of business together and he was a good man."

"You remind me of him in many ways." Galiena leaned closer

to Frode and whispered something for his ears only. Red didn't like not knowing what was being said, but it was Hunter who stopped him from going to her this time with a hand on his shoulder.

The affection between the older man and Galiena was evident. Red never knew his own father, but a fleeting memory of his mother flashed through his mind, his guilt over the loss of her still a sharp stab of pain in his heart.

"I do not mean interrupt," Anora said in a small voice, "but you said Tommy is in danger. Should we not do something about that?"

Galiena jumped, her hands flying to her face as though she'd just been startled. "Yes, Tommy!"

"I assume you mean the boy with a talent for lifting pouches," Hunter said. Red thought he heard a hint of admiration in his tone.

Galiena nodded. "He's a sweet boy despite his…talents. I don't want to see him hurt."

"I'll find him." Hunter was already striding toward the door.

"Do you need my assistance?" Red called after him.

"No," Hunter said, reaching for the door. "The lady is right. You are far too conspicuous."

"ARE YOU READY to tell me what happened?"

The stubborn Viking was pulling the fur cloak from his shoulders as he spoke, obviously intent on staying to question Galiena further.

Galiena held Red's ice-blue gaze as she decided whether she should take Frode's advice and trust him. She felt her resolve to push him away slipping as good sense prevailed. Her father had been a traveling merchant when she was a child, and together, they'd had more adventures than she could count. She had faced danger before, but this felt different. And more than she could face alone.

The men from the alley spoke of killing the heir—a baby—and mentioned the queen, but now she questioned if that was really what she heard. Only a fool wishing for a painful death would think of harming the heir of the king of England. A shiver slithered down her spine at the thought that if they were desperate enough to risk suffering the gruesome and agonizingly slow execution reserved for traitors to the crown, then they would not hesitate to kill anyone who jeopardized their sinister mission.

She slipped her hand under the flap of her long tunic, pressing her fingers to the pouches tied to her belt. The missive in her possession could be the key to stopping a traitorous plot and saving the queen from the pain of losing another child.

"Galiena, I asked if you were ready to tell me what happened," Red said, brushing a knuckle over her cheek in a soothing gesture.

"Aye," she nodded, her gaze transfixed on the floor in front of her as she thought about all that had happened and what to do next. Whatever it was, it would be dangerous. There was no doubt that she would need assistance. Perhaps the giant Viking, though she didn't know him, had been placed in her path by Providence. And if that was the situation, then really, how could she be in doubt of his trustworthiness?

She lifted her head to look at Anora and Frode. "But telling you what happened, showing you what I have, could put you in danger. I could not live with myself if either of you were harmed because of me."

"This old man needs to sit," Frode said, moving to a bench by the worktable, but he seemed more excited than worried.

Galiena looked at the large table where he sat, strewn with the tools of his trade, evidence of the business he'd built over his lifetime.

"You have so much to lose, and you have already been too kind to me. I cannot ask you to risk losing all this," Galiena said, sweeping her hand around the room. To her surprise, neither Anora nor her father looked the least bit unsettled by her words.

"If what you have to say proves to be that dangerous, then you will need our help," Frode said, almost echoing her thoughts, his tone as easy as if she had asked him to repair a buckle on her belt.

"If she stumbled into something treasonous, then it's better you know nothing about it," Red warned. She noticed he hadn't included himself in his warning, another revelation he was no ordinary man.

Galiena looked up at him; he was unblinking and calm as she met his intent gaze, a signal that he had correctly guessed the nature of the danger. She could tell by the way his lips tightened and his beard twitched with the flexing of his jaw that he understood she was admitting the situation was as dangerous as he'd thought even though she didn't say a word.

"If you will excuse my rudeness," Red said, turning back to Anora and Frode, "I would like to speak with Galiena in private and gauge the danger before she reveals it to you."

Again, she was struck by how this revealed the type of man Red was—a protector not only of women he'd unexpectedly kissed but of old men. Frode shook his head to protest, and Red's face tensed at his response, but then Anora's father held up a hand before the Viking could argue.

"I have seen much in my lifetime, Red, and I am not afraid for myself. But if Galiena is in danger, then she will need all the help she can get."

Red arched an eyebrow at the older man as he studied him for a long moment. "My apologies, Frode. I believe I have underestimated you."

"Accepted," Frode said before turning to her. "Galiena, tell us what this is about so we may help you."

Galiena looked at the faces in the room, two of them comprising the only friends and allies left to her. Nay, they were family. And Red...*well.* "I believe the hooded man is part of a plot to kill the queen's babe." She said the words in the barest of whispers. Saying it out loud, even if quietly, made bile churn in her stomach. "The child needs to be saved."

She had seen the much-loved queen a twelvemonth or more ago when the king and his army had passed through Oswestry on their journey to Wales. The king and queen had graced the local priest by stopping to pay their respects, and the queen, her belly rounded with pregnancy, had taken a walk with her attending ladies, a cadre of watchful soldiers in their wake. Her nursemaids followed her, carrying her baby daughter, a child not yet able to walk unassisted, while a little fair-haired cherub of a girl skipped along behind.

It had been nearly her undoing to see that little girl so much like her own. Now and again, Queen Eleanor would look over her shoulder at her daughter and give her a broad smile. The queen looked genuinely happy, and Galiena had wondered how she managed after losing so many of her precious babies. Galiena had lost one child, her only child, and it had irretrievably broken her.

Since then, the queen had given birth to a boy named after his father. By autumn, the new babe was the only surviving male heir to the king after their older son had died at the age of ten. He was the third male heir to die, and prayers were being said regularly that the new baby, Edward, would remain hale and grow to manhood to succeed his father.

"They must be warned to protect the boy," she continued as she removed the pouch from her belt and set it on the table, then carefully removed a small, rolled parchment and laid it gingerly next to the pouch. "And if what I have will help find the men responsible, then I must bring it to the king."

Nothing would ever bring back her own sweet child. She would never hold her again in her arms, and she would never forgive herself for failing to save her. But if she could save the queen from the despair of losing another child, of having her son's life cruelly taken by the hand of a monster before he had a chance to grow into a man, then she would do everything in her power to do so.

Even if it meant risking her own life.

A life she would have gladly given in exchange for her daughter's.

A life she would willingly give now to save another mother's child.

Chapter Five

GALIENA'S HEART SKIPPED a beat as a light rapping sounded on the back door. Red was at the door before Anora could get there, dagger in one hand as he carefully slid the small peep panel to the side with his other hand, just enough to peer out.

When he slid the bolt and opened the door, little Tommy the cutpurse was shoved through the back door, followed by Hunter, who quickly closed the door behind him and bolted it again.

"I found him lurking around the churchyard," Hunter said.

"I dinnit do nothin'," Tommy said with a scowl, crossing his arms protectively across his scrawny chest.

Galiena wanted to wrap the grungy little boy, with his mop of filthy brown hair, in her arms and tell him everything would be all right. But Tommy didn't think of himself as "little" and would push her away. Every time she saw him, she wanted to mother him, but she didn't know if it was for his sake or her own.

"You're not in trouble, Tommy," she said in a voice as gentle as she could make it. "We just want to talk to you about the man you took the pouch from today."

Tommy eyed her suspiciously. "Which one?"

Galiena put a reassuring hand on his shoulder. "The man who had the pouch you hid in the wall behind the tavern."

Tommy shrugged her hand away. "It weren't me." He

crossed his arms tighter and pressed his lips together in deter-mined defiance.

"Quit your whinging. We know it was you," Anora said, with no consideration for the tender age of the child whom Galiena guessed to be no more than eight years old. Appalled at her friend's lack of sympathy for the scared boy, Galiena shot her a pointed look, but Anora just responded with a small shake of her head and continued on. "We're not going to punish you, but we think you robbed the wrong person."

"Who be the *right* person?" Tommy asked with a cocksure grin.

Frode let out a hoot of laugher. "The boy has a point."

Anora continued to glare at Tommy, but the corners of her lips quirked up with amused admiration. "Some people are more wrong than others."

Tommy wrinkled his nose. "That don' make no sense."

"Tommy," Galiena interrupted. "Did you get a good look at the man who was chasing you this afternoon?"

The boy narrowed his eyes at her. "Maybe. Which one do ya' mean?"

"The one you thieved a pouch from and stashed behind the tavern." Galiena arched an eyebrow at him to let him know she was well aware he was being obtuse. She had to admit the boy was bold, which was probably a good thing considering he was an orphan who, despite the charity of the townspeople, had to scrape to survive.

"I remember him," Tommy said scratching his chin as though it was ages ago. "'E was braggin' in the pub 'bout 'is lord and how 'portent he was, and that 'e was the only one 'is lord trusted for a 'portant delivery. I figured he 'ad somethin' good, so I waited, and I took it."

Galiena shook her head at the cunning little scoundrel. "How did you manage that?"

"I followed 'im outta the pub and waited for him to get dis-tracted. He met up wit' a man in the alley, but they went different ways when they came back out. Didn't take long 'fore a pretty girl walked by and grabbed 'is attention." He shrugged as he spoke, as though he was talking about something as common as how he caught fish in the river.

Galiena's heart throbbed, looking at this skinny boy so wizened beyond his years, forced to learn the habits of men in pubs and the ways of thieving to survive. The thought of any child having to exist on their own as Tommy did made her want to cry. But she couldn't dwell on that now. "Did you hear what the men in the alley were talking about?" Galiena asked, a lump of fear in her throat that Tommy might know more than he should without realizing the danger.

Tommy shook his head. "Didn't follow 'em in there. I waited for 'em to come out. Then I nicked it." He suddenly looked suspiciously at Galiena. "How did ya' know about the pouch?"

"I was in the alley when you tucked it into the wall," she admitted. "I have it now."

Tommy's eyes widened. "Why did you take it? It's mine."

"Some might say that it belonged to him." She gave him a pointed look. But then she continued, before he decided it was best not to talk anymore, "It caught my eye. I decided to find out what it was about." In truth, had she not heard the men talking about the queen's baby and a plot to kill him, she wouldn't have even considered taking Tommy's hidden treasure.

"What was in it?" Tommy asked. "I could tell by the way the man kept feelin' for it in 'is pocket after 'e left the alley it was somethin' good."

Galiena shook her head, about to respond that it was best he not know what it was about—they didn't yet know themselves, but it was obviously important—when Anora said, "Nothing of value, just a letter to his sweetheart."

The boy's shoulders drooped. "I planned to get a bit of gold from 'im to give it back, but that's not worth nothin'." Then the cunning little boy brightened, showing a gap-toothed grin, "I know there were coins in the pouch, I could feel it. *Those* are mine."

"If you stay out of sight for a while, the coins are yours," Galiena said. "But you must stay hidden until the men leave town."

"That ain't no letter to a girl," Tommy scoffed, looking from Anora to Galiena, "not if you are wantin' to pay me to stay outta sight."

Red let out a snort of laughter. "Clever boy!"

Galiena couldn't deny that the boy was intelligent and also cunning. She hoped he found more to do with this life than just thieving, but as an orphan with no other family, his future was bleak.

"Put those deft hands of yours to good use by helping an old man with repairing mail," Frode said to Tommy, tipping his head back toward the shop. His sight was nearly gone, but the old man had deft fingers and the skill to do goldsmithing and the fine work of repairing chain mail by touch. "Are you strong enough to pound a hammer?"

"Aye," Tommy said with confidence, turning to follow Anora's father, his golden-brown eyes bright with excitement. "I'm good at poundin' things."

"I'll be the judge of that," Frode said. "A good smith must pound with precision. Can you do that?" He put a fatherly hand on the boy's shoulder as they passed through the doorway into the front room. Frode's gentle manner was what Galiena loved about him most, that, and the kindness he showed to people like Tommy who didn't have families of their own. Just as he'd done for her when she and Anora had become friends.

"I can lift a coin from your pouch without you knowin' I'm there. I think I can pound where you want me to." The arrogance of the child was as amusing as it was heart-wrenching.

Tommy could be heard a moment later chattering away to Frode, asking him the next question before the older man had even finished answering the first. Galiena let out a huge sigh of relief that he was safe—at least for now. But the man he stole the pouch from and the man he met in the alley were still on the loose. And probably looking for both her and the boy.

She turned to see Red, Anora, and Hunter all staring intently at her.

"Will you make me ask again for an explanation of what happened?" Red sounded impatient, but Galiena wasn't quite ready to tell him everything. Not before getting answers to a few of her own questions.

"First, tell me, are you a knight of the realm?" She crossed her arms in front of her and pursed her lips, just as Tommy had done, but not in a show of defiance. No, her stance was to remind Red and Hunter that she was still the master of her decisions and what would happen next.

Red's response was to immediately square off with her, legs akimbo and arms crossed across his chest. He faced her squarely as he matched her stance and demeanor. "No, I am not a knight. I am a warrior and I serve Lord Grogan of Hawkspur, or 'Hawk' as he's known."

Galiena had expected him to put up an argument when he moved to face her, that he would insist on asking the questions instead of answering them. She was mildly surprised and overwhelmingly pleased that he was answering her. "What is his relationship with the king?"

"He was the king's most favored knight for nigh on two decades. King Edward dubbed him 'Hawk' for his speed and ferocity after saving his life when he was nearly impaled by a Welshman's blade on the battlefield. The king reveres him enough to have recently granted him a Marcher stronghold." Red pressed his lips closed then, but kept his gaze locked with hers as he waited for the next question.

"Is he no longer the king's most favored knight?" She'd heard tales of a knight named Hawk, but if he'd fallen from favor with the king, then he would have reason to commit treason.

"He is still favored," Red said resolutely, his jaw twitching.

She tipped her head to the side as she contemplated his reaction, the implication clear in his words. "But no longer his *most* favored. You said he 'was.' Why?"

She heard Hunter huff out a deep breath, as though exasperated, as Red responded. "He defied the king for a woman. At least that is how King Edward judged the situation."

Galiena felt the gooseflesh rise unbidden on her skin. She didn't want to find the notion of someone defying the king exhilarating, but the devotion required to choose to anger the king for the love of a woman—it was an undeniable show of true love. "Who was the woman?"

Red's lips started to curve into that lopsided grin, as though he had just discovered a secret. "Lady Alyce of Hawkspur Castle, now his wife."

Her gaze flitted to Anora. They had heard the tales about the Lord and Lady of Hawkspur, and how the lord had been flogged for choosing his lady over his duty to the king, but she had assumed they had been exaggerated. When Anora had told her of the deed, it had reminded her of the romantic stories sung by bards she'd often heard while traveling with her father. It mattered not what part of Britain, Europe, or the Mediterranean they'd traveled through, every culture had rich tales of men being tested to prove their love.

She turned back to Red. "Did you agree with your lord's actions?"

"Aye," Red answered without hesitation.

"No," Hunter said, just as quickly.

Galiena ignored Hunter's response, but she felt more relief than she should that Red would have done the same for a woman. "How long have you served your lord?"

"Hawk has been my commander since I was a lad of twelve."

Galiena couldn't stop herself from lifting her brows in surprise. "*Twelve?*" Not much older than Tommy, she realized. An unbidden image of the rumpled, mischievous, red-haired, and blue-eyed boy he must have been rose in her mind's eye, making her heart soften. *No.* She pushed the image away.

"Aye. And he will have my loyalty to my last breath, even if it is given to protect him. I am not afraid to die for my loyalty to those who are deserving."

Galiena's breath caught in her throat at the words, and her heart felt like it may have skipped a beat. She knew Red sensed the impact of his words on her because he dropped his arms to his sides and stepped closer to her, forcing her to either stare at his chest or lift her gaze to his face. When she looked up at him, his expression was no longer stern. It was softer and warmer, and his eyes were…smoldering?

"The list of people who have earned my loyalty is short: Hawk, Lady Alyce, Hunter, and a few other soldiers," he said in a near whisper "And my wife and children will have the same loyalty. To my last dying breath."

Did she want that from Red? Part of her screamed *yes*, but then reason prevailed, and she remembered she was not deserving of such loyalty. Her husband and child had died despite her efforts, and she had not been able to give her last dying breath for them no matter how much she tried to keep them alive. God above knew she would have if it had been possible. She lived every day questioning why she hadn't been able to give her life for theirs despite her best efforts.

RED NOTICED THE way her breath hitched when he spoke of loyalty. He'd also noticed the way her skin heated with a blush when he said his wife and children would have the same until his death. It felt like a battle won, even if a small one, now that he was breaking through her resistance.

But then her face had hardened, and her eyes had become distant and filled with…sadness? Regret? He sensed the cause went far beyond what ever happened that day. He would be patient, but he would find out what brought her so much pain and how to ease her suffering.

Galiena peered into the other room where they could still hear Tommy asking Frode a thousand questions as the older man tried to instruct him on the proper way to repair chain mail. Tommy was sure he knew better ways to do everything and was not one to just take the goldsmith's word on how it was to be done. Seemingly satisfied the boy was in good hands, she turned back to Red.

"I will tell you what happened," she conceded. She held up a hand to stop the smug smile spreading across his face. *"But,* if you insist on being part of it, then you must promise to help me get to the king and queen before anything can happen to their son."

"The king and queen are on a procession through Wales now that the rebellions have been quelled." Red knew this because the king's plans were common knowledge. He wanted to see the land he'd conquered as well as be seen. "They started in Flint in the north of Wales in September and Edward is meeting with his vassals and touring the castles he ordered constructed along the way. They are traveling down the Welsh coast and are expected to be in the south of Wales by the end of December. It will not be difficult to determine where they can be intercepted."

"That is good news," Galiena said, elated. But her excitement was short-lived. "That also means the men who want to kill the queen's son can easily catch up to them, as well. We must be expedient if we are to succeed."

Her request wasn't practical or expedient. Hunter and Red could travel with greater urgency if left to their own devices, but having to escort another person, unused to hard riding or life on the road would slow their journey to the king. But he could tell by her expression she wouldn't accept his nay to her request. She might even follow along behind or even try to attempt to reach the king without his aid, and that would leave her unprotected. Every part of his body clenched at the idea of his she-wolf alone and on the road, with no one to keep her safe. Because of that, more than anything else, he had no choice but to agree. Red nodded agreement solemnly. "You have my word."

"Good." Her entire demeanor relaxed as she sighed her relief.

"Now, everything, from the beginning," he prompted her. He would wait until he had heard the entire story to judge if she was telling him the truth or holding back from him still.

"Yes," she said, "everything."

Anora cleared the tools and scraps from the far end of the worktable, then motioned everyone toward the benches. Red sat directly across from Galiena. He reached for the plate of candles placed at the center of the table and pulled them closer to where they sat so he could see every expression, every emotion, every flinch, every dart of her eyes.

It didn't take her very long to relay the events of the day, starting from when she decided to take a rest from her work in the narrow alley behind the inn to the present moment. When she repeated the conversation between the men in the alley, Red balled his fists on the table in front of him. The men were damn fools for not ensuring the alley was empty before talking about committing treason. And his little raven-haired vixen was damn lucky they didn't find her hiding in the shadows. Had they found her, letting her live wouldn't have been an option.

His she-wolf would have been dead and gone before he'd found her. That made him clench his fists even more tightly.

The biggest concern was that at least one of the men knew for certain she had the pouch with the missive, and likely assumed she had also overheard every word said. Red knew without a doubt that anyone planning treason who thought there was even the smallest suspicion someone had overheard them would never let that person escape alive.

But they'd have to get through him to get to her, and he would never allow that to happen. He'd tear anyone limb from limb who tried to harm even one hair on her beautiful head.

Now he just had to get her to quit resisting the fate that had brought him to her.

Red's hands were beginning to ache. His need to protect her was making him feel feral. He wanted to rip apart the entire village with his own hands searching for the men who were now a threat to her, and he would not stop until he found them and buried their lifeless bodies deep in the ground.

He forced himself to relax his fists as he watched Galiena touch the parchment with the tip of her finger to roll it over once. There was nothing on the outside of the little scroll. No seal. No markings. Nothing to indicate it was anything important. Her hand shook as it hovered above the missive, and she hesitated to open it. He reached and cupped his hand over hers to steady it. Her gaze flew to his as their hands touched but she did not pull away from him.

"It may be nothing," he said, trying to reassure her. "But if it is what you think it is, then everything changes."

She held his gaze as she considered his words, then nodded her head toward the scroll. "Open it."

Red did not let go of her hand as he picked up the parchment in the other and worked it open with his fingers. He stared at it for a long moment, feeling only slightly guilty for the relief that sent a thrill through his body as he took in the contents.

"Well?" Galiena asked. He could hear the nervous impatience in her voice. When he lifted his gaze to hers, he had to work to keep his face from revealing the excitement that had his blood pumping in anticipation.

"Tell me, Red!"

He met her gaze and held it, confirming what he had expected. "Everything changes."

Chapter Six

GOD HELP HER, but every nerve in her body was snapping with the exhilaration of the moment.

Of course, she was horrified that she had stumbled upon a treasonous plot to kill the heir to the English crown, but she felt more alive than she had in three years. She had definitely found an adventure, and the weight of it was tremendous, with the life of a child hanging in the balance. She would not fail in her mission to get to the queen before anyone could harm her son. There was too much weighing on the success of the mission.

But also, she wouldn't fail because it would be the modicum of redemption she needed for her own failure as a mother.

Admittedly, much of her excitement was the result of the man sitting across from her, holding her hand in his. She couldn't deny that she felt safe in his presence, and charmed by his easy, confident manner. Nor could she deny she'd been momentarily saddened, thinking about her future. If the missive had been nothing of import, he would have left Oswestry—and her—to continue on with his duties, and she would have been left behind to continue her mundane existence. But the anticipation she felt because her time with Red was not yet over felt like a betrayal to the husband who had always been kind and loving to her, had done everything he could to please her, and who had been taken from her too soon. She had loved him, loved their life together on the little farm, cherished being a mother, and been contented as Adam's wife.

She knew the church and society expected her to marry again, to find a husband who could provide for her so she would not be a burden to others, but she hadn't been able to do it. She barely survived on the wages she earned helping at the tavern and preparing the rooms above for travelers, but her pride would not allow her to beg for food or live off of charity. And she'd not even considered taking another man as her husband or trying to have a family again. It would feel too much like she was abandoning Adam and Nahara. There was no one else to remember them. If she didn't keep the memory of them alive in her heart and mind, then they would be forever gone, just like her father.

A reassuring squeeze of her hand brought her back to the present and she looked up to see Red studying her, his face etched with concern. He caught her gaze and held it, staring at her intently while he waited patiently for her to decide to continue. This man, with his ice-blue eyes that crinkled in the corners when he smiled his lopsided grin was dangerous to her. She felt herself thawing in his presence, felt her heart beginning to beat again, and felt the ember of hope that there was more for her in this life than what she'd lost burning deep within.

Anora broke into Galiena's thoughts. "Is what's in the parchment enough to convince the king that what Galiena overheard was true?"

Red splayed the parchment out on the table for everyone to see. Galiena, Anora, and Hunter all bent their heads forward to look at the rows of neat writing. The letters were so small that Galiena had to squint to see them clearly.

"I don't recognize the language," Galiena said, trying to make any sense of the letters and symbols. Because of her father's work as a merchant, it had been necessary to learn how to read and write rudimentary bits of the languages from many of the countries on the continent and the Mediterranean, but she couldn't decipher this.

"It's code," Hunter said.

Galiena gently pulled her hand from Red's, then turned the parchment to see from the correct angle, using both hands to hold it open. It was only a few finger widths wide, and about as long as Galiena's hand from the tip of her longest finger to her wrist. Inspecting the missive more closely, she recognized the letters from the Latin alphabet, used throughout Britain, but here they didn't form any discernable words and were interspersed with symbols made of patterns of dots.

"The boy is tired, but his stomach is rumbling," Frode said from the doorway to the shop.

Galiena had been so fascinated by the coded missive, she hadn't heard Frode enter. Red slid the parchment out from under her fingertips and rolled it back into a tight scroll as Tommy pushed past Frode into the room.

In a panic, she grabbed Red's hands before he could tuck the scroll under his cloak. "No. I must keep it." She would not let the missive out of her sight. Red and Hunter knew all that she did about the two men and the overheard conversation, and the only leverage she had remaining was the missive. If they had that, too, then they did not need her to warn the king of the danger. She knew it was selfish to insist she be the one to take the journey, but she felt in her heart that she must do this, as one mother to another, even if one of them was the queen of England. She also knew that Red could overpower her and take the missive if he so desired, but she was counting on him to keep his word and prove himself trustworthy.

Red slid the parchment back toward her with a nod, much to Galiena's relief.

Anora stood. "I will put a stew over the fire," she said moving to the hearth along the back wall.

The flames had burned down to embers and the early winter chill was seeping through the walls. She'd left her cloak behind at the inn in her haste to escape, but the fear and exhilaration from overhearing the men in the alley, stealing the pouch, encounter-ing Red, and running through the lanes to elude her pursuer had kept her warm—or at least, distracted from the cold.

She shivered now, as much from the chill in the air as from the growing realization of the danger she was in and that her life would never be the same again.

And if she wasn't careful, it may also be very, *very* short.

"THIS IS THE boy who used to tell me stories about his travels with his father?" Anora asked, looking at her father wide-eyed while gesturing toward Galiena.

Frode nodded. "Aye, the same."

They were sitting at the cleared end of the worktable near the warmth from the hearth, their bellies full. Tommy had finally grown tired, and Anora had put him to sleep in Frode's bed, which meant they also finally had a break from his incessant questions and boyish proclamations about his ability to take care of himself. It took some convincing, and a stern look from Red, to get the boy to agree to stay hidden at the goldsmith shop until they were certain his life was no longer in danger from the men in the alley. He'd protested during the bath that Anora insisted he take before getting into her father's bed but had relented when Anora reminded him that he'd agreed to the bath in exchange for the second large bowl of stew he'd somehow fit into his scrawny body. Red and Hunter were leaning against the wall on the other end of the room, as far away from them as possible, speaking in low murmurs.

Galiena had rarely discussed her childhood with anyone ex-cept her husband after her father died. Because of the vulnerability of being a woman traveling, her father had started dressing her as a boy from a young age.

"It's little wonder we became such fast friends when I met you as a grown woman. We already knew each other!" Anora put a hand over one of Galiena's. Her smile faded after a moment, and she surprised Galiena by giving her hand a gentle slap. "Why did you not tell me who you were when we met?"

Galiena blushed. "To be honest, I did not recognize you until you brought me here and I met your father. Then the memories of the few times I was in your shop as a child came rushing back. But you and your father had known me as a boy, and I wasn't sure if you remembered the times my father visited. Staying quiet about it was easier than explaining."

Red had straddled the bench next to Galiena and she suddenly felt overly warm, as though she was being suffocated. She looked pointedly at his knees on either side of the bench, one touching her knee and the other pressed intimately close to her hip as he sat facing her, then lifted her disapproving gaze to his innocent-appearing one. When he didn't get the hint from her glare that he was acting far too familiar for a man she hardly knew, she said, "There is ample room on this bench for you to sit a respectable distance away."

"If we are to travel together and pass as husband and wife, we should start acting the parts now," he replied, the skin around his eyes crinkling as his mouth lifted into that grin that she was finding more annoying than charming at this moment. Did this man take nothing seriously?

"No," she said pushing at his leg with her hand in a wasted attempt to get him to move. "We may have to travel together but we need not be this intimate. *Or* pretend to be married."

The decision had been made that Red and Galiena would leave before dawn on a course for *Llanbadarn Gaerog* on the west coast of central Wales. Hawkspur Castle was near the main road leading into central Wales, and they would rest there the first night. Red would request additional men from Hawk to ride with them into Wales to intercept the king and queen before an assassin got to their son, God willing.

"We will attract less attention if we tell others we are married, so I suggest you get comfortable with having me close," he insisted, obviously enjoying her discomfort.

"Not this close." She shoved against his chest with all her might.

He didn't budge. "For your own safety, you won't be staying in a separate room at the inns along the way, but the story will be your decision," he said with a shrug. "Of course, we can let everyone at the inns assume you are a harlot I've purchased for the night." His eyes crinkled and twinkled even as Galiena tried to push at him again. "But that story will make us more memorable. Or we can travel as man and wife. No one will care about that."

Annoying man. Before she could press the point further Red had turned his attention to Hunter, but he hadn't budged from his place beside her and had seemingly decided her protests were nothing to worry about.

"Unless you know where we can find another horse this time of night, we will need to take yours," Red said to Hunter.

"You can have it," Hunter readily agreed. "I'll find another."

It was Red's turn to be amused. "It's not like you to give up your mount so readily. How long are you planning to stay here?"

Galiena looked back and forth between the two warriors, wondering what the unsaid, but obviously understood, message was between them. It was as though they were having an entirely different conversation with the tones, looks, and gestures that passed between them at times.

"Until I know Frode, Anora, and Tommy are not in danger."

Had Galiena blinked, she would have missed the almost imperceptible glance Hunter directed toward Anora. She would have put it down to a twitch in his eyes, except she heard his muffled "oomph" that he tried to cover up as a cough and felt the movement of Red's leg as he kicked his friend under the table. Anora, as was true to her nature, was completely oblivious to the antics of the two men.

"Awfully chivalric of you," Red said, his voice thick with sarcasm.

Galiena would have sworn she saw the taciturn warrior's

cheeks redden lightly in the flickering candlelight.

"Frode, if you permit," Hunter said, "I will stay here until we are sure no one comes nosing around your shop looking for Galiena or the boy."

"You know you are welcome here," Frode agreed. "Sumayl is always on alert, but he will not turn away your added protection."

"Tommy will be difficult to keep under your roof," Galiena warned. "He'll get restless trapped inside and he'll sneak out if you don't tie him down. But I fear for him."

"I will keep him busy," Frode assured her.

That decided, Hunter looked at Galiena. "Do you know how to ride?" he asked.

"Yes," she said after a hesitation. She'd not ridden often, but she'd spent countless hours driving her father's wagon and she was not afraid of horses. Though she couldn't exactly recall when exactly the last time was that she rode *on* a horse, she felt sure it wouldn't be too difficult.

"He likes a light hand," Hunter said, his face etched with concern. "And whatever you do, don't kick his sides to make him walk or you'll be flat on your back in the mud and he'll be a furlong away before you catch your breath."

She swallowed a lump of anxiety, but she wouldn't let her fear deter her. Getting to the queen before something disastrous happened to her son was more important than her apprehension about being able to stay put in the saddle. She'd just have to hang on for dear life and make it work because the life of a child depended on it.

"Stand up," Red directed Galiena as he took to his feet. She looked at him warily, wondering what he planned to do. She didn't rise quick enough for his liking apparently because the next thing she knew he had scooped her from the bench and had her cradled in his arms. He bobbed her up and down in his arms a few times as though measuring her weight.

"Put me down, you ox!" she protested, trying to escape his

grasp to no avail.

"She isn't much heavier than a pair of saddle bags. If we take the barest of provisions, Hammer can carry both of us, at least until we get to Hawkspur, and I can find a suitable mount for her." Red set her back down on the bench.

"I prefer to ride a separate horse," Galiena said, feeling very indignant about being picked up like a sack of flour, and then plopped down.

"If you are not an experienced rider, Hunter's horse is not for you," Red said with a shake of his head as he took his place beside her again. This time, he sat facing forward on the bench instead of straddling it, but he was still sitting entirely too close for Galiena's comfort.

"I will hang on tight." She tried to elbow him a bit as she wriggled to make more room on the bench, but other than a smirk, he ignored her.

"Red is right, it will be better if you both ride Hammer," Hunter said. "The huge ox you call a horse will hardly notice another rider."

"You should get some rest," Frode interrupted, directing his comment toward Galiena. "The days ahead may be grueling."

Galiena didn't know if she could actually sleep with all the events of the day rolling around in her head, but she would at least try. The concern that was currently foremost on her mind was that she needed her cloak and at least one additional chemise and tunic from her little cottage. "Is it possible to go to my home before we leave so that I may get a change of clothing and my sturdier boots?" She really didn't have much hope for it, but she had to ask.

Red was shaking his head before she could even finish her question. "Can you give her some clothing and boots, Anora?"

Galiena laughed softly. "Have you not looked at us side by side? Even if we could hem one of her gowns, I cannot leave her without a cloak. Which would also need to be hemmed lest I ruin it by dragging it through the mud."

"You can't be that different in height," Red said, looking truly perplexed.

She stared at him, speechless. Had he really not noticed Anora and how different she was in height and appearance? Galiena didn't necessarily dislike her own short stature and curvy body, but she envied her friend's height and beauty. Anora was stunningly tall and willowy, with pale gold hair, sapphire blue eyes, and a ready smile. How anyone could not see the differences between them was beyond her.

"We can find you a cloak at Hawkspur, and there is a shoemaker who can make you boots," Red responded, seemingly confident he had resolved the issue.

"Am I to freeze until we get to Hawkspur? And we cannot wait an extra day while boots are constructed. We don't have the time. The queen's *child* doesn't have the time."

"You cannot go back to your cottage." The words were firm, but his expression was sympathetic. "I know you want your own things, but if the men you saw have even half a brain between them, they have learned your name and where you live. And they will be watching for you to return. I'll keep you warm under my cloak until we get to Hawkspur."

Galiena let out a frustrated sigh.

"Come with me," Anora said, rising from the table. "Let us see what we can find for you for the journey. And if you will be sitting astride a horse for long days, I suggest you wear braies under your tunic. We still have my brother's clothing in a chest upstairs. Perhaps we can make something of his work for you."

"Galiena," Frode said in a quiet voice. "Will you leave the missive with us, dear?"

She hesitated, fearful that once she gave it up Red would think he no longer needed her for the journey to the king.

"You will have it back," Frode promised. "But I may be of some assistance in this, even with my failing eyes."

She was too indebted to Frode to refuse him. Reaching into her tunic, to the pouch tied to her belt, she removed the scrap of parchment and placed it in his hand, giving his fingers a squeeze before letting go.

Turning to Red, she pointed a finger at him, schooled her face into the sternest expression she could muster, and said in her most commanding voice, "I am trusting you not to betray me and leave without me."

"I would not think of it, Wife."

She bristled at the endearment, but his serious expression and the hand he placed over his heart reassured her…somewhat.

THE DESPERATION HE heard in Galiena's voice, mixed with the fear he saw in her eyes, tugged at Red's heart. Obviously, she had more reason than just devotion to the monarchy compelling her to deliver the missive and the warning to the king and queen.

He watched as Anora took her by the hand and led her from the room. Though he could have traveled faster without her, he wouldn't leave her behind; this was too important to her, even if he didn't understand all the reasons why. He didn't doubt his ability to protect her.

When the women were gone, leaving only Hunter and Frode in the room with him, Red turned to his friend. "Is her hooded man one and the same as the man we seek?"

Hunter nodded solemnly and Red felt the blood in his veins turn to ice. He'd been looking for this man for the two decades he'd been in Britain. As a youth, he'd stepped off the ship onto English soil, and not even two full days had passed until The Executioner tried to take his life. His gut twisted with sharp anguish as he thought of his mother and uncle. They had not been as fortunate. They did not live to see another day, but Red had lived, each day since a reminder that he had survived and they had not. That he had failed to protect them. For a long time, he'd wished he'd died with his family instead of living with this need for vengeance that had taken root in his chest, eating at him for nigh these twenty-something years so that he could not rest until he found the man responsible for his anguish.

The Executioner. It was an apt name for a man so ruthless and cold.

"You will have your vengeance," Hunter reminded him, "but now he is involved in a treasonous plot that goes beyond him. With patience, we will get your man and the men plotting against the king."

Red ground his teeth together in frustration. Over a year ago, in a state of desperation and intoxication after nearly two decades of searching for the killer, he had turned to Hunter and his uncanny tracking skills for assistance. The man was the ultimate predator, and likely the deadliest man in all of Britain. He was privileged to call Hunter a friend instead of an adversary. Since he was his friend, he decided to beg the favor of helping him complete his quest for vengeance in the hope it would put the constant tightness in his chest to rest.

"Now that we found him, restrain yourself," Hunter warned. "Your best move is to get that missive to the king and find out who is behind it. Then you will have The Executioner *and* the men planning treason against His Grace."

Red inhaled deeply, letting the sagacity of Hunter's words penetrate the part of him that wanted to ignore all good sense and find the man to rip him from limb to limb. If he truly wanted to avenge his mother and uncle, then his every move needed to be timed and calculated.

"Can you understand the code in the missive?" Red asked Hunter, turning his attention back to the message that might not only save the king's heir but also reveal the identity of The Executioner.

"I know the basics of decoding and have not used the skill for some time," he admitted.

Red leaned forward for a clearer view as Hunter spread the missive out on the table next to a plate of candles. As before, the combinations of letters and symbols did not make any sense to

Red, and he feared that the only way to break the code was with a translation key—which only the author of the message and the intended recipient would have.

"There's definitely a pattern," Hunter murmured, studying the parchment. "It appears to be typical code with the dot patterns replacing specific letters. A common method of coding is to substitute the vowels with symbols or patterns. And to shift the other letters one or two positions in either direction the order of the alphabet."

Red pointed toward two sets of dot patterns near the bottom of the missive. "These dots look more like minuscule circles rather than actual dots. Does that mean anything?"

Frode laughed appreciatively. "You're no fool, Red. I am beginning to think Galiena may have chosen well."

"I knew that stoicism was hiding a deep appreciation for my wit and charm," Red said, clapping Frode on the shoulder.

"You have the wit and charm of a boar's balls," Hunter said with a smirk.

"Gads, how I have missed this." Frode cackled with merriment, wiping at his eyes. "I was once part of King Henry's army and I have some knowledge of the skills required for covert activities. Ah, but I miss the comradery and the excitement of those days." His face took on a wistful expression for a moment. "But let us return to the task at hand. Tell me about the circle dots. Are they throughout the message, or clustered together?"

"They are together," Hunter confirmed. "And they look to make up numbers, likely as part of a date. Looks like two numbers followed by a word and then four more numbers." He huffed out a sigh as he stared at the parchment. "Deciphering this by morn is possible—but there's work to do yet this night, if the men from the alley are still here."

Red narrowed his eyes at Hunter. "You think you can find them?"

"If they're still in Oswestry, I'll find them."

"I'll go with you," Red responded, knowing Hunter would

never allow it—he worked alone. In this, Red would be a hindrance more than a help. Which is exactly what the tolerant smirk Hunter threw his way conveyed.

"The men are looking for you and the lady; they know nothing of me. Stay here and do what you do best."

"Which is?" Frode asked.

"Watching over the ladies. You've always preferred courting to killing."

"You have always envied my ability to do more than grunt at a woman, turn the color of an apple, and then run away," Red said with a wink. "I'll be happy to teach you the ways of wooing a lady."

"No need," Hunter grunted, turning away from Red, but not before he saw the color rise in his friend's cheeks. Hunter rose from the table and searched for something on the work bench along the wall. A moment later, he returned with a piece of parchment, a quill, and a small bottle. He pushed the items toward Red, then turned the original parchment in his direction. "Make a copy of the missive while I'm out. You'd never guess it, Frode, but this lumbering lout has a steady hand with the quill."

Red studied the minuscule writing and symbols. "The letters aren't a problem, and I'll try to get the symbols as near as possible."

"The words on each line and the letter or symbol placement are also significant," Frode said. "The letter or word arrangement top to bottom can be as important as the order left to right."

"Good to know," Red acknowledged, opening the bottle of ink, and setting to work while Hunter slipped out the back door. He kept his head down, eyes focused on the task.

"Even a blind man can see the way Hunter is flustered around my daughter," Frode said, his voice wary. "Need I be concerned about having him under my roof, even if for only a few nights?"

"No," Red said with a shake of his head. "Hunter would never do anything to disgrace your daughter. He has too much self-control and values his honor above all else."

"And you?" Frode pressed. "Need I worry about Galiena's honor while in your company?"

Red stilled his hand and lifted his head to look at Frode. "I will treat her with honor, but I intend to make her mine."

"Already? When you've known her only this day?"

"Aye." Galiena running into his arms, looking at him with those mesmerizing eyes as she called him husband, and having the nerve to argue with him had sealed her fate to him as far as he was concerned. "My intentions are true and honest. She may not have admitted it to herself yet, but we are destined to be together, and I will not be deterred."

"Let an old man give you some advice," Frode said with a soft chuckle. "Give her a little room to breathe and let her come to you."

Red didn't like that advice. He had always said what he felt and taken what he wanted. Granted, when it came to women, he'd yet to find one he wanted to keep. But that had changed on this day.

"I can tell you will not be heeding my advice."

"I will think about it," Red promised.

"Galiena has no one left in her life who cares for her other than Anora, and now me. As such, I feel it is my duty to let you know that if I suspect you have tried to force her or coerce her, I will have Sumayl break your neck." Frode's face was hard as stone, and his voice was as sharp as a blade. His eyes may be unseeing, but his message was clear.

"Aye, sir," Red responded, an unfamiliar discomfort coming over him. They were not the harsh words Red expected from the old man, but he respected him for it. He hadn't been chastised in this way since he was a young man with nothing but a patchy beard on his chin. Hawk had been the only man Red had agreed to take orders from in nigh on twenty years. It gave him comfort to know Galiena had a man like Frode looking after her. As much as it galled him to capitulate to a man he'd known for an even shorter time than he'd known Galiena, he would do it.

For her.

Chapter Seven

I T WAS STILL dark when Red took Galiena's hand and led her from the goldsmith shop the next morning. There was a bite to the air that chafed her cheeks, but Anora had made sure Galiena was bundled from toes to teeth against the cold before letting her leave. She had on an extra pair of wool socks—which helped make the overly large boots fit more comfortably—thick braies and a second chemise layered under her gown. Her dear friend had stayed up all night hemming an extra cloak to a length that wouldn't trip her when she walked in it. And she'd added a slit up the back of the cloak that reached her upper thighs and could be held closed with a series of ties or left open to drape over each of her legs while in the saddle.

"You are the cleverest, by far. I am grateful to call you friend," Galiena had said to Anora, wrapping her in a huge hug. She clung to Anora for several long breaths. "Am I addlebrained to insist I be included in the journey to bring the news and the missive to the queen and king?"

"Yes," Anora answered with a mirthless laugh and an affectionate squeeze. "But no more addlebrained than a man would be in the same situation." She pulled back to look Galiena in the eye. "And who better to understand what a child means to a mother than you. I wager you would defy death, if needs be, to get to the queen and her babe, regardless of the perils you may face."

Galiena nodded her head and took in a fortifying breath. "If I'm going to get killed because of this tiny roll of parchment, I'd rather it be while trying to save the little prince than sitting in my cottage waiting for the people who are plotting to come for me." She touched her hand to her inner elbow where Anora had sewn a sleek pouch into the seam of her chemise, just wide enough to tuck the tightly rolled parchment safely away.

"You heard what Tommy said. Quit touching it, or everyone will know you carry something important," Anora scolded.

"Right," Galiena replied, deliberately folding her hands in front of her.

"Now, go save that little prince." Anora had turned Galiena by the shoulders then and pushed her toward the front room where Red awaited her.

With the wind tugging at her braided hair, she studied the huge horse in front of her. "Is that a saddle?" she asked, pointing to the blanket of fur strapped to the horse's back with a leather strap. She'd been expecting a proper saddle with a seat and something to hang onto for dear life. She imagined herself riding behind Red while she clung to…whatever the back of a saddle was called.

"No saddle," he confirmed. "We will be faster this way. Lighter. Just need the stirrups."

Her gaze followed his finger down to the metal loop hanging from a leather strap attached to a belt wrapped over the fur blanket and under the horse's belly. She assumed there was another on the other side. "I won't be able to reach those."

Red let out a low laugh as he twined his fingers together to form a cup and dropped them down in front of her. "Get up there."

Mumbling a reminder to herself that she was doing this for the queen, she placed her foot in his hands and waited for his next instruction. She heard his heavy sigh of frustration, followed by what sounded like a low growl. "The *other* foot."

"Oh." Thankfully it was still too dark for him to see the heat rise in her cheeks at her blunder.

"Grab my shoulders and swing your other leg over as I lift."

As she landed on the horse's back—none too gracefully—the beast bobbed his head and blew out a breath, sounding very much like his impatient master. Before she could comment on the similarities, Red grabbed the horse by his considerable mane and swung on to the horse behind her in one smooth motion. It was ridiculous to be offended by a horse, but it rankled that the beast didn't even make a sound when the huge Viking straddled his back.

"That was quite rude, Ham," she grumbled to the horse.

"Don't call him that," Red said, picking up the reins and nudging the horse to walk. "It's Hammer."

"You never shorten it to *Ham?*"

"That's insulting." As if on cue, Hammer nodded his head up and down.

"Did you make him do that?" she asked while she carefully wriggled forward to put space between her back and Red's chest.

"He's very astute," he said quietly.

Because it was still dark, and because Red couldn't see her face, she allowed herself an amused smile at his wry response and noticed some of the tension leaving her shoulders as his big frame protected her from the wind. She was about to say something about the benefit of a clever horse but stopped when Red leaned close to her ear to say in a low voice, "No more talking until we are away from the village."

A tingle of fear shivered down her spine at the reminder of the danger that may be lying in wait for them. It definitely wasn't the warmth of Red's breath on the sensitive skin behind her ear that brought up the goose flesh on her neck. She didn't resist when Red pulled her hood up over her head to hang low over her eyes, effectively hiding her from anyone who might be in the lanes.

They did not pass by the church or her cottage on the edge of the church yard. Instead, they took the lane that circled the western side of the village before passing by the last of the tradesmen's huts and riding away from town. She had been unsettled by Red's nearness, the way his thighs cradled hers and his chest pressed against her back. But she was grateful for the support of his body as the horse trotted faster and faster down the road. She just wished she knew how to keep from bouncing uncomfortably with each step.

Red snaked his arm around her waist and pulled her near until her back was snug against his chest. "Relax and let your body follow the rhythm of the horse." She didn't like to admit that it was easier to settle into the cadence of the horse's stride with Red's body as a guide to the movement and tempo.

Her father had explained to her that horses could see better than their riders at night because their eyes were so much bigger. This bit of knowledge, paired with evidence of the imminent sunrise in the graying horizon visible over the tops of the trees assuaged her fear that Hammer would misstep and launch them headfirst onto the hard ground, breaking their necks.

As they approached the first crossroads, Hammer broke into a rolling canter that made Galiena's stomach lurch with the rocking motion. Red tightened his hold on her but did not ease Hammer's pace. After what seemed an eternity, the horse turned sharply into the woods, forcing Galiena to jerk to the side so that Red's arm pressed forcefully against her belly as he tried to hold her in place. She felt the contents of her stomach, which was minimal considering they had yet to break their fast, rising into her throat.

"Please, stop," she begged, concentrating to fight a wave of nausea. The horse slowed and then came to a stop. Galiena opened her eyes to see they had ridden deeper into the woods and away from the road. "Please, let me down."

"No," Red said in a low voice. "Not until I am certain we are safe."

Galiena grabbed Red's arm with both hands to push it down, then leaned over the side of the horse and, to her complete and utter mortification, vomited. She let her head hang down for a long moment while she tried to gain control of her body.

"Slow, deep breaths," Red said with what sounded like sympathy as he lifted his arm high on her chest to support her. At the same time, he hooked a hand on her opposite shoulder so she could lean her weight into it. After a few breaths, he asked, "Are you done?"

"I think so," she mumbled, sitting up slowly. Red guided her until she was settled with her back against him.

"Rinse." She felt him moving around behind her and then he moved a stiff leather drinking pouch around to her front and held it up for her to take a drink. "Why are you ill?"

She obediently took the pouch and swished water in her mouth, then leaned over the side of the horse again to spit it out onto the ground. It was humiliatingly crude, but worth it to get the horrid taste from her mouth. "The rolling of the horse made my stomach queasy."

"I've seen people get sick riding a ship on the sea, but never have I witnessed someone get sick riding a horse."

"Don't sound so incredulous," she said irritably. "It was your fault. Your arm dug into my stomach when you turned."

"Drink," he said, holding the pouch up to her again.

She obeyed, then leaned back into him again, feeling depleted.

"This is going to be a long journey."

It wasn't Red who said the last, though she recognized the droll voice. Galiena slit her eyes open enough to see Hunter directly in front of them on his own horse.

"I'll take her back," Hunter said, unenthusiastically.

"No!"

"Not so loud," Red warned her.

"No," she repeated in a loud whisper. "I'll be fine. I just wasn't expecting him to turn so suddenly."

Hunter's expression remained bland as his gaze moved from her to Red, but she had the distinct feeling he did not believe her.

And he obviously did not think it wise for Red to allow her to continue. "Were we followed?" Red asked, changing the topic.

"No." It was the answer they wanted, but Galiena sensed there was more he wished to say.

"What news have you?" Red asked, his voice laced with the same suspicion Galiena felt. When Hunter hesitated, Red added, "You may speak freely in front of her. She is as much a part of this as we are now."

"Your pursuer is nowhere to be found."

"And…" Red coaxed.

"And the man he met in the alley is dead."

Galiena could feel the huff of breath that Red released at that bit of news against the back of her neck.

"How?" The tone of Red's voice as he bit out the one word sent a chill down Galiena's spine.

Hunter made the motion of a knife to the throat.

"Is that him?"

Galiena hadn't noticed the bundle strapped to the back of Hunter's horse until now. She fought another wave of nausea, knowing that Hunter, at least, would see it as final confirmation she wasn't to be allowed to continue. She swallowed the bile rising in her throat and looked away from the wrapped form behind Hunter. Think of the queen, she told herself. *Think of the queen.*

"I believe so," Hunter said. "But she got the best look at him. If it's not him, she'll know if it's someone from the village."

"I don't want her to see that," Red said more forcefully than Galiena thought necessary, even though the thought of looking at the dead man made her feel lightheaded as the blood drained from her face, but she steeled herself. *The queen. The infant prince.* This was no time to be squeamish. "I'll do it."

Hunter was already nudging his horse closer to them. He reached back and pulled the wool blanket from the dead man's upper body, then reached down to turn his head so she could see his face.

His hair was cropped short, and his face was colorless, but his neck was a mangled mess of dried blood and torn flesh. She forced herself to not look directly at his throat and concentrated instead on his face. When she'd seen the man, he was being choked, his features bulging with exertion. Now, his face was an ashen gray, making it difficult to tell if it was the same man. Pointing to the left side of the man's face, she said, "Can you turn his head so I can see above his ear on that side?"

Hunter easily swiveled the man's head so the left side was visible; Galiena could easily see the scar above his ear and the bald spot.

"That's him," she said, then averted her gaze. "He's not from the village and I've never seen him before."

Hunter let go of the man's head; she heard a thud and then another as, from the corner of her eye, she could see him pulling the blanket back over the dead man's head again. Bile rose unbidden to her throat once more but this time she couldn't stop herself from leaning to the side to retch a second time.

Oh, God, not again! She held out her hand for the pouch, which was promptly supplied, rinsed her mouth, and crudely spit it out, then took another drink.

"Are you sure?" She was certain Hunter meant the flat-toned question for Red.

"No," she bit out through gritted teeth as she sucked in a deep breath. "I'll not go back."

"She'll be safe at Frode's shop with Sumayl," Hunter argued, addressing Red as though he had been the one to protest.

"You're certain the other one is not still in the village?" Red asked.

"I couldn't find any sign of him," Hunter responded with a shrug as Galiena stiffened her spine. "She'll be safer there than anywhere else."

She clutched the arm he had wrapped around her middle and peered at him over her shoulder. "I can do this."

He stared back at her for a long moment. "If we stop every

time you get sick, it will take us a sennight to get to the king. By then it may be too late."

"I'll get better at this," she said, trying not to cringe at the desperation in her voice.

"And if you don't?" His dark red eyebrows twitched upward with the question.

"Then I'll learn to retch without Hammer breaking stride," she said, letting her irritation make her remark ring with sarcasm.

His lips quirked into a lopsided smirk. "You'll leave a trail, which will make my job that much more difficult."

"You'll figure it out and deal with it," she said with more confidence than she felt, but she knew she had won when he rolled his eyes heavenward with a slight shake of his head.

"Aye, *Wife*," Red conceded, "I'll deal with it."

She couldn't hide her own triumphant grin as she turned to face forward again, pointedly ignoring that he was back to calling her "wife" again. Or maybe, she conceded, she was starting to enjoy it. It had been a long time since she'd had a man flirt with her in a way that didn't involve him trying to immediately drag her to a corner for what he'd consider a dalliance and she'd consider something far worse.

"Please keep all of them safe," Galiena said to Hunter in a low voice, feeling self-conscious of his belief that she was not capable of completing the journey, and likely thought her a hindrance in getting to the king and queen before The Executioner. A small voice in the back of her mind suggested he might be right, but she refused to listen to it.

"I will," Hunter stated. "I will not let anything happen to Frode or Anora."

"Nor Thomas or Sumayl," she reminded him.

Hunter grunted and nodded once. "Sumayl is capable of protecting all of them, but I will stay until I am certain the danger has passed."

"Be careful," Red said, the warning earning him a peevish glare from Hunter. "The Executioner is a dangerous man."

"More dangerous than me?" Hunter asked in a growly voice.

"No," Red conceded. "But he's as close as anyone will ever come to being as lethal as you. You know that. You've been following him."

"He is proving elusive. I've yet to determine who he works for," Hunter said, setting his jaw in a hardline.

"How will we know...*The Executioner*? Is that what we are calling him?" Galiena asked. She hadn't seen his face and knew him only as a cloaked figure in a hood. She hoped she'd recognize his voice if she heard it. But if he was close enough for her to hear him, then he was close enough to kill them.

"You won't be going anywhere near him," Red growled.

Galiena looked over her shoulder at Red, shocked to see the hard, straight line of his lips under his beard and the gleam of pure hatred in his eyes. He stared over the top of her head, refusing to meet her gaze, and she found herself feeling very afraid and very alone for the first time since stumbling into the Viking's arms. The man she'd initially thought of as a giant, charming, joking oaf looked cold and deadly. She turned stiffly to face forward again, keeping her back straight so as not to lean into Red, and fought a shiver. She had no desire to get pulled into the storm of his dark mood.

"Both of you know who we are looking for, but I still do not," Galiena reminded them. "Who is this man?" When neither man responded, she added, "If this man is as dangerous as you say, then you put me at a disadvantage by not telling me what you know."

"Best of luck, Viking," Hunter said, then nudged his horse forward and rode into the cover of the trees.

The sun was above the tree line and dawn had become morning some time ago, and in the full light of day, Galiena found Hunter's uncanny ability to disappear unsettling, to say the least. "I don't think I like him." The words escaped her lips before she could stop them.

"Most people don't." Red's deep chuckle was unexpected. As

was the sudden relief that washed through her body at the rich sound, as though something lost had been found again. "I'll tell you what we know of this man."

She relaxed against him once more as he took up the reins and guided Hammer back to the road to continue the journey.

IF RED WAS a sensible man, he would have let Hunter take Galiena back to the goldsmith's shop. If he was a *wise* man, he would have forced her to stay under Sumayl's watchful eye and never agreed to bring her on this journey.

But when it came to Galiena, he was proving to be neither sensible nor wise.

His commander would understand without him defending his decisions. As much as Hawk used to jibe at him about his romantic tendencies, the man had lost all sense once he'd found Lady Alyce. Red was certain he would understand what it meant to make the wrong decisions for the right woman, so he would not have to explain his reasoning to Hawk.

Red knew his world had shifted in those first moments with Galiena. The challenge was going to be getting her to admit that she felt the same. His she-wolf was a feisty one when she wanted to be, docile and aloof when it suited her, and fiercely independent. He had no desire to tame her, but he had every intention of making her his. He laughed out loud, thinking about the challenge ahead and the merry ride it would be.

"Why do you laugh?" Galiena asked. Her hood had fallen back, and he could smell the scent of her soap in the thick, dark hair so close that he could bury his nose in it if he tipped his head forward. He had fought the urge to nuzzle her and hold her tighter to his chest, just like a kitten, but he knew he needed to censure himself lest he scare her away before he'd gained her trust.

"Nothing of consequence," he responded.

"Tell me of this Executioner so that I can at least know who is trying to kill me."

"He will not get anywhere near you." Red did tighten his hold on her then, and rested his chin on top of her crown, feeling an overwhelming need to protect her and soothe away her fears.

"I thought you said we had to keep our voices down."

Red hadn't realized he'd nearly shouted the words, but he was vehement that he would not allow anyone to harm her. "Are you afraid?"

"Of him? It sounds like I would be foolish not to be, but I will not let that stop me."

"You know I will not let him harm you." He spoke the words as a command and not a question, and in a harsher tone than intended, but he needed her to trust that he would protect her.

She turned to look up at him, studying his face as though searching for an answer to some question in the depths of his eyes. "I believe you."

He felt his chest swell with pride and nearly kissed her for it, but she turned to look straight ahead before he had the chance. A smile spread across his face, and he could do nothing to stop it even if he was sure it was a stupid grin and not at all befitting a warrior. He basked in the small triumph until she interrupted him.

"Now, tell me about this man so I may recognize him if we cross his path."

Red relented, though he hated the idea that she had to be aware of the despicable man. "Last time I saw him, he had a long, narrow face with sharp features and dark hair." Red didn't tell her about the way his lips twisted in a sneer as he watched his victims choke on their own blood, or the cold, evil glint in his eyes that matched the glint of his blade as he stabbed it through their necks. "We don't know yet who he works for, but we believe him to be a hired executioner."

"What is he to you, Red?"

It wasn't the question he expected from her, though he could have deflected it. But he didn't. He wouldn't tell her all of what he knew, but he did give her this: "He tried to kill me once. Would have succeeded if he hadn't been interrupted."

It was more than most people knew about him.

She was quiet for a while, then turned to look at him over her shoulder, her brow pinched with confusion. "Why did he not recognize you when he spoke to you in the lane?"

Looking over her head to avoid the distraction of her mesmerizing gaze, he said. "It was a long time ago. I was very young, didn't even have the first hair of a beard."

He was relieved when she turned to face forward again, not asking any more questions. It was on the tip of his tongue to tell her about his mother and uncle and all that had been taken from him the day they were murdered, but he held back. He'd only told two people what happened to his family the day they crossed paths with The Executioner: Hawk and Hunter. Hawk, because he'd saved him from death at the hands of The Executioner, and Hunter because he'd asked for his friend's help to find the man. To Hunter's credit, he didn't ask why before agreeing to help, but he told him anyway.

"Frode said you are alone in the world. Is that true?" He'd asked Frode to tell him what he knew of Galiena, but the old man refused to say anything more than that she had no family, that he'd known her father, and that the rest Red had to discover for himself.

"Aye," she responded, her voice clear and strong in the one succinct word. She had obviously accepted her plight, despite the hurt he sometimes sensed in her expression. He understood what that was like, to be forced to continue living life without the people who mattered the most but who one could never forget.

She didn't say more, and he didn't press her. She settled into the rhythm of Hammer's gait and didn't look back at him again until they stopped to rest the horse and stretch their legs.

"I've never seen a horse like Hammer," Galiena observed as they ate chunks of bread and sharp cheese from the leather bag

Red had strapped to his belt. "I've never seen a horse so broad in the back or thick in the shoulder as Hammer. His neck is like a tree trunk."

"I trust him with my life—and he's saved it more than once. He's as valuable to me in a battle as Hunter, or our commander, Hawk."

"Does he wield a weapon and protect your back?" she teased. "Is his aim true with a bow and arrow?"

Red liked seeing her like this, relaxed, and with an easy smile curving her lips and plumping her cheeks. "Like me, he prefers to hammer his enemies."

"Thus, his name," she said approvingly, looking up at him from where they stood side by side, eating their small repast and watching the horse graze.

"Hunter calls him 'Thunder' because of the way he pounds the ground with his hooves. He openly ridiculed his bulk until he saw what he could do in battle. Those hooves can crush skulls or knock a man farther than I could throw him."

Galiena raised her eyebrows in appreciation. "I suppose a good knocking is better than the head crushing."

"If you don't mind having all of your ribs broken and your breath taken away permanently," Red said with a satirical shrug and a genuine grin of pride.

"But you called him 'Hammer' even before you knew what he could do in battle?"

"In truth," Red confided, "I was going to name him 'Thunder' in honor of the god Thor, but after Hunter ridiculed his heavy steps, I decided to call him 'Hammer', which is Thor's trusted weapon of choice."

"And yours, I noticed," she said, nudging him with her shoulder. Her mouth curved in a broad smile, the white of her teeth dazzling against the pale pink of her lips.

He swallowed hard, drawing in a deep breath to keep himself from claiming those lips with his own. He'd wanted to kiss her again from the moment their lips touched the first time in the lane when she used him as a means of escaping The Execution-er—though neither of them knew then who the man was or how dangerous he truly was to her. But he wouldn't kiss her again until she was a willing participant, and he could take his time, lingering on her sweetness.

Instead, he nudged her gently with his elbow in a conspirato-rial way. "Don't tell Hunter, but I call him 'Hammer' because he sounds like Thor creating thunder."

"Not the stealthiest of horses, then?"

"No," Red agreed, giving a short whistle to call Hammer to his side. "But once we are on his back, the only thing that can take us down is an arrow. He will run down anyone who tries to come near, and I've yet to meet another horse powerful enough to knock him off his legs."

"Is The Executioner adept at shooting arrows?" she asked, her brow crinkling with worry.

"He prefers a dagger," Red said to soothe her. He didn't want to tell her that he carried a reminder of The Executioner's ability to hit a target with an arrow in the form of a puckered scar on his left shoulder.

She visibly shuddered, and he decided his attempt at easing her worry failed. Putting a finger under her chin, he tipped her head up until their gazes locked. "He will need to kill me before he can get to you."

"Is that your way of getting me to include you in my pray-ers?" she asked, lifting a sleek, black eyebrow at him. It was one of the most alluring things he'd ever seen a woman do and it made him speechless for a long moment. Still holding her chin between his fingers, he dropped his face close to hers until their gazes locked, then said, "My name on your lips as prayer is my most fervent desire."

Her eyes widened, and a blush crept up her cheeks. "I did not think you such a devout man."

He chuckled then. "Oh, kitten, it's not in prayer to your god that I want to hear you saying my name." He moved his lips close to her ear, inhaling the sweet scent of her hair as he placed his hands on her hips. "I want to hear my name on your lips as a prayer for more."

"More?" Much to his satisfaction, her voice was breathy and strained.

"Aye, more," he said nuzzling her hair with his nose. "More of me touching you."

He heard her swallow.

"Pleasuring you."

Her breath came quicker.

"In you."

"Oh, God," she said with a soft gasp.

"No, kitten, you can call me Red." He stepped back and lifted her onto Hammer's back before she could respond. "But in the right situation, 'Oh, God' will do."

He was enjoying the blush on her cheeks as he set her atop Hammer. And the spark in her eyes as she glared down at him.

"You overstep, sirrah," she chided.

"When I know what I want, it's what I do." He grabbed Hammer's thick mane and swung onto his back behind Galiena. "You will become accustomed to it, *Wife*."

"I am not your wife. You may call me 'Galiena', and nothing else," she retorted, but he was pleased to hear the mirth in her voice. "And I have no plans to become *accustomed* to your overstepping. Though, I suspect I shall have to learn to tolerate it until we complete this mission."

"Need I remind you that a declaration of being husband and wife is all that is needed to be married?"

"You've said as much, but need I remind *you* that we are not in your homeland. We are in England and without witnesses to vouch that the words were exchanged, it means nothing." She was getting more exuberant as she defended her argument. "And I did not declare you as my husband, I *called* you Husband, which is not the same. I might have well called you 'Hammer'."

It was exhilarating to see her so unafraid to speak her mind.

His mother had been the same—bold and enchanting. "You called me 'Husband' and I called you 'Wife', and until you can prove otherwise, we are married."

"If that's all it takes to be married, then it should be just as simple to div—"

He kicked Hammer into a gallop before she could finish her sentence. She grabbed the horse's mane to steady herself, but he had her caged in with his arms on either side of her. He let her bounce awkwardly while she found her balance, which didn't take as long as it did earlier in the day. Even with her riding improving, she would still be exhausted by the time they made it to Hawkspur, which he planned to reach by nightfall.

They stopped only two more times along the journey to attend to personal needs and give Hammer a brief rest. A full day of hard riding was tiring for an experienced rider, but for an inexperienced rider, it would make every muscle in the body scream for a reprieve. With each break, he'd noticed Galiena was getting stiffer and finding it harder to keep her legs from wobbling. When finally, they reached Hawkspur, long after the late afternoon sunset, he'd had to hold on to her for quite some time while she found the strength to move her legs. He could feel her quivering as she took her first steps.

"I can carry you in, kitten," he offered, knowing it would raise her hackles and make her more determined to walk into the castle on her own two feet.

"I am not your kitten," she hissed irritably.

"Aye, you are. You're wee and soft and feisty, just like a kitten." Before she could respond, he lifted his hands from her waist and her knees buckled again. "And I suspect you are wanting to scratch my eyes out right at this moment."

Scooping her up, he held her against his chest as the stable boys took Hammer to a stall to be wiped down, brushed, and fed. Normally, he would care for Hammer himself, but the stable master at Hawkspur was the best he'd ever known, and the horse was in very good hands.

Galiena squirmed against his chest, even as her arms were wrapped tightly around his neck. "I will have my legs back by the time you get to the doors of the keep. You can put me down there before anyone sees."

As he climbed the staircase leading up to the doors of the castle, he said "Tradition says a bride should be carried over the threshold by her groom."

"Stop with that, Red." She released her hold on him and pushed against his chest as he reached the top step. "Put me down now."

He set her on her feet, and she immediately placed a hand on the door to steady herself. Her legs were only a little less wobbly than before, and he was about to put his arm around her waist so he could help her into the hall when the heavy wooden door was pulled open from the inside. Before he could reach for her, she fell headlong into the arms of the man and woman standing there.

"Hawk," Red drawled, "Lady Alyce. I'd like you to meet my bride."

Chapter Eight

GALIENA WAS MORTIFIED. And if she'd had the strength, she would kick Red in the shins!

She carefully extricated herself from the man's arms, spreading her feet a bit wider as she stood up to better balance on her uncooperative legs. She tried to bow her head in deference to the lord and lady of the castle, but that just made her sway precariously.

Red's hands were on her waist before she could fall on her face again, pulling her back into his chest as he steadied her. It was not at all seemly, but the alternative was to fall into the arms of a stranger and his wife again.

"Please forgive my entrance," she managed to say without stuttering. "My name is Galiena, and I am *not* this man's bride."

The lord of the castle raised one thin, questioning eyebrow while he grinned at her as though she were a dancing puppet at a summer fair. He was as tall as Red, with angular features and hair as dark as her own. His arms were crossed over his chest as he looked from her to the elegant woman standing at his side.

Lady Alyce was tall and willowy with reddish-gold hair that framed her face in soft waves. She was stunningly beautiful. The twinkle in her eyes and the broad smile on her face were warm and welcoming, but Galiena still felt intimidated and out of her element. This was a woman of wealth and title, while Galiena was a meager widow who lived alone in a tiny cottage.

"I am so pleased, Red," Lady Alyce exclaimed as she reached for Galiena's hand and pulled her into an embrace. Then to her utter surprise, Lady Alyce slipped an arm around her and pried her loose from Red's hold. "Come with me to rest and get warmed. Hawk, my love, please have a tub and hot water brought to Red's solar. I am certain Galiena will appreciate a warm bath after supper to wash away a long day riding."

"N-no, my lady," Galiena said, embarrassment turning her cheeks even warmer than when she fell through the door. She could not let Lady Alyce tend to her this way. "That is not necessary."

"Nonsense," she insisted. "A warm bath will have you to rights in no time. I would suggest it before dinner, but I am afraid Red's bed chamber is two floors above us and will be a difficult journey for you in this state. I'd have Red carry you, but the stairwell is very narrow, and I fear you would have a battered head by the time he reached the top. Shall we sit by the fire for now?"

"Wart told us you had arrived," Galiena heard Hawk say to Red as Lady Alyce led her away. "And he said you had a pretty lady with you." This was a dire situation indeed.

"My lady," Galiena said as Lady Alyce helped her across the hall. "I have no desire to bathe or do anything else in Red's chamber."

Lady Alyce laughed. "The honeymoon cannot yet be over; I am convinced whatever he has done to irritate you will be smoothed over in no time. Gertrude," Lady Alyce said to a young woman as they passed by the buttery. "Please bring warmed wine for this dear woman to the table by the hearth." Turning back to Galiena she said through a wide, mesmerizing smile, "I want to know all about you. Red has been gone no more than a fortnight. He said he was on a personal mission, but he didn't tell us it was to bring home a wife."

"I am not Red's wife." She'd said the last louder than she meant to, but frustration and fear that the situation was careening out of her control made her desperate. As did the sudden and overwhelming pang for a home like Red's, surrounded by people who obviously loved him. Both of the women stopped and looked at her with expressions of surprise, which prompted the heat to rise in her face.

Again.

This was mortifying. She turned to glare over her shoulder at him, but the oaf was just smiling broadly as he followed behind her with his commander at his side.

Hawk let out a booming laugh and slapped Red on the back with a loud clap. "I had no idea you'd gone hunting for a wife. Too bad she's immune to your charm, Viking."

"She is as strong-willed as your Lady Alyce," Red said, apparently unaffected by the resounding slap on the back his commander had just given him. "But she will be sleeping in my chamber tonight."

"I will not," Galiena insisted as Lady Alyce continued to lead her through the hall toward the large stone hearth in the back, flanked by several heavy wooden chairs with high backs and the most luxurious-looking cushions. She almost groaned in anticipation of collapsing in the pillowy softness while she warmed her feet by the fire.

Lady Alyce stopped and looked at the two men following them. "Shoo, both of you. You can sit on the dais while we await supper. I wish to get to know this lovely lady. And dearest, please order a bath for Red after supper, as well." She continued toward the hearth, saying in a softer voice, "And I want to hear how you came to know Red."

"I'm sorry to say it will be a short stay, Lady Alyce," Red called after them. "We will be leaving at dawn."

Lady Alyce turned her lips down in a pout but did not argue. "I was hoping for a nice long visit, but I will take whatever time we have."

The thought of having to get on a horse again so soon almost made Galiena's knees buckle, but she managed to refrain from leaning any more of her weight into the kindly woman at her side. A warm bath would be heavenly, and the mention of food made her stomach rumble.

By the time they reached the cushioned seats, Galiena's legs were feeling less shaky, but the ache in her back was increasing. Or maybe she was just noticing her other pains now that her legs were no longer taking all of her attention. The noblewoman took her cloak from her and folded it before laying it over one of the chairs across from them. Then she motioned for Galiena to sit in the chair closest to the fire. Galiena sat as directed and stretched her feet toward the soothing heat, trying not to moan too loudly.

"There's definitely a wintry dampness in the air today. You must be chilled to the bone." Lady Alyce shivered as she said the last.

"My face and feet are chilled," Galiena admitted as she put her hands to the sides of her face. The heat of her prior embarrassments since entering the hall had warmed her cheeks somewhat, but they were still cold to the touch.

Lady Alyce's lips quirked in a smile. "Wart said Red had a bundle in his arms when he rode through the gate, and it wasn't until you were almost in the barn that he realized the bundle was a woman. The little scamp couldn't wait to tell us that Red had 'caught 'imself a lady'."

A soft burble of laughter escaped Galiena's lips at Lady Alyce's imitation of a young boy's voice. There had been several boys in the stable when they arrived, but she was too focused on trying to stand to pay them much attention. She'd remember to apologize in the morning for her rudeness.

"The truth is...." she started to explain but then stopped. Lady Alyce's husband was Red's commander, but did that mean they could be trusted? She assumed Red would discuss everything with Hawk, but what if there was a reason he didn't?

"The truth is," she began again, "we are not married. I must journey to Llanbadarn and Red has offered to escort me." An ironic laugh escaped her lips, even as she hoped Lady Alyce wouldn't notice the details she was leaving out. "Wait, that isn't the whole truth. The whole truth is Red didn't offer; he *told* me he was escorting me."

"That sounds more like the Red I know." Lady Alyce laughed. "He may be arrogant and commanding, but he's soft beneath it all, and if he says you are under his protection, you are in good hands."

Galiena was relieved Lady Alyce didn't ask more about the journey, and reassured by the ease in the woman's laugh and affection in her voice when she spoke of Red. Obviously, Lady Alyce truly liked and cared for him, and she tried to tell herself that the warmth blooming in her chest was relief that she would be safe with Red, but she feared his charm, even if boisterous, was beginning to work on her.

"Are your belongings still with the horse?" Lady Alyce asked, her voice laced with concern. "I thought Wart would have brought them in by now."

Galiena shook her head. "No, my lady. All that I have is what I am wearing. We had to…" She stopped herself, fearful of saying too much. "Well…we had to leave rather abruptly."

Lady Alyce nodded but did not ask more questions. Her face was kind and her demeanor welcoming, and Galiena felt the urge to tell the woman everything—but she didn't. Red could decide what to tell them of the events of the last two days.

"Thank you, my lady," she said quietly, "for your generosity." She looked Lady Alyce directly in the eye as she spoke, trying to convey the words she could not say. *Thank you for being so kind to me. Thank you for not asking me to say more. Thank you for knowing what to say to reassure me about Red.*

"Please, call me Alyce," she responded, her gentle smile widening.

She shook her head at Lady Alyce's suggestion. "I cannot do that. I am no one of consequence and you have been more than generous to accept me as your guest. It would not be proper."

"We are happy to have you as our guest." She reached out, placing a hand on Galiena's arm. "And I predict that you and I are going to be lasting friends."

The young woman from earlier appeared, setting down two tankards of mulled wine on the low table between them, the aroma of warm spices and fruit filling the air. "Supper is ready to be served, my lady."

Galiena turned to see a few men and women starting to congregate, and more were coming in from outside. A gaggle of young men and boys were laughing and pushing each other as they entered the hall, but quickly found their manners when Hawk let out a shrill whistle.

"That's better," he announced, leveling a stern look at the boys.

One of them separated himself from the rest and began to walk directly toward them. He stopped next to Lady Alyce's side, but he stared directly at Galiena with a grin on his face. She stared back at the scrawny boy with his mop of dirty blond hair, estimating him to be no more than seven or eight summers.

"Yes, Wart?" Lady Alyce coaxed gently when the boy didn't say anything.

"I, uh, I…" He continued to stare at Galiena as he scratched the side of his head as if trying to recall his reason for coming over to the women. "Is Henry coming down for supper?"

"Yes, he will be down very shortly. He finished his bath just before you told us Red had returned. Edna will bring him down soon."

Wart crinkled his nose in disgust and looked at his toes. "I don' like baths."

"I know, Wart," Lady Alyce said, giving him a teasing poke in the belly. "You have made that abundantly clear. But Cook is going to make a very special cake this week, and only boys who have washed with water and a cloth—and soap!—can have a slice."

"What kind o' cake?" he asked, lifting his head, and pinching his brows together, unable to hide his interest.

"Does it matter? I've yet to see you refuse any kind of cake."

He sighed. "True."

"It's a secret, but I'll tell you," Lady Alyce whispered, making a point of looking around to be sure no one else would overhear. "She's making a gingerbread cake."

"Wit' clotted cream?" Wart asked excitedly.

"For boys who wash from head to feet, yes, there will be clotted cream."

Galiena had kept herself isolated from most people for nearly three years. She'd been content with only Anora and her father as companions. It had been too painful to see the constant reminders of the family she'd lost. She'd thought about them and mourned them every day since they were taken from her. And being so near children felt like a knife to the heart, filling her with agonizing longing for her daughter. At this moment, she would give her own life if it meant Nahara could be here having a conversation about cake, looking so sweet and adorable. She bit her lip to quell the urge to pull the boy into her arms and hug him tightly.

"Was there anything else, Wart?" Lady Alyce asked kindly when the boy continued to stand there, looking from her to Galiena.

"Does the pretty lady belong to Red?" he asked unabashedly, staring at her with open curiosity.

Galiena shook her head and put her hands to her cheeks to be sure they weren't wet with unnoticed tears. "No. He is just a nice man who is helping me on my journey."

Wart raised his eyebrows, looking very skeptical. "He was holdin' you like a wife."

"I'm not his wife," she reassured him with a little laugh. He really was a precocious boy and hard not to like.

Much like Red.

"Yer pretty 'nuf to be 'is wife." Wart said the words very

seriously, not showing the least bit of shyness or embarrassment.

Galiena couldn't help but let a smile spread across her face. To her surprise, the tightness in her chest eased a bit, and a very small measure of the icy pain in her heart was replaced with a comforting warmth. "Thank you, Wart. You are very kind."

"No," he disagreed, saying matter-of-factly. "I'm strong an' mean."

"You can be strong and kind," Lady Alyce stated.

"Lord Hawk an' Red are strong and mean," Wart argued, raising his little chin as he spoke of the men he obviously thought of as heroes.

"Your lord and Red are very strong," Lady Alyce agreed. "And they can be mean when it is appropriate, but they are also very kind."

Wart seemed to contemplate this for a long moment…or he was contemplating his feet again. Then he looked up at the women with a disarming grin and winked at each of them.

Lady Alyce let out a gasp of mock surprise. "Where did you learn to do that?"

"Lord Hawk and Red taught me if I wink at pretty ladies, I might get a kiss." He pursed his lips and crinkled his brow again. "They tried to teach Hunter to wink but 'e can' do it. Or maybe 'e won't. I don' think 'e likes pretty ladies."

"That is a lot of information, Wart," Lady Alyce said with a sigh.

"I hafta go," he said looking over his shoulder. "Daniel will try to eat my portion if I'm not there to fight for it." With that, he turned on his heel and disappeared into the throng of people seating themselves at the benches along the trestle tables.

"Come, Galiena. You must be starving." Lady Alyce stood and gestured for Galiena to follow her to the table where Red and Lord Hawk were already seated. She couldn't remember the last time she was in a room with this many people. It was quite unnerving. At the inn, she cleaned the rooms when they were empty, and rarely assisted in the tavern, staying out of sight of most of the patrons. Even at the market, she waited until the throngs of people had made their purchases and left, making do with the picked-over items remaining.

As they drew near to the table, both men came to their feet. Hawk pulled out the highbacked chair to his left for Lady Alyce and Red signaled for Galiena to sit next to him in a smaller chair with a narrow, low back. She did as requested, but angled her chair toward Red so she did not have to look directly ahead at the crowd of people staring at them from the other tables in the hall.

Red sat down between Galiena and his commander but kept his attention on her. Leaning toward her he asked in a low voice, "Is aught the matter?"

"No. All is well," she said, her voice sounding tight and small even to her own ears.

Red looked out over the hall, surveying the people at the tables, then back at her. "There is no one here I don't recognize, but if anyone is making you uncomfortable, tell me now."

"It is no one in particular." She balled her fists on her lap, feeling foolish for how awkwardly she was acting. When had she become so afraid of people? She no longer recognized herself. She had traveled to the far reaches of the Mediterranean with her merchant father, and she had rarely been afraid then. Where was that courage now?

Red was studying her, the curiosity and worry evident in his eyes. "If you want to leave, I will request that we take our supper in the solar."

"I will not be rude to your commander and his lady wife. Lady Alyce has been very gracious, and I would not want her to take offense." She pushed her shoulders back and sat up straighter, feeling unsettled by the people looking at her, especially since she was still dressed in her dusty riding attire and Anora's boots, which were much larger than her feet. She had wished for a change in her life, an adventure, anything to break the monotony of her days—and she had gotten it.

Red grabbed the leg of her chair and pulled her close enough to him that their legs were touching. "You look beautiful, if that is what you are concerned about." As much as she hated to admit it, the look of genuine concern and caring in his pinched brows charmed her.

"I have no care if I look beautiful," she said to him, smiling to hide her discomfort. "I am not accustomed to being near so many people, let alone at the head of a nobleman's table in a castle." It was true that she did not care if the people in the hall thought her appealing, but there was a niggling awareness, a tiny hope, that perhaps Red thought her beautiful.

Galiena was startled by someone butting roughly against her arm. She looked down to see a small flaxen-haired child repeatedly bumping his head against Red's arm, and subsequently hers due to proximity. Behind the small boy was a large dog, sitting quietly but very attentively watching over the boy.

"Henry," Lady Alyce chided. "That is not how you greet Red and our guest."

"Listen to your mother," Hawk told the child, grabbing him by the shoulder to nudge him away. He leaned over to look the boy in the eye. "Let me show you how men greet each other. Do this," he said, balling his hand into a fist. The little boy imitated his father, folding his plump hand into a fist. "Then punch him as hard as you can in the arm." Which Hawk did to Red as he spoke.

Galiena heard a small grunt from Red and saw Hawk smile with satisfaction. When the little boy flung his fist into Red's arm, Red made a show of being nearly toppled from his chair as he clutched his bicep.

"Really, Hawk," Lady Alyce said, rolling her eyes at him, "the boy will never learn manners with you as a mentor."

Hawk turned to his wife, framing her face in his hands to kiss her quickly on the lips. "Manners can be taught later, Wife. First, he must learn to be tough."

Lady Alyce blushed and smiled, then put out her arms for the little boy to run into and scooped him up to hold against her shoulder. Galiena couldn't take her gaze from the toddler snuggled against his mother. The little boy looked to be about three years of age; she remembered how wonderfully affectionate her daughter was at that age, how warm she'd felt in her arms, and the sweet smell of her skin.

"Henry," Lady Alyce said. "This is Uncle Red's friend. Her name is Galiena."

Galiena looked from the boy to Lady Alyce, who was looking at her with those penetrating eyes that seemed to be all-knowing.

"Henry is very good at hugging," Lady Alyce said.

Henry lifted his head from his mother's shoulder to look at Galiena and nodded his head. Then he looked at his father and punched him in the arm. "Tough!" the little boy said.

"You can be tough and still give hugs," Hawk told the little boy, who immediately went from his mother's arms to his father's. After wrapping his arms around Hawk's neck and squeezing with all his might and a little squeal, he let go of his father and reached for Red.

That was too much for Galiena and she turned to look out over the hall, searching for anything to distract her attention. Watching Red pull the child into his arms made her think about things that were gone from her life, and she didn't think possible ever again.

"Hug."

Out of the corner of her eye, she saw a pudgy pair of hands reaching for her. Red had a protective arm around the boy's legs as he leaned in Galiena's direction with his outstretched arms. Both the boy and Red were looking at her expectantly.

She could do this.

She could give the boy a quick squeeze and then set him down to return to his mother and father. It would be over in an instant, and then she could feign tiredness and ask to be excused from the meal. It was impolite, she knew, but it was better than the alternative of trying to sit through the meal while she fought to hide the anguish that was likely to spring from her eyes.

Holding out her hands, she carefully took the little boy in her stiff arms, looking anywhere but at the child, as she awkwardly patted his back. But then his arms curled around her neck, and he pressed his head against her cheek and draped his warm body fully over her. She inhaled deeply and wrapped him fully in her arms, knowing the tears were dropping down her cheeks and that there was nothing she could do to stop them.

For a moment, she felt complete. For the first time in a long while, she didn't feel the bleak emptiness that had been her normal state of being for so long.

The little boy loosened his grip and pulled his head back to look at her face. "Down."

"Manners, Henry."

He turned to look at his mother, then back to Galiena. His pink cherub lips curved into a perfect bow. "Please."

Galiena complied with his wishes, but the moment his feet touched the floor and he scurried away with the dog in tow, she felt like her heart had been sucked from her chest and she was overcome with longing for her daughter, wishing she could hold Nahara in her arms again. Suddenly, she was uncontrollably cold. She wrapped her arms around herself and leaned forward fearing she may be sick.

Then she was in Red's arms, and he was clutching her to his chest as he carried her away from the table. She pressed her face into his shoulder and prayed for everything and everyone to disappear. She was overwhelmed with emotion and exhausted from all that had transpired in the last two days, which was why a hug from a toddler brought her to her knees. The weight of her grief for Adam and Nahara could bear down on her at unexpected times, and when it did, she was incapable of doing anything other than curling into herself and letting the darkness take her.

Chapter Nine

RED LOOKED DOWN at the woman in his arms, huddled against his chest. She still reminded him of a kitten, but this time it was because of the way she was trying to tuck herself into him as though she could not get close enough or small enough.

He held her in his arms, gently stroking her hair and murmuring soothing words in Norwegian to her. His mother used to do the same for her brother when the terrors seized him, and his eyes glazed with the fear of something only he could see. A blow to his head from a heavy beam while building a barn had left Red's uncle childlike, sometimes happy, and sometimes so fearful it wrenched the hearts straight out of his mother's chest and his own.

Galiena was doing the same to him now.

She wasn't childlike, but she was definitely overwhelmed by something. Whether it was fear or devastation, or both, he couldn't be sure—at least not yet. He would find out soon enough, but for now, he gave her what he thought she needed most at this moment: comfort and patience.

After a short while, he felt her body start to relax and unfold. He loosened his hold but still kept his arms around her as she stretched out her legs and lifted her head.

"Are you back?" He rested his chin lightly on the top of her head.

She was quiet for several breaths, then said, "Yes."

"Do you want to talk about it?"

"No," was her immediate and expected reply. She needed time to trust him, and he would be patient. He'd give her until the morrow, the next day at the most, and he would know what made her fearful so he could make sure it never happened again.

She pushed away from him, and he reluctantly released her as she stood, looking around with confusion.

"We are in Hawk's solar," he said in response to her unspoken question.

"I have made such a fool of myself," she said, burying her face in her hands.

Red put his hands on her waist and pulled her to stand between his knees so she would look at him. He was still seated in a chair by the fire, but she did not have to drop her gaze very far to look him in the eye. For a moment, he just stared at her face in the warm glow of the hearth, then he lifted a hand to glide his thumb over her cheek. "No, you did not make a fool of yourself."

It was meant to be reassuring, but she gave him a withering look in response. "I have, and more than once, starting with falling through the door and into your commander while his wife looked on."

Red quirked a smile at her. "It was a fine entrance and one they are not likely to forget."

"I could have lived with that mortification if it had stopped there. But then I went on to embarrass myself in front of everyone in the hall."

"If any of them say a word about it, I will have their heads on a platter." It wasn't much of an exaggeration. Red had already decided when Galiena rushed into his arms in the lane in Oswestry with the frantic look of fear on her face that he would kill anyone who tried to hurt her. That hurt included her feelings.

"I ruined supper." She huffed out a long breath. "And worst of all, I made Lord Hawk and Lady Alyce uncomfortable when they have been so generous and kind to me."

"You did ruin *my* supper," Red agreed, trying to lighten the mood. "But I can say with certainty that it will take more than a fainting woman to unsettle the lord and lady of Hawkspur. Hawk may be a seasoned warrior, but Lady Alyce is a force of her own." He'd watched Lady Alyce take command of the castle when her brother disappeared, then endured the sight of Hawk being flogged by the king, and later withstood the devastation of watching her treasonous brother be killed by her husband's sword.

"I did not faint," Galiena said indignantly. He didn't like it when she stepped back out of his reach but did not stop her.

She perched on the edge of the chair opposite him and focused on the fire. She appeared to be deep in contemplation, so he remained silent and waited for her to speak.

"Please do not let what happened in the hall taint your perception of my ability to complete this mission," she said, not looking away from the flames.

He was most definitely concerned about her, but he wasn't going to tell her that. And he didn't trust anyone else to protect her as he would. He almost sighed at his own foolhardiness, but he did not want her to think he was sighing his disapproval of her.

The truth was, he knew if he asked, Hawk would use his army and his castle to ensure Galiena's safety, and she was probably better off secured within the walls of Hawkspur than on the road with him. But he was not willing to leave her behind, despite his own selfish motives for wanting her near him.

She was a bundle of contradictions, and he was enthralled by her. She was bold, feisty, brave, outspoken, demanding at times. Then she was vulnerable, shy, contemplative, and even unsure at other times. When she pressed her lips together to concentrate, like she was doing now, he wanted to take her face in his hands and kiss away the worry he saw there. And when she challenged him, blissfully oblivious to her diminutive stature, unafraid to show him her irritation, he wanted to pick her up in his arms and spin her around in delight.

His breath caught in his throat when she turned to face him again, the pools of those wide silver-gray eyes of hers glittering in the soft light of the fire. He knew there was a well of thoughts and emotions behind her gaze and he wanted to know all of them.

"I am not afraid of the journey, or this man you call 'The Executioner'." She gave him a fixed look and her voice remained steady as she spoke. "For a long time, I prayed not to wake from my sleep each night; I thought it would be less painful than being left behind to live on without those I loved. Still love."

She did not seem to expect a response to her confession, and Red did not give one. He wanted to reach for her again, to pull her into his embrace and reassure her, but he did not do that either. She may not have liked being called *kitten*, but as with a timid cat, he knew the best way to gain her confidence was to stay still and let her come to him. In time, he would know exactly who she referred to and what had happened. Right now, he would be satisfied with the little she'd shared.

"I no longer feel that way, but now and again something reminds me of my loss, and it takes the breath from my lungs and makes me feel like my insides are being twisted in an iron grip." She looked down at her hands on her lap, her fingers rubbing nervously together, then took a deep breath and lifted her gaze to meet his again. "I'm not ready to say more about that, but you should know that I spent most of my childhood traveling with my father, sleeping on the ground under our cart more often than not. I can build a campfire as well as any soldier and make a meal out of what I can snare in a trap or catch in a stream. I'm not afraid of discomfort, and I will get used to riding a horse instead of driving one. Put me in a cart and I can guide a horse over even the most treacherous of roads." She smiled ruefully. "I've just never had the opportunity to sit on the horse's back over said roads."

Red leaned forward, resting his forearms on his knees.

"You're not frightened of them, then."

She shook her head. "I understand horses. I can sense when they are afraid, when they need encouragement, and when they need a strong hand to hold them back. I'm merely challenged when it comes to *staying* on their backs. Even so, I will endure what I must to make the journey." Her gaze was unwavering, the unspoken challenge visible in her eyes to defy her desire, her need, to see this through.

He adopted a stern look and addressed her as he would an eager squire. "The distance is not so far, but the journey will take two or three difficult days. If the gods are with us, we will get to the mountain pass *and* clear it on the second day. We will be cold, wet, muddy, and miserable at best." He thought of everything that could go wrong on the route to Llanbadarn. "We'll risk our horses slipping on icy trails. Or encountering thieves and bandits. Or catching a fever from the bone-chilling rain, sleet, and snow." *Or The Executioner finding them before Red found him.*

He'd hoped she'd change her mind after hearing the details of the journey, but she just nodded her head earnestly. "I've been cold and wet before. 'Tis a small sacrifice to save the infant prince."

"Your sacrifice may be much greater than a little discomfort." Red gritted his teeth to hold down the unfamiliar swell of panic filling his chest as he looked at her, so fragile despite her determination. "You are safer here. You've already shown more bravery than most: you risked your life to recover the missive, escaped when The Executioner returned for it, and found me to get the news and missive delivered to the king."

Her jaw clenched and her lips pressed into a thin line, but it was the disbelief and betrayal that flashed in her eyes that felt like a blade to the heart. He pushed away from the chair and closed the distance between them, dropping to one knee on the floor in front of her, burying his fingers in her hair to tilt her face up to his, and forcing her to see the torment she was putting him through.

"I couldn't live with myself if something happened to you. Stay here," he pleaded, despite the ache to keep her near, no matter where he was going. "Hawk can protect you until I return for you."

"And then what?" she asked in a strained whisper.

He pressed his forehead to hers. "Whatever you want of me for as long as you want me."

"None of this makes sense, Red. Your desire that I wait for you doesn't make sense. You don't know enough about me." Her hands were trembling when she touched them to his face to trace her fingers slowly over his lips and then his cheeks. They were cold against his skin, as were her lips when she pressed them to his in a brief kiss. His body tingled and in spite of the seriousness of her words, his heart sang. His she-wolf was warming to him. She held his face in her hands and said, "And my need to go to the queen, to see the child safe, doesn't make sense to you. But it does to me. I'm begging you to try to understand."

He pulled her into another kiss, stroking her lips with his tongue to warm her, to show her that it did all make sense. When she opened for him, he tasted the sweetness of her mouth. She was stroking her tongue against his, letting him in without hesitation, but there was a desperation in her response to him.

When he broke the kiss, she was taking quick, shallow breaths and her hands were clinging to his tunic, her fists twisting tightly into the material. She did not open her eyes to look at him. Instead, she rested her forehead against his as he smoothed his hands over her hair and down her back.

After her breathing slowed, she said, "I have been a shadow of the woman I once was for far too long. If I don't go on this journey, I fear I will never emerge from the darkness. If I stayed here, there would be nothing worthwhile left of me for you to come back to, Red." She kept her eyes squeezed shut, refusing to look at him as she spoke. "If we fail, my life is a small price to pay when I am hardly living as it is."

Red wanted to grab her by the shoulders, shake sense into

her, and tell her she was wrong, but her hands twisting tighter into his tunic as though he was her only hope for survival stayed his actions. Indeed, when she looked at him, there was no trace of fear. "If we succeed, I might be able to find the strength to forgive myself. To believe that there is a reason for my life to continue without…" she gave an audible swallow, "them."

She was ripping his heart from his chest and tearing it into fodder for the crows. He wanted to tell her she was wrong, that she didn't need to do this to be worthy of living. That she had him no matter what happened. But maybe it was more than that. She was broken and couldn't love him until she'd made herself whole again. Somehow, this task would achieve that for her. She touched his face again. "I must do this, Red."

He thought of how he'd been after The Executioner had taken all he had from him. Then he trapped his protest in his throat and nodded once because he knew that some healing had to be done alone, on one's own terms.

When she dropped her head onto his shoulder in relief and wrapped her arms around his chest, he lifted her as he stood and settled her into his lap again. He leaned back in the chair with his arms encircling her and clasped his hands together on her hip. "I have conditions."

She picked her head up to look at him, but she did not try to move out of his hold. "Name them."

"One: you must never be out of my sight."

She arched an eyebrow at him, and he knew she was already going to disagree with him. "I will need privacy to relieve myself; I still have my dignity."

He reluctantly relented. "Fair point. When you are not in my sight, you must be no farther than five strides away from me."

"Yours or mine?" she asked with an impish grin.

"Condition two," he said, refusing to reward her cheekiness with a response. "You will not make any rash actions or take any foolish chances. I will not watch you get yourself hurt. Or worse."

He tipped his head slightly and raised a warning eyebrow

when she opened her mouth to argue, cutting her off before she could speak. "Three—"

"How many of these are there?" She wrinkled her nose at him as she asked the question. To his chagrin, he found the action very alluring. And distracting. He took a deep breath. "Three: you may have the skills to survive the physical demands of the journey, but you will remember I am the one trained to fight, and even kill, if necessary. If we encounter anyone, you are to do everything I say without hesitation." She kept her lips pressed together, but he could see it took all of her restraint to do so. "Four: You will not argue with me every time I give a command."

The little vixen was staring at him as though he were giving her instructions on how to properly launder his tunics. "Did you hear what I said?"

"Yes, Red," she replied demurely, though she did not look the least bit obedient.

"You will do as I say if in danger, right?" He was used to ordering men about. Tiny women with large attitudes, not so much. He hoped he'd impressed upon her the importance of his commands, but he was almost certain he'd failed.

"Yes, I will." She laid her hand against his chest and looked up at him with a very serious expression on her face.

"Five—" Her fingers brushed against his neck as she picked at the neckline of his tunic, sending a jolt of heat straight to his groin. He trapped her hand in his own to get her to stop touching him so he could continue. "Five."

"Do you mean to be growling?" she asked smugly with a tip of her head.

He groaned with frustration. Not because of her interruptions but because all he could think about now was capturing her mouth in another kiss. He growled intentionally this time. "Five: you will not kiss me again the way you just did."

Her mouth dropped open, then closed again. She pursed her lips together as she studied him, then said, "You kissed me. If you do not want it to happen again, then you mustn't kiss *me.*"

"I did not say it would not happen again, kitten." He wrapped his arm tighter around her back to pull her closer, then leaned his face close to hers until their lips were almost touching.

"What did you say, then?" Her lips barely brushed his as she spoke.

"It isn't to be like the last kiss. It will be like this…"

He wrapped his hand around her nape, his thumb rubbing gently across the smooth column of her neck. He growled with satisfaction when her head tipped back, exposing the curve of her throat to him. Her skin felt like silk against his lips as he brushed his mouth along the line of her jaw. When he got to her ear, he sucked the lobe into his mouth to scrape his teeth over the sensitive spot. To his immense satisfaction, she shuddered at his touch. He wanted to discover every possible way to make her tremble and shiver with pleasure. He scattered kisses down her neck to the hollow at the base of her throat, relishing the little panting noises she made. He swirled his tongue in the indent between her collarbones, just above the thin material of her chemise, resisting the urge to tug both the chemise and her tunic over her head and bare her beauty to him. Instead, he licked a slow trail up the length of her neck.

God, but she tasted sweet.

When she dropped her chin to look at him, her eyes were glazed, and her lips were parted. He couldn't resist biting her bottom lip and giving it a gentle tug. Her sharply indrawn breath was another victory, another discovery, another secret uncovered.

A knock sounded on the solar door, and Galiena went rigid in his arms before scrambling off his lap. She scurried to stand at the fire with her back to the room as Red went to the door to open it.

As much as he resented the interruption, he was pleased to see the amount of effort it appeared to take for her to regain her composure.

$$\cdot\infty\diamondsuit\infty\cdot$$

Chapter Ten

GALIENA HEARD THE murmuring of voices at the door behind her as she held her hands to the flames. She turned to face Hawk and Lady Alyce as they entered the room, hoping that they would attribute her red face to the heat of the fire and nothing else.

"We thought you may want to take your supper in the privacy of the solar," Lady Alyce said.

Lady Alyce had her back turned to Galiena as she set the supper on the table in the center of the room, but she could see Red studying her face intently, then nodding his head. She could only imagine what the lady was silently asking Red, but she felt certain it had to do with the sanity of the woman who collapsed into herself and had to be carried like a child from the hall.

"We will leave you to dine together," Hawk said to Red. "When you are finished, we can determine what you need for the journey."

"I would like to speak to both of you about that," Red responded. "If you do not mind sitting with us while we eat, we can discuss it."

Galiena pushed the confusing thoughts about Red, the guilt over her feelings when he'd kissed her, and the surprising way she responded to his touch, out of her mind as she approached the table. Hawk and Lady Alyce were gathering documents, ink wells, and ledger books from the table to stack in a pile on the far corner, giving them plenty of room to eat their meal.

Red pulled a chair out from the table, indicating she should sit. "You may not feel up to eating, but you will need the strength."

He was right, her stomach and her emotions were in too much turmoil for food to be appealing, but she would be even more useless to Red on the journey if she did not keep up her strength. "I beg your forgiveness for my rude behavior when you have been so kind," she said to the lord and lady. "I was overcome with exhaustion."

"Nonsense," Lady Alyce soothed. "There was no offense."

Galiena felt awkward eating in front of the lord and lady, but necessity prevailed, and once Red attacked the food hardily, so did she though not with as much vigor. It was a chore to chew and swallow with her nerves on edge, but each time she stopped, Red would nudge another morsel of stewed meat or vegetables toward her and shoot her a look that said he wanted her to eat more.

"Tell us what you need, Red." To Galiena's surprise, it was Lady Alyce who gave the command, and Lord Hawk seemed content to have her take the lead.

"Food for three days," Red said around a mouthful of stew. "Another horse. One that is strong but steady. Galiena is not afraid of horses, but she is not an experienced rider."

"You work with the horses almost as much as the stable master; I'm sure you have one in mind. Whichever it is, take it." Hawk's obvious trust and ease with Red were apparent in his mannerisms and the way he spoke to him.

Red nodded, "The gray charger that you acquired in the summer. We've already determined that he is too easy-tempered to be a warhorse, but he is strong and sure-footed."

"Take him," Hawk readily agreed. "What else?"

"If you can spare four men as escort, that will be appreciated.

The Welsh rebellion may be quelled, but I don't care to take any chances."

Hawk nodded. "The king will remember you as one of my men-at-arms, but I will send a letter with my seal in case you need it to expedite an audience with the king and queen." He gave a derisive snort. "If his clerk is having a bad day, he tends to take it out on anyone who is not titled."

Red growled, narrowing his eyes, and baring his teeth, making Galiena smile in amusement. He obviously did not find it acceptable that anyone would dare refuse him, even a king.

"Edward thinks highly of you," Hawk said with a warning tone, "and even though the clerk does not care for me, he will not risk the king's wrath by refusing to deliver my message to him with the utmost haste."

"Has the king fully forgiven you for choosing Lady Alyce over your loyalty to him?" Galiena asked, a twinge of guilt gnawing at her for making the rude inquiry of the lord of Hawkspur, but she had to know if Hawk's relationship with the king would harm them or help them. Red's brows shot up disapprovingly with the question, and Galiena wondered if the Viking did not agree with what Hawk was rumored to have done for the love of his lady. Granted, she did not know the entire story, other than he did not fully execute the king's wishes and was nearly executed himself for it.

"I think it is *me* he does not forgive," Lady Alyce interjected.

Hawk put his arm around his wife and squeezed her shoulders, then turned his attention back to Red. "The king is more of a romantic than either you or me. He did what he had to, or he would have lost the respect of the realm. It's been more than a year and I still have the marks of the king's displeasure, should anyone doubt his leadership."

A pained look flashed across Lady Alyce's face as she put a soothing hand on Hawk's cheek, to which he responded by leaning in and unselfconsciously kissing her cheek. "You know I would endure it again daily if it is the price I must pay to have you."

"Daily?" Lady Alyce asked with a doubtful tip to her head.

Hawk shrugged. "Perhaps monthly. Or annually." Then he grinned, "Or at least once more in my lifetime."

The lord's wife flashed him a brilliant smile, her adoration of him apparent. "Once was more than enough."

An aching pang wrenched Galiena's chest as she watched Hawk and Lady Alyce together. She missed that easy comradery and warm jesting that couples share, remembering what it was like to have someone to lean on and someone for whom one would readily endure pain or worse.

"Now," Lady Alyce said, returning her attention to Red and Galiena. "I will instruct Cook to prepare the food provisions, but what else is needed?"

Red tipped his head toward Galiena. "Her friend in Oswestry loaned her clothing and boots, but Anora is significantly taller than Galiena. We will need boots that fit properly, warm gloves, and a warmer chemise and a tunic that fits if possible."

Lady Alyce nodded while she assessed Galiena. "I believe you to be similar in height and build as Gertie. She and Edna are warming bath water for you, but I will ask her to gather what she can from her wardrobe."

That is too much," Galiena protested, embarrassed over the fuss being made on her behalf. "I cannot possibly take her clothing. She will need it herself."

Lady Alyce shook her head, hearing none of it. "The boot-maker can have new boots for her in a day or two, and if needed we will have new clothing sewn for her in no time at all. Besides, I have reason to believe she will be preferring tunics with a little wider girth in them very soon."

"Already?" Red asked with a laugh. "Her husband wasted no time in getting her with child."

"I think it better to say *she* wasted no time in getting with child," Hawk retorted. "Once she had her heart set on Roger, there was no escaping for him."

"I did not see him protesting," Lady Alyce rebuked. "The eagerness was equally shared." She started to stand, and Hawk immediately pushed to his feet to assist her with the chair. She turned to Red, saying, "I had Edna prepare the room next to yours for Galiena. The baths should be ready in both rooms by now."

Galiena had eaten her fill and Red was quickly finishing the bits that were left, sopping up the gravy with a chunk of bread and popping it in his mouth. She reluctantly rose from the table as Lady Alyce beckoned her to follow, but Red reached for her hand and gave it a reassuring squeeze.

"I will be near," he said in a low voice.

Galiena nodded, then followed Lady Alyce.

"I will have Gertie fetch her boots immediately," she said to Galiena. "If they do not fit, our shoemaker is the envy of the realm; he will have a new pair ready by dawn if needed."

She was about to protest again, hating the idea of some poor man being forced to work the night through for her, but one look from the lady told her it would be folly to argue.

As luck would have it, the boots fit nearly perfectly. As did Gertie's gloves and tunic. Lady Alyce had inspected the cloak from Anora and deemed it sturdy enough. "But I would feel better if it had a lining of fur in the shoulders and hood for added warmth. If you will leave it with me, the alterations will be discreet, as we do not want it to tempt a thief." Once more, since she knew she had no choice in the matter, Galiena agreed.

Galiena had been bathed and brushed and was sitting by the fire, shaking out the strands of her hair to dry in the heat radiating from the flames. Lady Alyce and her maids fluttered about her, inspecting her clothing, and packing the extra items into a leather satchel.

Edna held up the heavy braies Galiena had worn under her tunic and chemise. "Clever girl! I must sew a pair like these for you, Lady Alyce. So much better than trying to tuck your chemise around your legs."

"They belonged to my friend's younger brother," Galiena said. When none of them looked at her like she was making an unwanted interruption, she mustered on, ignoring her instinct to stay quiet and unobtrusive. "He was training to become a blacksmith, hence the thickness. I am grateful she thought to give them to me to wear."

"Nothing so valuable as a good friend," Gertie said, then took the braies from Edna. "I will take these out to give them a good shake and wipe them clean. I do not think they will dry by morning if I wash them."

"A good shake is more than enough, thank you," Galiena said, giving the young woman a warm smile while trying to stay in control of the array of emotions assailing her. She had given herself over to the fussing of the ladies as they bathed her, dried her with a soft sheet, pulled a clean sleeping gown over her head, and brushed her hair. It had been unexpected, uncomfortable— and the most soothing, selfless thing anyone had done for her in a very long time.

She'd never had sisters, and before Anora, she'd never truly experienced the friendship of other women. She'd always been curious about the women gathered together by the riverbank or the town center as they washed and darned clothing while watching their children play, but she had never joined them. Instead, she had lived outside of town on the farm with her husband, content with the occasional exchanging of niceties with the men and women at the weekly market. Once she moved into the cottage on the churchyard near the edge of town, she had avoided the women and children—the women an awkward reminder that she didn't fit in, and the children a soul-wrenching reminder of her beautiful Nahara.

To be in the midst of Lady Alyce, Edna, and Gertie as they talked of and laughed about people they knew and things that happened, she was beginning to understand the appeal of the shared conversation and time together. She was at a complete loss as to how to be part of their sisterhood, but she was warming to the comradery. Of course, these women knew nothing about her or her past. They did not look down on her because of her unusual upbringing by her merchant father. Nor did they look at her with pity in the same way as the village women at home.

When Edna and Gertie had tidied the room and put everything away and prepared her clothing for the morning, they bid her good night and safe journey, then left her alone with Lady Alyce.

"I will not stay long, for you must get your rest. You have long days ahead of you," Lady Alyce said, seating herself on the rug before the hearth, facing Galiena. She had not expected the lady of the castle to sit on the floor with her as she dried her hair, and she started to protest, indicating they should move to the chairs, but Alyce shook her head and motioned for her to stay where she was by the fire. "I hope you do not take umbrage, but Hawk relayed to me the reason for your journey as told by Red."

Galiena was not surprised that Red had confided in his commander, nor that Hawk had confided in his wife. It was apparent in the little while she had been in their presence that the lord had great respect for his lady. She admired the confidence of Lady Alyce and the way she spoke freely, without fear of censorship.

She shook her head at the lady. "I do not mind, Lady Alyce. And I welcome any advice you may have for me."

"I was not just being polite when I said I prefer you to call me 'Alyce'," she said with a sincere smile. "There is no need for such formality between friends."

"Thank you...Alyce." It felt good to be thought of as a friend.

"I am not sure I have advice for you, but I have met the king and queen and can tell you what I know of them."

"Yes, please!" She had not wanted to admit to Red how terrified she was of speaking in front of King Edward and Queen Eleanor. Especially when she did not have good news.

"King Edward is intimidating and intolerant of anyone he feels is wasting his time."

Galiena felt a pit form in her stomach at Alyce's words. What would she do if the king did not believe what she had to say about the men in the alley? Would he think her being dramatic and seeking attention? Her gaze flicked to the pile of clothing on the chest at the foot of the bed. She had watched Gertie shake out and fold her chemise, but she had not found the little roll of parchment tucked into the cleverly sewn pouch attached to the inner seam of the arm.

"Do not let him scare you," Alyce continued. "If you treat him with deference but speak to him with confidence and aplomb, he will look upon you with favor. As for Queen Eleanor, be straightforward and immediately express your reason for speaking with her. She does not tolerate anyone mincing their words or flowery language. She wants you to say what you mean plainly and clearly."

Galiena nodded her head, taking it all in. She would need to practice what she planned to say so as not to stumble over her own words as she told the queen that someone was planning to kill her precious son. Not an easy conversation to have, and she feared saying it too plainly would send the poor women into fits.

Alyce patted her on her knee. "You will find the right words by the time you must face the king and queen. Red will demand a private audience with the king and tell him the worst of it, but they will want to hear you recount everything you heard and witnessed."

"Which is not very much," Galiena admitted.

"It will be enough. There can be no doubt as to the intent of the men if what Red relayed is accurate."

"I know it must seem very imprudent of me to insist on speaking to the king and queen myself when Red could just tell them what I heard and show them the missive—I assume he told Hawk about the missive?"

Alyce nodded. "Aye. He did say there is a coded message. And Hawk did inquire as to why he didn't leave you under our protection while he rode on, but Red said it was crucial to you to complete the journey and bring the news to the queen yourself."

The lady studied her with a somber expression.

Galiena waited for Alyce to tell her to trust Red to complete the mission, that it wasn't sensible for her to accompany him, and that she was being selfish for insisting on going to the king and queen herself. But she didn't say any of those things.

"Red trusts your reasons are sound, and that is all that is important," Alyce said with a quick shrug. Then a slow smile spread across her face. "Did you really throw yourself into Red's arms and call him your husband to escape the men after you?"

"I did," Galiena admitted, with an amused sigh and a deprecating roll of her eyes. "It was done in haste and without any forethought. And now I cannot rid myself of him!" Galiena was relieved when Alyce laughed at her jest. "That's not fair of me. The truth is, of all the men who could have been walking down that lane at that exact moment, it was my good fortune that it was Red."

"Aye, it was good fortune."

Galiena thought about what would have happened to her if it had been someone with nefarious intentions. Or even someone who was indifferent to a stranger in peril. "It surely does seem Fate played a part in putting Red there at the exact moment I needed someone with his...skills and connections. Lord above knows I tried everything to deter him once I thought he'd served his purpose."

"Sometimes the people we need the most are the same ones we push against the hardest."

"Did you push against Hawk?" As soon as Galiena asked the question, she realized her blunder. "I am sorry, my lady, I did not mean to pry, and I should not have asked such a personal question."

Alyce surprised her by reaching out her hand, which she tentatively took in her own. "Do not be embarrassed for asking. I don't always take to others, but I like you." She squeezed Galiena's hand. "And I have a good feeling this will not be the last time I see you with Red."

Galiena's gaze faltered, her stomach in turmoil over the expectation that she and Red belonged together. "I do not have many friends in my life, but I am honored to consider you among them."

"And I as well," she said with gentle understanding. "To answer your question, I did push against Hawk. I was a heartbroken widow determined to never marry again."

Galiena's head snapped up. "You are a widow?"

"I am. Judging from your reaction, you are as well?"

Galiena nodded as a lump started to form in her throat. It was not uncommon for women to be widowed, but Alyce was similar in age to Galiena, and she seemed so happy.

She continued, "I was afraid of being hurt again and had convinced myself I could not be a proper wife to anyone other than a doddering old man with no need for heirs—which seemed a worse fate than being alone. But the details of that story will have to wait for another time. Just know when I met Hawk, I did not think he could possibly love me as I was. And it felt like a betrayal to let another man into my bed and especially into my heart."

It felt like finally breathing in fresh air to hear Alyce speak about her experience and the things she feared the most. Galiena had felt so alone in her guilt and believed no one would sympathize with the struggles she faced. She wanted to hug the dear woman.

"I do not know your story," Alyce said, reaching out to cup Galiena's cheek in her hand, "but I do know it gets easier with time. And I am confident that despite whatever thoughts are in your head, you are deserving of love and happiness again."

Galiena could not stop the tears that rolled down her cheeks. She'd longed for the shared wisdom of a mother, or even a sister, while she was growing up, and especially when she married and became a mother herself. After a lifetime of learning how to navigate the world without the advice and guidance of another woman, Alyce's friendship now was worth more than treasure.

"Can I hug you?" Her voice was shaky, and she could hardly see for the tears clouding her vision, but she went gratefully into the other woman's arms as they closed around her.

"I knew there was a reason I thought we would be friends from the moment I saw you," Galiena heard Alyce say into her hair. "And it wasn't just because you fell through the door."

She laughed and hiccupped into Alyce's shoulder, soaking her tunic through with her endless flood of tears. It was like someone had pulled the cork from a keg, releasing the tension that had been drowning her for far too long.

"I think you and I have much in common and, when you are ready, you can tell me about it. If you'd like."

Galiena nodded her head against Alyce's shoulder. "I would," she said, the words muffled as she continued to cling to Alyce. It was a long while before they released each other, but finally, Alyce said, "Let us get you into bed. You must be exhausted, and you have a long day ahead of you on the morrow."

As they rose to their feet, Galiena said, "Please, Alyce, do not tell Red what I said about good fortune bringing him to me when I needed a champion. He is insufferable in his arrogance as it is."

Alyce laughed out loud. "You have my word," she said as she bid Galiena good night and closed the door behind her.

After the lady had left, Galiena thought about what they'd discussed and her fear that the king would not find her story credible. The key to it all was in that coded missive. But what did it say? What if the proof she needed was not there? She moved to retrieve the scroll to study it while she could, determined to make sense of it before they reached the king.

Chapter Eleven

R ED HEARD GALIENA pacing and murmuring to herself on the other side of the chamber door. The hour was late, but he'd wanted to brief the soldiers accompanying them and be sure all preparations for the morning were done before he took to his own bed. He wasn't going to disturb her, but once he heard she was awake, he tapped on her door.

Which opened almost immediately.

"You should take better care to know who is standing outside your door before opening it wide."

"No need to scowl at me," Galiena responded. "Anyone who wished to do me harm wouldn't have knocked."

Her reasoning was sound, but it still didn't please him. He stepped inside the room and looked down at her. "You have everything you need for the morrow?"

"Lady Alyce and her maids were very accommodating," she said with a nod, turning on her heel and moving to stand in front of the fireplace. She was barefoot, wearing a chemise, and wrapped in a woolen blanket that covered her from shoulders to shins. Her hair hung loosely down to the middle of her back, combed, and shining in the firelight. It was taking all of his concentration to keep from crossing to her, and wrapping the soft tendrils in his fingers so he could tip her head back to expose the creamy skin of her throat. His mouth went dry thinking of inhaling the delicate aroma that would still be lingering on her from the bath and tasting the sweetness of her skin and lips.

"Red?"

"What?"

"Did you hear what I just said?"

"No," he admitted. His lips tugged into a grin as he nudged the door closed and took a step closer to her. "I was distracted."

She put up a hand and shook her head slowly from side to side. "Don't come any closer, Red. I can't keep my focus when you're too near, and now is not the time."

He could feel his grin spread into an enormously satisfied smile. "Glad to know I have that effect on you."

"Don't look so smug," she chided. "This isn't a good thing."

"Mutual attraction is always a good thing."

"We have to stay focused." She was shaking her head again, a deep crease forming as she pinched her eyebrows together, her eyes looking anywhere but at him.

He had been about to step closer to remind her of the appeal she was trying to deny, but something in her expression stopped him. He sensed whatever was causing her reluctance had more to do with her than with him. As much as he wanted to pull her to him, he wanted more for her to feel comfortable with him. Lady Alyce had approached him after she'd left Galiena and warned him against overwhelming her, stressing the need to give her emotional and physical space to come to terms with what she was feeling.

"You have settled it all in your mind, that much is clear," Lady Alyce had said to him. *"But she may need time to be as certain about you as you are about her."*

His first instinct was to protest, to say how Galiena had responded to being held and kissed by him, to explain the certainty he felt when she first looked at him, that they were fated to be together, and that he knew she felt it, too. Before he could say any of that, Hawk had slapped a hand down on his shoulder.

"Listen to the lady. You don't realize how intimidating you are. And not just your size, but your tendency to see anything you want as something to conquer."

"Galiena," he said in a low voice. "Look at me."

She did lift her gaze to him then. To his relief, there was no fear on her face, but there was a wariness.

"I am not a man to hide what I want, and I want you. We both know that. But I want you willing and will settle for no less, nor will I force anything more." He thought he saw a measure of tension visibly release from her shoulders. "I may be twice the size of you but be assured you hold all the power in this." He waved a finger between them.

"Only for as long as you give it," she said, tilting her head and slanting her eyes.

"I give it to you freely and inalterably."

"And if I am never willing?" She stood straight as she asked the question, but he could hear the vulnerability in her question. He didn't believe she would *never* be willing, but he did believe she needed the reassurance that it would not change his conviction that she would never be forced by him.

"Then I will die a lonely and broken man, but I will take solace in the knowledge that I gave you what you desired."

"That is a bit dramatic." A bubble of laughter escaped her lips, but it did not reach her eyes, and she continued to scrutinize him for a long while. Still, he could see her demeanor softening and finally, she said, "I believe you."

"Good." He would not rejoice yet, but it felt like a small victory, like another door being opened.

"I mean I believe that I need not be fearful of you forcing your affections upon me," she said with a sardonic arch to one sleek, dark eyebrow. "But I will never believe that you will die alone, Viggo Algarssen."

Typically, he didn't like being called by his given name. Viggo didn't fit him well, and Algarssen meant nothing to him as he'd never known his father. He believed it to be a name created by his mother, along with the story that the man said to be his sire had married her, then died before he was born.

"When this mission is over, you will turn your charms toward some other woman. You are not the type of man to stay lonely for long."

"That may have been true of the past, but once the Norns pulled the threads of Fate and Urd brought us together, there can be no other for me." Though he didn't really believe in the old gods, and he had even less faith in the new one, he did believe in Fate. His mother had told him some things were preordained, and that you could push back against those things, or you could accept them. When Galiena looked up at him after running out of the inn and into his arms, he had been jolted to the core. If that wasn't Fate telling him Galiena was meant to be his, then there was nothing left to believe. "I was put in that lane at that moment when you needed me for a reason."

She looked leery and he expected he had said too much.

"What are the Norns and Urd? And do you really believe all of that?"

"The old tales say three sisters called the Norns weave the tapestry of Fate and every person has their own thread. Urd is the sister who guides each of us toward our destiny as the threads are sewn. I cannot say if we truly owe our existence and fortune, good or bad, to the gods—or one God as the Christians believe— but I only question Urd when she does not serve my purpose." He laughed then. "And in those times, the single deity I believe in is my sword."

There was more bitterness in his laugh than he intended, but it was true. He could believe that Galiena was meant to be his, but he refused to believe that his mother and uncle were meant to die cruelly at the hands of The Executioner. And he would fight Fate, Urd, the Christian God, or anyone else until his last dying breath if they tried to take Galiena from him.

She was staring blankly at his boots, and he wondered if she was horrified by all that he'd said. "If you believe me to be a heathen, or if I have offended you, it was not my intent to upset you."

"No," she said, jerking her head up to face him again. "I heard stories of many different gods as a child and take no offense to your beliefs."

He hadn't expected the vehemence in her response. Even more to his surprise was the intent expression she turned toward him, as though she not only understood what he was saying, but also felt understood.

"I direct my prayers to the Christian God because it is what is accepted here, and I can perform the rituals of the Church without hesitation. But if there is one thing that I cannot accept, it is that God—or any gods—would take the lives of others who have done nothing wrong because of some divine plan for me." She smiled sheepishly and whispered, "When the pain is too much, I choose to believe God isn't real…because if He is, He has forsaken me."

He did go to her then, and wrapped his arms around her before he even realized what he was doing. She looked so small, so vulnerable, and so dejected that his stomach clenched with the need to make everything right for her. But he knew too well that some things could not be made right, only endured.

She leaned her forehead against his chest and didn't resist his embrace. Though, to be fair, her arms were wrapped inside the blanket around her shoulders, and she likely couldn't use them to push him away if she wanted to with the way he was crushing her to him.

"Do you want me to let you go?" he asked, caressing his cheek against her silken hair.

"No. Just please don't try to kiss me right now." The words were muffled against his chest, but he heard them.

He grinned and resisted the urge to plant a kiss on the top of her head. "If it is your command, then it will be. But know this."

"What?" she asked suspiciously, pulling her head back to look up at him and narrowing her eyes even as her lips quirked into a hesitant grin to match his own.

"I *will* kiss you again." He said it with laughter in his voice, leveling a steady gaze at her as he spoke. "I am trusting Urd in this."

She laughed at him then and shook her head, but a wide smile lit up her face.

Another small victory.

GALIENA SHIFTED AND stepped away from Red while she still had her head about her. Before she could lose herself in the comfort of his arms. Or the appeal of the low, soothing tone of his voice. Or the way she could feel the laughter rumbling in his chest when she was pressed against him.

She moved to the chest where her clothes were stacked and picked up the little roll of parchment she'd tucked under her tunic upon Red's arrival. Bringing it back to where Red stood by the fire, she held it so that the markings were visible in the light from the hearth.

"I have been studying this and I have a theory."

"Tell me."

She half-expected he might laugh, or say something about it being too complicated, and not to concern herself with it, but he didn't and for that she was grateful. Pointing to the bottom of the message, she said, "I think this is a date. See how the dots are different than the others on the page? And the way they are clustered together, it looks like there are two different, distinct numbers, then a word, and then another set of numbers. If this is a date, and the word is a month, knowing which month could help to decode the letter swapping being used."

When she looked up at him, he was staring down at her, one brow cocked. "I am duly impressed."

She felt her cheeks redden at the compliment, feeling immensely gratified with his approval. And embarrassed that his appreciation should mean so much to her. She shrugged, trying to hide how much his words affected her. "To be of use to my father, I had to learn several different languages, or at least enough in each language to write inventories and tally numbers. I found it easier to learn if I looked for the patterns in each language."

He tipped his head and gave her a knowing look. "And this is just another language."

She nodded.

"I gathered from things you've said that your father was a merchant. Was that all, or like everyone else I've met in the last couple of days, do you have a past that is better kept secret?" He asked the question with a mock look of fright on his face.

She laughed sheepishly. "Until yesterday, I would have said there were no secrets, only disapproval from others. I only knew my father to be a merchant. I thought everything we did was an adventure, and the people we traveled with were fascinating. And I assumed the reason for not discussing with anyone the details of where we'd been or who we'd seen was to not raise suspicions about the contents of our cart. Typically, it was textiles and trinkets, but at times he was able to bargain for finer goods." She inhaled a deep breath of resignation. "And it appears he was also dealing in information."

"A very unusual childhood, indeed," he said. She looked at him warily, as though expecting him to judge her harshly but his only concern was for a woman traveling alone with her father. There were dangers enough for women, even when living in a village surrounded by familiar faces. A woman traveler was far more vulnerable. He brushed the backs of his fingers over her cheek, needing to reassure her with his touch. "It's an adventurous life, but also full of peril. Were you safe?"

"Oh, yes." She nodded vigorously. "Papa was very careful. We traveled with groups whenever possible, and he often served as a guide and sponsor to trustworthy men who wanted to make the journey to England from Turkey, Morocco, Spain, or other countries along the way. He only allowed men to travel with us who were vouched for and recommended by other merchants he trusted."

"Like Sumayl."

"Yes. And others, but I really don't recall much about any of them."

"None of them took a liking to you?" Red asked, struggling to keep his voice calm. Galiena had loved her father, which was apparent, but he wanted to throttle the man for putting his daughter in danger. She would not go unnoticed with her luxurious hair, pert nose, and curved lips. One look at her body, even as a maturing girl, and too many men would think about taking liberties and following through with their lascivious thoughts.

"No," she said with an impatient roll of her eyes and a smirk. "I dressed as a boy for nearly the whole of my childhood. It wasn't until my father was getting ill and began to worry about my prospects of finding a husband that I started to wear gowns."

Red leaned an arm on the mantel of the fireplace and crossed one foot over the other as he peered down at her. "There is so much more I want to hear about you as a lad," he drawled, enjoying the way her lips quirked in an involuntary smile and her cheeks colored.

"Another time, perhaps," she said, reaching for the parchment in his hand, giving him a glimpse of the thin, white chemise beneath the blanket covering her. "Tonight, this is more important."

"Tonight," he said, putting a finger under her chin to lift her face, "rest is more important." Before she could protest, he added, "On the morrow, we leave before the sun rises. Getting to the king before anything happens to the little prince is our priority. Decoding must wait until after we reach our destination."

"You are right," she conceded with a sigh as she rolled the parchment back into the small, tight scroll.

He watched her cross to the pile of clothing on a large wooden chest along the opposite wall, the breath catching in his throat. Her bare feet padded across the floor as the blanket trailed behind her, her hair loose, and her manner easy. For a moment, he imagined this was a shared room and the comfortable familiarity was something they shared every night, with her in her chemise and him appreciating her graceful calm. She would tell him stories from her childhood, and he would pull her onto his lap to inhale her scent.

The blanket slipped from one shoulder as she picked up an undertunic folded on the chest, and Red instinctively moved toward her to assist. He pulled the blanket up to cover her again, his fingers brushing against the smooth skin over her collarbones. The sharp intake of her breath was audible when he touched her, and he leaned closer to her, his own breath drawing deep when she leaned into his chest as it pressed to her back.

He crossed his arms over her, one hand wrapping around her waist, the other across the top of her chest, holding her to him as he drank in the clean, sweet scent of her hair. She let the garment and parchment in her hands fall back onto the chest, then her hands came up to his forearm where it rested beneath her chin, and she dropped her head back, as though surrendering to his protection.

And he would protect her. Satan's stones, but if The Executioner came anywhere near her, he would rip his beating heart from his chest and feed it back to him.

"Red," she whispered, her voice hoarse. "You should leave now."

She didn't loosen her grip on his arm, but he released his hold of her, slowly unfolding her from his embrace. He stepped to her side and picked up the parchment and undertunic. "What did you want done?"

She didn't look at him as she answered. "In the left sleeve, near the top but where the seam runs under the arm, there is an extra fold sewn in that the parchment will fit into."

He handed the parchment to her while he fumbled with the

undertunic until he found the little hiding place in the material. Taking the parchment to fit it into the fold, he said, "Clever."

"Anora is the clever one," she said, watching intently as his fingers worked the little scroll into the material until it was hidden from sight. He shook out the garment, confirmed it had not been dislodged by the motion, then attempted to fold the material into a neat pile and set it back on the chest.

"Get some sleep," he said, his voice gruffer than he'd intended as he moved toward the door.

"Red."

The word was barely perceptible, but he stopped and looked at her over his shoulder.

"Thank you." Every time she tried to steel herself, as she did now, with her back straight and her chin lifted, he wanted to go to her, stand at her side, and let her know that whatever in this world she faced, she didn't have to face it alone.

Instead, he nodded once. "If you need anything, just call for me. I'll hear you."

She turned and looked skeptically at the stone wall that separated her room from his.

He pulled the door open. "I'll hear you," he said again, then closed the door behind him before retreating to his own chamber immediately next to Galiena's.

He closed his own door and leaned against it. Hawkspur Castle was one of the safest places he could imagine with its fortified walls, the finest trained soldiers in the Marches garrisoned in the barracks, and Hawk to oversee it all with Lady Alyce at his side. Red knew that it was nearly impossible for anyone to get through the gates, into the keep, through the hall where several trusted and armed men slept on pallets, and up the winding staircase to the top floor. It always felt so good to sink into the huge, stuffed mattress covered in fine linen sheets, blankets, and warm furs, and he had looked forward to getting a good night of sleep without having to be on the alert even in his slumber. The fire was already lit in his room, and fresh water and a pitcher of wine were set on the sideboard near where his sword leaned against the wall.

None of that mattered to him.

He grabbed his sword, a blanket, and a fur from the bed, and walked back out into the passageway. He spread the fur on the floor outside of Galiena's door, reclined on it with his sword next to him, and then wadded up the blanket to prop up his head.

There was much to learn about Galiena's past, but what he did know was that her husband and her father were dead, and she had no one else. Galiena needed a champion, and he would be that for her. And he'd be damned if he was going to trust anyone else to protect her but him. He'd learned the hard way there was diligence required to protect those who were important to him. He would not let anyone else be taken from him.

She was his.

She may not have admitted it to herself yet, but he knew she was beginning to trust him. It was evident in the way she leaned into him and clung to his arm without hesitation.

He closed his eyes and crossed his arms over his chest, a triumphant grin on his face.

Mine.

Chapter Twelve

G ALIENA HAD A fitful night of sleep. Not because of concern about the mission, or fear for the queen's child, or worry that Anora and Frode were safe. She had a fitful night because she couldn't get the memory of Red's touch on her skin or images of him out of her head. When she did banish the thoughts of Red from her mind, then she was overwhelmed with thoughts of her husband and self-condemnation.

Adam had been a kind and loving husband. They had been content in their life together raising their daughter on the small family farm he'd inherited from his father. She loved him well when he was alive, and she did not stop loving him or her beautiful little Nahara after they were gone.

No one could ever displace Nahara in her heart, but what would happen to the love she had for Adam if she let another into her heart? She never wanted to forget Adam, and in spite of the kind words of Lady Alyce, she feared that if she ever loved another, the memory of him would fade until it was gone. And then *he* would be gone because there would be nothing left of him, and no one left to remember him.

But during the darkest and coldest part of the night, she realized that the real reason she would not let herself love another was because of her own guilt for not dying with her husband and daughter. It was a cruel fate to have failed to save them and then survive to relive the moment every day of her life. Every day she would repeat the memory when Adam went under the water never to surface again even as Galiena splashed through the flood to get to him. And then Nahara, who had been hanging on to the wagon, lost her grip and was swept away. Galiena had lunged for her, fighting the same current that had taken Adam, but she couldn't reach her baby girl before she was gone beneath the surface, too.

If only she hadn't made Adam stop so she could pick the flowers beside the riverbank, or if only she hadn't hesitated before plunging into the sudden and unexpected flood water, they might still be here with her. If only she'd been a better swimmer. If only…if only. But the truth was, she could change nothing, and her regret and guilt were as strong as the flood that had taken away the two most important people of her life, leaving her feeling as suffocated as if she herself had drowned.

After dozing sporadically, she finally rose and donned her clothing when the fire had burned down to a few embers. Dawn could not be so very far away, and she did not want to risk being left behind. Lady Alyce had found a saddle bag for her to carry her few belongings during the journey. In truth, nearly everything she had was borrowed, either from Anora or from Gertie. She wore the undertunic that Anora had sewn the hiding place into for the parchment, the braies that belonged to Anora's brother, as well as the boots and heavy tunic Gertie had found for her. She packed the soft chemise that Lady Alyce insisted she bring with her for the nights, as well as the simple gown belonging to Gertie of fine linen dyed forest green for her audience with the queen.

When she had everything packed into the satchel and ran her fingers over the missive tucked in her sleeve for the dozenth time, she blew out the candle on the sideboard and opened the door.

To her surprise, Red was already standing in the corridor. Bed coverings were wadded up in his arm, and his sword was gripped in one hand as he opened the door to his chamber with the other.

A surge of heated embarrassment—and disappointment—coursed through her veins at catching him returning to his room from what she assumed was a tryst. Although, why he didn't just bring the woman to his room, she didn't understand. Perhaps he felt it was an act of chivalry on his part to not risk her overhearing his love play with another woman after he'd been kissing her only a short while prior.

"Not a very restful night for you, I see," she said, meaning to keep her tone light. She had pushed him away and had no right to expect…what? Loyalty?

Unfortunately, her voice had an unintended edge to it.

"There are worse places to sleep than the floor."

She realized then that he'd slept in the hall in front of her door and flushed with embarrassment, feeling contrite about her hasty assumption that he had been returning from a tryst.

Wait there," he instructed as he withdrew into his chamber. He returned a few moments later without the blanket, shoulders covered in a fur, sword still in hand, and a saddle bag thrown over his shoulder. He took the satchel from her hand and flung it over his shoulder with his pack, then grabbed her hand and started toward the stairs.

"Why did you sleep on the floor?" she asked, perplexed by why he'd chosen discomfort if he had a bed in his chamber anything like the bed she'd just slept in—well, tossed and turned in, though that had nothing to do with the comfort of the bed and everything to do with the thoughts in her head.

"To ease my mind."

She barely heard his muffled answer because she was distracted by the broad expanse of his back as he dragged her along behind him. When he reached the spiral stairs, he changed the angle of his hand so as to give her a steadying hold as she followed him down the dimly lit steps.

Hawk and four other men were already gathered in the hall when they entered. She tried to pull her hand from Red's, but he tightened his grip and flashed her a quick grin. His possessiveness should have bothered her more than it did, but she found she was grateful for his reassuring presence.

"Good morn to you," Hawk said clapping a hand on Red's shoulder. "The horses are saddled and Cook just sent Wart out to attach the bags of provisions."

"Give her my thanks," Red responded, then turned as though to take his leave.

Galiena pulled back on his hand, refusing to budge. When he turned to look at her, she gave him a disapproving look and tipped her head in the direction of the men.

"They'll be riding with us," Red said, then started toward the door again.

Again, she stood her ground and pulled back on the obtuse man's hand. "Red," she said through tight lips.

This time he stopped to turn in her direction. "What?"

She tipped her head again toward the other men.

"They can be trusted," he said, still not understanding that she wanted to be introduced to the men.

"She's trying to tell you to quit being rude, Viking," Hawk said with a laugh.

Galiena nodded, adding in a low whisper for Red's ears only, "If we are to be traveling with these men, the least you can do is introduce me."

She heard a few stifled coughs behind her and turned to see two of the men smiling in amusement and the largest one shaking his head at Red.

Red turned to glare at the men, then grunted their names as he gave each a cursory glance over his shoulder. "Ox. Dane. Bard. Wolf."

She waited for him to tell them her name, and when he didn't, she decided she'd have to do it herself. She tried to turn to face the men more fully, but Red was walking toward the door again, hauling her along with him. Over her shoulder, she said. "My name is Galiena, and I apologize for Red's rude behavior."

Red stopped suddenly and she crashed into him. "Did you just apologize for me?" he asked, a comical look of indignation on his face.

"Aye, I did," she said, ignoring the laugher behind her. "These kind gentlemen are going to be traveling with us. The least you can do is tell them my name."

"Methinks he is afraid he will lose you to the charm of someone less ugly and oafish than him." The one called Bard said this, a dazzling and mischievous grin splitting his face. He had blond hair that hung in waves to his shoulders, chiseled features, and sparkling eyes that undoubtedly appealed to most women. Even she would admit he was a handsome man, but she preferred Red's more rugged features and his powerful intensity.

"He is most definitely not ugly," Galiena said with a snort of laughter at Bard's jest. "But 'oafish' is an apt description this morning. The daft man slept in the corridor instead of his bed, and I think he is a bit waspish because of it."

"Slept on the floor in the corridor, did he?" Hawk asked, with a knowing grin toward Red and a wink at Galiena.

"Mighty chivalrous of you, Viking," Ox said, his voice a deep rumble befitting his name.

Wolf and Dane did not add to the banter, but they were definitely enjoying the ribbing from their companions.

"Enough," Red growled. He released her hand, and for a moment Galiena thought he was embarrassed by all the attention—until he crouched down just enough to wrap an arm around the back of her thighs and lift her up. The men roared with laughter.

"Red!" she exclaimed, grabbing onto his shoulders to steady herself. She was the one embarrassed now. "Put me down." But Red only grunted in response, while the men laughed even more loudly.

As they approached the heavy wooden doors leading to the bailey, she thought he would surely need to release her to open the door since he carried the satchels and his sword with the other arm. But Wart chose to enter the hall at that very moment. When he saw Red coming toward him with Galiena hoisted on his arm, he pulled the door open wide and stood holding it with a smile on his face.

"The horses are ready," Wart said with boyish enthusiasm. "The pretty lady said she wasn't yours, but she was wrong, wasn't she, Master Red?"

"Remind me to give you a coin when I return, Wart."

"Aye, Master Red!"

Galiena let out a sigh of annoyance as she draped an arm over Red's shoulder and settled into accepting that she was going to be carried from the castle despite any amount of protesting.

"You are a scoundrel," she muttered, though she had to admit she felt enlivened and invigorated in a way she'd not felt for many years.

"You said I am most definitely not ugly," he said as he descended the stairs into the bailey. "Last night you said you couldn't concentrate when I was near you."

She had said both of those things and though she wanted to regret letting him know how much he really affected her, it was liberating to actually feel something other than sorrow and regret. "Aye, I did say that, but there is no need to get cocky about it. After all, that Bard fellow is quite appealing, as well."

He jostled her in his arms when she said the last, and called over his shoulder, "Wart! Tell Bard his service is no longer needed."

"I was only jesting, Red! His looks are too boyish for my liking. Don't embarrass him."

Wart was running alongside them now. "What did you say, Master Red? I don't think I heard right."

"Nothing of importance," Red conceded as he set Galiena on her feet next to a horse. "Wart, take this satchel and attach it to my saddle," he said, handing the boy his saddle bag. He strapped his sword to his waist, then tied Galiena's satchel to the saddle of what she assumed was going to be her horse.

Galiena eyed her horse, then compared it to the other horses as the men easily climbed into their saddles. "It's a very large horse, isn't it?" She tried to sound more confident than she was feeling. It wasn't the height that bothered her so much as the sheer size of the horse's chest and neck. It was obviously a powerful horse; she hoped it wasn't also obstinate.

She patted the beast on the neck, murmuring to it as a means of soothing herself, when Red returned to her side, crowding her against the horse's shoulder. He was standing so close, she had to tip her head back to look up at him towering over her.

"You can still change your mind," he said in a low voice. "Stay here under Hawk's protection while I ride to intercept King Edward."

The thought of how comfortable it would be to stay in a chamber that was as large as her cottage, sleeping on a luxuriously deep mattress with thick blankets as the fire burned in the stone hearth while Red and the others rode for long days in the cold and wet definitely had its appeal.

But then she thought about how hopeless and dark her life had become constantly living in the shadow of her grief over Adam and Nahara. If she did everything she could to save the life of the innocent baby prince of England, it would not bring her family back to her, but it would restore some of her faith in herself. "No," she said. "As I've said, I must do this for my own reasons."

He cupped her chin in his hand and brought his face so close to hers she feared he was going to kiss her right there in the open with his men looking on. "Do not forget it was your choice when you are cold and wet."

She swallowed, thinking more about the fact that part of her was hoping he would kiss her despite the audience. "My choice," she repeated, her words embarrassingly breathless.

"You want me to kiss you, don't you." It is an arrogant statement rather than a question.

She slowly shook her head though her heart was pounding

with anticipation in her chest. "I want to be on our way."

A small squeal escaped her lips as his hands came to her waist and pulled her closer. She clutched his forearms with her gloved hands, her breath catching as he closed the distance between their lips. When his mouth was so close to hers she could feel the warmth of his breath against her face, he said in a hoarse whisper, "Again, your choice."

Then he was lifting her off her feet and onto the back of the horse.

"Don't fall off, kitten," he said, slapping her on the thigh as he would one of his soldiers.

Chapter Thirteen

RED HAD WATCHED Galiena closely in those first hours. They had followed a familiar road until daybreak, with Ox and Dane leading the way and Bard and Wolf riding at his back. He'd chosen a horse with a broad back and smooth gaits to make the journey as comfortable as possible for her.

She hadn't complained or asked them to slow the pace. Instead, she had set her face into a determined scowl and concentrated on staying on the gelding's back. On the few occasions she looked at him, he'd nodded his approval at her.

Perhaps she would endure the journey better than he had anticipated.

After breaking for a midday meal and to rest the horses, they had veered off the main road and turned west on what was a well-beaten path at its best, and hardly a narrow trail at its worst. This part of the journey would be more difficult as the route was not so well-traveled, and they would encounter arduous climbs and descents along the way.

Still, Red was satisfied with the progress they were making and feeling optimistic about reaching Llanidloes by nightfall when they encountered their first obstacle: a narrow bridge of wood spanning a river which at this time of year would still be swollen from the recent rains.

Galiena halted her horse several paces from the bridge, looking apprehensive. Dane had crossed and yelled back that the bridge was sound enough if they crossed one rider at a time. Ox crossed next but when he reached the other side and signaled for Galiena to follow, she pulled back hard on the reins to restrain the gray. The horse pranced in place and tossed its head several times before Red got closer to settle it.

"There is nothing to be afraid of, kitten." Red saw the fearful expression in her eyes, which were wide and frantic, and his gut clenched. The color had drained from her face and her gaze darted in every direction as she looked from the bridge to the rushing river below, upstream, downstream, and even behind her. He sought to ease the terror that had seized her. "If the bridge can hold Ox, it can definitely hold you and your mount." When his words did not seem to penetrate her panic, he added, "Turning back is not an option. It would take us a full day to backtrack and take a different route."

She turned to him then, but her eyes were focused on something far beyond him. She squeezed them closed, dropping her face into her hands, tormented by demons that Red could not see. She was falling apart once more, as she had in Hawk's hall; seeing it again was torturous. There was only one solution for it; he reached for her and pulled her onto Hammer's back to ride with him, wrapping his cloak around her and holding her shaking body close to his chest. She grabbed handfuls of his tunic in her hands and pressed her forehead to his chest as she gulped in deep breaths of air.

"What is it, Galiena?" He rubbed his thumb in slow circles over her cheek to draw her attention away from whatever demons had taken hold of her. The wooden bridge wasn't the sturdiest he'd ever seen, but it did not appear unsafe to him either. When she didn't respond, he said, "I'll take you across."

"No!" she yelped, picking up her head to look out over the bridge and the river flowing below.

"This isn't the first bridge we've crossed," he said gently.

"What is it about this one that you fear?"

"It's the rushing water. The flooding banks. The wooden bridge…"

The river was significantly wider and the water flowing faster than any of the other crossings they'd encountered thus far. "Ah. We will not fall in, but can you not swim? Is that why you are so fearful?"

"I can swim," she said in a hoarse whisper, her gaze fixated on the gurgling water as if it would eat her as it swirled around the rocks and outcroppings along the riverbank. "But it wasn't enough."

He was about to nudge Hammer to walk over the bridge but stayed his command at the last of her words. "What wasn't enough?"

"I wasn't enough," she said, still staring at the water. "It was too cold. My fingers felt frozen. I couldn't hold on. The wagon slipped through my hands. *She* slipped through my hands."

Red's insides twisted at the sorrow in her voice. He didn't want to ask the question, didn't want to hear her answer, but he felt it was something she needed to say aloud. "Who was she?" he asked gently.

"My Nahara." After a long silence, she sighed and then turned to look up at him. Her face was bloodless, but her eyes were sharp, aware. "My daughter."

Red could think of nothing to say that would ease her pain. He dropped his forehead to touch hers and slid one hand around the back of her neck, and they stayed that way for several breaths. On the other side of the bridge, the men milled, their horses stamping and wheeling with impatience. Red could see them staring at them with curiosity and, he imagined, little sympathy. Still, he wouldn't force her; she needed his patience right now. He couldn't take away her pain, but he could lend her his strength.

"I'm going to take you across with me," Red said when her breathing returned to normal.

"No," she said, but with much less vehemence this time. "I

must do this." She let out a small, self-deprecating sound, not quite a laugh and not quite a sigh. "Else your men will think you daft for bringing a ninny-hearted woman on this journey."

"Next time," Red insisted. He didn't want her to face this fear alone. He wanted her to face it with him there to keep her safe. "There will be more bridges to cross as the day goes, but this is the worst. If your horse senses your unease with this crossing, it might communicate to him, making the rest more challenging than needs be. You will train him bridges are something to fear and that could take a long time to undo."

He didn't know how he knew, but he sensed that making Galiena focus on her mount's feelings instead of her own would help her to overcome her own fear. After a moment, he could feel her draw herself up, resolute, in his arms.

He helped her resituate herself on Hammer's back so that she was facing forward, tightened his hold on her, and then nudged his horse into a walk. As his hooves clopped on the wood, the hollow echoes disappeared over the water. She tensed and even trembled, so Red instructed, "Keep your eyes on the road on the other end of the bridge. Look where you want the horse to go."

She clutched Red's wrists, her gloved fingers digging into his skin as she pushed herself back against his chest. "Can you go faster?"

"Nay, kitten. If we trot, then his hooves slam down on the wood much harder. 'Tis safer to walk at a steady pace." He didn't think she could grip his wrists any tighter or tense her back any further, but she did. As a distraction, he leaned closer to her and said in a low voice, "What do you know of Anora and her father? It seems that he is more than just a goldsmith?"

"Now is not the time," she responded, her voice as tense as her body. "Concentrate on the path ahead."

He ignored her command, choosing instead to keep her thinking about anything but the rush of the water below or the creaking of the bridge as it swayed under Hammer's weight. His hooves rang hollowly on the wood planks, vibrating with each step. "You said your father was a merchant, but it seems there was more to him, as well."

"I imagine my father encountered a lot of people who were more than what they appeared; that doesn't mean he was anything other than a merchant." She continued to dig her fingers into his wrists, her arms stiff as she pushed back against him as though to brace herself against a fall.

"Mayhap it is in your blood to find trouble," Red said, purposely trying to raise her ire as a means of keeping her attention on him.

"I did not go looking for the trouble. It found me," she said peevishly. "Or rather, *he* found me."

"But then *you* found *me*," Red said, the anger rising in him at the thought of the despicable man coming near Galiena. "And I will protect you now."

"If the bridge collapses, no one can protect me," she said through panting breaths. They were halfway across, and she was pushing herself further up off the horse's back and into his lap with each step. If she stiffened her arms any further or lifted her knees any higher, she would soon be standing on the horse. She turned her head back and forth as she looked over one side of the bridge and then the other.

"The only way off now is straight ahead. Keep your focus on the road beyond the bridge," Red commanded. "Look where you want to go, and the horse will follow."

She snapped her head up to look straight ahead. "If there are more bridges, just hit me over the head before dragging me across them."

He laughed then. "Not a chance, kitten. The next will be easier."

"How do you know that?" Her voice was only a little less panicked as they drew near to the end.

"Because now you know you do not have to face it alone."

When Hammer stepped onto the road on the other side of the river, he signaled to Bard to cross the bridge with the gray palfrey in tow. Galiena was squirming in his arms, and he was just about to tighten his hold on her before she slipped off the horse's back when he heard the retching start. The poor woman leaned over the side of Hammer, spewing the contents of her stomach onto the ground below. He waited patiently for her to finish, then handed her his ale pouch to rinse her mouth.

"Good boy, Ham," Galiena said, patting his horse's neck as she straightened up again, gasping for breath.

"Hammer," he growled, but with no conviction as he was more concerned about Galiena than by what name she called his horse. The woman had the strangest reaction to stress.

"Why doesn't my horse have a name?" She had turned to watch Bard bringing her mount over the river. Her face was still pale, but some color was returning to her cheeks.

He decided not to mention the retching and answered her question instead. "He is proving too docile for a warhorse and will be used for other things, so I did not see the need to name him. But the stable lads call him Meddal."

"Metal? They must have named him before you discovered he was easy tempered."

"Not Metal. *May-thal*," he corrected, enunciating the word more clearly. "*Meddal* means 'soft' in Welsh."

"Oh," she said, disapprovingly. "Perhaps that is the reason he is docile. I think I will call him *Metal*, instead. That will make him feel stronger. Besides, he's the same color as metal, so it fits better."

Red laughed. "I'm sure that will fix him."

He took Metal's reins from Bard once they drew near, then lifted Galiena to settle her onto the gray's back. When she was situated, he took her chin in his hand and turned her to face him. "Are you all right?"

She nodded, and her eyes locked with his for a long moment. "I am embarrassed by my behavior, but I thank you for your kindness," she finally said, her voice quiet.

"I don't want you to ever feel embarrassed with me." He

hated seeing her like this, and he never wanted her to feel ashamed for being forced to do something that was so obviously linked to a horrible experience from her past. "I'll be your added strength whenever you need it."

Wolf had successfully crossed the bridge and had halted his horse next to Bard, both a discreet distance away from Red and Galiena. Ox and Dane were waiting farther along the narrow road, their mounts stomping restlessly.

She looked back at the wooden bridge spanning the river. "I can tolerate the stone bridges."

That explained why she'd not reacted the same way to the previous river crossings. Any tension he'd sensed from her during the prior day's journey he had attributed to the difficulty of a long ride on a shared horse. This was the first wooden bridge they'd encountered, and though it was sturdy enough, it did sway and creak with the weight of each rider as they crossed. If she'd had a bad experience on a wooden bridge, then every movement and noise would seem like a warning of imminent danger or as a reminder of a previous incident.

"There will be more bridges, most stone but some wood before we get to Llanbadarn Gaerog." He would not insult her by asking if she wanted to continue or if she would be all right. He knew she wouldn't turn back, and if she struggled again, he would be there to get her safely to the other side, especially now that he could anticipate her struggle and perhaps plan ways to distract her from her fear or prepare her for the crossing.

"Right then," she said with a determined sigh and a roll of her shoulders. "We best be underway. We have a lot of ground to cover."

He nodded his approval at her, then gently slapped Meddal—*Metal*, he corrected himself with an eye roll—on the rump to walk on before he gave in to his urge to scoop her off her horse and back into his lap to kiss her senseless. She looked so small to him, so fragile, and so earnestly resolute that it nearly broke his heart. He would kill anyone who tried to stomp on her pride or break her spirit.

Chapter Fourteen

G ALIENA HAD HOPED she would have time for her heartbeat to
return to normal before they encountered the next rickety
bridge, but there it was already. The last one had appeared
suddenly after a curve in the narrow road, leaving her with no
time to think about it before they were upon it. The next one was
still some way in the distance, but clearly visible, and like the last,
it appeared to be a spindly wooden thing with very little support.

It was a slow torture to watch the thing she feared most coming closer to her with each agonizing step of her horse, yet the
distance felt endless as the anticipation stoked her dread.

The narrow road had turned into a beaten pathway barely
wide enough for two horses abreast. It followed the bank of the
river and curved around the larger rocks and trees along the way.
They were riding along a straight stretch of the river, but it
curved out of sight just beyond the bridge. Folding her hands
together with the reins tucked tightly between them, she said a
prayer that the trail forked ahead, and they would ride in the
opposite direction of the bridge. To keep herself calm, she let
herself believe that another trail followed the curve of the river
and that crossing the bridge would not be necessary for where
they were going.

As was expected, God did not heed her prayers. Her father

had not been a devout man, and as a result, neither was she. She prayed when she didn't know what else to do, and her own lack of faith was obviously reflected in her prayers and noticed by God.

"Hell and damnation!" she exclaimed louder than she'd intended as Ox and Dane steered their horses onto the bridge, one right after the other. The trail did not split as she had hoped, the cliffs being too steep to traverse. This bridge looked just as wobbly as the last to her eyes, but the men didn't seem as concerned about it as they weren't even waiting to cross one rider at a time. Unless she wanted to turn around, the bridge was the only option.

She pulled back gently on the reins to slow Metal while she composed herself and worked up the courage to cross on her own, remembering Red's warning that letting her horse feel her fear could teach him to be afraid of bridge crossings. She didn't want to be the one responsible for causing him to learn fear. And especially, she would not let Red, or his soldiers think she was a spineless ninny. But before she could even take a deep breath to prepare herself, Red was at her side, taking hold of one of her reins and leading her mount toward the bridge.

"Red, no!" She needed a little time to gather her courage and to convince herself that since she'd crossed one bridge, she could cross another. But he wasn't giving her the opportunity, and when she looked down at the water, she felt the panic rising in her throat.

"I liked kissing you last night," Red said.

She was appalled that he would speak out loud about their private moment in the solar at Hawkspur. Her head snapped up so she could give him a good glare. Red had a wicked grin on his face; she had no doubt the other men could most definitely overhear every word he said.

"It is not appropriate to discuss that in front of your men," she said through gritted teeth. "Or anyone else."

His eyes twinkled and the corners of them crinkled. "I think you liked it, too."

"That's very presumptuous of you, Viking," she said, her ire rising.

"No need to shout. I can hear you."

"I'm not shouting." She didn't realize until the words were out that, indeed, she was shouting. But she couldn't seem to quiet her tone with her heart beating like a runaway horse. "It's your fault that I'm shouting. You didn't let me catch my breath before dragging me across the bridge and then you started talking about kissing."

She heard a snicker of laughter behind her but decided not to look back over her shoulder. The huge Viking had a way of unsettling her. She was having a hard time collecting her thoughts because of the way his leg was rubbing against hers as he guided Metal over the bridge. Despite his overbearing presence, she had to admit his nearness was also comforting, and she was grateful for it.

"Keep looking to the other side," Red urged in a low, mellow tone. "And keep thinking about kissing me."

"I am *not* thinking about kissing you. And quit talking about that or everyone will know it happened."

"Everyone knows now, kitten, with the way you're shouting."

She heard the men behind them snickering again. "Bard, Wolf, don't listen to what this big oaf is saying."

"It's you we can hear, my lady."

"I'm not a lady. I'm just Galiena."

"No need to yell, Galiena," Bard said. "We are right here."

She jumped in her saddle when he said the last, startling her as he drew his horse up to her other side. It took her several panicky breaths before she realized they'd stopped moving and she looked down to see the trail beneath her, then looked behind her to see they had cleared the bridge by several paces.

"Much obliged," she said to Red, her voice still overly loud as she brushed his hand from the rein and bumped Metal's side with her foot. "How many more of these do we have?"

"Not many," Red replied, catching up to her, but she knew he was lying.

"I'm glad to hear it because if there are many more, I will gladly let The Executioner get to me first."

Red's hand shot out and grabbed her wrist to stay her horse. "Do not jest about that."

The horrified look on his face wrenched at her heart. She had overstepped in her attempt to make light of a situation that was distressing to her forgetting that, according to Red, The Executioner had nearly killed him. It would only be fitting that he had a healthy fear of the man. "I am sorry, that was thoughtless of me after what he did to you."

"It's not me I worry about. I will not let him near you." The intensity in his eyes as he looked at her made her stomach flip flop in a way she almost did not recognize.

Almost.

She should have diverted her gaze immediately to break the intimacy, but in truth, she was beginning to take comfort in Red. He was everything one imagined of a Viking—big, intimidating, boisterous, inappropriate. That he was also appealing, attentive, sensitive, and gentle was unexpected.

He lifted his hand to stroke the back of his fingers over her cheek. She gave him a small smile, then dropped her gaze from his. She liked his nearness and familiarity, but was it because she had been lonely for so long and the fact that a man—any man— was giving her attention like she'd not experienced since her husband had died? Or was it that it was Red—and only Red—who she needed to jar her from the stupor she had been living in these three bleak years?

And what did this mean about Adam? Was it a dishonor to him that she did not want to be alone anymore? Did she need to forget about him to let someone else into her life? Would he disappear from her memory?

You are deserving of love and happiness again.

The words said to her by Lady Alyce the night before came to her mind. The kind woman had spoken of the loss of her own husband and the guilt she felt when she started to fall in love with Hawk, as though betraying his memory.

You are deserving of love and happiness again.

It was too much to think about at this moment. She lifted her gaze to the heavy clouds above as cold raindrops spattered her face. "Shall we carry on?"

"Aye," he said, reaching for her hood and pushing it up over her head. "Stay as dry as you can. Once the chill settles into your bones, it stays."

"I remember," she murmured, thinking about the times that she and her father had endured cold rains, snow, and everything in between. She'd learned to tolerate the frigid weather, but some days the damp wind was too much, and her teeth would set to chattering louder than the castanets she'd seen dancers clacking together in countries where the sun shone far brighter than in Britain.

"Were you out in the cold frequently?" Red asked as the horses walked quickly on.

"The cold is everywhere, so yes, my father and I traveled through every imaginable weather. Heat can be just as miserable as cold." She felt her lips curving upward as memories of her life with her father surfaced in her mind.

"Tell me more," Red encouraged. "Where have you traveled?"

She sighed contentedly as she thought about all the places she'd been. "My father bought and sold merchandise from Scotland all the way down to Morocco. Do you know of Morocco?"

Red nodded. "Aye. I've not been there, but I have read about it."

"Where did you learn to read?"

"Hawk teaches anyone in his ranks who is willing how to read. And write. He believes in taking every advantage possible.

And you?"

"My father taught me to read and write, at first just to make lists and tally numbers. But he always bought books to trade, and he liked for me to read to him during the long days driving the cart." The fond memories warmed her heart. She had not thought about the days traveling with her father in a very long time. Too long. She had let herself become numb and withdrawn. With Anora, she had started emerging from the dark place she'd been in; getting a taste of the world again made her crave more.

"I like to see you smile," Red said, flashing her his crooked grin.

"It feels good to smile." She felt herself blushing. "It has been a long time. It's also been a long time since I was kissed," she added quietly, not looking at Red. She hadn't expected to make this confession. But nothing was as expected of late. "I had forgotten how enjoyable it can be."

"Enjoyable?" Red lamented in mock offense. "A good roast is enjoyable. Mulled wine is enjoyable. A good *kiss* is breathtaking. Knee-wobbling. Heat-inducing." He accentuated each word by throwing his splayed hand in the air. "Saying it was anything less is the same as plunging a dagger straight into my heart."

"Perhaps you need more practice, Viking," she said. She did look at him then, tipping her head to see him clearly from under her hood and purposefully flashing him a teasing grin with a taunting arch of her eyebrows. She was shocked at her own coquettishness. And exhilarated.

She expected him to protest, mockingly bristle, and respond with his own barb. She did not expect him to reach inside her hood, wrap his long fingers around her neck until his hand almost completely encircled her throat, and pull her close so their lips almost touched, his breath warming her face when he spoke.

"You lie, kitten. I saw you trying to regain your composure standing by the fire after we were interrupted last night."

The horses did not break their stride, despite the fact that she dropped her reins in her surprise. A thrill coursed through her veins and warmth pooled low in her belly at his touch.

He kissed her then, pressing his lips to hers and sucking in her bottom lip to give it a sharp nibble before pulling back.

"But I'm not opposed to practicing, love," he said in a hoarse whisper with one eyebrow cocked. "Lots of practicing. On all of you until there isn't a part of your body my lips and tongue haven't practiced on."

She could hear the mischievous grin in his deep voice, which was smooth and seductive and made her weak in the limbs. Hell's fires, but he made her weak everywhere, including her determination and will.

When he released her, she cleared her throat and shook her head to rid it of the images he had put there, the increasing rain bringing her back to her senses. They had a mission to complete, an assassin to deter, and a child to save. That is what should be taking all of her focus. Not the red-headed Viking with his piercing eyes, tantalizing lips, and honeyed words that filled her with longings she thought never to have again.

"The mission, Red," she admonished, though even she could hear in her voice the smile that she couldn't seem to stop from spreading across her face—which she tried to keep hidden in the depths of her hood. "Let's not forget the reason we are together on this mission."

"Right now, let's not forget that the rain is only going to get worse," he said. "We need to move faster."

"I'm ready," she said with a bravado she didn't feel just before Red slapped Metal on the hindquarters. Clutching the reins with a death grip as her horse lurched into a canter, Galiena tried not to look down at the ground being churned up by the horse's hooves, imagining a similar fate for herself if she bounced off the side of Metal.

Chapter Fifteen

"THANK THE HEAVENS above," Galiena grumbled to herself. The blurry outline of scattered structures visible in the distance had to be Llanidloes. If it wasn't, she feared she might weep with disappointment—not that anyone would see her pitiful tears with the icy rain soaking her face. She'd kept her hood pulled down as low as possible for the last hour or more, but the rain had been so heavy and the wind so relentless that it had been impossible to stay dry.

She peeked from under her sodden hood at the riders and travelers ahead of them. As they'd drawn closer to Llanidloes, which was the last significant settlement before Llanbadarn, they had met more people making the same journey. She'd not expected so many to travel across Wales to pay their respects to a king who had recently conquered their land, but people seemed weary of the rebellions and constant fighting among the princes of Wales and ready for order to be restored.

There were a few who appeared to be lords, or men of a wealthy status, going to pay homage to King Edward, conqueror of Wales, even if reluctantly. Others appeared to be individuals or families making the pilgrimage, either on foot or in simple carts pulled by a lone horse, to see the king and queen of England. More were likely making the journey as entertainers or trinket hawkers, looking to profit off the throngs of people who would be crowding the city for a view of the king and queen.

Besides the fact that there were so many travelers, the driving wind and rain had slowed the progress of the horses to a walk, and they were forced to traverse at the same pace as those on foot for the final miles. She'd felt guilty riding a strong horse while others walked; the daughter of a merchant, widow of a farmer was not worthy of the distinction. To feel less conspicuous of the privilege, Galiena offered to take a young girl of perhaps six or seven up in the saddle before her, tucking the scrawny girl into her cloak to share what little warmth she had left. It pleased her immensely when Red took up the little girl's brother to ride behind him on Hammer, and Bard and Wolf took up two other children from the group of nearby travelers to ride on their horses.

It felt good to hold the little girl, who pressed up against her because they were so cold, both of them shivering. Emotionally drained from the day already, and too numb from the freezing wind and rain to feel the usual and ever-present pain in her heart, the memories of the past were mercifully quiet. Galiena was contented with the presence of the child and thought about nothing more for the time being.

Night was descending and the darkness would soon be complete. More buildings were becoming visible as they drew nearer, including a large church. She prayed there were enough inns and beds to house them all as she did not think any of them could possibly ride or walk any farther. The heavy clouds blotted out any sign of the moon and stars, and soon the night would be black as ink, making it a folly to continue.

They'd encountered several more bridges on the journey before joining up with the other travelers on the main road to Llanidloes, and though the driving rain and slick slats of wood had terrified her, there was no other option but to force herself to cross over them. She found that if she argued with Red over some mundane point, giving her the excuse to disguise her terror as frustration, it distracted her from thinking about where she was or what could happen. She knew he'd caught on quite early to her need to focus her anxious energy on some trivial matter, which meant he could be counted on to oblige her by taking a contrary stance to anything she said while crossing a bridge.

They'd argued about whether or not The Executioner should be assigned a name, something that could be used to refer to him without raising suspicion should anyone be eavesdropping. Red didn't see the point in it, preferring she not speak of him at all. She ignored his grumbling, insisting she wanted a name that would take away some of his power, something belittling—much in the same way she believed calling her mount Metal would bolster the horse's fortitude, though in the opposite direction. In the end, she decided The Executioner would be known as "Toad," even if Red refused to use the new moniker.

They'd argued about whether Lancelot caused the fall of Camelot, or if it was Guinevere due to the rift she caused between best friends, or if it was entirely the fault of King Arthur. The soldiers had even weighed in on this topic. Bard was the only one to agree with Galiena that it was solely on the shoulders of Arthur. The others agreed with Red's argument that if Arthur and Lancelot had not been divided by deceit and jealousy over Guinevere, then Camelot would never have fallen. That particular argument got them over the remaining bridges and a precarious stretch of the trail that edged along a steep bank of the river.

And if the howling of the wind and pounding of the rain had not increased to the point of being deafening, she would have continued to defend Guinevere all the way to Llanidloes as a distraction from her chattering teeth and frozen fingers.

As it was, she almost wept with joy when Ox and Dane stopped their horses on the lane in the middle of the village. It stretched for some length and was flanked by a number of buildings with lights shining through the windows. She was especially grateful to see what appeared to be three separate taverns with upper levels. With luck, not all of the rooms were filled as of yet.

The men dismounted from their horses, but Galiena was too stiff from the frigid weather and the long hours in the saddle to move of her own accord. Red approached and helped the little girl she carried to dismount so she could return to her family. Galiena didn't protest when Red grabbed her reins and led Metal to a barn behind one of the inns. Once they were under the roof of the barn, he took her by the waist and gingerly lifted her off the horse.

"I can't feel my legs," she whimpered—much to her shame— draping her arms around Red's neck as he helped her down. God help her, but Red would need to carry her again, just as he'd done the previous night. She should have been mortified, but she was too cold and too tired to care.

"Take her in," she heard Ox say. "Dane and I will bed down the horses and meet you inside."

Red cradled her to his chest as he hurried through the rain toward the inn. Bard got there first and yanked on the door, holding it open for them to pass through into the dim light of the tavern. The room was loud with talking and laughing patrons and smelled wonderfully of warm food.

"You may set me down now." Galiena couldn't be sure she would be able to stand, but the embarrassment of sinking to the floor would be easier to bear than the attention they were attracting at the moment.

Red, of course, ignored her wishes, pushing his way through the crowd instead to set her down next to the warmth of the hearth. The hoots and lewd comments that followed in their wake only served to put a grin on the Viking's face, although he did turn a menacing glare toward one young man whose remark was too ribald for his liking. Bard and Wolf added their menacing presence to his implied threat, and they quickly lost the amused attention of the other patrons.

Red kept his arms around her until she was steady on her

feet, while Bard and Wolf secured a nearby table and stools which they pulled closer to the heat of the fire. A plump woman with a linen kerchief tied tightly over her hair appeared and slid four tankards onto the table in front of them.

"My husband will be coming down any moment," the woman said to them, as though in warning should they be thinking she was alone. Smart woman, Galiena thought, recalling her own previous experiences working in a tavern; Red hadn't been her first "husband," though he'd been the first physical one she'd made up. When she'd worked in the tavern, any husband she talked about was purely imaginary. "We're near filled up for the night. Your men can sleep by the fire down here, but you and your wife can take my daughter's room above stairs." She looked Red up and down, then added, "Though I don't see how you'll fit. Your feet will be hanging off the end of the bed."

"I'm not his wife," Galiena tried to clarify through chattering teeth.

"What did you say, my lady? All I could hear was the chattering of your teeth," the woman said peevishly.

"She said she needs warm food and wine," Red interjected, still steadying her with his hands on her waist.

"Not much stew left," the woman said. "But I've got bread."

"We'll take what you have for six; two more are joining us," Red requested. "Show me to the room, then I'll return with the coin for the food and lodging."

The woman shook her head. "Eat first. When my husband comes down, I'll ready the room for you." This was not someone to be given orders, here in her own establishment.

Galiena guessed the woman had dealt with her share of demanding men in her lifetime as a tavern keeper, making it difficult for warriors such as Red and his companions to intimidate her. She looked up at Red to see his reaction to being contradicted and was pleased to see a smirk of amusement on his face.

"Thank you, good lady, for your hospitality," he said as a means of deferring to the woman's authority.

The woman seemed appeased by this as her manner softened and her voice took on a gentler tone. "This one is a mulled wine for the lady," she said, sliding one of the tankards apart from the others. "My husband warmed it for my old bones, but I think she needs it more."

"I thank you," Galiena said, the chattering of her teeth slowing. She thought she'd mention she wasn't Red's wife again when her shivering had stopped.

Red slowly released his hold on her, apparently watching for any signs that her legs would give out. She patted his chest reassuringly, then put her hands to her back and stretched from side to side. She was stiff from the long day of riding in the rain. And so wet. After peeling her gloves off her hands, she fumbled with the ties of her cloak, working to get the heavy, sodden garment off of her shoulders. She was relieved to hand it to Red, who took it from her to hang on a peg to dry near the hearth as she picked up the mulled wine, letting the warmth of it penetrate through her stiff fingers.

Bard and Wolf were already seated with drinks in hand, talking to the three men at the next table when Dane and Ox entered, carrying the saddle bags. Soon, they too were downing their ale and laughing with the other men.

Wooden bowls of watery stew and loaves of bread were placed on the table by the woman and her husband, who was as round and stern-faced as his wife. "You got the last room," he said in a gruff voice. "The flues are open to the above floor, but with this wind, you'll need each other to keep warm."

Galiena felt her face flush as she reached for a stool, focusing on the food to hide her embarrassment and discomfort. Having to share a room with Red had her stomach churning, and as hungry as she was, she feared anything she put in it now would come right back up. His kisses and flirting had been flattering, that she could not deny, and for a while she thought she might even enjoy a tryst—many widowed women did—and add some excitement to her life. But she knew herself, and she was not one to give her heart lightly. She did not think she could be a woman who gave herself to a man for a handful of nights and then watched him leave without it breaking her heart. Undoubtedly, an affair of months, or even weeks, would crush her when it ended.

Yet, the more she was out in the world again, the more horrible it seemed to return to her quiet, mundane life. She'd thought about it during the day as they rode, and she'd realized the thought of returning to days spent cleaning rooms and living alone in her widow's cottage brought her a feeling of suffocation. True, Anora gave her some respite from the boredom, but she couldn't expect her friend to take on the burden of being her sole companion and diversion from the tediousness of her days for the rest of her life.

With a hunk of bread, she scooped up some of the watery stew when Red pushed a trencher in her direction and ate it quickly. But the mulled wine seemed more fortifying, so she took a large swallow of it and used the opportunity to peer at Red over the rim of her cup. She sighed. He was seated next to her now, his body turned toward hers, one muscular thigh angled behind her as the knee of his other leg pressed against hers, surrounding her. It was becoming a familiar protective posture.

If she was truthful with herself, Red scared her. He had given her his strength on so many occasions in the days she had known him, she was becoming reliant on him. Just like the fear that filled her when she thought about resuming her former widow's life, a hollow feeling started in the pit of her stomach when she thought about what her future life would be like when this mission was over, and he had no reason to spend his days with her. She was fooling herself if she thought she could go back to the life she had before, letting the darkness envelop her again and dull the world around her. It was not possible after feeling the blood pulse through her veins as it had for the last several days, giving her life.

She had just lifted her tankard to her mouth for another warming swig when she felt Red stiffen at her side. The other men were suddenly alert as well, though they didn't break off their conversations. Looking around the room to see what had gained their attention, she saw a pair of men standing against the wall, periodically glancing in their direction. There were other people leaning against walls, drinking, laughing, and looking around the room, but there was something different about these men. They seemed to be studying the room, and, more specifically, studying *them*.

"Turn toward me," Red ordered in a low voice as he took a sip of his ale.

She did as he said, the hairs on the back of her neck standing up as a prickle of fear gripped her. Had The Executioner found them? "Who are they?" she whispered, looking up at Red.

His face was hard, as he stared directly at the two men. He put a hand on her back and leaned his body in toward hers, making it very clear that anyone who wanted to get near her would have to go through him first. Without thinking, she set a hand on his muscular thigh as a gesture of her trust in him, and to show she was not afraid. She hadn't realized what she'd done until his gaze suddenly turned to hers, fiery and hot.

"Who are they?" she asked again, lifting her hand from his leg, feeling flustered by her involuntary action. And his heated response.

He put his hand over hers before she could pull it away, wrapping his fingers around hers. "Dead men," he replied, keeping his gaze locked with hers, "if they even think of touching you."

The beat of her heart increased, and her breath hitched in her throat.

"Don't be afraid," he said, his eyes still trained on her, though she knew he was instinctively aware of every move the men made.

"I'm not afraid," she said, and she meant it. Her racing heart had everything to do with Red and nothing to do with the men watching. She had no doubt that Red would protect her from them.

He winked at her. "That's my kitten. You may be small, but you are fierce."

Fierce.

It was a good thing to be, she decided. In the days to come, maybe for all the days of her life, whenever she felt unsure, she would remember the way Red looked at her when he called her "fierce".

"Do you think Toad sent them?" she asked, tipping her head to the side, and grinning up at Red.

He grinned back and rolled his eyes at her. "It's a ridiculous name."

"Aye," she responded with a ripple of laughter. "It's difficult to be afraid of a Toad."

Chapter Sixteen

R ED WANTED TO kiss her nose when it crinkled as she called
The Executioner "Toad" and smirked up at him. But then
her face changed, taking on a serious cast, and he was mesmerized again. The woman couldn't hide anything. Everything she
thought and felt showed on her face, in the brightness of her eyes,
the curve of her lips, the set of her head. He'd always thought it a
flaw to reveal so much, but in her, he found it endearing.

Especially since he noticed she was not as expressive with
other people as she was when looking at him. That was a part of
her she shared with him, and he liked that.

"I don't recognize either of them," she said, her tone thoughtful. "I didn't get a good look at Toad, but I don't think either of
them are him."

He'd been distracted by Galiena, but he had been watching
the men covertly. Neither of them was Toad. These men were
meatier than the loathsome man, and not as tall. But they were
obviously looking for someone and seemed to think they had
found the person, or people, that fit the description. Perhaps they
had been hired and sent to look for them.

He didn't think he'd ever met these men or seen them before,
but it wouldn't take much for someone to find Red based on a
description. Or Galiena. He knew how conspicuous he was with

his height and red hair. And Galiena was not a woman to forget with her raven-black hair and distinctive gray eyes—though he doubted Toad had gotten close enough to her to know about them.

Red liked to think her eyes were for him only, the way they glistened when she was feeling feisty or darkened when she was angry. But he liked them best when they were silver, like the still waters of a fjord with the moon shining down into the depths—which is how they looked in this moment. He believed her when she said she was not afraid because they were calm and steady.

"Aye, I think The Ex—" He stopped, correcting himself. Toad was an idiotic name, but he had to admit it felt better to call him something associated with being small and warty. "I think Toad sent them, the way they keep stealing glances over here at you and me."

Ox, Dane, Bard, and Wolf still appeared to be casually drinking and talking but he knew they were on alert, waiting for a signal from him before they acted. Red contemplated the options, trying to keep a level head and not let his instincts take over. He wanted to march across the room, take both men by their throats, and smash their heads together. But that wouldn't get them to the man they wanted, the man they had to find before he found them.

"Ox, Dane," Red said as the two strangers pushed away from the wall to set their tankards on the bar before they headed toward the door, "Come with me. Bard and Wolf, stay here with Galiena."

Before Galiena could protest, he dropped a quick kiss on her lips, smiling at her worried expression as he stood. "Nothing to fear, kitten. I'll be back."

He followed Ox and Dane out the door into the street and quickly spotted the men a short distance down the lane. The rain had ceased, but there was still a howling wind. When the men saw Red and his men emerge from the tavern, their paces quickened, and then they started running. Red and his men were on them before they could reach the end of the lane.

"Dane, look for anyone watching out for them," Red commanded as he and Ox dragged the struggling men into a dark alley. They had both of them pinned up against the wall and gasping for breath before they could yell out for help.

"Where is he?" He bit out in a menacing voice to the man he had clutched by the neck. The man stopped struggling, a pained smile curving his lips.

"I'm not telling you anything," the man gasped as the veins in his throat bulged. "You think you can do anything worse to us than he will?"

"I can kill you," Red growled.

The man panted out a laugh. "Go ahead."

Red felt a moment of uncertainty. Ox was getting the same responses from his captive. Were these men truly more scared of what The Executioner would do to them than being killed in this alley?

"Is he here?" Ox's voice was even more menacing than Red's. The man was truly built like an Ox, broad and thick with a permanently intimidating grimace on his face. Red cringed when he saw Ox grab the man's fisted hand in his own meaty paw and squeeze, but he didn't disapprove. The man screamed when the first bone snapped but he still refused to speak.

Red punched his man in the gut, causing him to cough and sputter. "Kill me," he rasped.

"You're going to die anyway," Red said. "Tell me where he is."

The man tried to spit at Red, earning him a clap of his head against the stone wall of the building. He grunted as his eyes rolled back, but then he just laughed pathetically.

"Last chance," Red warned. "Tell me where he is now, and I'll spare you."

The other man was still howling in pain as Ox continued to crush his fingers in his hand, breaking them one by one. When both men still refused to say anything more, they knocked their heads against the wall and let their bodies slump to the ground. Picking up the miscreants, Red and Ox each threw a man over their shoulders and hauled them into the forest behind the village. Dane stayed a discrete distance behind them to ensure no one followed.

They walked for some distance, picking their way through the pitch black under the canopy of branches until they were a good distance from the village, then they dropped the men on the wet earth. Red felt for a pulse on the neck of the man he'd carried and found it to be very weak beneath his fingertips.

"If the elements don't get them, then the wolves and boars will," Red stated as they turned to retrace their steps out of the forest. As dark as it was, they had to rely on Dane's whistles to keep their bearings until they emerged again.

"Anything?" Red asked as they headed back to the tavern.

Dane shook his head. "A few drunks stumbling out, but no one that fit the description you gave us, scant as it was."

Red grunted his acknowledgment as he and Ox stopped at a trough of water to rinse the blood from their hands.

"Do you think he's here?" Ox asked.

Red shrugged. "My gut says he is."

"What do you want to do now?" Dane asked.

"We'll get what sleep we can. He doesn't like an audience for his deeds, so we'll be safe as long as we stay in the crowded inn. But I don't want him ahead of us on the road, waiting to ambush us. Be ready to leave before the sun rises." Red sighed in frustration, scrubbing his hand through his hair. "*Long* before the sun rises. If he's here and en route to the king, there is no other way to Llanbadarn than this road. I want to be well ahead of him."

"Now it's a matter of who gets there first," Dane said.

"And possibly who gets there alive," Red added, opening the door to the inn.

As he entered the tavern, his eyes were immediately drawn to the corner where Galiena still sat with Wolf and Bard. He felt the smile that came unbidden to his lips when he saw her sitting attentively, her face turned to the door as though she had been waiting and watching for him. When she looked at him, her shoulders visibly relaxed as she let out a long breath, and he swore he could feel the warmth of it wrapping around him. If the gods were on his side, he'd find The Executioner and kill him before he came anywhere near this woman.

"You have blood on your arm, Viking," she said to him as he sat facing her again. She looked neither angry nor appalled as she said the words, searching his upper body for any other sign of a fight. "As you do not appear injured, I gather it is not yours."

He couldn't resist stroking her cheek with the back of his fingers, enjoying the rosy hue of her skin and the almost imperceptible way she leaned toward his touch. "No, kitten, it is not mine."

"Good," she said with a small smile. It was not the response he'd expected, but it pleased him. "We will be leaving while the night is still dark." He dropped his hand from her face, only to find the end of her plaited hair where it hung over her shoulder. Winding the silky braid around his fingers, he marveled, not for the first time, at how small she was yet that she had more strength than she was aware. She knew those men had been sent to find them and kill them, or bring them to The Executioner, yet she was unruffled. And while she'd been petrified when they encountered the wooden bridges spanning the river, she'd pushed herself to cross them—even if it took her arguing with him the entire span of the water and then some.

"What are you smiling at?" she asked him.

"You."

She quirked a questioning eyebrow at him, the slim arch of it dark against her ivory skin. Tendrils of her hair had pulled loose from the braid and framed the roundness of her cheeks. "Are you always so jovial after a thrashing?"

He laughed then. "I hadn't thought about it, but aye, I enjoy a good thrashing as long as I'm not the one receiving it."

Her face turned more serious. "I assume it was not Toad or you would have said."

He shook his head. "No, it was not."

"Is he here?"

"I believe so," Red said without hesitation. She was clever enough to know the reality of the danger she faced, and he would not lie to her.

"Can we go to the room now?" she asked. He couldn't stop himself from gaping at her, and she laughed at his response to her request. "And bring a candle."

Red pushed to his feet, nearly toppling the table. "We are to bed, lads."

Chapter Seventeen

GALIENA ROSE TO her feet and put a steadying hand on Red's chest. "I merely wish to study the missive in private."

The way Red's handsome face fell with disappointment was comical, but she had to admit, warmth bloomed in her chest at the eagerness he showed when he thought she was suggesting something far more intimate than decoding secret messages.

"Ox, Dane," Red commanded, "sleep here but stay vigilant." When the men nodded, he continued. "Bard, Wolf, I'd like you to post yourselves in the corridor outside the room."

Galiena felt the heat of embarrassment creeping up her neck. She and Red would be entering the chamber together and everyone would assume that they were being...intimate. Granted, he had told the innkeeper they were husband and wife, but the soldiers from Hawkspur knew well that he was not married. What did they think of her?

"It's not what you think," she tried to explain to the soldiers, her mortification growing not only at what they must have been assuming about them but also at her shameless flirting with Red. "He's just trying to protect me. Nothing inappropriate is happening. In fact, we shall leave the door ajar."

"Of course, he wants to protect you, my lady," Wolf said. "Nothing to explain."

Bard nodded and said with a wink, "We heard that you proclaimed each other husband and wife; there is nothing inappropriate."

Galiena opened her mouth to protest, but Red already had his arm around her shoulders and was leading her toward the stairs before she could say anything more.

"Your bags, Red," Ox said, throwing a pair of saddlebags in his direction, which Red neatly caught in one hand.

"Last room at the end of the corridor," the innkeeper said as she strode past them with a handful of tankards, not losing a drop of ale as she maneuvered between the patrons.

The room was sparse, with a bed, a side table with a taper, and a few hooks on the wall. Red hung the bags on the hooks and took the taper to the sconce in the corridor to light. There was a small amount of heat coming up through a vent in the floor, but there was still a damp chill in the room.

Red overwhelmed the tiny space when he closed the door. His head nearly touched the ceiling, and if he stretched his arms out to each side, he'd touch both walls. She had to squeeze herself into a corner to let Red by with the candle to place it back on the table at the head of the bed. When he turned his attention back to her, she felt awkward and shy.

Realizing she looked much like a mouse cowering in a corner, she pushed herself away from the wall and reached inside the neckline of her chemise and into her sleeve to extract the rolled bit of parchment. Better to focus on the coded message than the very large, very brawny, very appealing presence of the Viking. Eventually, they were going to end up in that bed together, and if she thought too much about what might happen there, her nerves started to twitch. In truth, she wasn't sure if it was fear of what might happen or excited anticipation.

"I wish I had thought of making a copy of this before we left Oswestry," Galiena mused. "I do not expect the king will be willing to let us view it again after we hand it over to him." She started toward the table but then stopped, unable to get by Red in the cramped space.

He turned to face her, then stepped close until she had her head tipped all the way back to look up at him. She felt his hands settle onto her hips as he stared down at her with that lopsided smirk that made her stomach flip-flop. He slowly pressed his chest into her as he guided her backward with his hands.

"Don't do that," he whispered to her as his eyes darkened from ice-blue to the blue of the sky on a perfect summer day.

"Don't do what?" she asked, her voice more breathy than intended.

"Lick your lips like that." The words were said in a low voice that she felt rumble in his chest where it touched her. "Unless you're willing to give me a taste."

Her knees wobbled and she caught her bottom lip between her teeth to stop herself from licking it again. This earned her a growl as he backed her up against the wall. When he had her there, he caged her in by sliding his hands up the wall at her sides. Her hands went involuntarily to his biceps and her breathing increased to a rapid tempo. Every part of her body wanted to melt into his and her head felt like it was spinning with the sweet torture of waiting for him to touch her. All of her convictions that she was not a woman meant to have a tryst flew right out of her head, and all she could think about was how much she wanted Red to kiss her.

When his head dropped toward hers, she released her lip from between her teeth and lifted her face to meet him halfway. She expected a soft kiss, a tender pressing of their lips together, a taste of sweetness but a soft moan escaped her at the unexpected sensation of his tongue tracing her lips in an agonizingly slow circle, her body feeling boneless as heat swirled through her core. She gasped as his teeth pulled her lower lip into his mouth, giving it a playful tug before letting go.

"One taste will never be enough," he said, his gaze trained on her lips as he spoke. "I want to taste all of you."

Lord help her, she wanted him to taste all of her, too. Her

skin felt like it was on fire and only Red's hands and mouth touching every part of her would soothe her. She was about to tell him exactly that when he pushed away from the wall with a growl and grabbed the saddle bag hanging from the hook to the side of her head.

"Later," he growled. He reached into the leather bag and extracted something small. Holding it out to her, he said, "Your copy."

It took her a moment to clear her head and focus on what he was saying, but then she snatched the new parchment from his hand and scooted out from between him and the wall to sit on the bed so she could spread both parchments on the table beneath the light of the candle.

"Where did you get this?"

The bed sagged, nearly toppling her into him, as he sat next to her. "I made two copies while we were at the goldsmith's. I left one with Hunter and Frode and took the other."

"*You* did this?" It was an impressive copy, the symbols and lettering identical in size, placement, and character. Even the tiny symbol on the back was duplicated to perfection. "You could be a forger!"

He laughed then. "I'll keep that in mind should soldiering and training horses prove not so lucrative."

She liked it when he laughed. His entire face lit up, his beard twitched, and the corners of his eyes crinkled. When he grinned, it was endearingly crooked with the left corner of his lips curving up farther than the right. And when he smiled, the lopsidedness was still there, though less apparent, and his lips spread wide showing strong, straight teeth. There was a lightness that radiated from him, and it calmed her. She'd felt unsettled and apprehensive since the deaths of her daughter and husband, always on edge and not fully present in her own life but since Red had happened into her life, his nearly constant optimism, and his ability to make everything less serious, had brought a light into that darkness, and now it was perhaps what she admired the most about him.

"Unless you want me to kiss you again, you need to quit looking at me like that."

Galiena pressed her lips together to suppress the smile she realized was spread across her face and quickly turned to the missives on the table. They were flipped to the backside where the small design was inscribed in the lower corner.

"I've not seen this symbol before," she murmured as she tried to make sense of it. "It looks like three, triangle shapes inter-twined." She squinted as she tried to peer closer. "Are they three intertwined snakes?"

"Aye," Red said, his voice cold as ice. Galiena looked at him, surprised by his sudden change of mood. "It is a knot of Odin."

She tilted her head in question as she looked up at him, sensing there was more to the explanation.

All the light was gone from his face, and there was nothing jovial about him now. "It is the symbol for fallen warriors. The knot is a common Norse design."

"I've seen the snake used in many of the places I traveled with my father. In some places, it is a sign of life or healing, but in many, it is a sign of immortality. Or death." She looked down at the tiny drawing, remembering the many trinkets, plates, and pieces of jewelry made with the likeness of the snake, often with the tail wrapping back around to be swallowed by the same snake. "My father explained that it represented the cycle of life: birth, growth, healing, and eventually death."

"The snake is not a typical representation in the knot. It is an embellishment I've seen only once before."

His tone made the hairs on the back of Galiena's neck stand up as cold fingers of dread clutched at her throat. "Where did you see it?" she asked in a cautious whisper.

Red slid his hand into his boot and pulled out an intricate dagger. The blade was longer than his hand from fingertip to wrist, and the handle was thick and built for a man. A closer inspection of the silver hilt revealed an ornately crafted wolf crouched low on its haunches with the blade protruding from its wide-open jaws; it had red gems for eyes and an etched chain was wrapped around its body.

She leaned in closer to look at the design adorning the blade. Carved into the metal were various symbols, including the intertwined triangles of snakes. "Where did you get this?"

"My uncle made it. He made two of them and it was the only time I've seen snakes used to make the knot of fallen warriors." Red set the knife carefully on the table next to the pieces of parchment. In a quiet voice, he confessed, "I've never seen it anywhere else."

Galiena had been studying the knife, but she turned her attention back to Red. His ice-blue stare was intently focused on her, as though waiting for her reaction. Was the composer of the coded message Red's relative? "Where is your uncle now?"

"Dead."

Then not his relative. "So then…where is the other knife now?"

"The man who killed him took it twenty years ago." She saw the muscles in his jaw clench and instinctively reached her hand up to lay it along the side of his face.

"I'm so sorry, Red." He startled when she first touched him, but then she saw his face relax and some of the anger abate.

"He was my mother's brother, and I was named for him."

"Viggo?" she asked, letting her hand drop to his chest. She saw him nod from the corner of her eyes, but she was looking at his hand covering hers, pressing it to him. She could feel his heartbeat under her palm, steady and strong. Like the rest of him.

"He was a blacksmith and the closest thing I had to a father while growing up. But he got hit in the head with a beam while helping build a barn and was never the same after that. He made the daggers before the accident happened." He wasn't looking at her anymore but at the dagger. "He wasn't able to work as a blacksmith again. I did what I could to feed us and to help my mother, but we were barely surviving." He took a deep breath and looked at Galiena again, his face somber in a way she'd never seen before. "That's when my mother sent a letter to a cousin in England, asking if he would take us in and in return, we would work for him. He had a small estate, but it was far more than we had in Norway. He agreed and we took a ship to England. We encountered The Executioner the day after we landed."

"The Executioner killed your uncle?"

"And my mother."

Tears filled her eyes before she could blink them away. "Oh, Red. You were still a boy. I am so sorry." One of them spilled down her cheek.

He wiped it away with his thumb. "There's no reason to cry. It's done and over."

"But it's not," she said, her voice hitching. "He took so much from you."

"I won't let him take anything more from me." His voice had gentled, and his gaze had softened as he looked at her. "I vowed then that I would find him and kill him, even if it took the entirety of my days in this world."

The mild tone of his voice was in direct contrast to his words, and it sent a chill down her spine. She reached for the knife to look closely at the detail of the design on the blade. Then she exchanged it for the original missive and studied the tiny symbol on the back. They were nearly identical.

"So, Toad *is* the composer of the missive. At least, it would seem that way. Between the appearance of the man in the ally and the similarities between the…what you called the Odin's knot." In spite of these pieces of evidence, something about it still didn't make sense to her. "But who is he? What is his reason for doing this?"

"If my *hamingja* is kind, that's what the coded message will tell us," Red said, tapping his finger against the missive.

"*Hamingja?*" In all her travels, she'd never heard this word.

He laughed and explained, "Guardian spirits. Believers of the old Norse ways say that each of us has a *hamingja* who looks over us and determines how much luck and happiness we can have in our lifetime."

"Ah! Like a guardian angel," she said.

"Aye," he agreed with a nod.

"You believe in your *hamingja?*" she asked.

He shrugged. "Not really, but when it suits my purposes, I call upon her."

She nodded, thinking about what he said. She wasn't sure anymore what she believed about divine beings because she had lost faith in her guardian angel the day Adam and Nahara were mercilessly taken from her.

Turning back to the missive, she said with a weary sigh, "I thought I had made progress last night, but it didn't translate to the other lines." She pointed at the last line of the missive. "If the last line is a date—which it seems it is, based on the pattern of two symbols, then a series of eight letters, followed by four symbols—then this word can be narrowed down to the months with eight letters: February, November, or December."

Red leaned closer to see the parchment and nodded. "That's a logical start."

"If the other symbols among the letters are vowels," she continued, "the placement of them aligns with either November or December and since only one vowel symbol is used three times, December aligns with the pattern. If the last four numbers indicate the year, 1284, then the day would be twenty-eight: *28 December 1284.*"

"That's a good start," Red said excitedly.

"But here's where it falls apart. If I use this as the key to translate the letters on the rest of the message, it doesn't seem to work." She pointed to a set of letters on another line. "Look here. If I use the same letter translations on this line, it just produces nonsense. Nothing is even remotely recognizable."

Red groaned. "It's a different code than for the lines above the date. Maybe even a different code for each line."

Galiena dropped her head into her hands. "How will we ever

figure this out?" She cringed at the childish disappointment in her tone, but she felt completely defeated.

"Being able to write as you work would make this easier," Red said as he rubbed a soothing hand down her back. "When we get to Llanbadarn, I'll acquire the parchment, quills, and ink needed to keep record of your progress."

"Perhaps the king will have someone to decipher it," she said hopefully.

"Perhaps." Red rolled up the original message and handed it back to Galiena, then took off his boots and stood. He put the dagger and the copy of the missive into one of the boots and moved to set them by the wall.

When he turned back around, Galiena didn't know what to do next. She felt like she was on display and exposed, like the fabled Godiva riding her horse naked through a village. Feeling too conspicuous sitting on the bed, she pushed to her feet to stand next to the table. They both stood absolutely still looking at each other, the bed looming between them.

"Red—"

"Galiena—" he said at the same time.

She laughed and he sighed, scrubbing his hand through his hair, which hung in thick, fiery red waves down to his shoulders. "You should sleep, Galiena," he said, nodding toward the bed as he folded his cloak and dropped it in front of the door as though to use it as a pillow. "We'll be leaving in a few short hours."

Disappointed, she kicked off her boots and climbed under the blankets fully clothed as he settled onto the floor in front of the door. They had another long, difficult day ahead and she knew he was right; they should get as much sleep as possible. When she didn't hear him shuffling anymore, she blew out the candle.

Suddenly, the loneliness of the last three years overwhelmed her, a hollow feeling settling in the pit of her belly. "I don't want to sleep alone, Red." The words were barely audible, and she couldn't be sure he'd even heard her. She held her breath, listening for a response. Finally, his voice drifted through the darkness.

"Because you don't want to be alone? Or, because you want to be with me?"

She hadn't expected the vulnerable question, and she didn't want to hurt him, but in truth, she couldn't be sure which was the reason. She was lonely, but did that mean she would invite anyone who gave her any measure of attention to share the bed with her? Before she could answer, Red interjected.

"Don't answer that. It wasn't a fair question." From the sound of his voice, she could tell he had risen to his feet and was standing at the end of the bed.

The foot of the bed sagged under his weight, and in the darkness, she could barely see his form moving over her, warmth flooding her as he covered her with his body. They were both still clothed, and the blanket was between them, but tears unexpectedly welled in her eyes as the sensation of being safe and cared for enveloped her. She wished she hadn't extinguished the candle, wanting to see his face as he tugged the blanket down to free her arms. He leaned slightly to one side as he gently brushed his fingers down her arm until he found her hand, twined his fingers with hers, and slid their joined hands over her head. Then he did the same with her other hand, resting on his elbows with their hands clasped together above her.

She felt the softest brush of his mouth against hers, then the wet heat of his tongue licking at her lips, and she let out a soft moan of satisfaction. Or maybe it was a whimper. He chuckled then and deepened the kiss as all of the tension released from her body. She wriggled, trying to get closer to him and hating the layers of material separating them.

He lifted his mouth from hers and she tried to follow him but dropped her head back onto the mattress as his lips pressed to her jaw, then down her throat, eliciting gasps of pleasure from her. He kissed her slowly, deliberately, as though worshipping her as he nibbled and tasted her skin. His mouth burned a trail back up her throat to her ear, and he sucked its lobe into his mouth. She flexed her hands against his, wanting to touch him and rub her hands over his shoulders and down his back, but he wouldn't release her.

"I'm going to hold you while you sleep," he whispered as he tugged at her ear with his teeth, then rolled to her side.

"I want you to make love to me, Red." The words were out before she realized what she was saying, but she didn't want to take it back.

He brought his mouth back to hers, and between kisses, said, "You have no idea, love, how much I want to feel your skin against mine and to bury myself in you until we are both too exhausted to move." He pulled her bottom lip into his mouth, suckling it in a way that made her body feel strung tightly as a bow. She was panting when he released her lip. "But not tonight."

She whimpered in protest. Mortified by the rejection and her reaction, she turned her head away from him.

"No, kitten," he coaxed, "don't withdraw from me. And don't think I don't want you because I do." He nuzzled her neck. "God, I want you so much it hurts." He nudged her face back toward his and pressed his forehead to hers. "When I make love to you, I want to take my time. I want to savor you, linger on every part of you, and I don't want to stop until you are screaming my name."

She let out a sigh that was a mixture of satisfaction, frustration, and anticipation. At that, he tucked the blanket around her and pulled her close to his chest as he wrapped her in his arms. With two of them in the tiny bed, there wasn't much room to move. As the innkeeper's wife had predicted, Red's feet were probably hanging off the end of the bed, and she could feel the wall behind her.

"Sleep, my feisty kitten," he whispered, kissing her on the forehead.

She pressed her cheek against his neck and closed her eyes, feeling guilty as she prayed for a dreamless sleep, not wanting to be visited with images of the husband who was no longer of this world because of her.

Chapter Eighteen

THE RIDE TO Llanbadarn Gaerog was long, cold, and grueling. The wind, rain, and endless hours in the saddle were exhausting, but Galiena felt a twinge of pride when she was able to stand on her own accord after dismounting just outside the gates of the walled city. Her legs were shaking, and her fingers were stiff from clutching the reins, and often the mane of the horse, to stay astride. They'd galloped and trotted much of the distance, but she was determined not to be the reason they did not make it to the king and queen by nightfall. Or the reason The Executioner caught up to them—*if* he was behind them.

She wasn't expecting it when Red wrapped his arms around her waist and lifted her off the ground in a quick hug. She looked up at him as he set her down, the broad smile of approval on his face warming her chilled bones. "Three days on a horse and you've mastered it. You can ride with my company of soldiers any time."

She couldn't stop the wide grin that spread across her face or the way her heart swelled from his praise. She was also a bit embarrassed by his accolades and tried to deflect the attention. "It is because of your patience and tolerance that I am here."

"We still have obstacles ahead," Red said, taking Metal's reins. They had stopped on the edge of town where the lane was crowded with villagers, merchants, and soldiers in matching tabards adorned with the king's herald of three golden lions on a background of red. The sun was nearly set, and torches were being lit at the tavern doors. "We will have to wait with the throngs of others wanting an audience with the king, even with Hawk's letter."

"What happens if he won't see us?" It had never occurred to her that they would travel all this way and be refused an opportunity to speak with the king and queen.

"I won't let that happen," Red said with determination, then turned to his soldiers behind him. "Bard, come with us to see the king. Ox, Wolf, and Dane, see if you can find lodging and a place for the horses." The men nodded and horses were handed off. "Stay diligent. He may be here already," he added in a warning voice.

Taking Galiena's hand, Red led her through the gates to the city and into the throngs of people, Bard following closely behind. The castle was visible on the hill at the end of the wide lane that cut through the city straight to the gates of the massive fortress. The structure was daunting, with more fortified walls, a moat, and two massive towers flanking a heavy gate. As they drew closer, she could see the sharp points of a steel portcullis pulled high over the gate opening, which was lined with guards.

"State your business," one of the guards grumbled as they approached.

Red presented the letter from Hawk. "We seek an audience with the king on behalf of Sir Grogan, Lord of Hawkspur."

"No swords on either of you?" the guard asked.

"No swords," Red confirmed. He and Bard had left their swords with the other men, but Galiena suspected that Red still carried the knife in his boot and that Bard was likely equally armed.

The guards looked Red and Bard up and down, then commanded, "Open your cloaks."

Both men did as requested but Galiena stood still, uncertain if she should open her cloak to prove she was not armed. Perhaps they did not think a woman capable of carrying a sword.

"What about her?" another guard asked, tipping his chin in her direction. "How do we know she isn't carrying anything?"

Galiena felt Red tense at her side and saw he was about to speak, but before he could say anything they might all regret, she stepped forward and held up the sides of her cloak. "I am unarmed. No need for concern." As the guard stepped aside to allow them to pass, Galiena could hear a low rumble emitting from Red, as though he were growling at the man.

"Thank you, kind sirs," Bard said in a loud, jovial voice. She was sure he did it to mask his friend's displeasure lest the guards change their minds about letting them pass. When they were through the gates and making their way into the castle yard, Bard said, "You're not helping your reputation as a *berserker*, Viking. A little more tact would go a long way in convincing people you are not a barbarian."

Red bared his teeth and growled at his friend in response, but Galiena could see the crinkles around his eyes that showed he was not as miffed as he sounded. She smiled at him then, amused by the spectacle of him with his fur cloak over broad shoulders, towering height, flaming red mane, and boisterous voice. He was a frightening warrior to behold, yet all she could see was the protective, kind man who treated her with the same care as a fragile treasure.

"What are you smirking at?" he asked, turning his playful scowl in her direction.

"You," she said. "If I didn't know you, I would think you terrifying."

Red stopped walking to grab her hand and pull her back to him, spinning her so that she faced him. "But you're not afraid of me." It sounded more like a question than a statement.

Galiena looked up at him, surprised to see the question in his expression. He was a formidable force, but it softened her heart to know he had insecurities that required coddling. "No, Red," she said in a soothing tone. "I am not afraid of you."

He smiled at her then with that wickedly handsome, lopsided grin that made her insides swirl.

"Shall I sing a ballad while the two of you swoon over each other?" Bard asked in a sweet voice that did nothing to hide his sarcasm. "Or should we get on with our business? Personally, I'd like to get this over with and go find a hot meal, a strong ale, and a willing woman."

"Bard!" Galiena said with feigned shocked at his bawdy talk. "Do you not have a sweetheart waiting for you at home?"

He gave an overly dramatic and sad shake of his head. "No, dear lady, I do not. But I am holding out hope I will be as lucky as Red and one day a beauty such as you will run into my arms to claim my heart."

Galiena opened her mouth to respond but could not think of what to say. Had she really stolen Red's heart? It hadn't been her intention when she chose him to aid in her escape, but she couldn't deny that she had forced herself into his arms before she even knew who he was, or the kind of man he might be. Now that she did know Red, part of her hoped she *had* stolen his heart. But the other part of her was afraid of what it would mean to love a man who spent his life wielding a sword, constantly facing death. To love a warrior meant accepting that he may not come home from one of his battles—many did not, and many women were widowed because of it. She'd already been widowed and knew the pain of it too well. Was she willing to endure it again? It would be easier, and safer for her heart, to avoid it altogether.

"Let's go," Red grumbled, pulling her out of her thoughts and back into his side. He led her toward a large stone building with a multitude of people milling around the outside, presumably waiting for an audience with the king and queen.

Galiena was disheartened, fearing they may not be able to get the opportunity to appear in front of the king before the evening was over. Red pushed through the crowd until he found the king's clerk to give him the letter from Hawk. The clerk took the missive, then directed them to stand with the rest of the petitioners in the castle yard.

And then they waited.

And waited.

As the evening grew colder and their stomachs began to growl, Red pulled a few coins from his pouch to give to Bard to fetch food and drink for them, which they ate standing up. The crowd was beginning to disperse, some leaving after having their time in front of the king, others for more interesting pursuits as the sound of musicians performing and the voices of revelers drifted over the castle walls.

After waiting for what felt like hours, the clerk finally summoned Red and Galiena. They were the last to be granted an audience for the evening and the hall was nearly empty except for the king, queen, a handful of guards and clerks, and three men dressed in the fine garb of nobility. The king and queen sat on a raised dais with the noblemen seated to the side of the king.

"Your Graces." Red bowed to the king, the queen, and then the other men of rank sitting in attendance. "Lord Mortimer, Lord Tibetot, My Lord." Galiena followed his lead and curtsied while bowing her head to each man in turn.

"I am Lord Burbek," the third man said with an arrogant sneer. "You are?"

"Viggo Algarssen," Red said stiffly, "of Hawkspur. Sir Grogan is my liege."

Galiena could hear the irritation in Red's voice, but the arrogant lord only nodded and said nothing more.

"Your Grace," Red said, turning his attention back to the king and queen. "May I present Galiena of Oswestry."

Galiena felt like she was going to be sick again. She was trying not to let the sight of the king and queen intimidate her, but she had no experience being in the presence of nobility. She'd never met a lord or lady before Red brought her to Hawkspur Castle, and now she was standing in front of King Edward and Queen Eleanor of England!

Up close, the king was an imposing figure, with his tall stature and regal posture. Even seated, he towered above his wife as he peered down his long, thin nose at the parchment in his hand. Holding it up, he said, "Sir Grogan insisted that we grant you audience posthaste and in private."

Galiena felt her skin prickle as the king lifted his hooded gaze from Sir Grogan's letter to look at her and Red. She found herself staring at the king's eyes, the blue of them startling and the drooping of his left eyelid unsettling. It did not seem possible that a man with King Edward's reputation could have a physical flaw, and Galiena tried not to fixate on it. Instead, she lowered her gaze and tried to peer sidelong at the queen who was regal, serene, and appeared pleasant—just as she remembered from when she'd observed her in the churchyard at Oswestry more than a twelvemonth prior.

"There are few men I give as much credence to as the Lord of Hawkspur," the king continued. "I will assume you have good reason to insist upon seeing us so urgently."

"Aye, I fear we bring worrisome information, perhaps better shared—as my lord Sir Grogan wrote—in private," Red responded, and Galiena lifted her gaze to see the king's response.

"Tell me the nature of this...*information*...and I will decide." The king's tone sounded bored, but the expression in his eyes showed his sudden alertness.

Red met his gaze with squared shoulders and without showing any intimidation. She felt a flush of pride that a man with his stature and courage was protective of her even in the presence of the king. "We suspect there is a threat to your family."

"Why do you say this?" the king demanded.

"A conversation was overheard, and a missive was intercepted."

"You have this missive?"

Red nodded, but Galiena could sense his unease.

"Lord Mortimer, Lord Tibetot, Lord Burbek," the king said to the noblemen, his attention still focused on Red. "You are dismissed."

The three lords pushed to their feet and stepped down from the dais. All three of the men looked at them with curiosity as they walked by but as Lord Burbek passed by, his gaze lingered, causing the hairs on the back of her neck to stand at attention. She guessed him to be a man in his forties; he had sandy blond hair, dark eyes, and an arrogant air. She had been in the presence of many wealthy merchants when she was young, but never had she been in the presence of lords—or a king and queen—and she was finding it very unnerving.

After the men had left, leaving only a clerk and some guards lingering in the back of the hall and at the main doors, the king commanded, "Tell me what was heard. And who overheard it."

"Galiena overheard the conversation and was able to obtain the missive."

The king turned his attention to her after Red's statement, and Galiena almost took a step backward, wanting to shrink from his scrutiny. Instead, she dug her fingernails into her palms and steadied herself, not wanting to disappoint or disgrace Red.

"Is that so?" King Edward asked. Galiena thought she detected a slight lisp as the king spoke; the reminder that he was still a man even if anointed by God, calmed her nerves.

"Yes, Your G-grace." Her cheeks flamed in embarrassment at her nervous stutter and the shaking of her voice. But then she felt Red's hand close over hers as he shifted closer to her, and some of her confidence was restored.

That is, until the king dropped his gaze to their joined hands and then pointedly looked into Red's face. He arched one eyebrow but did not say anything more about Red's possessive gesture. When he returned his attention to Galiena, he waved her forward with a large, slender hand. "You may come forward as well, Red, as it does not appear you are going to let her out of your grasp."

Galiena took a deep breath and forced her legs to move despite their shaking beneath her gown, which she now realized was covered with a filthy cloak caked with mud from the road. She felt the heat rising in her cheeks again, embarrassed that she was meeting the king and queen in this state. And just when she thought things couldn't get any worse, the queen spoke.

"Why do you blush, dear girl?" The queen's voice was gentle and not at all mocking.

Galiena looked closer at the queen, astonished to realize that the woman was old enough to be her mother even though she had a babe under one year of age. She was every bit as regal and beautiful as one would expect a queen to be, with chestnut hair, dark eyes, and rosy cheeks.

"I realized the state of my attire, Your Grace," Galiena admitted, not wanting to lie to the woman. "I meant no disrespect and apologize for the filthy state of my cloak, but we did feel it was urgent to come to you straightaway upon arriving."

"And why was that?" Queen Eleanor coaxed in a soothing voice. "What is it that you overheard?"

Galiena thought it much easier to speak to the queen than to King Edward, but what she had to say was not comfortable, and she feared they might think her story a fabrication. Taking a deep breath, she decided it best to just be out with it. "I overheard two men in Oswestry discussing a plot to kill your babe." As Galiena spoke the words, the remembered pain of losing a child overwhelmed her. Tears sprang to her eyes and clogged her throat. She hated to be the one to bring the queen the distressing news that her son's life was at risk, but she was grateful that she'd been given the opportunity, mother to mother, to save the child.

Apart from the smallest gasp, the queen kept her composure. The king leaned forward in his chair, narrowing his eyes at her.

"Who were these men?" King Edward demanded. "What did they say?"

Galiena looked to Red, who nodded almost imperceptibly at her and gave her hand a reassuring squeeze. Turning back to the king, she met his intense gaze squarely and told him exactly what she'd overheard and witnessed in the alley and about the missive she took from the hiding place in the wall after it had been stolen from the men by young Tommy Cutpurse.

"One of the men is dead already," Red added before she could explain about being chased from the alley and running into Red's arms in the lane. "The other, we believe is on his way here. If he isn't here already. We fear he may be working with someone within the castle."

"Who killed that first man?" the king asked.

"I believe the second man from the alley," Red said. "Probably once he realized the missive had been stolen." He said no more; he just inclined his head and said, "That's why we're here, sir, and that's why we insisted upon a private audience."

Galiena had expected Red to say more about The Executioner, and the men who followed them into the tavern the night before, but decided he must have good reason for omitting that information.

"Boris," the king said in a louder voice, directing his attention to one of the guards. When the man came to the king's side, Edward said, "Post more guards in the corridor of the nursery. And put two guards in the room with the nursemaid. I want extra guards for the prince at all times, and no one is to enter the nursery other than those approved by the queen until we know what this is about." Turning back to Red and Galiena, the king asked, "Where is the intercepted missive now?"

"I have it," Galiena admitted. "It's coded. As yet we haven't been able to translate what it says." She released Red's hand and then turned to the side as she reached her hand into the neckline of her chemise to reach the sleeve to extract it. She wished she would have thought about transferring it to her pouch for easier access before they had entered the hall. At last, she was able to work the rolled parchment out from its hiding place and present it to the king. She blushed again when she realized the king and queen had both just watched her wriggling like a fidgety child beneath her cloak to get the letter out of the secret pocket above her elbow.

The king unrolled the parchment and studied it for a long moment before handing it to the queen.

"Perhaps Ferrando can decipher this," Queen Eleanor said to the king, handing the parchment back to him. "He is clever as well as scholarly."

"That he is." The king motioned for one of his clerks, and murmured in a low voice, "Fetch the queen's cousin and let him know I request his attention." The clerk nodded and hurried from the hall.

"I trust you have known Galiena for some time and can vouch for her character?" the king asked Red, smoothing a hand over his beard as he studied them.

Galiena felt the blood drain from her face. She could count the number of days on one hand that she and Red had known each other. Would the king discount her story once he realized Red had met Galiena only days before?

"I can vouch for her," Red confirmed, his voice steady.

The king eyed them both intently for several breaths, then tilted his head and asked, "How did you get involved in this matter, Red?"

"I was in Oswestry when the incident happened. She came to me for protection." Galiena felt the tension in Red's grip as he tightened his hold on her hand. "She was fearful the men might have come looking for her or the boy who stole the missive. I escorted her to Hawkspur, then to here."

"And the boy who stole the missive?" the queen asked.

Turning to the queen, Red said, "Hunter is ensuring the safety of the boy."

The king nodded his satisfaction. Looking at Galiena, he asked, "Would you recognize the man you overheard in the alley?"

The king's eyes were an even lighter blue than Red's, but they were far colder when he focused his piercing gaze on her. She couldn't help but shiver in response. But Red's tightened grip on her hand warmed her and gave her the courage she needed to respond without hesitation. "I did not see anything more than the tip of his nose as his face was hidden by a hood, but I believe I would recognize his voice." She hoped that was true. The men had been speaking in harsh whispers and strained voices, which could sound very different than someone's normal speaking voice.

"You will stay in Llanbadarn." It was not a question from the king, but rather, a command.

"Aye," Red agreed. "I have four of Hawk's men with me, and we are at your disposal."

"Stay alert," the king said. "If you see anyone resembling this mysterious man from the alley, tell one of my guards immediately."

Red nodded. "Of course, sir."

"In the meantime, the queen's cousin is a scholarly man with...*useful* skills," the king said. "I will instruct him to work on deciphering this message. You are dismissed, but I want to see you back here tomorrow afternoon. I will have more questions by then."

Red nodded, then bowed again to the king and queen. Galiena curtseyed, then followed Red's lead of backing away from the dais until they reached the door to exit the hall.

Bard was waiting for them in the castle yard. "Well?" he asked when Red took Galiena's hand and started for the castle gate at a brisk pace.

"Later," Red said, his head turning from side to side as they crossed to the gate. "We can talk when we are away from here."

The hairs on the back of Galiena's neck stood up as Bard searched the castle walls, both men suddenly alert and tense.

"What is it?" Galiena asked Red in a hushed tone as she increased her speed to keep up with his long, determined strides.

"I've got a gnawing in my gut telling me something isn't right."

Chapter Nineteen

"Tell me you found a place with a roof and real beds," Red said to Ox as they exited the castle gate.

Ox was leaning against the railing of the moat bridge, and Red was hopeful the relaxed look on his face meant they had found accommodations for the night that didn't require sleeping under the stars—or more accurately, sleeping under the clouds on the cold, wet ground. As soldiers, they were used to sleeping in harsh conditions, but he did not want to subject Galiena to the misery. Or worse, risk her catching the ague.

"Aye, we did," he said, pushing away from the rail. "Follow me."

Red knew that most people were intimidated by him and usually gave way when they saw him coming, but for Ox people scurried out of the way, leaving a wide path. He was a mountain of a man—the largest Red had ever seen—who had survived more battles than most, and he had the scars to prove it. He kept his gray hair cropped short, putting every scar, lump, and disfigurement on clear display. His nose had been broken so many times that the bridge of it was nearly flat. Most people found him ugly and frightening, which made him a very useful comrade in difficult situations.

As intimidating as he could be in battle, or when making his way through a crowd, he was often reserved around the fairer sex, shy and self-conscious, avoiding them whenever possible. Most women did not bother to even look his way, and those who did were often repulsed and fearful. But Galiena had not shrunk away from him when introduced. She'd greeted him warmly and smiled up at him as she did everyone. She'd shown no sign of thinking his looks distasteful or his size daunting, despite the fact that she looked like a child standing next to him. Red had wanted to hug her when he saw Ox standing a little taller after they were introduced and Galiena had not looked upon him with disdain or fear.

The streets were still teeming with people even with the late hour. Ox led them down the main street and then through several turns to a tall narrow house with a shop front on the bottom level.

"It cost a fair amount of coin," Ox said as Red inspected the outside of the building, "but the weaver was willing to move his family to a relative's home outside of the village for the right price."

"Where are the horses stabled?" Bard asked.

"Just outside the city walls. There is a stable with a master of good repute. I gave him a few extra pieces of silver as an incentive not to skimp on the feed."

"This will do," Red said and reached for the door handle.

"You should thank Ox," Galiena interjected, pulling on his hand. Turning to the big man, she said, "Please do excuse Red's rudeness. We really are grateful for all you have done."

Red looked down at her face, both amused and annoyed to see the chastising set to her pursed lips as she glared up at him. "Did you just apologize for me *again*?"

"Yes," she said in a hushed tone, pushing up on her toes to get closer to him. "You are very thoughtful and considerate with me, but do you know that to your friends you are abrupt and rude? You should show your men appreciation from time to time. It's important. I learned that from my father."

Ox let out a booming laugh and Bard nodded his head, a broad grin splitting his face. "She's right. You *should* show us more appreciation."

Red scowled at the two men who were getting far too much enjoyment from the situation. Turning back to Galiena, he said, "They are warriors, kitten. They do not need coddling from me."

He didn't expect the sudden blush that colored her cheeks. "You should only call me that in private, Red. Not in front of your men."

She was looking up at him with such an earnest expression that he almost laughed. Just a moment before she had been baring her claws and chastising him, which was a sharp contrast to her sudden shyness and obvious embarrassment. He ignored the soft hoot of amusement from Bard, and the way Ox turned away from them, as though he, too, were embarrassed by the exchange.

Red decided against being sympathetic to her discomfort and request for modesty, focusing instead on the fact that she'd given him her approval to call her by the pet name in private. He couldn't stop the grin that tugged at his lips as he picked up a lock of loose hair that had escaped her braid and wound it around his finger. Even in her disheveled state after a day in the saddle, he thought her breathtaking. She was a soothing balm for his warrior soul. Leaning closer to her, he said in a low murmur, "I can think of far better things to do in private."

She gasped, and her lovely lips formed an O just as the door opened, stopping her from saying anything more. Wolf swung the door wide and motioned for them to enter. "You better get in here before Dane eats what's left of the supper."

Red's stomach growled in response, the small bit of food they'd eaten while waiting for the king not nearly enough sustenance after the day they'd had. Giving Galiena a gentle nudge through the door, he followed her into the building with Bard and Ox directly behind him.

By the time Wolf dropped a heavy wooden bar into the

brackets on either side of the door frame to secure it for the night, Red's vision had adjusted to the dim light emitted from a doorway into a back room. A large loom took up one side and on the other side was a table covered in rolled swaths of fabric and cluttered shelves lining the wall. Entering the back room, he was pleased to see a hearth, a table, and a few shelves with dishes, cups, and other essentials.

Dane grabbed a scrap of leather left on the floor by the hearth for the specific purpose of wrapping it around the handle of a metal pot hanging high over the flames in the hearth and lifted it to the table. "I've been keeping yours warm. We have meat pies with turnips and currants. Lucky for us, I think the best baker in town has a shop on the corner of this street. We won't go hungry while we're here."

"But the ale is watered down and tastes like piss," Ox added as he set several tankards on the table, filling them from a large, clay jug. "Unless we are leaving soon, on the morrow I'll be on the hunt for better."

"We aren't leaving for at least another day, but probably will be here longer," Red said, pulling out a bench at the table for Galiena to sit. He took two meat pies from the pot, setting one in front of her as he took a huge bite of the other. It was hot and good. He swallowed it and took a swig of ale which tasted watered down as Ox had mentioned.

He gestured to Galiena to start eating as he said, "Edward ordered us to stay here and keep our eyes open for anything or anyone suspicious."

"Did you give him the missive?" Ox asked in his gravelly voice.

"Aye," Red said, taking another bite and chewing slowly while he tried to figure out why he felt uneasy. "He has a scribe who he thinks can break the code."

"But something is bothering you." Galiena's voice was quiet with exhaustion, and she chewed her food as though it was a daunting chore. She looked up at him through drooping eyelids, the heavy toll of the day catching up with her.

Slipping an arm around her back to help support her, he said, "I have a heavy feeling in my gut, but I can't say why. I thought someone was watching us, but I didn't see anyone unusual in the shadows of the hall, or in the castle yard."

"Do you think The Executioner is here?" Dane asked.

"Probably," Red admitted. He'd yet to tell the men of his connection with The Executioner. It had been a secret he kept from so many for so long because he wanted to face the man alone when he exacted his revenge, and he didn't want the pleasure of killing the despicable man taken from him. He justified his silence by telling himself that once he set eyes on The Executioner and could confirm he was the same man who killed his family, then he would tell them. Until then, knowing the man was a threat to Galiena and to the king would be enough for them.

Changing the topic, he announced, "Galiena has been working on decoding the missive, but if any of you think you have a skill for code-breaking, we'll take any assistance we can get." He reached down into his boot and pulled the copied message out to spread on the table. Red wasn't surprised when Bard was the only man to take the parchment in hand and study it under the candlelight. He knew Ox wasn't literate, despite his attempts to learn to read. And he suspected Wolf and Dane were limited in their ability considering they only recently started their reading and writing lessons at Hawkspur.

Bard blew out a low whistle. "I wouldn't even know where to start."

"That leaves you to break the code, Galiena. I don't know that I will be much help," Red said as he took the missive Bard held out to him, "but I will assist in any way I can. Just tell me what you need."

"Parchment, quills, and ink." She tipped her head and furrowed her brow in a way that was becoming familiar to Red. Then she dropped her gaze to the floor as though looking for something, examined the room, then finally focused her eyes on the table as she ran her hand over the smooth, wide expanse of wood. "Sand. I need sand and a sharp stick."

Red rubbed his own hand over the tabletop, understanding that she intended to use the sand as a reusable scroll while she tested theories. "This surface will do? Or do you need something with raised edges to keep the sand in?"

"This will do," she said, then let out a long breath as her shoulders slumped. "I might not be able to break the code, Red…but I suppose that won't matter if the king's scribe is able to decipher it."

"I have more faith in you than any scribe of the king's." He sincerely meant it. She had been resourceful enough to stay hidden and alert when the men entered the alley to discuss treason, and then to steal the missive when the opportunity arose. It took quick wits to run into a street, assess her options, and choose the right man in the blink of an eye to go along with her ploy of playing the drunken husband in order to hide in plain sight from danger. And because of her determination and refusal to be left behind, she'd succeeded in delivering the message to the king and queen of England that might save the life of the prince. He had no doubt that if she set her mind to it, she could decipher the code as well as the best scribes.

"I can find the parchment, quills, and ink on the morrow," Bard offered.

"I'll get the sand," Wolf said.

Red grunted his approval, then got up to inspect the doors and windows, pleased to see that any windows large enough for a man to get through were shuttered and barred. "How many rooms above stairs?"

"Four," Ox replied. "We will take it in turns to have one man sleep man here each night."

"Wolf lost the strength of arms test, so he has the first night," Bard said with a grin.

"Only because you helped Dane pin my hand to the table," he

grumbled while glaring at Bard.

"One finger, that's all I put on this hand, the rest was him," Bard said in defense, circling his forefinger in the air.

"I'd rather get it over with anyway," Wolf said, pounding Bard heartily on the back as he reached for the pitcher of ale. "After tonight, I know I have a soft bed awaiting me for—I hope—at least three nights straight. How long will we be here?"

Red shrugged. "Until the king decides otherwise. I'd prefer to stay until The Executioner is caught and Galiena is no longer in danger." Having completed his inspection of the lower level, Red stopped behind Galiena, putting a hand on her shoulder before he even realized what he had done. It was becoming a habit to touch her. "Is there water for washing?"

"Aye," Dane replied eagerly, pointing to several buckets on the floor to the side of the hearth. "I will warm some over the fire and bring it up to you." He'd been part of Hawk's force for nigh on a twelvemonth, but he was still like a pup, always trying to prove himself and seeking approval.

"Thank you, Dane," Galiena said sweetly before Red had a chance to respond.

"Aye," Red grumbled, though inwardly he was amused by the woman's need to constantly make up for what she saw as his rudeness. "It's appreciated." He sighed when Dane stood a little taller after hearing his words of approval. Perhaps his kitten was right.

He looked down when he felt Galiena's shoulders and head rest back against him, pleased by the trusting gesture, especially since they were not "in private," as she had insisted earlier. It only took a moment to realize her reason for seeking his support was because she had actually dozed off. He glanced at the stairwell along the back of the room and determined it was too narrow for him to carry her up the stairs without bobbing her head against the wall.

"Best get you upstairs," Red said to Galiena, "before you fall asleep on the table."

"I'll take the first night," Galiena mumbled as she slumped forward on the table to rest her head on her arms.

"No, kitten," Red said with a chuckle. "That means I'd have to sleep down here, too, and I'd rather not."

"You can have the bed, Red. I'll be fine right here," she said through a wide yawn.

"I'm sure as hell not sharing a bed with Dane," Red drawled. "You can stand up of your own accord, *Wife*, or I will be forced to put you over my shoulder and carry you up." He knew calling her "wife" would rile her nerves, and he suspected the threat of being thrown over his shoulder would prick her temper long enough to give her the energy to get up the stairs.

He was wrong.

"You wouldn't," she said drowsily. "And just because I called you 'Husband' once doesn't mean we are married."

Without hesitation, Red hauled her up from the bench, then crouched to wrap his arms around her legs and lift her off the ground. Ignoring her weak protests and the hoots of the men, he started toward the stairs. It wasn't as chivalrous as cradling her in his arms to carry her, but it was the best he could do in the narrow passageway.

The fact that he didn't slide his hand up her leg to grab the tantalizing curve of her backside as she was draped over his shoulder was all the chivalry he could muster at the moment.

Chapter Twenty

GALIENA SLIT HER eyes open in the early hours of the morning as dim light was just beginning to creep through the slats of the shutter covering a narrow window. She vaguely remembered Red leaving her alone to wash, and then she'd climbed under the blankets of the bed. She must have fallen asleep immediately because she didn't remember anything more after that.

It was only when she'd lifted her head to look around the room that she realized she had been lying on Red's chest with an arm draped over his stomach—which was still clothed, much to her relief. Further inspection revealed that she was in the chemise she'd put on the night before and was wrapped in a blanket. Red wore a clean linen shirt and braies. He was lying on top of the bedding, his booted feet hanging off the end of the bed, covered only by a fur thrown over their legs.

"Oh, saints above," she whispered to herself when she realized that she had one of her legs crossed over his. The blanket wrapped around her, and Red's clothing, provided a barrier between their bodies, but that did little to lessen her embarrassment at the familiar way they were lying together.

"You're awake." Galiena felt the vibration of his chest against hers as he spoke, his voice gravelly with sleep.

"Yes," she said hesitantly, trying to gather her thoughts. Despite the warmth radiating from his body, she decided the seemly thing to do would be to roll away from him. Which she tried to do but was immediately thwarted by the weight of his forearm wrapped around her back. She let out a sigh and squeezed her eyes shut at the realization that she must have wedged her way into the crook of his arm and draped herself over him in her sleep. It was the way she and Adam had often slept. She waited for the searing loss of her husband to scald her as always, but instead, she only felt the comforting warmth of the Viking's body next to hers. Then she cleared her throat and turned her head to face him.

She had every intention of letting him know that she did not think it wise for them to continue to behave as though they were a married couple when they were not, but all the thoughts in her mind flew away like so many sparrows. His head was resting on his folded arm, and he was looking at her through hooded eyes. The sleeve of his shirt was pushed up almost to his shoulder, putting his muscular bicep and forearm on full display. She couldn't seem to tear her gaze away from the bunching muscles or the smattering of dark red hair visible where his arm tapered toward his wrist. She swallowed hard and forced herself to look up and away from his very appealing and very masculine form, only to be greeted by the cocky tilt of his lopsided grin.

"Take your time, kitten," he said with an arrogant drawl. "I like the way you look at me."

Protesting was futile as she knew she had not been in the least bit subtle. In fact, she probably looked like a fox drooling over a tasty rabbit, the way she had slowly perused the length of his arm from his chest to his wrist. "Don't make too much of it, Viking. I was just taken aback to find you in my bed."

She would have argued that she had a reputation to protect, but most people in Oswestry hardly noticed her existence. She had no relatives or acquaintances beyond Anora and Frode to judge her actions, and by the way they'd readied her for the journey and practically pushed her out the door and onto Red's horse, she suspected they were dabbling in matchmaking. Especially since Red had already announced they were married, even without a vow spoken between them or the blessing of a priest.

Now, he reached for a pewter cup resting on the table beside the bed and offered it to her. "Wine to wet your throat?"

She took the cup from his hand, taking a sip before handing it back to him. It quenched her thirst and moistened her dried throat almost better than a mouthful of stale water. He watched her as he brought it to his lips, and swallowed a mouthful, then set the cup back on the table and repositioned his hand behind his head with a smug smile and a satisfied exhale. He tipped an eyebrow at her.

"If you want me to leave, tell me now," he said in a low voice that sent shivers down Galiena's spine.

"And would you go if I asked?"

"I'd walk through fire on the way out the door if you asked me to."

She believed him. It was a powerful feeling knowing this huge man was willing to let her be in control whenever they were alone. "If I kissed you and then asked you to go, would you?"

His gaze was locked on hers as he nodded, the blue of his eyes dark in the dim morning light. "It would be a pain worse than the flames of hell, but I would—and will—do it without hesitation if you ask."

"And if I ask you to stay?" She couldn't stop the smile that curved her lips when she saw his throat bob, the hair in his trimmed beard rippling as he clenched his jaw.

"Then I will do it. And anything else you ask of me."

Her mouth went dry at his response, and she licked her lips, not realizing exactly what she had done until she saw his eyes widen as though seeing a feast.

"Ask me," he said hoarsely.

"Ask you what, Red?" she teased, knowing well what he

meant.

"Ask me to stay and ask me to kiss you."

"Will you stay?" she asked, her voice soft and coaxing, bolstered by the confidence of knowing he wanted the same thing she did.

"Aye," he said gruffly, pulling his hand from behind his head so that he could wrap it around her neck. He caressed her neck with his thumb in slow circles while his other hand slid up her back.

"Kiss me, Red."

His mouth was on hers before she could even take a breath. She wriggled her body higher on his chest to get closer to him, his low growl of satisfaction vibrating through her as she gently rubbed her tongue against his, tasting the sweetness of the wine as she explored.

The blanket wrapped around her suddenly felt too confining, the layers separating them too much. Lifting her head, she looked down at him, the passion in the depths of his gaze vivid and his breathing as labored as hers.

"Are you asking me to stop?" His hand was rubbing a slow, soothing track up and down her spine.

She shook her head. "No."

"What do you want, Galiena?"

"I want…" she paused. If she said what she wanted from him, everything would change—at least for her it would change—and there was no going back from it. She had been worried that what she was feeling for Red wasn't real, that her craving for intimacy had more to do with being alone for so many years than with the man looking at her now with an intensity that took her breath away. And her doubts.

Red had helped her regain her confidence by trusting her when she ran into his arms in the street, by not questioning her ability to make the journey, by bolstering her courage when she didn't feel brave, by believing she was as capable as the king's scribes to break the code.

By making her feel not so alone.

By making her feel alive, again.

By making her feel safe. And feel she was home.

He smoothed his hand over her hair. "Whatever you want, it's yours."

"I want you." The slow smile that spread across his face felt like the sun shining down on her after a long storm. "All of you."

A peal of laughter escaped her lips when he flipped her onto her back suddenly and unexpectedly. He nuzzled her neck, nipped the sensitive skin of her earlobe, then took her mouth in a long, slow kiss that made her head spin. When he pulled away to look down at her, she felt dizzy, like she'd drunk too much wine.

"Do you know what you are asking?"

She nodded her head, then lifted her hands to cup his face, his beard soft against her palms. "I want you to touch me, Red. I want to feel your skin against mine. I want all of you."

He kept his gaze locked with hers as he pushed himself off the bed to stand, then held his hand out for her to take, which she did without hesitation. When she was standing next to him, he gently pulled her closer to him. Galiena could feel the heat from his ragged breaths as he brushed the back of his fingers over her cheek and down her neck. He was moving excruciatingly slow, his touch reverent. When he reached the top of her chemise, he caught one of the ribbons at her neck in his fingers, tugging until the bow came undone, then hooked the ribbons where they remained crossed, dragging his hand down until they hung loose.

She shivered when he traced the line of her collarbone as he pushed the chemise aside, baring her shoulder. His lips followed, warming her as he pressed molten kisses from the base of her throat to the top of her arm. He set his hands on her waist, bunching the linen in his hands until the hem of her shift was at her hips, and then he lifted it over her head, baring her completely.

"You're beautiful."

Her apprehension disappeared at his whispered words, spoken with so much awe. Feeling emboldened, she slid her hands under his shirt, pushing the material up as her fingers skimmed over the hard plane of his stomach to the wide expanse of his chest. He reached over his shoulder to grab the back of his shirt and pulled it over his head in one smooth movement, then slid his arms from the sleeves and let it drop to the floor. Her throat hitched at the sight of his muscles bunching and rippling as he moved. A patch of hair covered his chest, tapering down to his stomach and she reveled in the feel of it under her fingertips, gloriously coarse and crinkly. Knicks and scars were scattered across his torso, tokens of his life as a warrior.

Not the body of a farmer.

She closed her eyes for a long moment, banishing the guilt that tried to worm its way into her heart. She would not compare this man to the other. And though she would never forget Adam, now was not the time for memories.

When she opened her eyes again, Red was standing still, his expression relaxed as though he was patiently waiting for her to come back to him. She gave him a reassuring smile. "I want to see all of you."

He obliged, first slipping the dagger from his boot, and tossing it onto his discarded shirt on the floor before kicking off one boot and then the other. She pulled the binding from the end of her braid as she watched him untie his braies, and she shook out her hair until it floated in loose waves over her shoulders, watching as he pushed the braies down his narrow hips and stood naked before her. Her breath caught. His body was magnificent, every part of him exuding strength and power.

"*You* are beautiful," she whispered in awe.

He closed the short distance between them, wrapping his arms around her waist as he pressed her to his chest and picked her up. She draped her arms and legs around him as he lifted her, the steely thickness of his cock pressing against her core, sending heat spiraling through her as her entire being began to pulse in anticipation of the dance that was as old as time.

He covered her body with his own as he set her down on the bed, bracing his weight on his elbows. She arched up against him, loving the feel of his weight pressing into her.

"Slow down, love," he rasped in her ear. "I plan to take my time with you." He shifted to her side as he spoke, smoothing his hand up the curve of her hip and over her ribs. His thumb brushed along the underside of her breast, sending unexpected zings of pleasure through her.

"Red," she gasped, wanting him to quit this slow torture. When he put his mouth to her, laving the tight nipple with his tongue, she buried her hands in his hair, pressing into him. He slid his hand down her body to the place she wanted him most, his fingers teasing as he brushed them over her. She lifted her hips as he slid a finger inside her, his thumb rubbing slow circles over the sensitive nub at the apex of her slick folds. She arched her neck and dropped her head back. A soft moan escaped her mouth as he inserted another finger to stroke her in a steady rhythm.

"I want you now, Red," she panted, digging her fingers into his shoulders.

"Patience, love," he murmured as he brushed his lips over the tip of her other breast.

"I need you inside me now." She was coming undone, and she wanted him with her. His hot breath scorched her skin as he licked his way to the base of her throat, swirling his tongue in the indent between her collarbones before planting hot kisses up the column of her neck. When he stopped kissing her, she looked up to see him hovering above her. He grabbed her hand with his, sliding it along the bedding until he had it pinned just above her head. Then he did the same with her other hand, his eyes locked with hers as he held her there, pinned to the bed.

"I want to see your face when I take you." He shifted his hips between her legs, and she bent her knees to bring them up on either side of him. The tip of his cock pulsed against her core as she lifted her hips to his, her body clenching around him, stretching to adjust to his thickness as he entered her.

She tightened her grip on his hands as she arched her body against his, then lifted her knees higher to wrap her legs around his back and take him even deeper. Her eyelids fluttered as the sensation of heat coiled in her center and started to spread through her body, but she kept her gaze locked with his. His eyes darkened as he slowly pulled his hips back, then sank into her again, his speed increasing and her body clenching tighter around him with each long stroke. The delicious tension in her belly started to spread throughout her body as the friction increased.

Just as the intimate intensity of looking into his eyes while he filled her was becoming overwhelming, he dropped his forehead onto hers and growled, "You feel so good, Galiena."

She dropped her head to the side, gasping her pleasure, and he nipped at her neck. Releasing her hands, he planted his on either side of her as he straightened his arms, arching his back as he lifted himself above her.

"Deeper, Red." She reached to grab the hard muscles of his buttocks and pull him into her, wanting to be closer to him. Wanting more of him.

The tension in her core curled tighter as waves of pleasure started to roll through her body. He continued to rock against her as he lowered himself over her, covering her mouth with his as she cried out from the ecstasy exploding in her like a thousand shooting stars, and then Red withdrew from her as a low guttural sound emitted from his throat.

Galiena wrapped her arms around Red as he rested his forehead on hers. Balanced on his elbows, he covered her still and she could feel the beating of his heart against hers as their breathing steadied. In the quiet, she heard rain drumming down on the roof in a constant, soothing rhythm. She felt warm and safe.

"What's wrong?" Red asked, his voice laced with concern as he lifted his head to look down at her, brushing a tear from her cheek.

She didn't know when the tears started, but she could feel the wetness on her cheeks, and she couldn't seem to stop them from falling.

He rolled with her until she was stretched out on top of him. His hands were on either side of her face as he held her still so he could look at her. "Did I hurt you?"

She laughed, but it sounded more like a sob. "Of course not." She tried to smile at him, but the tears just flowed faster. She wasn't hurt and she wasn't sad. She felt lighter than she'd felt in such a long time, like a shroud had been lifted and with it the dull gray fog that never seemed to leave her. Until recently, she had doubted she would ever feel anything other than sadness, despair, and emptiness.

Red had changed her life, and the only thing that scared her more than admitting that she'd fallen in love with the Viking was admitting she loved him to herself. He was possessive and protective, but that was his warrior nature, and she loved that strength and fearlessness, even as she feared it. He led a danger-ous life, and she didn't think she could survive losing another person she loved.

He wiped a thumb across her cheek, his other hand rubbing soothingly up and down her back. He was patiently watching her in a way that made her feel like she was more important to him than anything else, and that he would give her all the time she needed to work through what was in her heart.

"You need to quit looking at me like that," she said as he wiped another tear from her cheek.

"Like what?"

"Like you already know what's going on in my mind but you're just waiting for me to make sense of it."

He smiled then, slow, and easy. That was when she realized she'd made a terrible mistake. This man had already started working his way into her heart, and if she was not careful, he would break the fragile shell of it into a thousand pieces.

She needed to divert herself with a different topic, something that would remind her why falling in love with him would only lead to heartache. She stacked her hands on his chest and rested her chin on them. "Tell me about some of these scars on your chest. How did you get them?"

He studied her for a long moment, then said, "Most of them are old, remnants of a time when I was young, cocky, and stupid. Which one do you want to know about?"

She picked her head up to look at his upper torso, tracing a finger over a faint line arching over the end of one shoulder. "This one."

"That one is courtesy of Ox."

Galiena's mouth dropped open in surprise. "He was your enemy once?"

Red shook his head. "After my first battle under Hawk's command—which we won—I returned feeling arrogantly over-confident. I told Hawk I was ready to train with his elite warriors, actually demanding that he let me prove myself. Ox took it upon himself to show me that I wasn't as tough as I thought." He laughed at his own folly. "It was a good lesson."

Galiena could feel the pleasant vibration of his chuckle where her body was flattened against his, making her very aware of the large, warm, naked man beneath her.

"Tell me about this one." She touched her fingers to a puck-ered scar high on his chest, just beneath his shoulder. When she looked back at his face, his eyes were ice-cold.

"That is from The Executioner."

Thunder rolled outside as the wind and rain increased, forc-ing a cold gust of air through the small window. Galiena shivered and Red rolled onto his side, still holding her to him, then reached down to pull the blankets over them. She cuddled against his chest, as he draped a leg over hers.

"How did you escape him?" she asked quietly. When he'd told her about his mother and uncle, he'd not said anything about what happened to him, and she hadn't pressed him for the details.

"Hawk." He was silent for a breath, then continued. "The Executioner ambushed us on the road. We were on foot and alone, and the coward shot me from the cover of the trees. When he emerged from his cover, my uncle drew his dagger and tried to defend us, but The Executioner jumped from his horse, wrestled the knife from him, and used it to kill him. My mother tried to run, but he chased her down before I could get to him and killed her, too, with my uncle's dagger."

Galiena's gut clenched with horror. "How old were you?"

"Twelve. He would have killed me, too, and was about to finish the job, when Hawk came upon us. He'd heard my mother's screams and arrived just as The Executioner was standing over me. I'd fallen to my knees. He'd grabbed the front of my shirt and was about to rip my throat apart like he'd done to my mother and uncle, but he didn't get the chance. Hawk was barreling down on us, blade drawn, and The Executioner chose to jump on his horse and escape rather than meet his own death."

"And you've served Hawk ever since?" She knew the world was violent and full of cruel people, but it was painful to think of any child having to watch their mother and uncle being killed before their very eyes. "What of your mother's cousin?"

"Hawk was a young warrior, with little experience and no desire to take on the responsibility of an attendant. But he didn't have the heart to leave me to fend for myself in a country I knew nothing about. He helped me find my mother's cousin, but the man was already dead—murdered—by the time we arrived at his estate. Fortunately, in the two days we traveled together, I impressed Hawk with my strength and fortitude, and we've been at each other's side ever since." Red shrugged nonchalantly as he said the last.

"And you are sure the hooded man from Oswestry is the same man?"

"After failing to track him down for nearly two decades, I enlisted Hunter to help me find him, and he says it's him. I didn't get a good look at him because of his hood, but he was similar in build and had the same swagger."

"I'm so sorry, Red," she said, gently circling the scar on his chest with her finger.

"Let's not speak of him now," he murmured and pressed his lips to the top of her head. "It's storming a gale out there and there's nothing to do but stay right here until it passes."

She had forgotten how wonderful it was to lay in bed with a man, limbs tangled together and sharing each other's warmth. Sharing secrets and dreams. Slipping her leg higher between his, she hooked her heel on his calf and wriggled closer. "Tell me something else about you, Red."

"What do you want to know?"

"Hmm," she hummed, contemplating. She just wanted the comfort of hearing him talk as he held her like this. "Do you have a home? Or do you live at Hawkspur?"

"Both." He tightened his arm around her waist, pressing her closer to him. "Hawk has granted me a small manor house on the edge of the village at Hawkspur as payment for my service. When the time is right, I will furnish it and make it a home, but for the time being, I stay in a room at the castle."

"Is there ever a right time for a warrior to settle down?" she asked with a teasing laugh.

"Aye, there is." The tone of his voice was full of promise and hope.

And it scared the hell out of Galiena. There was so much that could happen, so much that could go wrong. No one knew better than she that those promises and hopes could be gone in an instant.

Chapter Twenty-One

R ED LOVED THE way the blush colored Galiena's cheeks every time he looked at her. And the way she couldn't seem to stop the corners of her beautiful lips from curving into a small smile. He couldn't help but smile himself, remembering the feel of her in his arms, and the way her body responded to his when he'd made love to her a second time. He'd been reluctant to leave their bed, and he was finding it difficult to concentrate as he fought the urge to carry her back up the stairs and strip her naked to worship her with his body again.

"Red," she chided, the wide smile taking the sting out of her tone. "Quit looking at me that way and focus on the missive."

"Looking at you what way?" Bard asked, emerging from the stairwell.

Galiena's face turned scarlet, and she immediately dropped her attention to the parchment opened on the table.

"If you mean like he's dreaming of a home filled with your bairns," Bard continued, ignoring Red's glare, "rumor has it he's been looking at you that way since he carried you into Hawkspur."

"I've called her 'wife' since the moment I met her," Red said, "but she doesn't believe I mean it."

"How could it mean anything?" she asked with a laugh. "You

didn't even know my name yet."

"You called me 'husband' before you knew my name," he countered.

"Ho!" Bard hooted in amusement. "Well, then it is true. Time to start filling that house with little, stubborn, red-headed babes."

Sensing that Galiena's embarrassment was turning to true discomfort, Red put an end to the topic. "Bard, aren't you meant to be looking for parchment, quills, and ink?"

"On my way," he said, with a dramatic bow and a sarcastic grin.

Red got up to lock the door again after Bard left, then returned to the table and straddled the bench to sit at Galiena's side. He was about to say something to goad her about being his wife but noticed that her spine was unusually rigid and that she was staring intently at the parchment as though not wanting to look at him. His instinct was to touch her, to ask her what was bothering her, but he sensed she did not want his attention at the moment.

It was a stark contrast to the smiles and blushes from only a short while prior, and it felt like knives lodged in his heart. Had Bard's jesting about her filling Red's house with children caused her unease? She'd told him about losing her daughter, and he couldn't imagine there was anything more painful. It would be enough to make a person vow never to have children again, the fear of another loss being too great.

Red had known from the moment this woman ran into the shelter of his arms that Fate had brought her to him. What he hadn't thought about was the consequences of finding the woman decreed by Fate as his mate, when Fate didn't decree him as hers. Galiena had jolted him to his core from the first moment he saw her, and it was up to him to convince her she was his she-wolf. What they could be together measured more than the risk of loss and pain.

But first, he had to bridge the distance she had put between them. And in this moment, the best way to do that seemed to be reining in his urge to overwhelm her with his presence. He pushed himself back on the bench, giving her physical space. He was searching for something to say when a pounding on the door echoed through the shop. Red rose, pulling the dagger from his boot before moving to the door. "Aye?" he called through the door.

"It's Ox and Wolf," Ox replied in his gravelly voice.

Red quickly removed the wood bar from the brackets and opened the door. The two men entered, carrying casks of ale and buckets of sand. He secured the door behind them and followed them into the back room of the shop.

"The sand is wet," Wolf said. "I took it directly from the beach."

"That is perfect, Wolf," Galiena said, flashing the young man a strained smile. "It will be easier to work with."

Red looked at the young warrior standing next to the table, grinning down at Galiena. It shouldn't gall him so much to see her smile at someone else, and he couldn't blame Wolf for his dazed response, but he didn't like it one bit. He jostled Wolf with his shoulder to get his attention, then ordered in a gruff voice, "Put the buckets down and look for something sharp she can use to write with in the sand."

Wolf had the decency to look abashed when he realized he'd been caught staring at Galiena. He set the buckets on the floor and hurried into the front shop to sort through the weaver's tools.

"How much sand do you need spread out?" Red asked, scooping the heavy, wet grains with his hands.

Galiena spread her hands about shoulder width apart over the end of the table. "About this wide, and the width of the table, but leave room around the edges, please."

Red did as she asked, then handed her the large couching needle Wolf had found.

"This will do nicely," she said, inspecting the tapered metal tool that extended the length of her hand. She stood to make it easier to work in the sand without dragging her sleeves over it, then drew neat letters across the top of the square, starting with the twenty-three Latin letters in standard order and ending with the three symbols for *th*, *wy*, and *eth*.

"Have you been able to discern any more of the code?" Ox asked, pouring ale into tankards from one of the casks and setting them on the table.

She shook her head, still studying the parchment. "I think I need to see the alphabet written in order."

"You believe this can be done without a key?" Ox said, leaning over the table to peer at the parchment.

"If the date on the last line is translated correctly by shifting the letters one position, then it would follow that the other lines are a shift, as well," Galiena responded. "The other lines may possibly be shifted by more than one position." She scratched the last line of the message in the sand as written. "These symbols appear to be numbers and if the dot patterns are vowels, then this group of letters and symbols would translate to 14 December 1284."

She pointed to each letter as it appeared in the alphabetized row, then wrote the letter directly to the right of it under the line of coded letters, substituting an *e* for the repeated symbol of three stacked dots. "But if I apply this same pattern to the other lines, it doesn't form any discernable words."

Ox looked at the scrawled letters in the sand for another moment, then took a long swig of ale. "I'll have to take your word for it. None of it is discernable to me."

"Doesn't the king have someone working on that?" Wolf asked.

"Aye," Red responded. "But it may take a while for his scribe to decipher the code, and..." he paused, looking at the men thoughtfully, "I have reasons of my own to know who wrote this."

Both Ox and Wolf nodded once, neither man asking for any more details. They knew if he wanted them to know more at this time, he would have told them.

He sat on the bench opposite Galiena and reached for a tankard of ale while he watched her work. She'd written the first line of the message into the sand, and beneath the line, she wrote as if the corresponding letters were shifted up two positions. When that didn't work, she wiped a hand over the sand to smooth it, then repeated the process, shifting the letters three positions. She'd gone through the process nearly a dozen times with no luck, when she dropped the heavy couching needle on the table and plopped down on the bench, huffing out a sigh of frustration.

"Maybe Ox is right," she said. "Maybe the scribe used a key known only to him and the recipient."

"Have some ale and bread," he insisted. Bard had returned with the parchment, quills, ink, and fresh loaves of bread, which the other men were eating in the front room while Red and Galiena worked in the backroom. "And tell me what I can do to help."

"It would be helpful if you would copy the message out onto another piece of parchment, but this time leave space between the lines to write the translations." She took a drink of the ale he pushed toward her, then wiped the sand off the palm of her hands. She picked up a chunk of bread and bit off a piece, chewing slowly as she stared at the line written in the sand.

"Perhaps try shifting backward," Red suggested, pleased at the way her face lit up with renewed energy.

"I'd not thought of that." She pushed to her feet, still gnawing on the bread, and started scratching the letters below the line from the missive in the sand, using the letter shifted one position to the left. When that didn't work, she started the process again, shifting the letters two positions to the left. This time, a recognizable word began to form.

"Look, Red," she said excitedly, pointing to the first word she'd written in the sand. She'd left blanks where the symbols for the vowels were located. "*L*-blank-*n*-*g*-*s*-*h*-blank-*n*-*k*-*s*," she repeated.

He'd been watching her write each letter, his senses starting to tingle as soon as she'd translated the letters. "Longshanks," he confirmed. He'd known then that the first word referred to the king of England, proof that the message would be damning for whoever wrote it. "The king is known as 'Edward Longshanks'."

Galiena gave him a sidelong glance of confusion. "I thought he was Edward Plantagenet."

"He is, but he's also known as 'Longshanks'." He stood and circled around the table to look over her shoulder at the letters in the sand. "If the second word is also shifted two positions backward, it says *seeks*."

Galiena wrote the letters into the sand, then continued with the translation, substituting the known vowels for the symbols. *"Longshanks seeks to weaken,"* she read out loud before turning to look at Red. Some of the color had drained from her face, and he knew she understood as well as he did the gravity of what they were uncovering.

"Try the next line," he suggested, but the pattern of shifting two letters to the left did not work. Galiena tried shifting the letters three positions to the left but came up with nothing legible again. She repeated the process three more times until they were shifted five positions to the left, but still, it did not produce anything that made sense.

"Let's try shifting to the right again," Galiena said, wiping the sand clean below the original line, and restarting the process again.

He'd started to think they were on the wrong track again when finally, the fourth shift to the right yielded results. He watched, not saying anything until the entire line was written in the sand. Only then did he read it out loud. *"Old ways are threatened."*

Red grabbed the parchment he'd finished copying the coded message onto, and added the translations below the first, second, and last lines, adding an arrow indicating the correct direction along with a number to indicate the number of positions shifted for each line. "There doesn't seem to be a pattern yet as to how many positions or which direction to shift for each line," he said, showing his work to Galiena.

"We will have to just keep repeating the pattern, trying first one direction and then the other." She put her hands on her lower back, leaning backward to stretch.

"The king is expecting us to make an appearance before evening," Red reminded her. "We need to wipe the sand back into the buckets and put away the parchments until we can work on this again. I don't want anyone to happen upon this."

"Do you think we are being watched?" Galiena asked, her eyes wide with concern.

"I don't know," Red admitted, "but I can't rid myself of this gnawing in my gut."

Bard entered the back room as Red said the last and turned a sharp look at him. "We've regretted it when we didn't heed your gut before, Viking."

Chapter Twenty-Two

"ALL OF YOU may enter," the guard grumbled at them.

Galiena was relieved. She felt better with Ox and Bard accompanying them, and at least inside the inner bailey, they could stand under the wooden wall walk, and get some refuge from the rain. Wolf and Dane had remained at the house as a precaution, although against what, she was not exactly sure. Red had instructed them to be on the lookout for anything unusual or anyone lurking around the house.

To her surprise, they were admitted to the great hall immediately, however, from the number of people milling about waiting to speak with the king, it would be some time before they were granted an audience.

"Give us your cloaks," Ox said. "We will watch from over there." He tipped his head toward the side wall where they could see everyone entering and exiting the room from the main entrance and the inner doors.

King Edward and Queen Eleanor were again seated on the dais at the far end of the hall. Red took her by the hand and led her toward the line of people waiting for an opportunity to speak with the king and queen. They didn't have to wait long as a clerk soon pulled them out of the line to bring them to the front.

"Chairs," the king ordered with a wave of his hand, and two

wooden stools were placed on the dais to face the king and queen. "And remove everyone else to the castle yard so we may have some privacy."

Galiena darted a glance at Red as he muttered, "I'd say the king has much to discuss with us."

After they'd given the proper greetings, they each sat on a stool at the king's request. "I want to hear this story, again," he said and leaned forward as though ready to listen intently.

Galiena started telling the story, careful not to leave out any details. After her description of the men she'd seen behind the inn and what transpired between them, the king held up a hand to stop her from saying anymore.

"Does the description of the man from the alley who turned up dead match anyone you know, Red?" King Edward asked.

"I saw the man after Hunter found his body. I did not know him."

"Continue, Galiena," the king commanded in a gentle tone.

She was beginning to feel less intimidated by the king as she continued the retelling of events while he and his wife listened intently. When she got to the part about running into Red, she blushed as she admitted that she had called him Husband, hoping the ruse would provide her refuge from the man chasing her.

"How many days ago was this?" the king asked, one eyebrow arched.

Sensing she said something wrong, Galiena stiffened her spine as her stomach flipped nervously. Before she could answer, Red responded. "Five days, Sire."

The king turned a cold sidelong glare toward Red. "When I asked if you had known the woman for long, you told me you could vouch for her."

"Aye, sir. I do vouch for her. As does a close friend of Hunter's who has known her since she was a child." What Red said wasn't exactly a lie. Frode had known her since she was a child, but he had thought she was a boy then, and they had only been reacquainted for nigh on a year. She looked from the king to

Red, fear pricking her nerves at the way the two men were staring at each other.

"None of Hawk's men are conventional," the king conceded. "I've given him and his elite force—including you—much leeway because he has never failed me." The king paused. "Except the once when he put his lady-wife before my command, but he succeeded in the end. Do not fail me, Red, as I may not be so lenient with you." Turning back to Galiena, he said in a tight tone, "Proceed, dear lady."

Galiena swallowed, her fear a palpable lump in her throat. She finished the story, answering the king's questions as she went, finally ending with how they took refuge with Anora and Frode.

The king asked Red if he saw the man's face when he spoke to him in the lane.

"No, Sire. He wore a hood pulled low over his face. He did not want to be seen or recognized by anyone." When the king said nothing more, Red said tentatively. "May I ask, Sire, if your scribe has been able to decipher the message?" When the king shot him a sidelong glance, Red quickly added, "I am not asking the content of the message. I am only hopeful that you will be able to determine who is conspiring against you. I know I speak for Hawk when I say we are at your disposal in any way you deem necessary."

The king appeared appeased by Red's explanation, but before he said anything more on the matter, he gave his wife a quick nod and the queen immediately pushed to her feet, as did Red and Galiena. Galiena couldn't hide her shock when the queen took her hand and smiled sweetly at her.

"Please accompany me to the nursery, Galiena, while the men continue their discussion. You can see for yourself the child who will one day be King of England after his father."

Galiena curtseyed to the queen. "I would be delighted."

But she wasn't delighted. She didn't like being separated from Red and she was suspicious as to why the king did not want to divulge whether the message was being deciphered by his scribe.

Not daring to defy the queen, she obediently followed after darting a glance over her shoulder at Red. She could tell by the hard set of his jaw he was not pleased to see her leaving, but like her, he dared not say anything to the contrary.

The queen led her to a door at the side of the dais, which a guard immediately opened for her, revealing a stone tower with winding stairs. Another guard inside the door led the way up the stairs as two more guards followed behind them. Galiena conceded she was probably safer with the queen than anywhere else in the entire kingdom.

"Tell me, Galiena," the queen said pleasantly over her shoulder as they climbed the stairs, "do you have children?"

For three years, when anyone asked her this same question, she had replied that she did not, but after the king chastised Red for not telling the complete truth, she felt compelled to be completely honest. "I had a daughter, but she died."

"What did you call her?" the queen asked, her voice gentle and caring.

"Nahara," Galiena said. It felt good to say her daughter's name out loud, to have someone else hear it and know of her existence.

"And did she favor you, or her father?" They had emerged into a landing with a heavy wooden door flanked by two more guards, and the queen stopped to look at her as she asked the question.

"She had black hair like mine, but her father's green eyes." Galiena felt warmth blooming in her chest as she spoke of her beloved daughter. "But my husband said she was every bit as stubborn and bold as me."

"She sounds beautiful," Queen Eleanor said with a genuine smile.

"Yes, the most beautiful thing I've ever seen," Galiena said, feeling a measure of pride that she was able to speak of her daughter without breaking down into a flood of tears. She hadn't spoken to anyone about Nahara in this way since the day she died. No one had asked her.

Or perhaps they had, and she had been too numb to hear the questions.

"I knew from the way you teared up telling me about the threat to my son that you were a mother also. I've lost ten of my children, and it never gets easier. I cried for days at the passing of my precious Alfonso just four months past." The queen had a wistful gaze and a sad smile on her lips. She was silent for a moment, then sighed deeply. "God has blessed me with five daughters who are hale and healthy, and now another son. But I can say with certainty that Nahara will never be forgotten because she will have a place in your heart until you draw your last breath."

"Thank you for your kind words," Galiena said, putting her hand to her heart. "I can only aspire to be as brave as you, Your Highness."

"You have already proven to be brave, dear girl," the queen said, cupping Galiena's cheek. "You risked your life to bring us the missive and tell us of the threat."

Before Galiena could reply, the queen nodded to one of the guards, and the door was opened for her. She saw a room with bright tapestries hanging on the walls, probably for added warmth. It was furnished with an intricately carved wooden cradle, and another, simpler bed along with a cushioned bench that Galiena assumed was for the wetnurse. She looked around, expecting to see the little girls who had traveled with their mother through Oswestry more than a year prior in what was obviously a nursery, but the only other people she saw in the room was another guard standing by the narrow windows along the outer wall and a woman—the wetnurse—sitting on the bench holding a bundle in her arms.

The wet nurse immediately pushed to her feet.

The queen reached for the babe, cooing to him as she pulled the blanket back to reveal his face, which she turned toward Galiena. The child was looking at his mother as she continued to coo and whisper to him, a broad smile on her face. Galiena could not help but smile as well when the baby mimicked his mother's expression with a wide grin, his little tongue barely sticking out past his gums.

"He is proving to be hale, like his father," the queen said, beaming proudly at her son. Then her tone turned melancholy. "Soon he will join his sisters in Windsor, and I will follow my husband on his next campaign." Forcing a smile, she looked up at Galiena, saying, "I miss my children terribly, but it is what must be done for them to thrive."

Galiena couldn't imagine being away from her baby for so long or letting someone else raise her child for her, but she knew it was the way of royalty and nobility. She watched Eleanor looking into the face of her son, her gaze so full of adoration and love, and thought about the strength and courage it took to be the queen—and the sacrifices. It was a life she would never wish for, and a reminder to her that a simple life was something to be cherished.

A pang of guilt stabbed at her chest. She hadn't had nearly the heartache and limitations on her life that the queen had had to endure. She'd loved her simple life with Adam and Nahara. They'd worked hard on the farm, and they'd been tired at the end of the day, but they'd had each other and a home that was full of laughter and love.

She wanted that again.

The queen handed her son back to the wet nurse. "Let us return to the hall. I have no doubt Red is keen to have you returned to him." She gave Galiena a sly, womanly look that made her flush from the top of her head to the tips of her toes.

Galiena followed the queen back down the stairs, thinking about her new revelation. Given some more time, she thought, she would be ready once again to start a family. But was Red the right man for the life she wanted? She wanted simple, and he was anything but simple. He was an overbearing warrior who led a dangerous life. She would worry every day about his safety, wondering if he was coming home again or if something had happened to him in some far-off place.

"Cousin," the queen said in a jovial voice.

Galiena looked up to see a tall man dressed in the garb of a friar standing at the entry to the winding stairs from another level of the tower. The nursery had been on the uppermost floor of the tower, and the next floor down appeared to be that of a solar. The door was still ajar behind the friar, revealing a large table in the center of the room stacked with parchments, books, inkwells, and quills. There were several chairs scattered around the room, along with smaller tables and chests along the wall.

"Cousin," the friar said, lifting Eleanor's hand to his lips. "You are looking as majestic as ever."

Queen Eleanor laughed, looking affectionately at her cousin. "You always know how to cheer my spirits." Turning to Galiena she said, "Galiena, I would like to introduce you to my dear cousin and trusted advisor, Friar Ferrando. We grew up together, and I was so pleased when he joined the Order of the Dominican Friars and pursued studies here in England at Oxford."

"As a patron of the order, they were honored to lend you my services as your advisor," Friar Ferrando crooned, his voice mellow and smooth.

"I am pleased to meet you, Friar," Galiena said, bowing her head. Something in his manner gave her the impression he was not a very sincere man, and she didn't like the way his smile never reached his eyes.

"Ferrando," the queen continued, "this is the remarkable young woman who risked her life to bring us the missive."

"Is that right?" the friar asked, his steely, black gaze sharp as he looked down his long nose at her. He drew back his lips, exposing his teeth in what she supposed was meant to be a smile, but it appeared more sinister than convivial.

Galiena nodded uncomfortably and she suddenly wanted to be away from the man as quickly as possible.

The queen didn't appear to feel the same trepidation. "My

cousin is a renowned scholar," she boasted, her pride in him obvious. "He is in great demand and is often away, lecturing students, and debating the great philosophers of the land. In fact, he has just recently returned from the friary in Caermarthen, where he shared his vast knowledge. We are fortunate, indeed, that he was able to join us, and at such an opportune time when we require his expertise."

Galiena didn't like the way the friar kept staring at her. Not knowing what else to do, she forced a tight-lipped smile on her face, nodding in acknowledgment of his accomplishments.

"Have you made any more progress on the missive?" Queen Eleanor asked the friar.

"It is a difficult code to break," he said in a condescending tone, "and will take more than a day."

"I have complete faith in your abilities, Ferrando," the queen said. "It is imperative that we discover as quickly as possible who is threatening the future king of England."

"You can trust in me, dear cousin," Ferrando said with the slightest bow of his head.

"In this, I am your queen," Eleanor said with a regal lift of her chin. "The future of the realm is at stake."

"My queen," Ferrando agreed, but Galiena could have sworn she saw the muscles in his jaw ticking as though holding back irritation. "Please, let me escort you to the hall."

Ferrando preceded the queen down the stairwell, turning his body slightly toward her and offering his hand for assistance as they descended. Galiena followed, uneasiness turning her stomach inside out.

When they reached the bottom of the stairs and emerged into the hall, Ferrando held out his bent arm to the queen, who hooked her arm in his, a genuine smile on her face and her expression once again full of affection. He turned to Galiena next and extended his bent arm in invitation. She felt herself recoil, but then remembered he was the cousin of the queen, and it would be an insult to be rude to the man. Reluctantly, she lightly hooked her hand in the crook of his elbow.

As they approached the king, Galiena watched Red turn to look in her direction. The look on his face was one of displeasure at seeing her on the arm of another man, but then his eyes narrowed as his expression changed to wary bewilderment, and finally pure, thunderous fury and hatred.

The friar had stopped walking as he returned Red's stare, and Galiena thought she saw recognition register in the man's eyes.

"Galiena," Red said in an angry voice as he pushed to his feet, "come to me now."

$$\cdot \infty \diamond \infty \cdot$$

Chapter Twenty-Three

R ED LOCKED EYES with the man he'd been searching for nigh on two decades, the man he'd watched kill his uncle by stabbing him through the neck with his own knife, ripping through his windpipe until his lifeblood drained out in a gush and then a dribble. He'd watched the same man chase down his mother and do the same to her. The force of the arrow lodged in Red's shoulder had knocked him off his feet and rendered him useless. It had hurt like hell as he'd pushed to his feet and tried to get to the man before he got to his mother. But he'd failed.

He'd never forget the terror on her face as the man grabbed her and spun her around, then gripped the front of her cloak as he drove the dagger into her neck. She'd looked fearfully at Red as he was running toward her, her hand waving him away feebly before she was thrown to the ground like a useless carcass.

Red had kept running toward the man, his vision clouded with fury. As a lad of twelve, he'd been taller and broader than most boys his age, but he was not yet the size of a man. The killer had easily pushed Red aside when he tried to ram him with his good shoulder, the pain excruciating as he fell to the ground, landing on his injured side, the arrow burning with the intensity of a red-hot poker digging into his shoulder.

The man had grabbed him by his shirt front and jerked him

into a sitting position as he sneered, "You're a gutsy one, aren't you, boy?"

Enraged with pure loathing, Red had spit at the man, fully expecting it would be his last act in this world.

"You have a hatred in you, boy," the man said with a twisted grin. "If I didn't have to kill you, I'd take you with me, mold your hatred into something useful."

That hesitation on the man's part, the need to linger with Red and toy with him, is what saved his life. Hawk had rounded the bend and, seeing what was happening, pulled his sword and bored down on them. The man heard the hoofbeats in time to roll away before Hawk could strike him with his sword. Hawk rounded his horse, then leaped down to come at the man, but he had run immediately for his own horse and galloped away before Hawk got to him.

Hawk had saved Red's life, and Red had been fighting loyally at his side since.

And now the man who had killed his family was staring at him with the hand of the woman he loved hooked onto his arm. The Executioner, whom he'd vowed to kill with his own hands once he found him, was standing in the presence of the king and queen of England, surrounded by the royal guard. Effectively untouchable.

He had the same sinister grin, long nose, and evil eyes as he did twenty years earlier, though he had more wrinkles in his skin and gray strands threaded through his dark hair than he did then.

"Galiena," Red said, barely able to control his fury at seeing The Executioner, or his fear for Galiena, "come to me now."

"The queen has just introduced me to this lovely lady, and I am reluctant to let her go yet." The Executioner, garbed as a friar, spoke with slow deliberation, his tone sinister and threatening—at least to Red's ears.

"Let her go now," he bit out, seeing the way he was pressing Galiena's hand to his ribs, tethering her to him. The only reason he didn't already have The Executioner's throat in his hands was because of the king's castle guards, who would have killed him before he could get to the man.

The king let out a booming laugh. "No need for jealousy, Red. This is my wife's much-loved cousin, Friar Ferrando. He will not steal your woman away." Turning to Galiena, he added, "You better do as Red says before he does something he will regret. The man is not known for his patience."

The Executioner slowly lifted his arm to release her, his gaze still locked with Red's. "I can see he has been molded into a dangerous man."

"That he has," King Edward agreed. "He is one of Sir Grogan's finest."

"Is that so?" the friar said with a slight tilt of his head.

Red could feel his teeth on the verge of cracking as Galiena scooted to his side, her face pale, and her eyes wide. He immediately pushed her behind him, not wanting The Executioner to look upon her a moment longer.

"Show some courtesy, Red," the king warned in a low voice. "Ferrando is my wife's family and the best man I know to decipher the missive. We are fortunate he is with us when we need him most."

Red remained silent for a long moment, unable to speak. Finally, he managed to say in a barely controlled voice, "Do you require anything else, Sire?"

"You are dismissed," the king said, though it was clear by his tone and demeanor that he was irritated. "As before, do not leave the city until I grant permission."

"Aye, Your Grace." The only thing that kept Red from being overcome with rage and leaping at The Executioner to strangle him was the need to protect Galiena and the knowledge that he risked being escorted straight to the dungeon instead of to the castle gate if he acted rashly.

He backed away from the dais, keeping Galiena behind him as he went. Once they were far enough away from the king that others started to fill the space between them and the dais, Red turned, putting his hands on Galiena's shoulders to keep her in front of him, and guided her quickly toward the door and out into the bailey.

"Who is he?" she asked in a hushed voice as he grabbed her hand and started toward the gates of the castle at a brisk pace. He searched all around them as they went, trying to see everywhere at once. He did not wait for Ox and Brad; they would know to wait and would join him when they were certain no one had followed them.

"We can talk about it once we are back at the house." He did not look at Galiena as he spoke, knowing that if he saw the fear in her face, he would want to sweep her up in his arms and reassure her. But there was not time for that, and he had nothing reassuring to say. He needed to get her to safety, then determine the next course of action.

He didn't take a direct route back to the house, using instead the narrow alleys and passages when possible. Once they were a few buildings away from the house, he stopped in a narrow gap between two buildings and tucked Galiena safely behind him while he watched for Ox and Bard. As they turned the corner onto the lane, he let out a short, shrill whistle. When Ox gave the signal, he emerged from the dark alcove, pulled Galiena into his side, walking as fast as he could without Galiena falling behind until he reached the weaver's house, pounding quickly on the door and calling out to Wolf and Dane to let them in.

When they were safely within the walls of the house with the door barricaded, Red pulled Galiena to him and wrapped her in a tight hug. He could feel both of their hearts pounding in their chests and realized he had not experienced fear like this since the first day he'd met The Executioner. Seeing Galiena in the man's grasp had nearly caused his knees to buckle and his sanity to snap. It galled him that, after all these years, when he finally came face to face with The Executioner, he could not take his planned vengeance right then and there. But now, Galiena's safety had to come first.

That didn't mean Red wasn't going to have his revenge, though. He most definitely would kill The Executioner, but he would have to be strategic and patient.

"Who was that man?" Ox asked.

"He is known as 'The Executioner'," Red said. "Until now, few knew of his existence, but many have died by his hand."

"He is the man Galiena overheard in Oswestry?" Bard guessed.

"Aye," Red grunted.

"I understand now why you trust your gut," Galiena said, looking up at Red, the dazed look of suffering a shock still evident on her face. "As soon as I saw him, I got a sick feeling that there was something wrong with the man."

Red searched her eyes as he cupped the back of her head in his hand. "He didn't hurt you?"

"No. The queen introduced him as her cousin. She said he was a scholar and a trusted advisor. He is who they gave the missive to for deciphering." Her voice was thick with dismay, and fear was etched on her face. "They will never believe us. He will lie to them about the coded message and kill the baby."

"But why hasn't he killed the king's son already?" Bard asked from behind her.

"There are so many guards in the tower," Galiena explained, "including two at the nursery door, and even one in the nursery. It would be impossible for him to get near the babe without being caught." She paused for a moment, then looked up, her eyes lighting as she appeared to remember something else. "The queen said he just recently returned from Caermarthen."

"Depending on how privy The Executioner is to the king's business, or how friendly he is with the guards posted around the city, it will only be a matter of time before he discovers where we are. And the king will have our hides if I try to leave the city with Galiena." Red sighed in frustration. His instinct was to get Galiena as far away from here as possible, but even Hawk couldn't protect them if the king proclaimed them fugitives.

Looking at the other four men, he said, "We will need to stay on guard."

Galiena rested her cheek against Red's chest, and he could feel her shivering. "It will be impossible to convince the king that the friar is The Executioner," she said, her voice muffled. "What are we going to do?"

Red was silent for a long moment as he looked down at the woman in his arms. Finally, he admitted, "I don't know yet."

He'd meant it when he said he would die before he let anything happen to her. He wasn't afraid to die. But he was afraid he'd fail to protect her. He'd walk through the fires of hell for Galiena; would it be enough to save her?

❖ ———— ·◇◈◇· ———— ❖

Chapter Twenty-Four

R ED SENT WOLF and Dane out for food and more tapers as he and Galiena set to work on deciphering the message with renewed urgency. Ox and Bard were above stairs resting in preparation for guard duty from the late-night hours until morning. Red was taking every precaution possible, but he was still uneasy. The fact that The Executioner had the favor of the king and queen drastically changed the balance of everything and did not bode well.

Decoding the missive was more important than ever considering The Executioner had been tasked by the king to decipher it. They went painstakingly line by line, with Galiena shifting the letters along the alphabetical order to the right, first by one position, then two, and so one, until the letters started to form something recognizable. At the same time, Red worked on the same line but with shifts to the left. They'd solved the first two lines earlier in the day and were now working on the third.

"I have it," Red finally announced.

Galiena walked to Red's side to peer down at the words he'd scratched in the thin layer of sand spread across the table. "*If Marcher law is replaced,*" she read. Picking up the parchment where they'd transcribed the first two lines, she read the lines together. "*Longshanks seeks to weaken. Old ways are threatened if*

Marcher law is replaced."

"It would appear Edward's victory of Wales may be more precarious than he believes," Red said as she handed him the parchment. Red spread it out under the light of the taper and transcribed the translation for line three, adding the notation of the shift six positions to the left.

Galiena jumped when a knock sounded on the door, and Red put a reassuring hand on her shoulder before moving silently to wait by it until Wolf said the agreed-upon word, then slid the bar from the brackets to let them in.

Wolf set some meat pies on the sideboard in the back room and Dane ran up the stairs to fetch Ox and Bard while Red poured tankards of ale for each of them. When everyone had picked up a meat pie and tankard and seated themselves at the table, Red decided it was time to tell the men of his connection to The Executioner after the developments of the latest audience with the king and queen.

"Here's what you need to know: the man we're avoiding— for now—and I have a history that goes back twenty years. Bard and Ox already know it was he who Galiena overheard in the alley in Oswestry, and that it was he who chased after her before we escaped the city for Hawkspur, but there is more to this story. He is known as The Executioner for good reason, though it wasn't I who gave him that name."

Red proceeded to tell the story in detail of his first meeting with The Executioner, the deaths of his family, and the years he'd spent looking for the man. "I finally enlisted Hunter to help me find the man more than a year ago. Based on my description, and Hunter's nefarious connections, he discovered that there was an assassin favored by the more questionable nobility to perform their lethal deeds; that's where he got the name The Executioner. He has a particular way of violently ripping through a person's throat, cutting through their windpipe, and nearly severing the neck entirely. It has become his signature."

He saw Galiena set down her meat pie and take several deep

breaths with her brows pinched together. He put a hand on her back and murmured, "I'm sorry, kitten. I should have waited to give the men the details after you had gone upstairs."

She shook her head. "No, we all need to know who we are up against. Go on."

He should have remembered that she was full of spirit, his little she-wolf. Red stood and put his foot on the bench. "There is one more thing." He pulled his knife from his boot, so he could show the men the intricate design of intertwined snakes on the blade. "This same symbol is replicated on the back of the original missive. It's called the warrior's knot, a well-known Norse symbol, but I've never seen it depicted by snakes until my uncle etched it onto two daggers he crafted. One of which is this dagger that I have, and the other is the dagger stolen by The Executioner from my uncle."

As Red was answering the questions of the men, he watched as Galiena continued to study the parchment with the deciphered lines, then started to work on decoding the next line of the missive. He had noted a pattern in that the first line shifted two positions to the left, the second line four to the right, and the third line six to the left. He was about to tell her to try shifting eight positions to the right for the next line, but she had already come to the same conclusion.

She was a clever and admirable woman, and he would do well to remember that about her. Red continued to watch Galiena work, suddenly stopping midsentence once she had the phrase fully written in the sand below the coded line: *Submission not an option.*

"What does it say?" Ox asked.

"*Submission not an option,*" Galiena recited.

Red picked up the parchment to read the other decoded lines to the men. "I thought the message would reveal another planned Welsh rebellion, supported by a few sympathetic English barons. But this points to the Marcher lords."

"Why would the Marcher lords rebel against the king?" Galiena asked, her brow furrowing as she tried to make sense of the puzzle. "Doesn't the king support them?"

"Aye," Red responded, "the king does support them. But the Marcher lords have their own laws, which are different than English laws. And though King Edward is their liege, they suffer very little interference from the king, and have rights that extend beyond what any other English lords are allowed."

"They are very powerful," Ox added, "and powerful men do not like to give up their authority."

Red sighed and looked at the men around the table. "This goes no further, but in this situation, I know Hawk would approve of me telling you that there have been rumblings among some of the Marcher lords that they fear the statute signed in Rhuddlan this spring by Edward will supersede the Marcher customs. They do not trust Edward when he says he will not reduce the Marcher lords to the same level as other English barons. They fear imposing English common law throughout Wales is just his first step toward stripping them of their power."

"They would be fools to start a war with Edward," Bard said, shaking his head in disbelief. "They would need every Marcher lord to agree to a rebellion—which Hawk would never agree to— and even then, they would be outmanned if Edward calls up his entire army."

"It doesn't make sense," Red agreed. "What does the rest of the missive say?"

Galiena had been working on the next line, following the pattern, and shifting ten positions to the left. "*Beware Tibetot and Gifford.*"

"Robert de Tibetot and John Gifford," Red confirmed. "Both played important roles in quelling the rebellion and are loyal to the king. They were there with the king during our first audience with him."

"Hmm." Galiena tipped her head, a perplexed look on her face. "I tried to shift the next line twelve positions to the right, but it doesn't appear to be working."

Red studied the letters but couldn't discern any recognizable words.

"I'll start again at one," Galiena said with a heavy sigh, the exhaustion evident on her face.

Red gently took the couching needle from her hand and set it on the table. "You need to rest."

She shook her head. "This is too important."

"Let me work on it," Bard offered. "I see how you are testing each shift until you find the right number. And I can write the line and the number on the parchment, as you have been doing."

"Good man, Bard," Red said, clapping his friend on the shoulder, but he could see Galiena hesitating. "I trust him as much as I do you, Galiena. Let him work on it while we get some rest. We all need to keep our wits about us in the coming days and lack of sleep will not help."

He grabbed his sword from where it leaned against the wall and beckoned for Galiena. She reluctantly put her hand in Red's outstretched one as she stifled a yawn and followed him up the stairs. When they reached the room, he barred the door, setting his sword to the side of the doorframe, then took the dagger from his boot and set it on the small table beside the bed.

When he turned around, Galiena was standing at the foot of the bed, chewing on her bottom lip, and looking around the room as though she didn't know what to do. The sight of her uncertainty while alone in his presence was like a knife to the gut.

"Galiena." She looked up at him, a telltale crease marring her brow that he wanted to smooth his thumb over while he fixed whatever was upsetting her. Except it seemed to be he who was the root of her distress. "I will do anything you ask to ease whatever is troubling you. If you want me to sleep on the floor, I will. If you don't want me in the room, say the word and I'll sleep in the corridor."

"No, I don't want you to sleep on the floor," she said, but the crease deepened, and she did not move from where she was standing at the foot of the bed, out of his reach.

"It's killing me to see you in distress, and if I have caused it, it was never my intent." His palms itched to touch her, but he held himself back. Instead, he quirked a deprecating smile at her. "I've been told I can be overbearing when I set my mind on something...or someone," he added with a slight tip of his head in her direction.

To his relief, her lips curved up slightly and she laughed quietly. "Subtlety is not one of your strengths."

"No," he agreed, his smile broadening, "but if it is what you desire, I will work on it."

Her gaze softened, and the furrow in her brow eased. "I wouldn't have made it here without your overbearing lack of subtlety. To be honest, I had every intention of dressing as a man and traveling on my own to the king. I realize now what a foolish idea it was."

He tried to imagine her dressed in braies and a tunic with her pert little nose, rosy cheeks, mesmerizing eyes, and curves that made his mouth water just thinking of them. "You would have fooled no one."

"I used to be quite good at passing myself off as a boy," she said defiantly, putting her hands on her shapely hips.

"I believe you could as a child, but now?" He raked his gaze down her body, lingering on the swell of her breasts and the flare of her hips. "Not a chance."

Her cheeks turned pink, and she dropped her hands to her sides. "As I was saying, I owe you and your overwhelming persistence my gratitude for so much, including making me feel alive again. Really alive. Not just existing. That is what I was doing until the day I ran into your arms, and you looked at me with something other than pity, like I was someone other than the woman who lost her husband and wasn't able to save her child, as I'm known in Oswestry."

He stepped toward her, but stopped himself from reaching for her, sensing she needed to say what was on her mind without his interference. "You have never been someone to pity in my view."

"The truth is it is I who must learn to stop pitying me." She moved to sit on the edge of the bed with her hands folded in her lap. "Until today, I thought I would have to leave the memory of Adam and Nahara behind to move forward. That letting someone else into my life meant replacing them." She looked up at him then. "But knowing Lady Alyce has found happiness again after her husband died, and seeing the queen's love for her children even when she knows she must let them go to be raised by someone else made me realize they will always be in my heart, no matter what happens or what I do. Adam and Nahara will still be a part of me, even if I love another man or another child."

Red moved to stand in front of her, then knelt on the floor, taking her hands in his. "As they should be."

"Adam was a good husband," she said evenly, looking him in the eye and lifting her chin. "I loved him, I will always love the memory of him, and I am not done mourning him. I may never be done mourning him."

Red didn't like to hear her talking about loving another man, but he knew it was his own selfish needs that made him feel that way. "I will accept that."

"I will want to talk about him and Nahara when I am missing them," she said, her gaze intent as she watched his face.

He nodded. "And I will listen."

"I don't know if I can get past my guilt," she admitted. "When Queen Eleanor held her baby in her arms, she looked so happy, despite having lost so many children. I want that, but I don't know if I can be as strong as she."

Red lifted a hand to cup her cheek as he looked into her eyes so she could see he was sincere. "You are stronger than you know. I've seen it."

"Sometimes the pain is too much." A tear dropped from the corner of her eye, and Red swiped it away with his thumb. "My husband and my daughter died because I stopped to pick flowers. Adam drove the cart slowly over the bridge because he was waiting for me. If I had been with him, he would have crossed it more quickly and been on solid ground before the flood came and the bridge collapsed. I tried to get to them in the river, but the current was too strong."

"It wasn't your fault." Red didn't intend for his voice to sound so gruff, but he wanted her to stop blaming herself. "If the bridge was weak, it would have collapsed even if he drove the cart faster, and you may have died with them. You risked your life trying to save Nahara. That in itself is proof of how much you loved her. You did all you could."

She closed her eyes and leaned her forehead against his chest. "Maybe someday I will believe that."

"I'll remind you as many times as you need," he said gently, wrapping his arms around her as he dropped a kiss on the top of her head.

"I don't know that I can give you what you want, Red."

"How do you know what I want?"

"You want a wife to fill your house with children," she said, the words muffled against his chest. "That's what the people who know you have said several times."

"Yes, I would like a house full of children. But only if that's what you want because I want you first. And if I can only have you and nothing more, it is enough." He sighed. "You are my she-wolf, Galiena, and we are meant to be together."

She picked up her head to give him a stern look, pressing her lips together as she tried not to laugh. "You've already forgotten about being more subtle."

"Mmmm," he hummed, tightening his hold around her back. "I did say that. But that was before I was touching you."

She shook her head at him as her grin widened. "At least put forth some effort."

"I'd rather put my effort into getting you naked and giving you pleasure."

"This doesn't mean I have agreed to be your wife or have your children," she reminded him, but her tone was playful.

He lifted the hem of her gown up over her knees and nudged her legs apart with his body until he was kneeling between her legs. He nuzzled her neck as he slid his hands up her thighs to her hips. "Then you do agree with getting naked and indulging in pleasure."

She tipped her head to the side, giving him access to her throat. "It depends on what pleasure you have in mind."

He growled against her neck as he nipped the skin. "The pleasure of you on your back while I lick every part of you."

"Oh," she said, her breath hitching in her throat—much to his satisfaction.

"I want to taste you." He trailed kisses up the side of her neck, "with your knees over my shoulders and my tongue inside you," he bit softly on her earlobe, "until you are quivering."

"That's not subtle," she said breathlessly.

"And after I make you come with my mouth," he continued, moving to the other side of her neck, "then I'm going to fill you with my body and ride you until you scream my name."

He could feel her rapid pulse under his lips and heard her breath get heavier as he kissed the base of her throat. Satisfied that she agreed with his plan, he reached down to untie her boots and slip them from her feet. Then he stood, pulling her to her feet with him to loosen the ties at the sides of her tunic and pull it over her head. Her chemise quickly followed, as did his own clothing and boots.

She lifted her hands to his chest and slowly ran her fingers across the expanse, leaving a trail of heat where her fingers skimmed lightly over him. As much as he craved her touch, he wanted to give her pleasure more. He untied the worn strip of ribbon on her braid and ran his fingers through her hair until it was cascading in dark waves over her shoulders. Scooping her up, he carried her to the bed, pulled back the coverings, and laid her down on the linen sheets. He stretched out next to her, looking down into her face.

"I've never seen anything more beautiful than you," he said, tracing the curve of her face with his fingers. He kissed her, savoring the sweetness of her mouth and the way her tongue felt brushing against his. His hands were sliding along her silky skin, caressing every curve and contour, but when she reached for him, he stopped her.

"Not yet, sweet." He pushed up on his knees and lifted one of her ankles in his hand as he grazed his lips over her calf. "I'm not done with touching you, yet, and it requires my full concentration."

The slow, sensual smile that curved her lips as he kissed and nipped along her leg would be etched in his mind until he took his last breath. Moving between her knees, he set her leg on his shoulder, then picked up the other, licking and nuzzling at a sensitive spot he discovered behind her knee before working his way along her thigh.

He inhaled the intoxicating scent of her, groaning with satisfaction when she gasped and arched against him as he licked a slow path along her core, separating the folds there with his tongue. Cradling her hips with his hands, he sucked at the sensitive nub that made her writhe in the most satisfactory way until she was panting his name. Then he plunged his tongue inside of her, tasting her as her body clenched and undulated. He couldn't get enough of her as he pressed deeper, the wild response of her body igniting a fire in him.

When she grabbed his head to hold him to her, he opened his eyes to watch her as she cried out his name and her body arched against his mouth. She was beautiful in her ecstasy, and he nearly came to completion himself at the sight of her.

She tugged on his hair after her muscles relaxed, and he obediently crawled up the length of her body, kissing and licking as he went. She still had her hand buried in his hair as he sealed his mouth to hers in a long intoxicating kiss, the taste of her body mingling with the sweetness of her mouth. He guided her knees to his hips, entering her slowly as she wrapped her legs around his waist despite his desperate need to feel her body taking him into her.

"Galiena," he groaned when he was fully inside her and she tightened around his cock, hot and wet and perfect. He buried his face in her neck, biting at the skin there as his arms slipped under her arms to grasp her shoulders for leverage while he thrust into her. Every stroke was bliss, the tight friction of their joined bodies moving in rhythm driving him wild.

"Look at me, Galiena," he rasped on the brink of losing control. She opened her shimmering silver-gray eyes, locking her gaze with his. "Mine. Say you're mine."

"I'm yours," she gasped.

Satisfied, he drove into her hard and fast until the sensation intensified to the point of snapping. But he held onto his last shred of control, rocking against Galiena until he felt her body squeeze tight, pulsing with her pleasure before he found his own release with a lusty growl.

He supported the weight of his body on his elbows and buried his face in her hair until their breathing slowed while she trailed her hands up and down his back. When his heart was no longer hammering in his chest, he rolled off of her but then gathered her in his arms to hold her closely. She sighed and he smiled, kissing the top of her head.

When he could hear the slow, even rhythm of her breath as she slept, he closed his eyelids and let himself fall asleep, feeling more contentment than he'd ever known because she'd said she was his.

IN THE COLDEST part of the night, they'd made love again. He'd awoken with her stretched out on top of him, her soft skin pressed to him from his chest to his knees. He rubbed slow circles along her spine as she was waking up, his heart nearly exploding when she propped her chin on his chest and smiled at him. She was radiant and happy, and he never wanted her to be anything else.

He was about to tell her that, but then a mischievous gleam sparkled in the silver of her eyes and her smile changed to a wickedly sensual grin. She planted her hands on either side of his chest and started kissing a trail down his chest to the flat of his stomach, her body gliding against him as she moved lower. Then she took him in her mouth, and he thought he'd died and gone to heaven.

When the pleasure became too much and he couldn't wait any longer to be inside her, he reached down and pulled her up until she was straddling his hips. Reaching between them, he stroked her until she was wet and writhing against his hand. Positioning her over his cock, he lifted his hips and thrust into her in one swift movement, his neck arching as he gasped at the feel of her taking him inside her. He slid his hands up her ribs and cupped her breasts, losing himself in the splendor of her face and body as she moved with him.

When he felt himself about to explode inside her, he put his hands on her hips as he tried to control his rhythm until she threw her head back and moaned with pleasure. Then he gripped her hips and thrust, taking his pleasure with her.

She collapsed on his chest, their bodies still joined as the last blissful waves coursed through them in slow pulses. He stroked her hair and her back as their hearts slammed against their chests in unison.

"You are my breath," he whispered, "and my heart." She lifted her head and looked down at him. He couldn't tell if the bewildered look on her face was one of happiness or if he'd completely overwhelmed her again. He brushed a strand of hair behind her ear, saying gently, "You don't have to say anything, Galiena."

He rolled with her then, tucking her against him as he curved his body around hers. "Sleep. You need your rest."

His heart ached as he wished for the pain in her heart to cease. He knew she had yet to reconcile her guilt about moving on from Adam with what she was feeling for Red, but he was confident she would find the balance. She'd said she was his when they were making love, but when her passions cooled, she still grappled with the memory of the husband she thought she was betraying.

He had to believe she would be able to move beyond her remorse and guilt. And he had to accept that Adam would always be a part of her. But that didn't mean she wasn't his she-wolf, and until she realized that he would have to be patient.

Unfortunately, patience was something he had yet to master.

Chapter Twenty-Five

GALIENA DIDN'T THINK she would ever again have to endure a day even half as horrible as the day she lost Adam and Nahara. Or that she would survive if she had to endure it. But she was wrong on both counts.

She'd awoken in the early hours of the morning to find the bed empty of Red. The sense of loss was like an icy chill skimming over her body. He'd left his dagger on the bed near her, but the door was unbarred, and his sword was gone. Sliding from under the covers, she found her chemise, tunic, stockings, and boots, which she hastily donned. She ran the comb that Lady Alyce had given her while at Hawkspur through her hair, plaited it, and tied it with the usual piece of worn ribbon.

She could hear the low murmur of voices through the floorboards, hope springing in her heart that Red was below stairs with the other men and not gone. Her stomach did a little flip and her heart beat a little faster when she saw Red as she entered the room, his mouth curving into that uneven smile that she loved so much. She hadn't realized that she was standing still, staring at him until he rose from the table and walked to her.

When he was standing in front of her, he put his hand on her waist and pulled her closer to him. "I like the way your whole face brightens when you look at me," he murmured, looking at her intently.

"And I like the way you smile when you look at me," she whispered back.

He kissed her on the nose and took her hand to lead her to the table where the other four men sat. The table had been wiped clean of the sand, and only the two pieces of parchment were sitting on the table. "Bard decoded the remainder of the missive following your method of shifting one position at a time until words formed."

Galiena almost couldn't breathe. "And does it implicate The Executioner?"

"No," Red said with a frown. "But it does implicate two lords who have pledged their loyalty to King Edward. One of them was with him the first night we met with the king."

"Which one?"

"Lord Burbek," Red said. "He was the last man to step off the dais when they were leaving."

Galiena remembered him. "He made me uncomfortable, but I attributed it to his arrogance of being nobility."

Ox chuckled. "'Arrogant' describes most noblemen."

Red spread the parchment on the table for Galiena to read. "Here it is."

Longshanks seeks to weaken.

Old ways are threatened

If Marcher Law is replaced.

Submission not an option.

Beware Tibetot and Gifford.

Rhys to be blamed.

Burbek and Wright gathering forces.

Bring armies.

Meet in

14 December 1284

"If you look at the number of shifts per line," Bard explained, pointing to the numbers written to the side of each line with arrows depicting the direction of the shift, "there is a pattern. There are ten lines total and if the lines are numbered by alternating bottom to top, you get the number of shifts to make. The line on the bottom is one, then the line on top is two, then the next line from the bottom is three, and the next line from the top is four, and so on. The top line shifts left, then next right, and they continue to alternate all the way to the bottom."

Galiena studied the message. "Where are they meant to meet?"

"That's what we don't know," Red admitted, frustration showing on his face. "I copied the message exactly as it was written. That line was short and there was nothing more written on the parchment."

"We need to bring this to the king," Galiena insisted excitedly.

"There's one problem," Bard said. "Two, if we consider the king may not be pleased with us having a copy of the message or that we did not trust his advisor to decipher it."

Galiena's heart sank as the understanding dawned almost immediately. "There is nothing here that ties this to Friar Ferrando. At least, nothing we can prove."

"That's the problem," Red said, blowing out a heavy breath.

"What do we do?" Galiena asked, feeling just as desperate and frustrated as Red. "King Edward and Queen Eleanor will never believe me if I say the friar's voice is the same as the one I overheard in the alley in Oswestry."

"If he wasn't the queen's cousin, I would have killed him already and this would be over," Red said through gritted teeth. "I still haven't ruled out that option."

"We've been discussing other options," Ox said, slanting a warning glance at Red. "Dane is leaving at first light to return to Hawkspur to find Hunter—if he's not already on his way here—and to inform Hawk of what has happened. Hunter has been tracking The Executioner and may know something that we can use to connect him to all of this."

Galiena glanced at the narrow window high on the wall, the first rays of dawn creeping through the opening. A new dawn was meant to be a sign of hope, but she couldn't shake the feeling of foreboding that had settled like stones in her stomach.

Red must have sensed her uneasiness because he poured her a tankard of ale. "This will put some color back in your cheeks," he said, sliding close to her on the bench as he wrapped a protective arm around her waist.

She took a sip, then asked, "What are we to do while Dane fetches Hunter?"

"That's what we've yet to decide," Red admitted. "Ox thinks we should bring the missive to the king to show him Lord Burbek is involved and suffer his wrath for not trusting his scribe. If Lord Burbek is arrested, he may reveal the others involved."

"Aye," Ox said with a nod. "The rats will scurry when the ship starts to sink. Burbek may even point his finger at the evil friar once his life is on the line."

"Everyone knows what was done to Daffydd when he was deemed a traitor by Edward," Wolf said, affecting an apprehensive shiver. "The king has proclaimed that the standard punishment for anyone who dares defy the crown."

Galiena looked around the table to see if she was the only person who didn't know what he was referring to. The rest of the men were either crossing themselves or grimacing. "Dare I ask who Daffydd is and what happened to him?"

She saw Red shoot a sharp stare at Wolf when he opened his mouth to elaborate. Turning back to Galiena, he said, "Daffydd was the brother of Llywelyn ap Gruffydd, the last Prince of Wales killed a year past. Daffydd betrayed King Edward, more than once, and suffered a prolonged and difficult death for it."

"Prolonged and difficult?" Galiena asked. She was reluctant to know the details but felt it necessary to fully understand the consequences should the king feel betrayed by anyone. "I would know exactly what that means."

Red sighed, then said, "It means he was dragged behind a horse to the place of execution, hung by his neck until nearly dead, then taken down to have his entrails cut from his body while he was still breathing. Finally, his limbs and head were severed from his torso, and his head was placed on a pike at the king's palace in London while his arms and legs were paraded through the kingdom to the four corners of the realm as a warning to anyone else who might think of betraying King Edward."

Galiena shuddered at the image. She knew who Llywelyn was, and when he was killed by the English, it effectively put an end to the last rebellion, but she'd been so absorbed in her own grief over her husband and daughter that she'd given little attention to the horrible details that were an inescapable part of war and treason.

"If we go to the king with what we have now," Red said, "we risk Ferrando not being implicated, and escaping. However, if we withhold what we have found, the royal heir may lose his life." Red pursed his lips. "I fear we do not have a choice but to bring the king the translated message."

"Then what will you do about the friar?" Galiena asked Red, a sick feeling in the pit of her stomach. The Executioner had taken so much from him, and she knew the depths of the loathing he had for the man. If Red killed him, he faced execution himself for murdering one of the queen's family.

Red held her gaze for several breaths, his jaw set, but there was a vulnerability in his eyes. "Whatever is needed to keep you safe."

A chill ran down her spine at his words. "But not at the cost of you."

The tension between them, and the discomfort of the other men, was growing in the silence that ensued until Ox interrupted. "The sun is up, Dane. Best make haste while you can."

Dane pushed to his feet, then picked up a saddle bag resting against the wall and slung it over his shoulder. "Let's hope

Hunter is already on his way here and that we return soon. Otherwise, look for us in four days."

"Godspeed," Ox said.

Four days? It seemed an eternity. Galiena said a silent prayer that it would be soon enough.

And that Red would not do anything to get himself killed before they returned.

"I DO NOT understand why the king would not be pleased that you are bringing him the message decoded," Galiena said, her cheek pressed to Red's chest as they embraced, saying their goodbyes. She didn't like that he was going to see King Edward without her to present the message, but she understood his reasoning that she would be a distraction to him if trouble should arise.

"It is his pride," Red said, stroking his hand over her hair, "as with all kings. He did not grant us permission to make a copy of the missive, nor did he task us with decoding the message. By doing so, it seems we do not have faith in him or his chosen advisors. We make them look foolish."

She did not want to think about what might happen to Red if the king was angered by their actions. It was her idea to decode the message, and it was because of her insistence that they were now in this situation. It did not seem right for Red to face the consequences of their actions alone, but she would respect his wishes and stay at the house under the protection of Wolf and Bard. "I trust you will be able to smooth over the king's pride."

"May I be worthy of your trust," he said with a chuckle, giving her a squeeze.

"And I am trusting you to come back to me safe and hale," she added in a quieter voice. It was taking every bit of her control not to show Red how panicked she was about him being taken away from her by some terrible twist of Fate.

He put a finger under her chin and tipped her face up to brush a kiss across her lips that jolted her all the way to her toes. He looked down at her. "I will always come back to you. I cannot breathe without you." He kissed her again, this time more deeply, the taste of his lips and the warmth of his mouth like a balm for her soul.

He looked regretful when he finally broke off the kiss. "I will be expecting you to be right here when I return, ready to finish what we've started."

"With pleasure, Viking," she said, smiling up at him despite the fear churning in her stomach and making her feel ill.

Reluctantly, she released him, and he went to the bedside table to get his dagger. He looked at it in his splayed hand for a long moment, then said, "I think it would not be in his favor to have it found on me if the discussion with the king does not go well." She imagined he would feel vulnerable without it tucked into his boot. He slid it under the mattress for safekeeping, then reached for her hand and led her away from the shelter of their shared room and down the stairs to where Ox, Bard, and Wolf were waiting.

She was still clutching his hand, hesitant to release him, as he picked up the rolled parchment with the translated message from the table and slid it into his boot. To Bard, he said, "If we are not back by midday, or if I have not sent word, take Galiena to Hawkspur by the route we discussed."

"It will not come to that," Galiena said adamantly around the lump of fear and dread clogging her throat. "I will come to drag you from the castle myself if I have to."

"My ferocious she-wolf." He pulled her to him, kissing her hard and quick. The welcome sting of the force of his kiss still pulsed through her lips when he turned away from her and lifted the latch from the door. "Let's go, Ox."

ONCE OUTSIDE, HE waited until he heard the bar slide back into place, then set off for the castle with Ox at his side. The sun had been up for more than an hour, but with luck, they would arrive before the throng of petitioners who sought an audience with him daily.

They were winding between the buildings when they noticed the people on the street were moving toward the main lane stretching from the castle gates to the edge of town, the crowds beginning to gather as some spectacle captured their attention. Fearing the king may be venturing out from the castle, which would delay obtaining a meeting, they followed the crowds to see what was happening.

"Is it the king?" Ox asked someone as they drew near.

"The king left at dawn for a hunt," someone replied. "A contingent of the castle guards just marched past. They seem to be on a mission."

Red felt his blood freeze in his veins. He turned and started to run toward the house with Ox on his heels. He made a silent plea that the soldiers were not en route to the weaver's house as he slipped into a narrow passage between two buildings, then emerged on the street that passed by where they were staying.

The soldiers had turned off the main lane and were marching directly toward the house. Fury burned within him at his own failing: he had underestimated The Executioner.

"Stay back, Ox," he commanded in a low voice. "I will need you on the outside if they arrest the lot of us." Then he took off running toward the soldiers in the vain hope that they would take him and leave Galiena and the others alone.

They were already pounding on the door of the house, and Red knew it may be the death of him, but he yelled to get their attention. When the soldiers saw him, they drew their swords, and several started advancing toward him.

Red held his hands out to show he was not armed. "What is this?" he demanded.

"You are Viggo Algarssen, otherwise known as Red?" one of

the soldiers asked, though it was said more as a statement than a question.

"What do you want?" Red demanded again.

"The queen has ordered you be brought to her for questioning," the captain announced. Red recognized him from the first night they spoke with the king and queen.

"For what reason?"

"She will ask the questions. Not you," he sneered, motioning for two soldiers to grab him. Red did not fight, though the urge had his fingers itching and his veins bulging.

One of the soldiers continued to pound on the door of the house.

"You have me," Red said. "Let's get this over with."

"Open up!" the captain yelled at the door. When there was no response, he turned to Red and said, "The woman is also to be brought to the queen."

"No," Red bit out through gritted teeth, rage blurring his vision. "She has nothing to do with this."

"That is not for you to determine," the captain said with a sneer. "Tell whoever is in there to open the door now or we will be forced to break it down and drag her out."

"I'm the one you want. Take me to the queen," Red argued. If he could get the soldiers away from the house, then Galiena had a chance of escaping the city before The Executioner could get his hands on her.

The captain pounded again. "Open the door now!" When there was still nothing from within, he turned to Red and drove his fist into his gut.

Red let out a muffled *oomph* but gritted his teeth against making any further sound.

"Did you hear that?" the captain called out. "That's your lover being beaten. Open the door now or it will continue."

The captain turned to Red again as the other two guards continued to hold his arms and punch him repeatedly in the face and stomach. Red steeled his jaw and tightened his stomach muscles, but the continuous pummeling was taking its toll on him. He clenched his teeth to bite back his grunts, knowing that every sound he made would be torture for Galiena.

He heard the bar sliding out of the brackets and the front door opened to reveal a castle guard. "They tried to escape out of the back," one of them said as he pushed Galiena through the door and out into the street. The captain had stopped punching Red, but his knees nearly buckled as he watched Galiena being led from the house, her face contorted into a mask of rage. "There's no reason to take her," he grunted, his jaw aching and his stomach heaving as he tried to speak.

With a sword at his back, Bard was pushed through the door next, followed by two more guards. His hair was tousled and the skin around one eye was discolored and puffing. Wolf was nowhere to be seen and Red hoped he had been able to escape before the guards arrived and that he wasn't lying dead or dying somewhere in the house.

"Search the house and search them," the captain of the guard ordered. Several of the men entered the house, and other men searched Red and Bard.

"Don't touch her," Red growled as one of the men moved toward Galiena. She squared her shoulders and glared at the man like an angry feline. Pride burst in his chest; his kitten may be small, but she was fierce. The guard hesitated, looking back and forth between Red and Galiena. "I will hunt you down and kill you if you touch her."

"You are not in a position to be making threats," the captain sneered.

Red kept his gaze locked on the guard near Galiena, even as another guard was running his hands over Red, looking for weapons. "Eventually, I'll be released and what you do next will determine if I let you live or die."

The guard slowly stepped back from Galiena, his hands still at his side.

"No weapons," the guard searching Red declared. "Only

this." He handed the rolled parchment to the captain of the guard, who stuck it in his belt with a satisfied nod.

After ransacking the house, the guards returned with Red's dagger. One of the men held it out to the captain, who studied it carefully, then asked, "Where did you find this?"

"Under the mattress in what looks like the woman's room."

"It's mine," Red growled.

"We have what we need." The captain looked at Red with smug superiority, then said, "Bring them all."

Red wanted to howl in frustration as he watched Galiena being forced to walk down the lane with him by the guards. Her demeanor was bold, her back straight, and the set of her jaw brave, but it still felt like a knife to Red's gut, knowing how afraid she must be under her mask of defiance.

The queen was a wise woman, much loved by the king, and not prone to rash deeds. And the king, though known for his temper, was fair and just. But both were being poisoned by Friar Ferrando, a man they loved and trusted, unaware his heart was fueled by pure evil.

Red had watched the queen look upon Galiena with kindness, even gratitude, for the risks she had taken to bring them the missive and the knowledge of the threat made toward their son. He had to cling to the hope the queen would not forget now what Galiena had done for her.

Chapter Twenty-Six

R ED TOOK HIS watchful gaze off Galiena just long enough to inspect his surroundings as they entered the castle. With the king absent, the great hall was devoid of petitioners, and the large wooden thrones set out for the king and queen were empty. His blood boiled in his veins when he saw the only person in attendance was The Executioner who stood with his elbow resting on the back of the king's ornate chair. As they approached the dais, the evil friar locked eyes with Red, his face an expressionless mask of stone.

Red flexed his fingers as he imagined closing them around the friar's neck and squeezing until the man's face turned purple and his eyes bulged. He bucked against the guards holding him, but they had anticipated his reaction and tightened their hold.

Once they were directly in front of the dais, the captain of the guard stepped to the edge of the platform and held out the rolled parchment. Friar Ferrando stood upright from where he was leaning against the chair and walked slowly across the dais to the guard. He took the parchment, unrolled it to read, looked up at Red, and clucked his tongue as though he was addressing a petulant child.

Red felt like his teeth were about to crack, he was clenching his jaw so hard. After The Executioner killed his family and had been a heartbeat away from taking his life, he'd sworn he would never allow anyone to put him in that position again, at least not without a fight. And now he had walked directly into the man's grasp without any resistance and with his arms restrained in a failed attempt to protect Galiena.

He slid a sidelong glance in her direction. Her face was stoic, and she held her chin high, but he thought he detected a shred of fear in her expression when she glanced his way. It was killing him to see her bound by the hands of the guards and vulnerable to The Executioner. He would sacrifice his life, if that's what it took, to get her out of this situation unharmed.

The door from the tower stairs opened and the queen glided across the dais with her guards behind her, attracting everyone's focus, including Red's. But not before he saw the friar tuck the parchment into his sleeve. The guards, their captain, the friar, and the prisoners all bowed in acknowledgment of the king's wife.

The queen lowered herself onto her throne with regal poise and assessed the prisoners in silence. "I'm gladdened to see the lady looks unharmed, but what happened to them?" she asked the captain of the guard, tipping her head toward Red and Bard.

"He resisted," the captain said, pointing to Red, "and he tried to escape out the back of the house with the woman."

"That's a lie," Red growled in protest.

"Hmm." The queen looked deceptively calm as she studied Red, looking suspicious of him. Red lifted his chin in response but felt it wiser to say nothing more. She turned to her guard and asked, "What did you find in your search?"

"Just this." The captain of the guard held up the dagger. "It was found beneath a mattress in the woman's room. The Viking says it belongs to him."

"Bring it to me," she ordered.

Once the guard handed it to her, she studied the intricate details of the hilt, then placed the blade flat across her palm as she looked closer at the symbols engraved there. Looking up, she said to Red, "I recognize this symbol with the snakes. The same design is on the missive the lady found. Tell me what it means."

"It is a Norse knot representing fallen warriors," Red said. He didn't miss the way the friar straightened and focused intently on the knife as it was handed to the queen. The Executioner's intent gaze lifted slowly, and a wicked grin spread across his face as recognition dawned.

"Like everything," The Executioner drawled, "it has more than one meaning. Tell us the other, Viking."

Red glared at the man, images of plunging the dagger into the man's black heart filling his mind. "Death."

"Of which you are well acquainted," Friar Ferrando said. "I can only imagine the number of men, women, children perhaps, you've delivered as an angel of death."

"I don't kill women or children," Red growled, trying to lunge forward, but the guards at his side held him in place. Keeping his eyes locked with The Executioner's, he said through gritted teeth, "As I'm sure you know, only an evil coward would take the life of a defenseless woman or attempt to kill a child."

"Enough," the queen said sharply. Nodding toward the prisoners, she asked, "They are unarmed?"

"Yes," the captain of the guard said, then shifted uncomfortably. "But we did not search the woman."

"I am not concerned about her." With a dismissive flip of her hand, the queen said, "Remove your hold from the prisoners while I speak to them."

"Is that wise, cousin?" Friar Ferrando asked. "The Viking is a dangerous man."

The queen turned a sharp glare at the friar, staring haughtily at the man. After a long silence, the friar bowed his head slightly and conceded, "My queen."

"When I want your counsel, I will ask for it, *cousin*." Queen Eleanor's tone was like ice.

Red felt a small surge of satisfaction at the queen's obvious show of power. Perhaps the cousin was not as beloved and trusted as it first appeared. From Red's vantage point, he could see the evil friar's jaw harden and his expression turn cold as the queen directed her attention back to him, Galiena, and Bard.

The castle guard hesitated, looking to their leader before releasing them. If Red had not already been watching The Executioner, he might have missed the subtle nod he gave to the captain of the guard before the other man signaled for his men to do as the queen asked.

Red moved to Galiena's side as soon as the guards released him, pressing his shoulder against hers and looking down at her. "Are you hurt?"

"No." Her shoulders were squared but her eyes were wide and her face pale. It killed him to see her frightened, but he was grateful and proud of her for the courage she was showing despite her fear.

"Do you know why I had you brought to me?" the queen asked.

Red had no doubt The Executioner had falsely decoded the message to implicate him, but he was in no mood for a game of guessing. "With all due respect, Your Highness, I ask you to be forthright."

The queen eyed him for a long moment, then nodded once. "Friar Ferrando deciphered the missive. It would seem there are Marcher lords who are fearful my husband, the king, will strip them of their power now that Wales is conquered. Sir Grogan is named."

"That's a lie," Red growled as Galiena drew in a sharp breath.

"There was a time when I would have believed Hawk incapable of such treachery," the queen said evenly, "but Hawk is a changed man, as evidenced by his act of defiance when sent to Hawkspur to find a traitor to the crown. He let the prior lord of Hawkspur slip through his fingers because he fell in love with Lady Alyce. How am I to know she hasn't convinced him their way of life is in danger if he does not do something about it?"

"Hawk is devoted to his wife, and he is loyal to his king," Red said. "Neither he nor the Lady Alyce endeavor for more power or riches than the king has granted them already. He is a faithful and true subject of King Edward, and no one could persuade him to betray his king or his country."

"I do hope you are correct in your assessment," the queen said, peering down at him with imperiousness. "However, my husband and I have been betrayed by those close to us before. We understand the lure of power and riches and know well how it can change a man. Or woman."

Red could feel the tide changing, and not in their favor. King Edward and Queen Eleanor had held the throne of England for nearly two decades, a feat requiring cunning, fortitude, and a large measure of cynicism. As with Daffydd, they were swift to mete out punishment if crossed—a policy that deterred treason for all except the most foolhardy.

There was a pounding on the doors of the hall and the muffled humming of raised voices from the castle yard. The pitch of the voices rose as a guard opened the door. After conferring with whoever was on the other side of the door, the guard turned back to the queen. "I beg your forgiveness, Your Grace, but there is a man here to speak with you and he has something you will want to see."

"Bring him forth," the queen instructed.

A large man with pocked skin and a balding head entered the hall, followed by another man pushing a wheelbarrow draped by a coarse blanket. The pocked man removed his cap as he drew near the dais, twisting it nervously in his hands as he affected a clumsy bow. "Your Grace," he said, his voice raspy.

"You are?" the queen asked.

"I am Aengus, master of the stable."

"And why have you come here?"

"I found a man behind the stable this morn, Your Highness. He had been murdered."

Red's stomach dropped, a deep foreboding humming in his ears.

"Who is the murdered man?" the queen asked.

"He had said his name is Dane. Was Dane, excuse me, Your Grace," Aengus said. "He and another man arrived two days past, requesting care for their horses and those of their companions. A full count of six horses."

"No," Galiena whimpered, sagging against Red. He put his arm about her and pulled her into his side.

"Is that him there?" The queen motioned toward the wheelbarrow.

"Aye, Your Highness."

The queen looked to Red. "You or your companion may look to confirm what the stablemaster claims."

Bard put a hand on Red's arm to stay him, "Stay with Galiena." He stepped to the wheelbarrow and lifted the blanket to look. When he dropped the blanket back in place, he squeezed his eyelids closed and sucked in a deep breath.

Red felt like a knife had been plunged in his chest as Galiena tried to stifle a sob at his side. Dane had been a good man, and he had the makings to be a great man. He was eager, loyal, even-tempered, and far too young to die.

"His throat has been ripped apart," Bard said, his tone low and his voice shaking with anger as he returned to stand beside Galiena and Red.

Red's vision went red with fury. Another person in his life dead at the hands of The Executioner. He pushed Galiena toward Bard, then lunged toward the dais. "You did this," he said in a booming voice. Immediately, the castle guards were on him, restraining him from getting any closer to the queen. "Does the queen know what you do in your spare time? Does she know that you butcher people?"

"It looks to me," Friar Ferrando said coolly, "that you are far more capable of butchering a man with that dagger you carry than a simple man like me who carries nothing but rosary beads."

"I'll kill you," Red roared. He lost his control, allowed his composure to snap, and now The Executioner had the advantage. When the vile man smiled, Red knew it and he was disgusted with himself for letting it happen.

"Did the lad refuse to take part in your treasonous plot?" Friar Ferrando continued. "Is that why you killed him?"

Red pressed his lips together and stayed silent, knowing there was nothing he could say that would make any difference. He turned his focus to the queen and stared at her earnestly as she seemed to contemplate him in return.

The castle guard stepped forward to address the queen. "Your Highness, it takes a large blade to kill a man as this man was killed. A blade like the one found in the possession of the Viking."

"I did not kill him," Red bit out. Fury blurring his vision at the sound of Galiena's gasp, but he kept his voice even and his focus on the queen.

"He could not have killed him," Galiena interjected. She had come to stand behind Red and grabbed his arm as if trying to keep him anchored to her. "He has not been out of my sight for days. Even if we had not been together every hour of the day and night, Red could never do something so heinous."

His heart swelled with pride at Galiena's defense of him and her show of confidence in his character. He wanted to wrap his arms around her and hug her to him, but he could not afford the distraction. Not when The Executioner thought he was about to snare them both in his trap.

"That will have to be decided by the king," the captain of the castle guard snapped authoritatively at Red. Turning back to the queen, he said, "My queen, I suggest you detain these people until the king returns on the morrow for the safety of your child, yourself, and your subjects. When word spreads through the village of this murder, the people of Llanbadarn will demand justice. They will want to know the man responsible is locked up and is not going to slit their throats in the night." He paused, then added, "And until we can be sure the woman is not complicit, she should be detained."

Galiena had stiffened as the captain was voicing his ridiculous opinion, and he could feel the fear thrumming through her. Red glared at the captain of the guard, certain that The Executioner had found an ally in the king's ranks.

When the captain opened his mouth to speak again, Queen Eleanor held up her hand. "Quiet, Boris," she commanded, pushing to her feet.

The captain's face reddened but he held his tongue.

"I must think on this without your blathering. Aengus, I thank you for coming forth. You may leave now. Boris, put the body somewhere cool until the king returns, and bring the rest of your guards back into the hall. I am retiring to the solar to consult with my advisor. I will return with my decision shortly. Until then, Red, you and your companions are not to leave the hall."

The guards closed in around them as the queen left through the door to the tower. Red pulled Galiena into his arms, wrapping himself around her, offering what little protection he could.

"Red," she whispered against his chest as Bard stepped closer to them. "We must find a way to show the queen the true translation of the message."

"I fear she will not believe it," Red murmured against her hair.

"If we survive until the king returns," Bard muttered in a low voice, "we may be able to convince him the friar and the captain are behind the treason."

"You came to that conclusion, as well," Red said to Bard, gratified to know he was not alone in his suspicions. Tightening his grip on Galiena, he said, "What happened to Wolf?"

"He was able to get away from the house before the guards caught up to us," Bard said.

"Ox will have found him. If I can convince the queen to let the two of you go, I want you to get her out of the city and to the safety of Hawkspur."

"No!" Galiena gasped. "I will not leave you."

He stroked a hand down her back as he spoke in a near whisper. "The stables will be watched. Get away from Llanbadarn then purchase horses."

"What are you saying over there?" Boris, barked, stepping closer.

"I am merely soothing the woman," Red said.

"No talking," Boris grunted at them.

The scraping of the tower door alerted them of the queen's return, Friar Ferrando following behind her as she strode across the dais to stand next to her throne. The triumphant smirk on The Executioner's face sent a chill down Red's spine, and he instinctively pushed Galiena behind him.

"I am a mother as well as a queen," Eleanor said evenly, "and I will not risk the life of my son, the heir to the throne of England, when there is so much uncertainty as to the true meaning of the missive, and now there has been a brutal death. Upon my husband's return on the morrow, I will present Edward the deciphered message. He will undoubtedly want to speak with you once he has met with Friar Ferrando. Therefore, while we await the return of the king, I must insist—"

"Your Grace," Red said in a clear voice. He knew he risked the wrath of the queen, but it would be worth it if it meant getting Galiena safely away from The Executioner. "I beg your indulgence that you will allow me to speak."

"You do not get—" Friar Ferrando's words were cut off by the queen's harsh rebuke.

"I decide who gets to speak in my presence." Queen Eleanor's voice was stern and laced with irritation. "Not you, cousin." Turning back to Red, she said, "Carry on with what you wish to say and make it quick."

"I offer myself as hostage if you will let Galiena go and allow my companion to accompany her for protection. I will be your prisoner until the king returns to hear my testimony." He felt Galiena's grip tighten on his arm, heard her choking protest. "Galiena is no danger to anyone. She risked her life to bring you the missive, warned you of the threat to your child. She is not capable of malice or lies."

The queen seemed to be contemplating his words as she fixed

her gaze on Galiena where she clutched Red's arm. Finally, she said, "I do owe Galiena a measure of gratitude. I saw the tears in her eyes when she warned me of the plot against my son. The sincerity of her concern was unmistakable." She paused, then announced, "I will grant your request, Red. Your companion may take her back to the weaver's house."

Red bowed to the queen. "My deepest gratitude."

"I can be merciful, Red, but I will not be foolish."

"Of course, Your Grace," Red responded, realizing he had underestimated the queen; to ensure the cooperation of Galiena, she would make Red as uncomfortable as possible while they awaited the king's return.

"Galiena and your companion will accompany you to the castle yard to see you restrained," the queen declared. Turning to Galiena and Bard, she warned, "If you try to leave the city, or do anything to interfere with the king's process, my mercy will cease, and his suffering will be increased. Boris, remove the prisoner to the inner ward and use the restraints along the west tower."

Red grabbed Galiena by the waist and kissed her before the guards pulled them apart. "Do not fear for me. I will be all right."

Chapter Twenty-Seven

HER HEART WAS being ripped from her chest as Red was led away.

He had not resisted the guards until Friar Ferrando stepped to Galiena's side and forced her to take his arm while he led her into the castle yard. Bard had tried to interfere, but the queen threatened to have him chained to the wall with Red if he did anything stupid.

"I said I would protect you, Galiena," Bard bit out. "I'll be right behind you."

Red, on the other hand, was not able to see reason as long as The Executioner was touching her. He ripped out of the hold of the restraining guards and launched himself at the friar, nearly getting to him before every guard within reach had pounced on him and wrestled him to the ground.

In the confusion during the scuffle, Galiena wrenched her hand free of the friar's and tried to get to Red, but he was completely hidden by the pile of guards holding him down. "Red, don't fight them," she wailed as fear threatened to choke her.

Bard pulled her away, yelling to Red that he had her and would get her to safety. Feeling helpless, she closed her eyes and buried her face against Bard's chest, not wanting to see what they did to Red.

The queen stepped forward once the guards had Red restrained and on his feet again. "You leave me no choice, Red." Turning to the captain, she said. "Remove his boots and strip him of his tunic. A night in the cold should cool his temper."

The castle guards ripped off Red's tunic and boots, leaving him barefooted and clad in only his shirt and a braies. They clapped irons around his wrists and ankles, chains leading from the cuffs to metal rings mounted on the stone wall of the castle yard, forcing his arms to be suspended at an angle above his head and his feet to be shoulder width apart.

It killed Galiena to see him like that, but she could see that her distress was only making matters worse for Red. Breathing deeply, she lifted her chin and met Red's furious stare. Her chin quivered and she could not speak, but she tried to tell him with her eyes that she would be strong for him.

"You will stay here until the king returns on the morrow," the queen announced.

When he was fully restrained and the guards stepped away from him, Galiena started walking toward him before she even realized what she was doing. She hesitated, fully expecting the guards to restrain her, then looked at the queen when the men hesitated to touch her.

"Please, Your Grace," she pleaded, "I fear for his safety. Let me stay with him until the morrow."

"No," Red protested.

"The castle yard is open," the queen said. "I will instruct the guards not to interfere if one of his men wish to remain, but they are not to speak with him or go too near him."

"Thank you, Your Grace," Galiena said, relief washing over her.

"Say your farewells quickly," Queen Eleanor said with a wave of her hand, "then return to your accommodations until the king beckons you on the morrow."

Galiena rushed to Red and ran her hands over his torso. "Are you all right, Red? Did they hurt you?"

"Don't worry about me," he growled. "Go with Bard and stay out of sight."

"Enough," the queen snapped.

Galiena stood on tiptoe to kiss Red quickly, then Bard grabbed her hand and pulled her away. Her heart broke in half, a physical anguish that caused her legs to weaken.

The pain of seeing him like this, not knowing if she would ever hold him in her arms again, was like molten lead burning in her belly. She managed to make it through the castle gates before her knees gave out and she collapsed against the railing of the bridge, heaving the contents of her stomach into the moat below.

Chapter Twenty-Eight

RED COULD TOLERATE the cold and rain, but being restrained and rendered incapable of protecting Galiena from The Executioner was making him feel as powerless and violent as a baited bear. His shoulders were burning despite wrapping his hands around the chains to carry some of the weight of his body.

The storm had passed, and the night was now still, but a dampness still hung in the air. The castle yard was dark and nearly empty, save for a few guards and Wolf. Hawk's soldiers were as loyal to each other as they were to their liege, and he was grateful that at least one of them was standing watch over him. He had to admit that if The Executioner should decide to slit his throat while he was in this position, he was helpless to stop him. Wolf's presence during the dark hours of the night was reassuring that he stood half a chance of surviving to the morrow.

He knew it was just a matter of time before The Executioner sought him out to finish the job he'd failed to complete twenty years ago, and it was only fitting that it would be during the coldest hour of the night. His first clue that a meeting was imminent was when the guard on duty was relieved by the captain, the same man who had given The Executioner the translated missive.

His current guard had started his shift only a short time prior and had been dozing as he sat on a wooden stool, leaning against the cold, stone wall, his head tipped back, and his chin tilted skyward. Wolf had found an old plank of wood that he'd thrown on the ground to sit on with his back to the hard wall a short distance away.

"Before you take to your bed, show that one to the gate," Boris said to the leaving guard, hitching a thumb in the direction of Wolf.

Fuck.

Wolf did not go willingly. It took both Boris and another guard to expel him from the castle yard as he yelled and scuffled with them the entire way. The disruption drew the attention of the guards on the wall, though most of them returned to their posts once the excitement was over. Red noticed one of the guards on the wall lingering in the shadows of a tower. Another of The Executioner's miscreants, no doubt, on the lookout for unwanted witnesses.

"What was your price to conspire against your king?" Red asked in as bored a drawl as he could muster when Boris perched himself on the stool near the wall, his sword still unsheathed.

Boris's back was stiff, but he said nothing in reply. He stared straight ahead as if he hadn't heard Red's comment. Red continued, "Or is it that you will pay with your life if you don't follow the friar's commands?"

"Shut your mouth, Viking," Boris said through gritted teeth. *Ah.* He'd landed a blow close to the truth of it.

"Do you have a wife, Boris? Children? Perhaps it is for their lives that you serve him?" From the dim light of a distant torch, Red could see the way the man stiffened. A blow even closer to the truth. He could use what he learned against the man. "I suppose it is better that you die a traitor's death than let The Executioner get to your family."

"I said, *shut your mouth,*" Boris sneered.

"He'll kill you and your family when he's done with you anyway."

"You know something about that, don't you, Viking?" said a familiar voice.

There were not many people who could put fear in Red, but the quiet, taunting voice of The Executioner immediately brought him back twenty years, turning him from a seasoned warrior to a scared twelve-year-old boy struggling in the bend in the road where he'd first come face to face with the evil man. He emerged from the shadow of the wall like an apparition, practically floating as he moved soundlessly toward Red. He appeared as he did less than a sennight past in the streets of Oswestry—a tall, slim, haunting figure with his face hidden in the folds of his hood.

"Boris," The Executioner said as he stopped directly in front of Red. "Take your stool and move farther away." He flicked his hand dismissively at the guard as he regarded Red from the depths of his hood. "You, of course, will stay here. Now. You're the one that got away," The Executioner said as he stepped closer.

So close, Red could smell the rank stench of his breath. He gave The Executioner a smug smile and said, "Bested by a boy."

The friar slipped his hand into his cloak and pulled out the dagger Red had not seen in twenty years. The dagger was the match to his own, save that the eyes were green gems instead of red. In the dim light, he couldn't see the emeralds, but he remembered them well, remembered watching with fascination as his uncle crafted the blades. They were true works of art, built strong to last a lifetime, meant to be heirlooms, but The Executioner had tainted them.

Now he turned it over in his hands, then held it up so the light from the torch could reflect off the silver of the hilt, making the jeweled eyes of the wolf glitter. "I've kept this for nigh on two decades and it's served me well. Used it too many times to count."

Red felt the fury burning in his gut, climbing his gullet, threatening to choke him.

The Executioner touched the cold tip of the blade to Red's throat, then slid it along his collarbone, the sharp edge stinging against his skin.

Red clenched his teeth together and growled, "At least have the decency to look a man in the eye as you kill him."

The Executioner lifted a hand to his hood and pushed it back just far enough for Red to see his face, his beady eyes locking with Red's as he continued to draw the blade over his skin and carving a shallow path toward his left shoulder, where he stopped and looked at the scar left by the arrow he'd shot at the young Red. He smiled a cold, teeth-baring grin. "I see I *did* leave you with something, a small memento to remember me by." The friar trailed the tip of the blade to the collar of Red's shirt, then lifted it with his finger and slit the knife through the material from his neck to his waist. He pushed the torn edge back, baring the scar on Red's left shoulder from the arrow, a smirk of satisfaction pulling on his thin lips.

From the corner of his eye, Red saw Boris push to his feet, his head moving from side to side as he tried to get a better look at what was happening, though he made no move to interfere. The friar obviously wanted to talk, or he would have killed Red already, and since there was nothing else to do to get out of this situation, he decided to keep the man talking to buy time.

And possibly, buy a miracle.

"You have a face like a weasel," Red said, smiling mirthlessly at the man. "Makes it easy to recognize you."

The Executioner laughed as he prodded the scar with the point of the dagger, digging it into Red's flesh. "I had rather hoped you would have succumbed to an infection. Fever. Neglect. Anything that would have caused you suffering and death."

"I had the same wish for you," Red replied, keeping his tone even. He would not give the man the satisfaction of seeing him rankled. The scrape of the knife over his collarbone and the thin trail of blood left in its wake was hardly noticeable after his many battles, but now it required a bit more concentration to ignore the tip of the blade digging into the twenty-year-old scar The Executioner had given him with the arrow. He could feel blood beginning to pool and then drip.

The Executioner *tsked*. "Looks like I will be getting my wish first."

"As a boy," Red said, deliberately speaking slowly, "my mother allowed me to exact revenge on boys who tried to taunt me as long as I still had a bruise or mark from their beating. Once the mark was gone, I could no longer get retribution." Tipping his head to get a better look at The Executioner, he said, "Fortunately, the scar from your arrow will be with me for this life and into the next, so there is no end to my ability to gain my retribution. I thank you for that."

"Ah, yes," The Executioner said, as though recalling an important point. "You heathen Vikings aspire to die in battle and earn your place in Valhalla, scars, and all. Does that mean you think to seek your vengeance in the next life?"

Red kept his voice low and unafraid. "I think to seek my vengeance in this life."

The Executioner pulled the blade away from Red's shoulder and held it up between them, the metal tip dark with blood. He looked at it with a type of fondness. "Do you know why I killed your family?"

"Bloodlust?" Red asked, working hard to keep his tone expressionless.

"That, and because it proved lucrative." He shrugged. "Although, the only gain I got from killing your family was this knife," he lifted his attention to Red's face, "and the pleasure of killing the man who hired me to kill all of you."

Red couldn't stop himself from reacting in surprise, jerking his head back. He'd never realized they'd been targeted. He'd always assumed they had just been unlucky, in the wrong place at the wrong time, the victims of robbery and the bloodthirst of an evil man. They knew no one when they'd landed on English shores and had given no one reason to want them dead. Except…

"My mother's cousin," Red said.

"Aye," The Executioner confirmed. "The churl had a new wife and didn't need more mouths to feed. He was the first man to hire me to do his dirty work. He also holds the honor of being the first man to try to cheat me of what I was owed." He arched an arrogant brow. "And the last."

Red felt no remorse for his mother's kin. He'd gotten what he deserved.

"It's rather poetic, don't you think?" The Executioner asked with a tilt of his head. "The first person I executed for coin was your brother—"

"Uncle," Red corrected, though he didn't know why he felt the need.

"It makes no difference," the evil friar said dismissively. "What matters is that I stole this dagger from him, killed him with it, and then your mother." A sadistic smile crossed his face as he said the last. "And it's been my weapon of choice ever since."

His eyes had blurred with rage when The Executioner spoke so nonchalantly about killing his mother. Only a coward would kill women so callously.

"My only regret was that I didn't get to kill you with it." He cleaned the blood off the tip of the blade by wiping it on Red's shoulder. "But that is about to change."

"Once you use it to kill the king's heir," Red said hastily to keep him talking, "it will be your last execution." Red laughed then. "Well, the last you commit, but it will end with the king executing you. Slowly. And if I know Edward, he will give the executioner that knife to cut your entrails out while you watch. Who can possibly be paying you enough gold to kill your own kin, the son of your cousin, the queen, and to risk enduring the king's wrath?"

The Executioner laughed. "You really think I would tell you?"

"You seem to be in the mood to talk," Red said with a sarcastic smirk.

The Executioner pressed the tip of the knife under Red's chin, leaning his face close to peer into Red's eyes. "I am savoring this kill. I cannot tell you how satisfying it will be to finish executing the only person who has ever escaped my blade. You should be proud of the honor."

"There is no honor where you are concerned." Over The Executioner's shoulder, Red saw Boris walking toward them now, sword in hand.

"Ferrando," Boris said in a low voice, and Red saw the anger creep into The Executioner's face at hearing his name.

"Shut up," he hissed at the guard.

Boris moved to the friar's side. "You didn't say anything about killing him."

"It is not your place to question me," The Executioner said, his irritation rising.

Leaning his face close to the Executioner's, Boris frantically whispered, "If you do this, it will look like I am responsible."

The sound of boisterous talking reached their ears as several drunken guards stumbled out of one of the towers across the castle yard, laughing and slapping each other on the backs. They seemed to be on a course for the back gate of the castle, which would take them very near to where Red was chained to the wall with The Executioner's knife poised to rip his windpipe from his throat.

The Executioner disappeared into the shadows of the wall, but Red wasn't so foolish as to think the threat of having his throat slit to be gone. As soon as the men passed through the back gate, he fully expected The Executioner to return and finish the job.

Only this time, he wouldn't waste his time talking.

To his last dying breath, Red's only regret would be that he never told Galiena that he loved her.

Chapter Twenty-Nine

GALIENA WAS IMMEDIATELY granted access to the great hall while she awaited an audience with the king. He had returned to the castle only a short time earlier and she had expected to be forced to wait long hours, possibly even refused. When she was shown in almost immediately, she took it as a sign that her *hamingja* was favoring this day.

There hadn't been time to go to Red, but she saw him across the castle yard, still chained to the high wall, but his shirt had been ripped open and there was something dark along the ridge of his collarbone. Ox and Bard had told her there was an incident during the night, but they did not give her details, only assuring her that Red still breathed and stood on his feet of his own accord.

Her chest had swelled with pride to see him standing strong, a defiant look on his face, and her heart had nearly burst with longing to go to him. When he noticed her being escorted to the hall by the castle guard, he'd jerked on the chains and shouted her name. She'd kissed her hand and held it over her heart as she looked at him, and mouthed, "I love you," to him, but the distance was great enough that she didn't know if he could see the words her lips formed.

"Please go to him, Bard," she'd begged. "Tell him I am not

afraid and that he must trust in me."

"Come to the hall after you've spoken to Edward," Ox instructed. "I want both of us there in case things do not go as planned. Wolf is to stay with Red until we return and then I will relieve him of his post."

After they entered the hall, Galiena put a hand on his forearm. "Thank you, Ox."

Ox put his hand over hers and squeezed lightly. "You are one of us now. I will stand by you and protect you for as long as I have breath in my body, just as I do for Red, Bard, and Wolf." She was moved to see his eyes mist as he dropped his head and added, "I failed Dane, but I will not fail you."

"You have failed no one, Ox, and I am humbled to call you 'friend'."

A muscle twitched in the jaw of the giant man as he looked down at Galiena. She smiled up at him. Before anything more could be said, there was a disruption as the guards in the hall came to attention.

King Edward, Queen Eleanor, Friar Ferrando, and the queen's guards had appeared; the king and queen took their seats on the large, intricate thrones on the dais. Galiena cringed to see Toad standing just behind the queen's chair but swallowed her fear. She closed her eyes, picturing Red's face smiling down at her, the image giving her strength and fortifying her resolve. This was the most pivotal moment of her life, and Red's future—and possibly her own—depended on what happened next. She had failed to save those she loved in the past. Now the arrogant, boisterous, overbearing Viking was her heart, her breath, her life. She would not fail him. A deep calm flowed through her.

Bard had entered the hall during the commotion and now stood beside her. "Red said to tell you not to fuck this up by throwing up on the king's boots."

Galiena smiled as warmth bloomed in her chest. He knew a prick of anger would heighten her focus and determination. "If he were here, I'd tell him to shut his mouth before it gets him killed or I'll have wasted my time."

Bard and Ox both chuckled softly and then Bard added, "He also says to tell you he loves you."

She felt the tears welling in her eyes, gladdened that he had seen the words she'd mouthed to him. But now was not the time to dwell on sentimental feelings. Lifting her chin, she said in a haughty tone, "If he loves me, I will hear the words from him, not from one of his mates."

"That's exactly what I told him," Bard said with a glint in his eye. "Now go save the insufferable man's ass."

The king called across the hall, his tone sharp and bitter as he motioned Galiena to come forward. "Have you come to beg for the Viking's life?"

Galiena walked to the dais and dropped to her knees in front of the king and queen of England, bowing her head low. "I am here to request a bargain."

"A bargain?" King Edward asked. "What could you possibly have that I would want?"

Galiena hardly dared breathe as she lifted her face enough to look up at the king. "I have the key to decoding the missive."

"Friar Ferrando has already decoded the message," the king growled.

She swallowed hard, drew a deep breath, and said the words that would either save the man she loved or land her in chains next to him. "Friar Ferrando purposely did not decode the message correctly."

The king's brows arched high. "You dare accuse the queen's cousin of deceit?" He bit out each word, though his tone was deceptively calm.

Galiena tried to ignore her racing heart. "Yes, Your Grace, I am accusing Friar Ferrando of deceit."

"She is lying," Friar Ferrando sneered.

"That is a bold accusation to make of my trusted advisor," the queen said testily. "Our mothers are sisters; I have known him since we were children."

The king narrowed his eyes at Galiena. "You stand by this accusation knowing Friar Ferrando is kin to the queen?"

"Yes, Your Grace," she said. Her stomach churned and she said a silent prayer that she would not be sick this very moment in front of the king and queen. Or on the king's boots.

"This is a very serious accusation, Galiena," the king said sternly. "What proof do you have?"

"The friar told the queen Sir Grogan was implicated in the translated message. But I know that he was not named in the message. Although a lord in your attendance the first night we met with you *was* named."

"And how do you know this?" the king asked.

"Because, Sire, I decoded it with the assistance of Red and Bard," she said, lifting her chin high even as her heart pounded so hard in her chest that she was sure her shaking was clearly visible. Think about Red, she told herself. *I cannot fail. I must save him.*

"That's impossible," the friar said with a mirthless laugh.

"Why did you not bring this information to me before?" King Edward stared down his long, regal nose at her as he spoke.

"Red was on his way to bring you the message when your captain arrested us and took the decoded message." Galiena had to remind herself that though this king was known for his temper, ruthlessness, and swift justice if wronged, he was also known to be a fair man, respected by his lords, and tolerant of commoners testifying against those who had wronged them, even if noblemen.

The king looked at the castle guards lining the wall. "I expected Boris to be in attendance. Where is he?" There was an ominous tone to King Edward's words that left Galiena feeling like there was more to this situation than of which she was aware.

One of the guards stepped forward from his post at the foot of the dais. "Sire, we have not been able to find him this morning. A contingent of guards is searching for him as we speak."

"What is your name?" King Edward asked the guard, his voice tinged with irritation.

"William, Your Grace."

"William," King Edward growled, "Who saw Boris last?"

"I cannot say for certain, Sire, but I saw him relieving the prisoner's guard during the night."

The king arched an eyebrow. "Is that so? Not the typical duty for the captain of the castle guard."

The hairs stood up on the back of Galiena's neck. The guard must have been part of whatever happened to Red during the night when Wolf was forced from the castle yard. She saw William swallow hard, his lips pressed into a thin line and his face pale as he nodded once.

"Sire," William said, a shake barely perceptible in his voice. "Permission to speak with you privately."

The king studied him for a long moment, then motioned for the guard to follow him as they walked a handful of paces away from everyone else in the hall. The guard could be seen speaking earnestly, his voice a low murmur. The king's face turned from wary to intent as he listened. He appeared to ask the guard some questions, then nodded at the young man and directed him back to his post.

"Which of you were with Boris when he arrested the Viking?" the king asked as he returned to stand on the edge of the dais.

Three of the guards stepped forward from their positions along the wall.

"Did any of you see a missive confiscated?"

"Aye, Sire," one of the guards admitted. "It was taken from the prisoner's boot and given to Boris for safekeeping."

"Did any of you see what he did with it?"

"No, Sire," all three guards replied in unison.

"Was anything else confiscated?"

"A dagger, Sire," one of the guards responded.

"I have it, Husband," Queen Eleanor said. She snapped her fingers and one of her guards brought it forward and set it in her outstretched palm. She turned the dagger so that her husband could see the blade. "They recovered a dagger with snakes engraved in it that match the intertwined snakes on the missive."

The king nodded slowly, then turned back to Galiena. "Does this knife belong to Red?"

Galiena felt her heart sink. She did not want to say anything to make things more difficult for Red, but she dared not lie to the king. "Yes, Sire. But there is an explan—"

The king held up his hand. "Until Boris is located, we do not have the document that you claim Red was bringing to me, nothing to prove you translated the message. But we do have a knife engraved with an incriminating design and owned by the man you are proclaiming is innocent."

Galiena felt her stomach knot. If she did not proceed carefully, all could be lost. "Your Grace, if you will allow me to demonstrate to you how to decode the missive, you will see the true message." She hoped that if the king agreed to her request, she would then be able to explain the reason for Red possessing a dagger with the same design as the coded message. "I am confident if you ask Friar Ferrando to do the same, he will not be able to demonstrate the method he used because he falsified the message he gave you, to serve his own purposes."

"Your Grace, she knows nothing about which she speaks," Friar Ferrando said, throwing up his hands as he stalked forward. "She is lying to save her lover. A woman of weak morals cannot be trusted. Decoding is excessively complicated, requiring a master scholar of my training to comprehend."

The king motioned for his wife to lean closer to him, then said something into her ear. The queen pursed her lips as the king was speaking but nodded in response. King Edward turned his sharp gaze back to Galiena, then directed his attention to Friar Ferrando. "The logical solution is to have Galiena demonstrate her method." He held up a hand when the friar started to protest. "Since it is complicated, as you say, and she can't possibly comprehend the methodology required, then you have nothing to fear, yet she has everything to fear."

The friar looked like he wanted to protest, but instead, he

clenched his jaw, giving one reluctant nod of agreement.

"What is it you require, Galiena, for this demonstration?" the king asked.

Galiena released a huge breath, relief coursing through her body—though she wouldn't indulge in feeling triumphant until Red was released and the full extent of Toad's evilness was exposed. "Parchment, ink, and quill. Two pieces of parchment, if I may be so bold. And the encoded message."

"Fetch what she has requested," the king said to one of the queen's guards standing behind them. "The copy of the message that Ferrando was referencing is in the solar; bring that as well."

Galiena was still on her knees in front of the king and queen, the discomfort a small price to pay for the king's attention, and nothing in comparison to what Red had endured for the last day and night.

"Rise, Galiena," the king ordered. "Am I correct to assume the bargain you are proposing is to gain Red's freedom in return for decoding the message—*if* I deem your translation to be correct?"

"Your Grace." Galiena paused to muster her courage. "I mean no disrespect, but if you deem my translation correct, and it proves Sir Grogan is not named, is that not proof enough to release Red?"

The king studied her for a long moment, a small smile on his lips. "Well said, dear lady. However, there is the small matter of him threatening the life of my wife's cousin and trying to attack him in the presence of my wife. How am I to know he was not intending to also harm the queen for ordering his capture?"

Galiena slid a sidelong glance at Toad where he stood on the edge of the dais. A shiver ran down her spine from the cold look on his face. She feared he might try to escape, but there was nothing she could do about that now. She would have to trust the king to order his guards to stop him if he attempted to leave. "If you will allow me to hold my request until after I have proven the message was decoded incorrectly by the friar, I would be grateful, Sire."

The king set his lips in a straight line, obviously displeased with her request. "I give you no promises that I will honor your request in the bargain if you are not willing to tell me now what it is you want."

"I understand, Your Grace, and I am willing to risk the consequences if you are willing to indulge my request and trust it is for good reason." Her legs were shaking beneath the layers of her gown, and her knees felt like they were about to buckle. The king had been tolerant of her forthright speech to this point, but she knew his tolerance could end in the blink of an eye.

"She has pluck, my love," the queen said to her husband, though her voice was loud enough to be heard by all. "Red has chosen well."

The king put his hand over the queen's where it rested on the arm of her throne, letting out a throaty laugh. "I cannot fault him, as I know well the value of a bold woman."

The queen smiled lovingly at the king as her gaze locked with his, and for a moment, it was as though they forgot about everyone else in the room as they looked upon each other with devout admiration.

The guards returned with the supplies, breaking the spell between the king and queen. "Bring a table and a chair for the lady," Edward ordered. When four of the guards had muscled a trestle table onto the dais, he motioned for them to set it in front of the thrones and for Galiena's chair to be placed opposite of them. "Be seated, Galiena. Let us see how you deciphered this code. You, as well, Ferrando. Someone fetch him a chair," the king ordered.

As she took her seat and reached for the supplies, the king instructed the castle guard to retreat to the far end of the hall near the doors, out of earshot. The queen's guard was instructed to move to the back of the dais, but Toad was sitting uncomfortably close, his chair situated only an arm's length away from her. Her hands trembled and she had to take a deep, steadying breath, reminding herself that the future of the man she loved, whether he lived or died, depended on what she would do next.

The king drew her attention when he directed a question to Galiena as he motioned toward Ox and Bard. "Are they privy to the contents of the message you translated?"

"Yes, Sire," Galiena said sheepishly. "They have been charged with my protection in Red's…absence."

"I see. They do not look very willing to be out of reach of you." Slanting a warning glance at the two men, he said, "Out of respect for Galiena, I will allow you to stay. Beware, Ox and Bard, you will be placed in shackles along with Red if I am not convinced Hawk is innocent of wrongdoing. Or if you do anything to raise my ire."

Other than Ox and Bard, Galiena was now alone with King Edward, Queen Eleanor, and The Executioner.

She positioned the ink well, a quill, and two pieces of parchment in front of her on the table, then placed the copy of the coded message to the side where she ensured the king and queen had as clear of a view of it as she did. When she was situated, she lifted her head to see Toad staring intently at her, his eyes dark with hate. She held his stare for a moment, refusing to be intimidated by the loathsome man, and then she looked at the king and queen. "Your Graces, with your permission I will explain to you my process for deciphering the missive as I am working."

"Granted," the king said.

"There are ten lines in the message, comprised of letters and symbols." She pointed to the symbols composed of dots, explaining they were the vowels within the words, then pointed to the symbols composed of small circles in the last line of the message. "If these are numbers, then the last line appears to be a date. That is where I started."

Toad scoffed and said, "That is not at all how it works."

Galiena lifted her head to see the deep lines of concern etched in Toad's face, despite the flippant tone of his remark. Good, she thought. When she looked at King Edward and Queen Eleanor, they were both leaning forward, attentive as they watched her work. "Continue," the king instructed, ignoring the queen's cousin.

She explained how she deduced the final line was a date, and how she narrowed it down to the month of December based on the one repeated vowel symbol throughout the word. "When I wrote 'December' under the letters and symbols, it became apparent that the code was a shift of one position to the right along the alphabet." She went on to explain each line varied in the number of positions shifted along the alphabet and alternated the direction of either left or right.

As she spoke, the king motioned for one of the queen's guards, waving him close to whisper in his ear. Galiena could not discern what had been said, causing dread to prickle along her spine as the guard retreated from them and exited the hall. Focusing on the task at hand, she forged ahead with the translation. When she got to the sixth line of the message, she counted out loud the shift of nine positions to the right, proving that the lords implicated were Burbek and Wright.

She lifted her face to see Toad's reaction to the proof that Grogan was not one of the lords named in the message. He was staring at her with the intensity of a man ready to kill someone with his bare hands.

"Cousin?" the queen said, puzzled. "How did you come up with Sir Grogan's name? She has matched your translation line for line until this point."

"It is nothing more than a misunderstanding, Your Grace," he said in a voice devoid of emotion. He turned toward the queen. "An error resulting from my haste to decode the message. I am deeply concerned about the life of my dear cousin's babe and wanted only to find the men who dared threaten him."

"I think Sir Grogan would not be pleased with your error," the queen said evenly, looking directly at her cousin.

"My sincerest apologies, my queen," the friar said, placing a long, slender hand over his heart.

Galiena had expected the gratification of seeing Toad stutter and his usual smug superiority replaced with a pale look of fear, but when she looked at him, his face was hard with cold calculation. She shivered as he fixed a deadly stare on her.

"Sir Burbek is not here to defend himself," the king said. "He left yesterday for his manor in the south of Wales." He turned to one of the queen's guards. "Tell the stable master to ready forty horses with provisions for a journey of two days."

"Yes, Sire!" The eager young soldier was already running for the door as he called out his response to the king.

"Continue with the translation," King Edward said, waving his hand at the missive. "I wish to see what else Ferrando translated incorrectly."

Galiena continued through the translation until all the lines were transcribed. "The one line that doesn't make sense is the ninth. It just says *Meeting at*, nothing more, and the next line is the date."

"What did you find for this line, Ferrando," the king asked.

The queen answered before the friar had a chance to speak, "*Hawkspur on…*"

"I question that the girl's translation is even correct," the friar said, his voice shaking with anger. "It is coincidence that her method even produced a translation, and a matter of luck that some of it was correct."

"Is it?" the queen asked, staring up at her cousin.

"With your permission, I will retrieve my translation notes to demonstrate my findings to you." The acquiescent expression on his face was in direct contradiction to the fury reflected in his eyes.

"I think not," Edward interjected. "Perhaps later, when you are giving me a detailed explanation as to the incompetence of your translation."

Friar Ferrando's face had turned a deep shade of purple, and Galiena feared he might come over the top of the table at her if the opportunity arose.

Reaching into his tunic, the king pulled out a leather pouch, which he opened, extracting the original rolled parchment Galiena had given to him a few short days prior. He spread it out on the table in front of them, looking from the copy to the original. "There does not appear to be anything omitted from the original when the copy was created."

Galiena was about to agree with the king, but something caught her eye. She leaned forward to see the parchment better, noting there were ink splotches scattered over the missive. At first, it appeared to her to be nothing unusual or uncommon, but upon closer inspection, she could see a pattern forming. "Sire, I believe the ink splotches are deliberate. See how there is a spot of ink directly to the right of the words that translate to *meeting in*? If you look at the lines, there is one ink drop on each, over a specific letter."

She picked up the quill and wrote on her translated copy the letter with an ink splotch from each line: *G-l-a-m-o-r-g-a-n.*

"Glamorgan," King Edward read aloud. "The most southerly region of Wales. There are several lords residing there who claim to be loyal to me—including Lord Burbek."

The king nodded thoughtfully as he studied the missive. When he looked up again, Galiena could see the anger in his ice-blue stare. "I want to know *who* wrote this missive."

"Sire, if I may be so bold?" Galiena stared at the evil friar, remembering the despair in Red's voice as he told her of the day The Executioner killed his mother and uncle, thinking of Dane and the horrible suffering he endured at the hands of this man, and knowing that if given the chance he would just as surely rip out both Red's and her throats without hesitation.

"Is there something you wish to say, Galiena?"

"Yes, Sire." She glared at Friar Ferrando and then faced the king. "I would like to request what I want from you in this bargain."

✦ ⋅◦◊◦⋅ ✦

Chapter Thirty

S HE WAS A fucking queen!

No, she was better than a queen; she was a goddess.

She was Freyja, goddess of love, war, life, and death. She had won his heart, and he would love her until his dying breath. She had waged a fierce battle of wills with the king of England, and she was prevailing. She'd wagered for Red's life at the risk of her own death. His heart was on the verge of exploding with pride for this woman that he did not deserve.

He wanted to go to her, to take her in his arms and tell her he loved her, but he dared not distract her. She was still facing the king and queen, unaware that he had been led into the Hall, though still flanked by guards ready to cut him down with their swords if he proved a threat.

His arms felt like they'd turned to stone after being suspended since the prior day, and he was flexing his fingers to get the feeling back in his hands. Definitely not much of a threat. *Yet.*

Not more than an hour had passed since he'd watched Galiena enter the hall from across the castle yard. His instructions to her, and to Bard and Ox that she was to stay away, had been clear. He did not want her anywhere near The Executioner when he could not be with her to offer his protection.

In truth, he'd had a deep foreboding that he would not be

able to convince the king Sir Grogan was innocent in a plot to hobble the king's authority over the Marcher lords. And he'd had an even deeper foreboding the king would not be sympathetic toward his reason for wanting to kill the queen's cousin with his own hands.

Regardless of what was to happen to him, he did not want Galiena to be punished for his actions. He'd tried to convince Ox, Bard, and Wolf that they needed to take her from Llanbadarn and leave him to face whatever consequences would come of it. They had refused, insisting Galiena had resolutely rejected their attempts to make her leave. Instead, she'd put up a fierce fight. Red had wanted to chastise them for bending to her will, but he knew well that holding her back was about as easy as trying to force a hissing kitten into a burlap sack.

Still, when he'd seen her walk through the castle gates, his relief had been immeasurable. He'd feared The Executioner would try to get to her when he was thwarted from killing him. Even so, not knowing what The Executioner had planned caused his sanity to teeter on the verge of splintering, especially when he watched her walking into the hall.

But then she'd kissed her hand and held it over her heart, while her lips formed soundless words—words that he'd convinced himself were her affirmation of love. He'd decided then that he had to trust in his kitten. She was intelligent, cunning, and fierce. With her resolute stance, the determined look on her bewitching face, and the luxuriant rope of hair flowing down her back, she looked as fierce as Freyja. Now, as she faced down The Executioner and stood up to the king, he thanked his *hamingja* that Galiena had chosen his arms to run into when she needed protection.

He couldn't hear what Galiena was saying, but he could see her bent over the table with quill in hand. The king directed his attention at Red and signaled for him to come forward.

The Executioner was looking at Galiena with death in his eyes, and Red's palms itched to wrap around the man's neck as he walked closer to the dais, stopping within arm's reach of where Galiena sat with her back to the hall. Ox and Bard stood at the side of the dais, watching everything as it unfolded. Wolf had entered the hall with Red but stayed back when the king beckoned Red to come forward.

He'd moved within earshot of Galiena just in time to hear her solve the riddle of the meeting location and saw the king studying her intently as she pressed him to hold up his end of the bargain. Edward looked up over her shoulder at Red, then returned his attention back to her. "What is it you want from me?"

"I want you to listen to a story."

The king and queen both looked taken aback at the peculiar request. "A story?" the king asked skeptically.

"Yes, Sire. It is a story about a young boy—Red, as a matter of fact—who survived an encounter with a man known as The Executioner, after watching his mother and uncle be assassinated by the man."

Galiena had yet to notice Red was standing behind her, so intent was her focus on showing the king and queen her method for deciphering the message. From where he stood, he could see the king was duly impressed. The queen was maintaining a straight face, likely because this did not bode well for her cousin and trusted advisor.

"Go on," the king encouraged.

She repeated the details of the story as he'd told her, including the revelation that The Executioner had stolen a dagger during the encounter. "It was one of a pair of daggers made by Red's uncle, both engraved with that symbol of the intertwined snakes, Odin's knot, in a design of his making. You saw that same design as depicted on the original missive." She tipped her head toward the parchment on the table. "By coincidence, divine intervention, or the work of a *hamingja*—as Red would say—I ran into the arms of Red as I was trying to escape the very same man who killed Red's family twenty years ago. The Executioner was the man in the alley discussing the plot to kill your son."

The friar's gaze was shifting between Galiena, Red, and the king and queen, his increasing discomfort visible on his pale face. Red watched the man bedecked in the typical attire of a friar with a brown tunic, belted at the waist, and a long cowl with a deep hood draped over his shoulders. As was also typical of a friar, his hands were folded beneath the cowl in what was meant to be a pious posture, but Red feared it was not a rosary that he had hidden under the long flap of the cowl.

"And do you know where this...*executioner*...is now?" the king asked Galiena.

Red kept his gaze focused sharply on Friar Ferrando, watching his every move. If he made even the slightest motion toward Galiena, Red would have the man's neck in his hands before anyone could stop him. He'd likely be killed by the guards for attacking the queen's cousin, but he would make sure the evil friar's neck was broken before that happened.

From the corner of his eye, Red saw Galiena slowly nod in response to the king's question. The veins in the Executioner's neck bulged, as his gaze darted around the hall.

The king picked up Red's dagger, which had been sitting on the table between him and the queen. He turned it over in his palm, admiring the intricate work. "Fenrir, from Norse mythology," he said matter-of-factly. "Doomed to live in chains because it was known that only evil could be expected of him." As the king walked slowly around the table toward Red, the evil friar started backing away from the table.

Red noticed the queen's guards flanking the door to the tower had stepped together, effectively blocking the door. The contingent of castle guards were lined up at the end of the hall with several stationed near the main doors as they watched the drama unfolding on the dais. Even if they could not hear what was being said, it was obvious from everyone's posture that the meeting was tension-filled.

As the king circled the end of the table and stepped down from the dais, Galiena turned to watch Edward approaching and then noticed Red standing behind her. She let out a gasp, then pushed to her feet and started toward him. For the length of a breath, Red turned his attention from The Executioner to Galiena, but his warrior instincts still prevailed. From the corner of his eye, he saw the friar pulling his hand out from beneath his cowl.

"No!" Red shoved King Edward to the side and launched himself at Galiena, tackling her and wrapping her in his arms as he twisted to protect her from the impact when they hit the wooden planks of the dais. The chair she had been sitting on toppled and skidded to the side in the mayhem, and Red felt his head connect with the edge of the table on the way down to the floor, and pain radiated through his shoulder.

"Are you hurt?" he asked Galiena in a strained voice and tried to roll onto his back in case The Executioner tried anything else. Oddly, he couldn't completely make contact with the floor; only then did he realize the burning he felt was from the embedded blade of the dagger.

"I am fine," she panted. "Are you hurt?" She rolled to her feet and reached for him.

"I'll be fine," he grunted, looking around him to get his bearings as the sounds of shouting and scuffling boots filled the hall. Over Galiena's shoulder, he saw Bard kneeling down to assist them, while Ox stood with his feet braced apart, ready to fight anyone who came near them.

"Take her away from here, Bard," Red said, pushing Galiena into Bard's arms as he sat up.

"You have a—" Bard started to say, pointing to his shoulder.

"I know. Leave it." He grimaced.

"What are you going to do, Red?" Galiena asked in a panicked voice as she looked up at Red with wide eyes.

Instead of answering her, he grabbed her chin with his thumb and forefinger and kissed her quickly. "I love you."

The noise around them had died down except for muffled grunts. Red got to his feet to see the queen surrounded by her guards, and The Executioner being restrained by more guards. The king was staring at the man, his expression like thunder as he ominously flipped Red's dagger over and over, catching it neatly in his hand after each rotation. He leaned to the side to look at the dagger protruding from the back of Red's shoulder, then stepped behind him to inspect the hilt.

"I believe we have found the missing dagger," the king said.

"Aye, Sire," Red acknowledged as the king circled back in front of him.

"Do you have a preference as to which one we use?" the king asked, his voice like ice.

Red tilted his chin toward the dagger sticking out of his back.

"I agree," the king said with an approving smirk, then raised his voice to call across the hall, "William, send someone for the surgeon."

After the guard had dispatched someone, the king motioned for him to come forward.

"Yes, Sire?" the guard asked. "How may I serve you, Your Grace?"

The king gestured to him, and the guard's gaze met Red's. "I wish to introduce you to Red." Turning to Red, he said, "This young soldier is William. He was on guard duty during the night."

Red nodded to the soldier.

"On the castle wall," the king added, looking pointedly at Red. "You see, on still nights, such as last night after the storm had passed, sound carries, and he overheard a most interesting exchange between you and a cloaked man."

Understanding dawned. This man had saved his life. "I have you to thank, then, for the drunk soldiers who stumbled from the tower and then camped out along the wall until morning."

William blushed with embarrassment. "Aye. I recruited some mates from the guard tower. I'm pleased our ruse worked."

"So am I," Red said with a chuckle. "Any later and this knife would have been stuck in my neck last night instead of my shoulder now."

"Fresh wound," William grinned. "According to what I overheard, your mother would say it means you are still allowed to take your revenge."

"Aye, she would," Red said. Truth be told, he would have preferred to kill The Executioner himself, but he would have to be satisfied with whatever the king chose to do with him. The fact that he would use the same knife The Executioner had used to kill Red's mother and uncle, and apparently, every victim after would have to satisfy him.

"I must speak to the queen while we await the surgeon," Edward said, "and it appears you have someone on the edge of her patience waiting to speak to you."

Red turned to see Galiena standing a short distance away with Bard and Ox at her sides. She had tears on her cheeks, a grim set to her quivering lips, and her eyes were blazing. He wasn't sure if she was overwhelmed with sadness, joy, or irritation.

He held out his good arm to her and she immediately came to him, wrapping her arms gingerly around his waist and reaching up to kiss him. He kissed her back, then pressed his forehead to hers when she broke off the kiss. "I was so scared for you, Red."

"There was no reason to be scared when I had you fighting for me."

She pulled her head away from his so she could look him in the face, anger flashing in her silver-gray stare. "What were you thinking, jumping in front of a knife? You could have gotten yourself killed!"

"I was thinking of you," he whispered, wrapping a hand around her neck to bring her face close to his. "I am nothing without you."

"And I am nothing without you," she said, as a soft sob escaped her lips.

"Kiss me, *Wife*."

She pressed her lips to his, kissing him gently, breathing life into him again. After a moment, she broke off the kiss. "Red?"

"Yes?"

"I'm still not your wife," she said, unable to hold back her smile. "Just declaring it doesn't make it so."

"You're right, kitten. You have to declare it, too."

"Let us retrieve that dagger," the king said, interrupting them. He was standing at their side with the surgeon, who directed Red to a stool at the table.

Red gave Galiena a squeeze before he let her go. "We'll finish this discussion when the surgeon is done, but I know that you love me and—I will have your declaration," he said, brushing a knuckle under her chin.

"That's a bold assumption, Viking," Galiena called after him as he sat on the stool and leaned over the table.

The surgeon pulled an iron from his satchel and handed it to William, nodding toward the hearth along the side of the hall that butted up to the castle wall. "Stoke the flames and set the end directly in the hottest part of the fire."

Ahead of him, Red could see the friar sitting in a chair near the back wall of the dais while two men restrained his arms, and another leveled a sword at his chest. His face, which had been purple with murderous rage not that long ago, was now a pale mask of arrogant defiance. He stared back at Red with glittering black eyes.

He was relieved when the king stepped into his line of vision, effectively blocking his view of the despicable friar. Though, he wouldn't truly feel at ease until The Executioner was chained to a wall awaiting his slow and painful death.

"Tell me, Red, what declaration do you await from Galiena?"

It was not the question Red was expecting from the king. He grimaced as the surgeon prodded his shoulder but managed a chuckle. "To declare me her husband. I've declared her my wife, but she believes it to be in jest only."

"She is a woman with her own mind."

"Aye, Sire, that she is." It was what he loved most about her.

"Galiena, come, stand by my side," the king commanded.

When she had skirted the table and was standing next to Edward, he said, "Is this true? Do you think him to be jesting?"

"It is a complicated situation," Galiena said, clutching her hands together in front of her so tightly her knuckles were white. Red found it amusing that she would still be nervous with the king after all that had transpired in the last hour.

The king held up his hand to stop her from saying more. "Do you love the Viking?"

A terrible stinging ripped through Red's shoulder, robbing him of his breath. Fortunately, Galiena's attention had been on the king, and she hadn't witnessed his response to the pain, but her gaze flew to him at his indrawn breath, concern etched on her face.

"I am fine, kitten. The worst is over," he said, stealing a glance at the dagger the surgeon had dropped onto the table, the blade slick with his blood.

Her eyes widened as something behind him caught her attention. Red swiveled his head to see William walking toward the surgeon with the cauterizing iron in his hand, the tip glowing red.

He may have been too hasty in saying the worst part of this was over. He turned his attention forward and clenched his teeth in preparation for what was to come. He would not give The Executioner the satisfaction of hearing him react to the pain.

"The king has asked you a question, Galiena," Red reminded her, focusing his attention on her instead of what was about to happen.

"Do you love the Viking?" the king asked again, and Galiena turned a pale face in his direction.

"Yes, Your Grace," she admitted. "I do love him."

Red felt his lips tug into an involuntary smile. He was quite sure she'd expressed her love for him when she was entering the hall to meet with the king, but the distance had been far, and he worried he may have dreamed it in his half-crazed state.

"And do you want him as your husband?"

Galiena turned to look at Red, her expression softening as she focused on his face. "I do want him as my husband."

Red closed his eyes, his teeth near to cracking as he clenched them against the scalding pain when the surgeon pressed the iron over the wound left by the dagger thrown by The Executioner.

"Say it again," he bit out in a low voice, his teeth still gritted as the smell of burning flesh filled his nostrils.

Galiena grabbed Red's hands in her own, squatting down so her face was even with his across the table. "I choose you, Red. I want to be with you, and no one else."

The surgeon applied a salve to the burn that did little to dull the stinging of his flesh, but her words were a balm to his heart. And his soul.

"There has been no one else for me since you ran into my arms, accused me of being drunk, and called me 'Husband'." Red pulled their joined hands toward him and pressed his lips against the back of her fingers. "From the moment I looked into your eyes, I knew I would do whatever it takes to have you as my wife."

The surgeon stepped back from the table, his work completed. Red stood and walked around the table to Galiena, placing his hand on the small of her back and positioning his body so that The Executioner could no longer see her. He wanted to get Galiena out of the friar's sight and far away from the man as soon as the king allowed.

"Red and I have unfinished business. I want you to leave us, and I will return him to you within the hour," King Edward told her then.

Galiena looked to Red, her face paling.

"It will be all right," Red assured her. "Ox and Bard will take you back to the house. Wolf will wait outside and return with me."

"Galiena," the king said as she turned to leave. "You are brave and clever. The queen and I are indebted to you for endangering your life to save the life of our son and the heir to the throne. Thank you."

Red knew that *thank you* was not something the king said often, and he doubted Galiena truly understood the depth of the king's gratitude. But she said, "You are welcome, sir. I am only sorry the queen had to endure the shock of discovering her cousin was behind the plot."

"As am I," the king responded.

Galiena performed a graceful curtsey and Red watched her she backed away respectfully along with Ox and Bard at her side, before they reached the door and left the hall. Once she was away, he turned his attention back to Edward. The queen had come to stand by the king, her guards at attention a short distance away.

"We have William's accounting of what happened last night, but I want to hear it from you."

Red explained in detail everything that had transpired and everything he had learned, but he did not have any satisfactory answers as to why Ferrando would betray his cousin the queen, or the extent of the plot to undermine the king.

"Wait here," the king instructed Red, turning to stalk toward The Executioner with the queen and her guards behind him.

While the king interrogated the friar, Red picked up both daggers from the table, wiping the blade of the bloody one on his breeches to clean it. He looked at them both side by side, one in each palm, running his thumbs over the smooth hilts, clear memories of his mother and his uncle rushing back to him. He had mourned them every day of the last twenty years, longed for their counsel at times, and regretted the things they had missed because their lives had been cut short.

His mother had never had an easy life, abandoned with a babe in her belly by a man who cared only for her beauty and nothing for her. As a boy, his purpose in life had been to make his mother's life easier. And when his uncle had gotten hurt, he'd wanted to do the same for him. But he'd been too young, too naive, and he had failed.

He was older, wiser, and stronger. He would not fail Galiena.

Seeing The Executioner defeated while the king of England hovered menacingly over him provided a small measure of satisfaction. But Red wouldn't breathe easy until the man was dead and no longer a threat to Galiena.

Red was impatient to go to her, and he was uncertain why the king had not dismissed him already, especially after he'd heard the details of Red's encounter with Ferrando. He had no other information to offer, and being in the same room as The Executioner sickened him.

To know the man had been contracted to murder them somehow took some of his desire for revenge from his heart. Or perhaps he only felt that way because he knew The Executioner's time was now short. It didn't matter. He didn't care what the man had to say anymore; he'd heard enough from him. But as the friar's voice grew louder, it was impossible to ignore the way he was practically spitting out the words, spewing his hatred and jealousy of the queen, and his resentment of the king. In his mind, they were the reason why he didn't have the riches and respect he felt he deserved. He'd become an assassin because he enjoyed the kill and the coin he received for his services. He'd earned even greater wealth when he joined forces with the Lord of Glamorgan in the south of Wales to undermine the king's power and hurt the queen. Lord Burbek was an underling of the Lord of Glamorgan and had been tasked with doing his nefarious deeds.

When the king was satisfied that he'd heard all he needed to know, he requested the queen's guard to take her away from the hall, which she did willingly, not wishing to look upon her deceitful cousin any longer. The king dismissed the remainder of the guards in the hall, as well as Wolf, leaving only him alone with Red, The Executioner, and the three guards detaining him.

"I find myself in a predicament, Red," the king said leaning against the table at Red's side. Both men were staring at Friar Ferrando, who was looking back at them, his angry glare full of rage and evil. "I must away immediately. I have business to attend to in the south of Wales with the Lord of Glamorgan and

Lord Burbek. Which means I do not have time to prepare for a proper execution for the queen's cousin." He paused, crossing his arms over his chest. "Are you feeling hale and fit after your ordeal?"

Red nodded as he rolled his bad shoulder. It was uncomfortable, but he could still move it; the stiffness would settle in later.

The king motioned to the guards to release the friar, then turned to Red. "It would expedite matters if you would do me the honor of executing The Executioner on my behalf."

Red looked at the man who had kept the flame of vengeance burning in his belly for twenty years. He'd pictured killing him thousands of times in thousands of different ways, each slow and painful. He looked down at the daggers still in his hands and realized he just wanted this to be done. He wanted to be rid of the anger and the hatred, of the memories that had haunted him since the day The Executioner changed the course of his life.

Then Galiena had barreled into his life and into his arms, creating a new course for his life, one of joy and love. All he wanted now was to follow that path and forge a life with her.

The sooner this was over, the sooner he could be with her. He lifted his gaze from the knives in his hand to meet the eyes of the king. "My uncle crafted these daggers because of a small boy's fascination with the tale of a mythological wolf. Fenrir, as you stated. It was a tale I made him tell me again and again. They were meant to be a thing of beauty. Something he and I shared, besides our name." Red flickered his gaze to The Executioner before returning it to the king. "The friar changed that."

Red spun the dagger with the green-eyed wolf in his right hand, then wrapped his palm around the hilt. He thought of all the souls The Executioner had ushered into the next world with it. "For my uncle and my mother," he said in a low voice.

His left shoulder still felt like there was a blade embedded in it each time he moved it. The pain was a reminder of how close The Executioner had come to taking another person—this time, the most important person—that he loved from him. He spun the red-eyed wolf dagger in his left hand, then gripped the familiar hilt. "For Galiena."

A mirthless laugh escaped his lips as he walked toward the man shrinking away from him, his eyes seeking an escape that did not exist. He'd been stripped of his hooded cowl, but the wooden cross yet dangled satirically from the rosary beads looped over the belt at his waist.

Toad.

That's all he was now. Gone was the arrogant air of a scholar, the pious righteousness of a friar, and the depraved superiority of an assassin. The Executioner had ceased to exist, and there was nothing left but a man with the ugly warts of evil on his shriveled soul. "I'd tell you to pray to your God, Friar, but I don't think even He will forgive you. And now it's time to meet Him." He slipped the blade home, watching without pity as the life left The Executioner's eyes and his body crumpled to the floor.

The deed was done. He returned to the king, holding the dagger the queen's cousin had stolen so many years ago by the bloodied blade as he presented it to Edward. "This dagger no longer represents my uncle."

The king nodded his silent approval as he took the dagger by the hilt, the silver body and green eyes of the engraved wolf splattered with crimson.

"Do with it what you will, Your Grace," Red said, reaching for the remnants of the shredded shirt the surgeon had removed from him before cauterizing his wound. He wiped the blood off his face and chest, then from his own blade, rubbing the hilt until he was sure nothing of the friar remained. Then he bowed to the king and left the hall, tossing his shirt into the flames of the hearth as he passed.

— ∞ —

Chapter Thirty-One

A COLD, STEADY rain was pouring down again when Red finally emerged into the castle yard, but Galiena did not care. Bard had tried to convince her to return to the warmth of the weaver's house, assuring her Red would return there as soon as he was able, but she stoutly refused.

She picked up the hem of her gown and ran toward him as the doors to the hall swung closed behind him, stopping when she was within arm's reach. "Are you hurt?"

He shook his head. He was staring at her as though she was the first spring flower after a long, dark winter. "I told you to wait at the house, kitten," he said, placing his hands on either side of her face to tip it up to him. "You'll catch your death in this rain."

"It matters not. I won't leave without you," she said wrapping her arms around his waist as that lopsided grin she loved so much spread across his face. She let out a delighted gasp as he wrapped his arms around her and spun her in a circle. "Put me down before you hurt yourself. *Husband.*"

She saw the change in his expression as he slowly lowered her to the ground. "What did you say?"

"I said, put me down before you hurt yourself." She looked up at him, her eyes wide with feigned innocence.

"After that," he growled, turning her so his shirtless body

blocked the icy rain and wind.

She smiled up at him. "I said, *Husband*."

"Bard, Ox, Wolf," he called in a loud voice without taking his gaze from hers. "Come closer. I want you to bear witness." When they were standing in a circle around them, he grinned down at her, his face smug with satisfaction. "Say it again, in front of witnesses, *Wife*."

"*Husband*," she said with a laugh. "I am proclaiming you as my husband."

"We heard it," Bard confirmed, draping Red's fur over his shoulders.

"Say it again," he said to Galiena as he wrapped them both in the warmth of his cloak.

"I am nothing without you, *Husband*." She said, looking into his handsome face. She meant every word of it. He'd stood by her side, holding her hand, and he'd patiently waited for her to find her way out of the darkness and despair that had been her constant companion since losing Adam and Nahara, and he'd proven her heart was big enough to love them *and* him.

"And I am nothing without you, *Wife*."

He kissed her, thoroughly and carefully, as though he was drinking from the well of life. She sighed with contentment when he lifted his head to look into her eyes again.

"Take me home, Red," she whispered.

"To Hawkspur?" he asked, his voice filled with hope but his face vulnerable.

"Yes, to your home in Hawkspur," she said.

He caressed a thumb across her cheek as he looked at her. "Our home. Yours and mine. We will fill it with all the furniture and comforts you desire. With a big, soft bed where I can wake up next to you, my wife, your beautiful face the first thing I see each morning. And anything else you desire."

"All I need in a home is you and me," she paused to smile up at him, "and a houseful of children."

A jubilant smile spread across his face as he wrapped her in his arms and spun her in another circle. "I'll give you the wedding you deserve when we get to Hawkspur so we can get started on having sons and daughters."

"I don't want a wedding in Hawkspur," she said, laughing softly when his face fell. She pressed her lips gently to his. "This was perfect, *Husband*. I can't imagine a wedding more beautiful or vows more perfect than what we just shared."

"*You* are perfect," he said, looking at her with so much love in the depths of his soft blue eyes, she thought her heart would overflow.

"Kiss me again, *Husband*."

He pressed his lips to her hair, murmuring, "My kitten." She felt her lips tug into a smile at the endearment.

He nuzzled her neck. "My she-wolf." The words sounded like a possessive growl, and her skin shivered.

"My wife," he whispered, finally pressing his lips to hers.

Epilogue

August 1286

"A SMALL CHEST was delivered from Hawkspur today," Galiena whispered after Red placed a gentle kiss on her lips. It wasn't the kiss he wanted, but it would have to suffice for now if he did not want to wake the babe in her arms.

The light of a single taper illuminated the look of contentment on her angelic face. It was a look that Red would never tire of, and a look he expected was reflected on his own face at this moment.

"Ani was fussing," she said softly with a smile so full of love that it made his heart twist in his chest. "I think she needed her mama to hold her."

"I think it is fair to say it is her mama who needs to hold her." He chuckled gently, as he reached down to pick up Ani's sleeping twin brother, Erik, and cradle him against his chest. He had not protested when Galiena wanted to name the little girl after her dearest friend Anora, and she had agreed to name the boy for his commander and closest confidant—though she preferred Hawk's given name of Erik for the boy instead of the moniker of "Hawk". Red would have been satisfied with either.

Galiena scoffed quietly. "As if you are any better! I've woken many times in the night to see you with one or both of them asleep on your shoulders."

Red could not deny it. After his wife, the next best things to have in his arms were his son and daughter. He'd been ecstatic when Galiena had informed him the previous autumn that she was with child. But when her belly grew so distended and heavy that he doubted her ability to stand upright without falling forward, he'd started to get fearful. If the baby took after him in size, surely it was too much for a woman so petite to birth. But Lady Alyce had assured him that many women smaller than Galiena had birthed large babies and both mother and child flourished.

He'd spent many hours in those last days before the babies came with his arms around his wife, cradling her swollen belly in his hands to take some of the weight of it off her. It had driven him almost mad with worry while she labored to deliver the first baby, and then to find out there was another!

He'd been terrified that it would be too much for her tiny body to birth a second baby, and then he'd worried that the tiny babies would never grow hale enough to thrive. But like their mother, who had the strength of Freyja coursing through her veins, the little warriors grew stronger with every day, their hardy wails soon filling the manor at all hours of the night and day.

Anora and Erik had survived the cold, wet days of early spring and grew fatter with each passing day. Red had felt some of the fear and panic release their iron hold on his chest as mother and babies gained in strength and vitality in the months since the birthing.

"At least when they are asleep, I don't have to worry about you throwing them up in the air until they are breathless with giggling," Galiena chided, though the curve to her lips told him she was not bothered by his playing with the babies.

He put Erik back into the cradle, then reached for Ani as he raised a questioning eyebrow at Galiena. "Are you ready to put her down?" When she nodded and held his daughter up for him to take, he took the tiny girl in his big hands, and marveled at her little bowed lips and the puff of fine, dark hair on the top of her head, which he kissed before placing her next to her brother.

Galiena stood and he wrapped her in his arms as they both stared down at their babies. The children had taken after their mother in coloring, both with dark hair and grey eyes, but already Erik was beginning to outgrow his sister and was becoming a hefty boy. Secretly, Red hoped his son would be as big as his father so that he could protect his little sister when Red wasn't there to look after her. Even if he wasn't big, Red had nothing to worry about because he knew Hawk would ensure Erik would be trained by the best warriors in the kingdom, even if he wasn't there to see it.

He dropped a kiss on the top of Galiena's head and then whispered. "Will you come to the solar with me?" The babies had been sleeping in their chamber from the day they were born and neither mother nor father were ready to move them to their own bedchamber as of yet. Though the babies were too young to take notice of their parents' activities, when Red wanted his wife completely to himself, he took her to the solar where they could take their time making love on the fur before the hearth.

Galiena looked up at him with a seductive grin on her lips and the sparkle in her silver-grey eyes that still made his breath catch in his throat. "Has my husband missed me today?"

Taking Galiena's hand, Red pressed it to his lips. "Always, even when I am away for only the day."

He led her from their chamber and down the stairs to the solar. He'd already stoked a fire in the hearth and brought up tankards of wine. He guided her to one of the pair of cushioned chairs that faced the fireplace and set a cup of wine on a low stool within her reach.

"Tell me what the wee little ones did today," he urged, taking a long drink of the fragrant wine. As much as he preferred ale, he'd learned to appreciate the drink that was his wife's preferred choice in the evenings.

"Ani is trying to crawl," she said with a wistful smile. "But Erik is very contented to lay on his belly and watch her scoot across the floor."

He laughed at the image of his determined daughter and carefree son. "He can take his time. There will be plenty of years to come where he will long for idleness."

Galiena smiled and nodded, but he could see the apprehension in the creases around her eyes. She would never get over the pain of losing her first child, Nahara. He'd always been sympathetic to her loss, but now that he had children of his own, he better understood the fierce protectiveness they invoked and the constant terror of losing either of them. He could not fault parents who resisted forming too strong of an attachment to their children because they were as likely to survive to adulthood as not. But it was too late for him to adopt that frame of mind; he was as smitten with Ani as he was with his wife, and the pride he felt swelling his chest every time he looked at Erik was overwhelming.

Deciding it best not to dwell on thoughts of gloom, he instead looked at his wife's serenely beautiful face, as she sipped her wine and relaxed into the chair. She sighed and her lips relaxed into the smile that had become his reason for living from the first day they'd met.

"Tell me of your day, Husband," she said, turning those mesmerizing grey eyes in his direction, the light from the flames making the silver specks in their depths dance.

"The breeding pair Hawk purchased from Spain arrived," Red told her.

"I'd forgotten that you had requested horses from Spain," she said. "Are they what you hoped?"

He nodded. "They are. Once they settle in, I will show Hawk why they are superior to anything else for warhorses."

"He is not convinced?" she asked, raising a sleek, black eyebrow at him.

"He trusts my opinion when it comes to breeding and training horses, but I'll feel better when he can see the value of what he paid for the pair."

"He tasked you with creating the strongest and best warhorses in the kingdom," she said with a smile full of pride. "If you say they are the best, then they must be."

He loved her unwavering confidence in him.

He loved her.

He reached for the pouch at his side, but his hand was stayed when she said, "I am dying of curiosity, Red. Will you not open the cask on your desk? Lady Alyce seemed to think it was from the king."

He laughed as he stood, "If you were so curious, you need not have waited for me to open it." He pulled the dagger from his boot and pried the lid off the wooden cask. He turned the dagger over in his hand before returning it to the sheath on his calf, as always admiring the intricately carved, ruby-eyed wolf. While the knife had been a gift from his uncle and had been the instrument that brought an end to the man who took the lives of his mother and his uncle, it had also saved his wife from meeting the same dire end at the hands of that same murderous man; Red had carried it since the day he'd lost his family and one day when Erik was old enough, he would pass it on to him, along with the history of the knife's origin and the deeds attributed to it. The knife's twin, with its similarly carved wolf bearing emerald eyes, had been left with the king; it had been in the possession of the evil man—the queen's cousin—for so long and used by him in so many heinous ways, Red had not wanted to keep it. The ruby-eyed wolf was enough of a legacy to pass on to his son.

He set the lid to the small wooden chest aside and looked down at a rolled parchment sealed with the royal seal and nestled in a bed of straw. Carrying the box over to Galiena's chair, he kneeled next to her and held it out. "You should finish opening it."

She picked up the parchment and broke the seal, then unrolled it to read aloud, "We are returning your family treasure to you, but it's been crafted into a new form in honor of the new lives you've brought into this world. May the pain of the past be put behind you and may the Lord bless your children with health and renewed hope for their future." She tipped the parchment toward him, pointing toward the two elaborately designed and intertwining E's.

"Edward and Eleanor," he confirmed.

She set the parchment aside and then peered tentatively at the bed of straw, hesitating before lifting a handful of it away to reveal the contents. Then she gasped, her mouth dropping open as she reached in and scooped up the gifts to hold up to the light from the fire. In each hand, she held a beautifully crafted silver cup. Each of them was adorned with the profile of a wolf, each facing the other when held side by side. The wolves had their front paws propped on a stone as they stretched their necks heavenward with their mouths parted in a howl. Each had a dazzling emerald for an eye, and at their feet were the links of a broken chain.

"Fenrir's broken restraints and his pups to carry on his legacy," Red said, admiring the work. He blinked hard to clear his blurring vision, then cleared his throat. He stood and gently took the silver cups from her hands so he could place them on the mantle of the fireplace, the green eyes winking in the flickering light from the fire. Then he sat on the large chair next to the hearth and held out his hand to Galiena. When she placed her delicate hand in his large palm, he tugged so that she would come to him, then settled her on his lap.

Other than when she was naked in his arms, this was his favorite time with his wife, alone in front of the fire with her on his lap, safe in his arms. As she always did, she draped an arm around his neck and stroked his cheek with her other hand. "Are you happy with what the king did with the dagger?"

He cradled her shoulders in one arm and gently tugged on the ties at the neck of her thin chemise with the other. "Aye. It had been turned into something evil by the queen's cousin, and I did not want the memory of it. But I like that it has been melted down and turned into something representing the hope of the future—our future, and our children's future—but is still a reminder of my uncle and my homeland."

"Hope," she repeated in a whisper as she rubbed her thumb over his bottom lip. As distracting as her touch was to him, her solemn tone indicated her words required attention. "It is something I thought I would never feel again." A small smile curved her lips as she lifted her gaze to meet his. "But you changed that."

"No, kitten, you changed that—" he stared into her wide, silver-gray eyes—"when you burst into the lane and into my arms and chose me as your husband."

She laughed. "I *called* you 'husband' to escape a ruthless killer. You thought I meant it."

"Why would you not, kitten? I knew the moment I saw you that you were to be mine." He dipped his head and nuzzled the side of her neck. "I could only assume you knew the same the moment you saw me." His words were muffled against the delicate skin behind her jaw, just below her ear where he knew her to be sensitive to his touch.

"It took some convincing," she said, tilting her head to give him better access, just the way he knew she would. "I might need more convincing."

"Is that so?" he asked, nipping the lobe of her ear between his teeth.

"Love me, Husband," she gasped, "before the babes awaken again."

With her cradled in his arms, he rose from the chair, then lowered her onto the plush fur spread before the hearth and showed her in every way possible just how much he worshipped her.

About the Author

Lois dreamed of becoming a writer since she was a child making up her own bedtime stories. She started writing after getting her master's degree in English literature, though the road to becoming a published author has been long and fraught with many of life's interruptions.

Medieval history, Great Britain, knights, and castles have been a passion of hers for as long as she can remember, but it wasn't until she was in her thirties that she became an avid reader of romances. After reading The Wedding by Julie Garwood, she was hooked on medieval romances and soon started writing her own. She loves writing about bold women, broody knights, and vexing Vikings.

She currently lives on the US West Coast with her husband and dog. They love traveling, visiting their son (also a writer!) in Los Angeles, and dreaming of living abroad.

Website – www.loistemplin.com
Instagram – instagram.com/lois.templin
TikTok – tiktok.com/@loistemplinauthor

www.ingramcontent.com/pod-product-compliance
Lightning Source LLC
Chambersburg PA
CBHW060432310726
48977CB00001B/150